W9-AKD-308

HARRIS COUNTY PUBLIC LIBRARY

YA Moldav
Moldavsky, Goldy,
The Mary Shelley Club /
$18.99   on1155484551

THE MARY SHELLEY CLUB

THE MARY SHELLEY CLUB

Goldy Moldavsky

Henry Holt and Company
New York

Henry Holt and Company, *Publishers since 1866*
Henry Holt® is a registered trademark of Macmillan Publishing Group, LLC
120 Broadway, New York, New York 10271 • fiercereads.com

Copyright © 2021 by Goldy Moldavsky
All rights reserved

Library of Congress Cataloging-in-Publication Data
Names: Moldavsky, Goldy, author.
Title: The Mary Shelley Club / Goldy Moldavsky.
Description: First edition. | New York : Henry Holt and Company,
2021. | Summary: "A deliciously twisty YA thriller about a mysterious
club with an obsession for horror"— Provided by publisher.
Identifiers: LCCN 2020021771 | ISBN 9781250230102 (hardcover)
Subjects: CYAC: Clubs—Fiction. | Mystery and detective stories.
Classification: LCC PZ7.1.M6396 Mar 2021 | DDC [Fic]—dc23
LC record available at https://lccn.loc.gov/2020021771

Our books may be purchased in bulk for promotional, educational, or business
use. Please contact your local bookseller or the Macmillan Corporate and
Premium Sales Department at (800) 221-7945 ext. 5442 or by email at
MacmillanSpecialMarkets@macmillan.com.

First edition, 2021 / Designed by Rich Deas
Printed in the United States of America

10   9   8   7   6   5   4   3   2

*For my sister, Yasmin, my favorite person
to watch scary movies with*

Beware; for I am fearless, and therefore powerful.

—*Frankenstein*, Mary Shelley

PROLOGUE

RACHEL SAT AT her desk like a pretzel, ankles tucked beneath her, knees up and pressed against the hard edge of the wood. She stared at the wiki for Nellie Bly, the historical figure she was supposed to be writing a paper on, but all the words made her eyes glaze over. It wasn't that she wasn't interested in Nellie Bly; Rachel could get behind any badass journalist with a zippy name. But there were just too many distractions around.

Spotify blared the latest Taylor single, and no matter how many times Rachel put down her phone, determined to start reading about Nellie, it would chirp again with a new text from Amy and she had to pick it up. Like now.

i wonder what he's doing rn. we should go to his house and SPY

i'm not about to stalk, Rachel texted back, and put down her phone for real this time.

But even as she read Nellie's truly interesting bio, Rachel's mind kept wandering.

She wasn't going to spy but . . . what *was* he doing right now? Was he out with friends, or playing video games, or studiously doing homework like she was supposed to be? Whatever he was up to, Rachel was sure he was definitely not thinking about her. He barely knew she existed. Well, except for the fact that they'd actually had, like, a legitimate conversation this morning. It didn't last more than three minutes, but it was real. And there were smiles. Mutual smileage was had.

Rachel grinned just thinking about it. And even though she was alone, she buried her dopey, blushing face in her hands.

A string of new messages furiously beeped from her phone and Rachel picked it up, Nellie Bly all but forgotten.

U likee him!!1 Amy wrote.

U luv him!!!

U want to have his BEBEEES!!!111!

Rachel groaned and hurled the phone onto her bed, then shoved it under her pillow. She did not want to have his *bebees*, and she seriously never should've told Amy about her crush. Back to Nellie. Rachel sat up straight, readjusting the laptop, like getting the right screen angle was the trick.

As Rachel ignored her phone even harder, she caught sight of someone outside. Her desk sat flush against the window, where she could see the front lawn. It wasn't unusual to spot someone walking around, but it was past nine in the suburbs. Nobody was out past nine.

That wasn't what made Rachel pause, though. It was that this person had stopped in front of her house, still as a statue. He wore dark pants and a black parka, and although she couldn't see his face very well, it seemed unusually pale.

Goosebumps crawled up Rachel's arms, but she wasn't sure why. The logical part of her brain kept telling her that it was just a person on the street—a neighbor, maybe—nothing more.

A muffled dinging came from under her pillow. Rachel grabbed her phone, glancing down at Amy's latest text.

STALKERS CAN'T BE CHOOSERS GURRRL

Out the window, the man had gone. Rachel breathed a sigh of relief.

As Taylor's voice faded and Rachel's phone finally stopped beeping, she decided to get back to work. But then she heard another noise. This time, it wasn't from any of her devices. It came from downstairs.

Heavy and deliberate, like a footstep.

But that was impossible. She was alone in the house. A new song threatened to start, but Rachel quickly muted the melody. She sat perfectly still, like a puppy anticipating the arrival of a stranger at the door. She waited a bit, ears straining as a long beat of quiet stretched out endlessly.

And then a noise blasted through the room. She startled, nearly falling off her chair at the shrill chirp of a new text. This time Amy had sent just a GIF of a bearded Chris Evans breaking out in a hearty giggle. Rachel would've laughed too, but there was that nagging uneasiness that pulled at the hairs on her neck. Actually, given the circumstances, the longer she looked at the GIF—an infinite loop of explosive, silent laughter—the more it creeped her out.

Right as Rachel was about to text back, she heard the noise again. This time, it was louder and she was sure it was a footstep. Someone had stepped on the creaky spot in the hardwood between the couch and the coffee table.

Rachel took a deep breath. "Mom, is that you?"

Her mom was supposed to be out in the city for a girls' night with her friends. But she had only left an hour before and she couldn't be back yet. Maybe she'd turned around, forgotten something.

Rachel clung to this thought even as her heart started pounding. But in the back of her mind she knew she would've heard her mom's car pull into the drive-way, heard her dump her ring of keys loudly on the console table, heard her messily toe off her boots as she announced she was home, the way she always did.

Rachel put her phone down and made her way to her door, opening it slowly.

"Mom?" she called out again.

When no answer came, Rachel stepped out of her room and crept down the hall toward the stairs. Her socked feet padded lithely on the carpeted steps until she entered the living room.

Someone was there. It wasn't her mom.

The man from outside was standing across the room, dressed all in black. Even his hands were gloved. As Rachel stared at his face, she realized now why it had looked so pale before. What she'd thought was flesh was actually a white mask.

Then Rachel caught sight of the other man. He stood by the TV, dressed just like the first. They stared back at her, their faces scarred and rubbery.

The brain does curious things when suddenly presented with something it cannot comprehend. Rachel's very first thought—a flash—was to offer the men a glass of water, like she'd been taught to do for all guests. And then, just as quickly, she understood. These men were not guests.

5

Rachel's first impulse was to call for help, but anything that wanted to come spilling out of her got jammed in her throat, frozen along with the rest of her. She felt like she was suddenly sinking in quicksand and any movement would only thrust her deeper into the muck.

Two things happened very quickly and all at once.

One of the men charged out the door, blasting through it like he was swept up by the wind. The second man moved too, but not for the door. He lunged toward Rachel, and just like that she broke free of her paralysis and ran. She thought only of the back door in the kitchen, picturing herself opening it, breaking through to the crisp backyard air, and escaping. In a moment, she didn't have to picture it. She was in the kitchen, she was reaching for the door, fingertips an inch from the knob.

But then his hand was a vice around her arm. She was caught.

1

ONE YEAR LATER

I OPENED THE door and Saundra was there, her smile and outfit sparkling.

"Get dressed, Rachel, we're going to a party."

I'd only known the girl three weeks but here she was, showing up unannounced at my apartment like she'd been doing this for years.

"Sorry, can't." I was in my sweats and getting ready to relax with my favorite comfort movie of all time, *Night of the Living Dead*. Also, I hated parties. "My mom doesn't want me going out on a school night."

Like an apparition in a bathroom mirror, my mom appeared behind me. "Sunday's not technically a school night, is it, Jamonada?"

Jamonada was a pet name my grandmother had given me because I was such a chubby baby. I'd tried to give it back but there were apparently no refunds, and anyway, my mom loved it. It was Spanish for "ham." Not like "That girl is so funny and precocious—she's such a ham!" Like literal lunch meat. And now Saundra had heard it, so there was that.

"Hi, Ms. Chavez!" Saundra said.

"There's school tomorrow," I muttered. "So, yeah, definitely considered a school night."

"But you didn't have school today," my mom countered. "I'd say the jury's still out."

Saundra nodded emphatically while I stared at my mom like she hadn't raised me for sixteen years. At first, I honestly could not figure out her angle. And then it hit me: My own mother was worried about my friendless-loner-patheticness.

"But you want me rested and refreshed for school tomorrow, *right*, Mom?" I did that clenched-teeth thing people do when they want someone to take a hint.

My mom did that bright-smile thing people do when they ignore hints. "You had the whole weekend to rest and refresh, honey."

We were at an impasse. I wanted to spend the night with the living dead, and my mom wanted me to spend time with the actual living. Time to bring out the big guns.

"Saundra, tell my mom where the party is." It was a risk. For all I knew Saundra wanted to take me to

Gracie Mansion to hang out with the mayor, and with the circles she ran in, that wasn't entirely implausible. But chances were good that the setting for this party would suck.

Saundra hesitated, but I pressed on. "Go on, tell her."

"An abandoned house in Williamsburg," Saundra said.

I swiveled back to my mom, glinting with triumph like a freshly polished trophy. "*An abandoned house in Williamsburg.* Hear that, Mom?"

It was a game of chicken now. My mom and I stared each other down, waiting to see who would give in first.

"Have fun!" Mom said.

Thwarted by my own mother. She'd had only two rules for me when we moved to New York City: 1) Keep my grades up, and 2) make friends. The fact that Saundra had shown up here should have been enough proof that I'd made friends. Well, one friend. Either way, I'd accomplished the impossible task of making a new friend as a junior at a new school. But to my mom, a party meant more possible friendships, so that meant I was being dragged to Williamsburg.

I got changed (I refused to take off my tie-dye pajama shirt, despite Saundra's protests, but I dressed it up with cut-off Dickies and a jacket) and we left.

"We could walk," I suggested. We were in Greenpoint, just one neighborhood over, and the weather was nice.

Saundra snorted. "What, and get murdered?"

"It's pretty safe around here."

Saundra dismissed me and the borough of Brooklyn with a laugh and took out her phone. "Yeah. *Sure.*"

The Lyft arrived in less than three minutes.

We sat in the backseat, Saundra multitasking by taking a dozen selfies, updating all her social, and telling me who'd be at the party. This also happened to be our lunch routine, where she told me all the gossip about people I still barely recognized in the hallways.

Saundra had decided we would be friends as soon as I walked into Mr. Inzlo's history class at Manchester Prep. When I sat down, Saundra had leaned over and asked if she could borrow a pencil—a total front, I knew, since I'd spied a pencil in the open front pocket of her lavender Herschel.

At first, I'd wondered why Saundra wanted to be my friend, but I quickly realized that Saundra had started talking to me because she couldn't handle the notion that there was somebody in her class who she knew nothing about. Because as I soon discovered, Saundra Clairmont's defining characteristic was her burning compulsion to know absolutely everything about absolutely everyone.

So that day, I fed her some morsels about myself. Before Manchester, I went to public school on Long Island. I lived there with my mom until we decided to move to New York City.

Unlike the majority of the students, I was not rich or a legacy or technically a scholarship kid. I only got in because my mom was the ninth- and tenth-grade American History teacher. So, yeah—my mom had a knack for getting me to go places I didn't want to go.

But now, as Saundra and I sped toward Williamsburg, I'd gone from not wanting to go to this party to dreading it. The thought of seeing all those people, not a single one of whom would talk to me—it made my throat tighten. Worst of all was knowing that I'd have to pretend. Pretend to be a part of their world, to be like them. I was about to tell Saundra that I wasn't feeling that great, but then the Lyft pulled up to the place. Saundra bounced out of the car and I scrambled after her.

We walked up to the abandoned house, which looked straight out of a late-'80s urban horror movie. All of the windows were boarded up with weathered, graffitied wood and there were multiple signs stuck to the door, with tiny print that was surely warning us to stay away. It was crammed between a closed warehouse and an empty lot with a FOR SALE sign on its chain-link fence.

But there was one bright spot. A girl sat on the stoop, dressed goth-black, her ghostly face hovering over a book. Her fingers blocked the title, but the sharp corners of Stephen King's name peeked out on the cover. I liked Stephen King movies. Maybe I could strike up a conversation with this girl. Maybe this was my kind of party after all.

"Hey, Felicity!" Saundra said. Felicity looked up from the book, glaring from underneath micro bangs. She didn't return Saundra's greeting.

"Okay then, bye." Saundra looped her arm through mine and pulled me up the steps. "Leave it to Felicity Chu to bring a book to a party."

The living room was packed with a couple dozen people laughing, joking, and sloshing drinks in their hands. The inside of the house wasn't much better than the outside. The wallpaper was moldy where it wasn't peeling, the floors were sticky linoleum, the only light came from heavy-duty construction lights, and you could practically smell the asbestos in the air. But nobody seemed to care.

I didn't know exactly what I had expected at rich-kid parties, but this wasn't it. I found it kind of ironic that they'd all left their cushy palaces to get their thrills in a house that was falling apart.

"Gonna grab a drink," Saundra yelled over the music.

"I'll come with you." But when I turned around, she was already gone, swallowed up by the crowd. The only thing worse than going to a party you don't want to be at is being at that party solo. I wasn't gonna hang around as the lonely buoy lost in a sea of friends. There was only one thing left to do: hide in the bathroom.

Walking up the stairs was like entering a portal. The sounds of bottles and bad pop music faded away, eclipsed by a dank darkness that thickened with every step. Usually, my anxiety dissipated once I walked away from a crowd and into a pocket of quiet. It was like breathing into a paper bag, a quick way to calm myself down. But not this time.

I stood at the top of the stairs, waiting until my eyes adjusted to the dark and I was able to make out shadowy shapes. I clicked my phone on for some light, enough to see that the hallway was covered in a flowery wallpaper. As I felt my way down the hallway, though, the faded blooming petals turned creepy, like wrinkled, witchy faces.

My breath hitched at the sight of a door slightly ajar. The crack was so black it was impossible to tell what was inside that room, and holding my phone up to it didn't help. There could've been a person standing right there, watching me, and I wouldn't have known. This place was getting to me.

I should've turned around and left, but I was at a party. I wanted to be carefree and normal and stupid. Not someone jumping at every shadow. So, I pushed my fears aside and shoved the door open.

It was the bathroom after all. No one inside. The lights didn't work, and neither did the faucet, but it was quiet. I pulled out my phone and pulled up Instagram. Nothing good ever came from going to his page, but I couldn't stop myself. I knew it was bad for me, but I downed the poison anyway.

I clicked on the picture of him and his best friend in their soccer uniforms. My eyes traced the strands of his hair, his dark amber eyes, nearly shut with glee. And the dimples. His wide, dimpled smile was a sucker punch to the gut. Below the post were hundreds of comments from his friends. I'd read every one of them, multiple times. If I started to read them again now, I could lose hours.

But then I heard a voice. It was indistinguishable at first, but it had an angry cadence.

I was clearly not the only one upstairs. I quietly left the bathroom and followed the voice to the room next door. I realized there were actually two people speaking in hushed, insistent tones. An argument.

The door swung open and I had just enough time to get out of the way as Bram Wilding stormed out of the room, his creamy skin flushed red. He didn't notice me. But when I turned back around, I knocked right into Lux McCray. I'd never actually met either of them, but they were high school royalty, the kind of popular that you don't need to meet to already know everything about them. Lux and Bram were Manchester Prep's resident power couple.

My phone slipped out of my hand and bounced on the carpeted hallway floor. It illuminated Lux, finding her the way that light always seemed to, and highlighted the sharp angles of her face so that she looked like the heroine on a V.C. Andrews book cover. Her eyes rounded in surprise, but then narrowed.

"What the hell?" Lux demanded. "Were you *spying* on us?"

"No?"

"I don't know what you think you heard—"

"I didn't hear anything."

Her glare roved over me, from my Zappos slip-ons to my messy bun of thick brown hair, then lingered on my sandy face. Maybe Lux was asking herself why

I had so many freckles and couldn't I have found a beauty tutorial that would get rid of some of them?

I stared back at her. To Lux, my natural freckles probably looked like dirt compared to her fake ones. I could tell Lux's freckles were fake because they were too round, uniformly small, and perfectly spaced. The kind you drew on gingerly with a brow pencil. They skittered over the bridge of her nose, fanning out above the tops of her cheeks. A beautiful constellation.

I got a whiff of her perfume. Miss Dior. The preferred eau de parfum of future disgraced political wives. Her peachy skin glowed, soft and toned, beneath the straps of her Brandy Melville tank and her hair was the color of whisked butter. She was the kind of blond and pretty that died early in horror movies.

But then Lux's gaze diverted to my phone on the floor. She picked it up and looked at the screen long enough to see not only the post but also the Instagram handle. "Maybe watch where you're going instead of stalking *Matthew Marshall*."

A heavy ball of anxiety burrowed in my chest, threatening to expand to the rest of my body. It happened quickly like that, the way fear took over sometimes. One minute I could be fine and the next I'd start feeling uneasy, jittery, my fingers and toes tingling in a bad way. She wasn't supposed to know Matthew's name.

No one was. I pounced for my phone, and Lux looked shocked and offended, as though it was *her* phone. I managed to snatch it out of her hands.

"Freak," she hissed, shouldering past me and disappearing down the dark hallway.

It was an instant reminder of what I was. Not normal. A freak. It was obvious to everyone, including Lux. Yeah, I was officially over this party.

I headed downstairs to find Saundra so we could get out of there, but the unnerving darkness and the weird encounter with Lux followed me like a tablecloth I'd accidently tucked into my waistband. Nobody was supposed to know Matthew's name. I'd known it was a bad idea to come to this party. I'd known it.

My brain swarmed with dizzying thoughts and it felt like I was going down the stairs both too fast and too slow. I pushed my way through the crowd, my tunnel vision zeroing in on the front door.

I was outside in a second, swallowing the crisp night air. I needed to get my mind right, do literally anything else but think about what had just happened. I needed to do something stupid. Reckless.

My eyes hooked onto the only person outside. I walked over and tapped him on the shoulder. In times like these, I could be a character in a possession movie if I needed to: lose all control and let something else

17

take over. I barely waited for him to turn around before I grabbed a fistful of his shirt and pulled his face down to mine.

I hated the part of myself that did stuff like this. Reckless and wrong.

But it worked. As soon as our lips touched, all thoughts of Matthew Marshall and Lux and how stifling the house had felt were washed away. And in that moment, I didn't care. I could chalk it up to high school party shenanigans. I could pretend I was drunk, be a wild girl, morals be damned. I was pretty sure this was what normal kids did at normal parties.

Soon I wasn't thinking about anything at all, and as my thoughts quieted, my senses took over. There was the sound of his breathing; sharp as he inhaled through his nose and then soft as he sighed. I took in the scent of his shampoo, something woodsy. Pine and lime. And then even those senses fell away and I was left with only two. There was just the feel of his lips, and the taste of them.

When we both pulled away, breathless, I finally got a look at who I'd been kissing.

At the sight of him, my mind—serenely blank just a moment before—blared loud with a big resigned *fuck*.

"Rachel?" Saundra called as she came down the stoop.

I couldn't tell if Bram Wilding was horrified or repulsed by what I'd just done, but he gave me the courtesy of staying stone-faced. So that was good to know. Bram, *Lux's-boyfriend-who-I'd-just-basically-assaulted-because-I-was-a-criminially-innapropriate-freak-like-Lux-said-I-was*, was courteous. He turned and walked away before Saundra could see him.

"Who was that?" Saundra asked when she reached me.

"Nobody."

She quirked an eyebrow. "I just saw you talking to somebody."

"It was no one. A ghost."

"It's funny you should say that," Saundra said, the tips of her fingers twiddling together. "'Cause there's gonna be a séance!"

2

SAUNDRA LED ME back through the house, her arm linked tightly through mine to prevent any attempt at escape. "Why are we doing this?" I asked.

"It's a *séance*," Saundra and I both said at the same time, though our tones were polar opposites.

"What could possibly go wrong?" Saundra asked.

"You've obviously never watched *Night of the Demons*."

Saundra stopped walking and turned to face me. She gently put her hands on my shoulders and looked at me very seriously. "Rachel? No one gets your references."

I sighed. That was fair.

"It'll be fun," Saundra said. "And anyway, this is how you make your mark at Manchester. This is how you get to know the heavy hitters." She dropped her hands and squeezed my elbow. "This is how you find your people."

Who knew that all I needed to do to find my people was conjure up some dead spirits? There was already a group forming a circle on the living room floor. By now the party had quieted down, leaving about fifteen of us still there. Unfortunately, one of them was Lux. My stomach knotted up as she glared at me. I was already on her bad side—I prayed she would never find out I'd just kissed her boyfriend.

Someone had shut off the construction lights, so the only light came from the center of the circle, where some kid was lighting thick block candles set on the floor. When the room was sufficiently eerie with flickering candlelight and everyone was sitting in place, the guy stood up. "My father owns this place, so this séance better not mess anything up."

"Rodrigo, your father bought this place so he could demolish it and build luxury condos," someone reminded him. "Let's raise hell!"

There was a smattering of laughter, but I must've missed the joke. One girl raised her hand. She looked different out of her school uniform, but I recognized her instantly because she was always assertively raising her hand in Earth Science. Just like she was now. "What kind of séance will this be?"

"A past-life séance," Thayer Turner suggested. His father was the state's attorney general and as Saundra had informed me, the Turners were practically the next Obamas. Admired, beloved, perfect in every way. Even now, at this party, Thayer was dressed impeccably in a purple blazer that looked great against his dark brown skin.

"What's a past-life séance?" Raisey-hand asked.

"It's when you look in a mirror and you see what your past life was," I said.

Thayer turned to look at me. In fact, everyone turned to look at me. It was probably the most words any of them had heard me say since I'd infiltrated their school. I'd been joking when I mentioned the séance in *Night of the Demons*, but as I looked back at their ghoulishly lit faces, it was starting to feel more like a prediction.

"Yeah," Thayer said slowly, taking an extra beat longer to examine me. "New Girl's right. Lucky for us I saw a mirror in the hall closet!"

"What were you doing back in the closet?" someone said. I shot the guy a dirty look. There was a sniveling jeeriness to his tone, which Thayer hadn't missed. His shoulders squared as he headed for the hallway.

"Ha ha, funny, Devon," he called back.

When Thayer came back into the room, he was holding a full-length mirror. He leaned it against the fireplace. The glass was murky with age and decay, and everyone scooted around it to get a better look at themselves.

"It might take a minute," Thayer said. "You have to concentrate."

If this were anything like the movie, a bony demon would appear any minute now. But there was only a group of bored teenagers tilting their faces to show off their best angles.

Of course I knew that there wasn't going to be a demon popping out at us, or even that we'd see our past lives, but still, I was starting to feel the familiar prickling sensation at the back of my neck. I didn't believe in past lives, but I had a past. What if I looked in this mirror and they were all able to see who I really was?

"Nothing's happening," Raisey complained.

"Well, I guess you don't have a past life," Thayer said.

"To go along with your nonexistent love life," snickered Devon, the asshole. People laughed again, and I began to wonder if I wasn't in fact seeing a bunch of demons in the mirror after all.

"Settle down, children," Thayer said. "Why don't we forget the past-life thing and try to communicate with *actual* spirits?"

"Like our great-grandparents?" someone said.

"Like the people who lived in this house," Thayer said.

"I thought it was abandoned," Devon said.

"Well, someone had to live here first to abandon it, smartass." Thayer leaned forward. It was a subtle move, but it quieted everyone down and made them lean forward, too. "There was a couple who lived here, Frank and Greta. Typical hipsters—I'm talking vegan cashew cheese and terrible style. All's well in Hipsterville until one day Greta starts to hear a buzzing."

"Buzzing?" somebody asked.

"Like when a fly whizzes by your ear," Thayer said. "At first it was just once in a while, like maybe a bug got in through the kitchen window and couldn't get out. But then it was more constant. Insistent. Greta realized the noise was loudest whenever Frank was home. Anytime they'd be together, she'd hear it. The buzzing. She asked if he was making the noise on purpose. Frank said he couldn't hear anything. But Greta kept hearing the buzzing and eventually she couldn't take it anymore. Greta broke down and begged him to please stop buzzing and Frank looked her straight in the eye and said he didn't know what she was talking about.

"But Greta didn't trust him. The buzzing was too loud. She didn't believe he couldn't hear it. And as Greta began to spiral, she no longer just thought he was lying about the buzzing. She thought he *was* the buzzing. Greta became convinced that Frank was wearing a skin suit—that underneath it, he was just a million flies, buzzing and swarming and out to get her."

Some people (Devon) snorted, but they still listened, waiting for Thayer to continue the story. I leaned in. I wanted him to continue, too.

"Frank tried to reason with Greta, of course, but Greta couldn't stand to be near him, what with all that buzzing. Some mornings, as he ate his cereal, she'd see a fly crawl over his earlobe and he wouldn't even be bothered. At night she couldn't sleep because Frank slept with his mouth open and anytime she closed her eyes, she imagined the flies pouring out."

Thayer opened his mouth, letting his jaw drop low, stretching it as far as it would go. No flies came swarming out, of course, but he held on to the pose, staring us down. I could feel Saundra squirm next to me. When he clamped his mouth shut with a click, a few of us startled.

"Greta couldn't stand it anymore," he continued. "One day she took a meat cleaver and swung it right into Frank's neck."

Saundra gasped dramatically.

"She was trying to free the flies. But she just ended up killing Frank. And when Greta saw that there weren't any flies, she offed herself next. And the scariest part of the whole thing is that Frank and Greta were"—Thayer made his eyes go wide and lowered his voice to a whisper—"registered Republicans."

I snorted, but nobody else seemed to find it funny.

"Okay, that was a joke, but the rest is totally true!" Thayer went on. "It was a week before anyone even discovered their bodies. Neighbors heard buzzing at all hours of the day and it just kept getting louder and louder. Someone finally called the police, and when they broke down the door, guess what they found?" The pause was dramatic. "Flies. Hundreds of thousands of them, crawling all over the house—and the bodies."

"You're full of it," said one girl, but beside her, a guy swatted his neck and shivered.

"So what, are we gonna, like, try to talk to the people that died here?" Lux asked. "Don't we need a Ouija board or something?"

Another girl, Sienna Something, cleared her throat. "I've been part of séances before. I know what to do." She made a show of sitting ramrod straight and locking hands with the people on either side of her.

I didn't know whether I was supposed to be impressed or disturbed, because séance*s*, plural? But I didn't have time to dwell on it as the girl next to me grabbed my hand.

"Go on, then," Thayer coaxed, amused. "What do we do next?"

"We have to concentrate on nothing but also open our minds and souls to all the possibilities that the universe presents to us," Sienna said, sounding like a YouTube wellness guru. She raised her chin toward the broken chandelier in the center of the ceiling and took a deep breath. "Greta, we come to you with love and concern in our hearts. Your death was untimely and, like, totally brutal and stuff, and that sucks. And we're aware that you had that small issue of killing Frank or whatever, but I also believe in giving women the benefit of the doubt and I *know* he was probably buzzing all day under his breath to tick you off. We're here for you and we love you. If you can hear us, send us a sign."

My mind and soul were open and all that, but a deep crease formed between my eyebrows. The only thing I knew about Greta was that she was one hundred percent a made-up person in a made-up story. But I seemed to be the only one to take issue with this.

Around me, everyone closed their eyes, the only sounds in the room the quiet strains of people trying to stay still or hold their breath. Definitely no signs from Greta. And yet we waited for what felt like way too long a time. I thought about sneaking out, but I didn't want to be the one to break the spell. I was pretty sure that wasn't what Saundra had meant by finding my people. But thankfully, I didn't have to do anything

27

because someone spoke up for all of us. "Okay, this is obviously—"

A thud in the ceiling interrupted him, and more than a few heads snapped up at the noise. It was loud and strong enough to make the chandelier crystals chime like this was a breezy day on a North Carolina wraparound porch and not an abandoned house in Williamsburg.

"Is there someone upstairs?" somebody hissed.

"It's Gretaaaaa," Thayer said, his voice vibrating spookily.

"Greta, is that you?" Sienna asked. "Tap once for yes and twice for no."

Everyone waited again, listening closely for more sounds. After a moment, another thud. "Greta," Sienna said. "Are you okay?"

Another moment, another thud. And then, just in time to make Sienna's smile flicker off, a final thud. Two taps.

"She's not okay," Saundra whispered.

There was a moment of restless silence as we all snuck glances at each other, looking to see who was scared and who believed.

"Greta, how can we help you?" Sienna asked.

"That isn't a 'yes' or 'no' question. How's she supposed to answer us?" Lux said, rolling her eyes.

Then a new noise came from above. Not another thud, but more of a rumbling, like a bowling ball being hurled across the floor. Dust fell from the popcorn ceiling. Then all at once other things started to happen. It wasn't just the ceiling now, it was the walls too, knocking, pounding, as if the house was coming alive. The candles went out and I heard a piercing crash. The mirror had fallen, spraying us with glass.

Screams broke out, loud enough to match the growing cacophony of the crumbling house. Saundra's scream was shriller than everyone else's and she yanked my hand suddenly, pulling me up so fast that my feet slipped as I scrambled to stand. The sounds of people rushing around in the dark mixed with the thunderous roar still coming from the ceiling and walls. And then the noise morphed into something else.

Something much closer.

A swarm.

A buzzing.

As though a hundred thousand flies were crawling all over us.

The screaming started in earnest then, particularly from one person. "*Get them off me!*" she screeched. "*Get them off me!*"

The bright fluorescence of the construction lights flickered back to life and illuminated a totally transformed room. There were people bottlenecking at the doorway, yelling and frantic to get out. But mainly we all stared at Lux, who was in a full-blown panic. She was wildly pulling at her beautiful blond strands, crying hysterically for someone to help get the flies out of her hair.

But there weren't any flies. The light ushered in a stillness, and out of the corner of my eye I saw the only other person who wasn't freaking out. Not one strand of his loose, curly hair was out of place. His thick-framed glasses were not askew. I watched as he clicked a portable speaker and slipped it into his pants pocket. And just like that the buzzing came to a halt.

I clamped my lips shut. I tried not to let it out. The rest of the people in the room swore and caught their breaths, but something else was bubbling up inside me. Finally, I had to let it go.

I laughed. Hard. I laughed so loudly that soon, people turned to look at me like *I* was the weirdest thing in the supposedly haunted abandoned house.

Lux's eyes locked onto mine. She was breathing hard, her fists full of blond clumps, like sad bouquets. I thought for a moment she'd pulled out her own hair, but then I noticed the clips at the edges. Hair extensions.

"You did this to me!" Lux pointed at me as if *I* had been the one to snatch her bald.

I shook my head, and though I was trying to be serious, little laughs continued to slip out.

"This was your stupid prank!"

I looked around, trying to spot the guy with the portable speaker, but he hadn't stuck around to see Lux chew me out. Everyone else was riveted, though.

An angry, guttural sound came from Lux's throat and she threw her extensions on the floor. "Laugh it up now because you're *done* at this school." And with that she stomped out of the house.

I had stopped laughing by now. When I turned to Saundra, her face was frozen in a grimace. I waited for her to say something. Like all the encouraging things she'd told me when she said this party would be "totally fun" and that I'd "find my people." But all she said was, "This is not good."

3

I COULD FEEL how *not good* my situation was the minute I walked into school the next morning.

Manchester Prep was a private high school, and you could tell how exclusive it was by its location alone. Manhattan. Upper East Side. Basically on Museum Mile. It was four stories high, with the kind of intricate Gothic details carved into its facade that attracted tourists and their cameras. It was pretty on the outside, but cramped within.

We wore uniforms. Oxford shirts and gray blazers with the school crest. The boys wore slacks and the girls wore pleated gray skirts that were meant to chastely kiss the knees but more often than not grazed the thighs. I'd made the mistake of ordering my uniform online instead of having it fitted like everybody else, so my hemline scraped along my shins. The uniform was starchy and chafed and bit into the soft parts of my waist, and the whole thing was a big metaphor for how much I did not fit in here.

A part of it was the money thing. As in they had it, I didn't. You'd think it wouldn't make that big a difference when we all wore the same clothes, studied the same things, but as soon as they opened their mouths you could tell we belonged to two different worlds. They loved to talk about their things: how expensive they were and how many of them they had. They had unlimited credit cards and wore Cartier jewelry, and for some reason that I will never understand, they all had the exact same Celine Nano designer bag. I once saw one of my classmates try to buy a Twix bar at a deli on Second Avenue using a hundred-dollar bill.

So yeah. There was *me* and there was *them* and the chasm between us was the size of Manhattan.

But now, as I took the same route I always did to get to my locker, I felt like I didn't fit in for a completely different reason. People were looking at me. Like, really stopping to look. Some sneered; others leaned into their friends to whisper, their eyes never leaving me.

I didn't have to hear them to know what they were saying. *That's the girl who crossed Lux.*

I'd worked so hard to not call attention to myself at this school, to blend in, that when all eyes were on me, I felt it as acutely as a sudden change in temperature.

Everything went cold. Even the people in the alumni portraits that trimmed the high-ceilinged walls seemed to be watching me. They were mostly angry-looking dudes from back when Manchester was exclusively angry-looking dudes. The school became co-ed in the '80s, and my locker was directly beneath the Technicolor portraits of two female alums with fanned hair. One had become an astronaut and the other a B-list sitcom actress. Both seemed way too interested in my being a newly anointed social pariah.

I didn't see Lux, but I felt her presence all around, like a ghost haunting me. I felt it most strongly in my Women in Literature class when I saw Bram at his seat. Our gazes locked for an infinite moment in which I was yanked back to the kiss. I felt my face redden and I wondered if he'd told Lux about it and if I should expect my already-ruined life at Manchester to get exponentially worse. But then he looked away and so did I, and we both went back to pretending that I didn't exist.

I tried my best to stop thinking about Bram, but unfortunately, he was Saundra's favorite conversation topic.

"Were there any guys in your old high school who were as gorgeous as Bram Wilding?" Saundra asked as we sat down in the cafeteria.

I put down my sandwich. My stomach suddenly

hurt but Saundra didn't notice my loss of appetite. She ate distractedly, her gaze locked on the center of the room. It was the prime real estate of the school's upper echelon. Saundra watched Bram and his friends like they were doing something truly remarkable instead of the same eating and chatting as the rest of us plebes.

Thanks to Saundra, I learned everything I never wanted to know about Bram. He was the product of Andrew and Delilah Wilding, a publishing magnate of Scottish descent and a former model from Cairo, respectively. But I knew something about Bram that Saundra couldn't know. Like what his lips felt like.

"All the guys in my old high school were ogres," I said. Saundra was doing me a solid by not talking about the elephant in the room (my sudden notoriety and social ostracism), but I desperately needed to change the subject. "Could we talk about literally anything else?"

"Okay, we can talk about the party, which I am legit still not over. We got to find out that Lux's legendary locks are actually extensions?" Saundra looked up and sighed. "You pray to the scandal gods, but you just never think you'll get a response, you know?"

"You didn't think it was a mean prank?" I asked.

"Oh, don't tell me you believe those rumors."

"What rumors?"

Saundra's eyes lit up. If there was one thing she

liked to talk about more than Bram Wilding, it was rumors. "I forgot you're new and you don't know all of Manchester's dirty secrets." She swept her plate to the side, as though she needed to make space for the enormity of what she was about to say.

"People think there's some big prankster in school pulling the strings behind everybody's biggest humiliations. Like one time, Erica Belcott got locked in the basement pool at the Y and when they found her, she was curled up in the fetal position on the diving board. She said someone had been flicking the lights on and off. Another time Jonathan Calden woke up in a dumpster behind a Red Lobster without knowing how he got there. And there was that one time when Julia Mahoney swore somebody was leaving her creepy notes written in red lipstick all over the place, and when she found a tube of lipstick in her backpack in AP Chem, she freaked out and knocked over the Bunsen and nearly set the class on fire.

"Hence, the prankster theory. People think it's all connected, that one person is behind it all. They'll say, 'That asshole got me.' But it's like, uh, no, Jonathan, how about some personal responsibility? Waking up in a dumpster is your own fault for going to that Red Lobster in Jersey."

Usually when Saundra dropped a bunch of names on me I zoned out like it was white noise. But a mysterious menace on the loose, screwing with people's lives? "Tell me more."

"It's been going on forever," Saundra said. "I heard about the 'prankster' before I even started high school. But it's just one of those urban legends."

My mind went to the boy I'd seen when the lights came back up at the abandoned house. The one who'd discreetly shut off his portable speaker while everyone was distracted. I'd found out his name—Freddie Martinez. A look around the cafeteria and I spotted him, the sight of the loose curls cresting over his light brown forehead unmistakable. He sat surrounded by a group of friends.

"Who are those guys?" I asked Saundra.

"Ugh. The Tisch Boys. They're in the Film Club together. They're all going to the Tisch School at NYU to study movies—sorry, *film*," said Saundra. "And one of them *is* actually a Tisch. Careful—they might try to recruit you on account of their club not having a single girl in its membership. It's a huge optics issue. Once, Pruit Pusivic was trying to flirt with me and for a minute I was into it but then it hit me, like, Wait, do you really like me or are you just trying to get me to join Film Club? It really gave me trust issues."

"Oh."

"Exactly," Saundra said. "They think they're cool, but they're just pretentious nerds."

I didn't think Freddie looked all that nerdy, though. Yeah, there were the thick glasses frames, but I kind of liked them. Plus, he had the relaxed posture and easy smile of someone with a healthy amount of confidence. And there was that jawline. Sharp enough to light a match on. His clothes were kind of messy—the uniform oxford shirt wasn't ironed like the other boys', and his shoes were scuffed and in need of polishing—but I got the feeling all of that was on purpose. A look he cultivated.

"And what about that guy?" I said, jutting my chin in Freddie's direction.

"Freddie Martinez?" Saundra asked. "Why?"

"Just curious."

The look on her face said there were much more interesting people to gossip about at this school, but Saundra was always happy to show off her encyclopedic knowledge of the student body, even if it was only Freddie Martinez. She took a deep breath and launched into a list of Freddie facts.

I learned that he and I had something in common: In a school of one-percenters, we fell somewhere in the ninety-nine. He was a scholarship kid. His mom was a caterer who he helped out on the weekends, but he also sold cheat sheets and term papers. And apparently, for the right price he'd even take your standardized tests for you. Around here that was a lucrative side gig.

"Basically, he'll do anything for a buck, which is so tacky, but I guess it comes in handy if you suck at algebra or something." Saundra took a breath. "There's also rumors he deals drugs, but personally I find those rumors so racist."

It was a good thing she wasn't spreading them, then.

Freddie was deep in conversation with the guy sitting next to him. I wondered if the two of them had come up with the prank, or if it had been just Freddie. I wondered if Saundra was wrong. Maybe there *was* someone messing with the students of Manchester Prep.

That would be awful.

It would also be the most interesting thing to have happened since I arrived.

4

MY FAVORITE WAY to blow off steam was by watching horror movies. I considered them a sort of exposure therapy. Which was ironic because my former therapist hated the idea. But I found the horror soothing, almost cathartic. Maybe it was the knowledge that everything I was seeing was fake and would be wrapped up neatly in under two hours. If I could train myself to sit through scary movies, face all different kinds of horrors head-on, then maybe I could transform into a calmer, more serene version of myself.

That was the plan, at least. I started watching horror movies last year, after I was attacked. At first they creeped me out. When I saw *The Exorcist* I had to look away anytime there was a close-up of Linda Blair's frothy, veiny face. And after I watched *The Ring* I refused to answer my phone for a week.

Scary movies made me feel everything they were

designed to make me feel. I got scared, then I got over it. If I got chills, they eventually exploded over my skin like a splash of cold water. You get the jolt at first, but then you're clean and refreshed and all the happier for having taken the plunge.

But over time, I got addicted to the feeling, and after I watched most of the mainstream horror movies, I started stumbling into the subcategories of horror that were more campy or cheesy than scary. The stuff with bad makeup and worse dialogue. I wasn't immune to horror or anything, but lately, scary movies just weren't cutting it.

Tonight's fare—a movie called *Rabid*—included. It didn't help that I kept getting distracted by my phone.

I thought I'd left the weirdness at school behind, but that had been naïve. The moment with Lux and her hair extensions lived on in social media, played out in all kinds of different iterations. I was being tagged in Instagram posts where people either crossed out my eyes or wrote long, rambling captions about how I was the worst person in the world for what I'd done to Lux.

I sighed as I scrolled through my notifications and found a TikTok in which a boy dressed as Lux (I could tell by the blond wig) and another boy dressed as me (freckles drawn on as big as moles all over his face) wrestled each other to the ground.

All of this because I'd been laughing at a dumb prank. But of course, to everyone else it looked like I'd been laughing at Lux. And maybe a part of me *had* been laughing at her, had found joy in her fear, taken pleasure in her distress. I let the TikTok play again and zoomed in on the cackling face of "Rachel."

A year ago, before fear and anxiety became unwelcome friends of mine, the monster side of me had reared its ugly head. Ever since then, everything I did was an attempt to keep it hidden. But for that brief moment, when the lights came on in the abandoned house, I'd been exposed. And now this monster was popping up all over social media for everyone to see.

But the worst posts—the ones that felt like a finger-blade glove had just sliced through my stomach—were the ones that explicitly made fun of *Lux*. Snide anonymous tweets about her fake hair, Photoshopped images of Lux with a bald head. It was those posts that signaled that this, as Saundra had so succinctly put it, was *not good*. I could feel the dread clawing its way down my throat, and it had nothing to do with the movie I was watching. I felt bad for Lux, but even in our brief interactions, I had gotten the sense that Lux was not a girl who took humiliation lightly. She would want revenge.

My mom's dread was definitely coming from the movie, though. She sat at the other end of the couch with a stack of ungraded papers on her lap and both her hands covering her face, peeking out only to see if the gore was still on the screen.

"Do they have to show so much . . . cheek muscle?" she asked.

Rabid was about a woman who gets most of her face torn off in an accident. We were at the part where doctors were showing her the damage. Lots of wailing ensued, both from the patient and from my mother. I'd never seen the movie before.

"Yes. They have to show it all," I said. I put my phone down and grabbed a fistful of microwave popcorn from the bowl balanced on my thighs.

I'd never once invited my mom to watch movies with me, but she always insisted on joining in. I was pretty sure she considered this mother-daughter bonding time.

"This is so gross," my mom said. "And gratuitous! Why do these movies always have to show violence against women?"

"It's directed by two women. The Soska sisters."

"Really?"

"I can watch it in my room if you want."

My mom shook her head like I knew she would. I think she indulged my scary-movie habit because she probably saw this as my dealing with "my trauma" from what happened last year. But she didn't have to like it. Which she made clear during every horror film we watched together.

Instead of looking at the screen, Mom busied herself with her papers. Out of the corner of my eye, I saw her uncap her red pen and draw three successive question marks in the margin of some kid's essay. My mom looked up when the screaming started again and winced.

"Should I be worried, Rachel?"

It took everything in me not to slide off the couch as I rolled my eyes. "We need to stop watching movies together."

"Is there something going on at school?"

"Nope."

"'Cause I know you like to watch these movies after you've had a hard day."

"School's delightful," I said, stuffing my mouth and voice full of corn.

"I'm serious. This movie makes me queasy and you're watching it like it's the Thanksgiving Day Parade."

"I find this much more interesting than balloons and marching bands, Mom."

"Exactly. How you can watch this stuff and snack at the same time is beyond me. You're practically licking the butter off your fingers."

My mom had to love me. The whole unconditional

thing, it was in the Mom Handbook. But sometimes, like right now, she slipped up. I could tell she loved me *despite* the fact that I scared her. She must've thought that I was defective. And a part of me knew she watched these movies with me because she felt guilty. About what happened last year. For leaving me alone that night. For not being there.

"Are you saying I have no feelings? Like a psychopath?"

"Rachel—"

"Because that's what it sounds like." I didn't want to argue with my mother, but sometimes it was easier than answering her questions. Sometimes you had to lean into the argument. I kept my voice flat. Like a psychopath's.

"Jamonada," my mom said softly. "Please don't say that."

I swallowed and grabbed my phone again. I'd only been joking. Kind of. Whatever it was, I'd picked a fight with my mom and I felt sorry. "I'll find another movie."

My mom shook her head again. Mother-daughter bonding time was too important. "It's fine. It's not that scary."

My phone dinged. A new text from Saundra.

Heyyyy, just fyi stay off the internet for tonight?

The ball of dread in my stomach grew larger. I did her one better: I deleted my Instagram. I hardly used it anyway. I'd only signed up for a new account when I transferred to Manchester because it felt like the protocol. A normal teenage girl would have an Instagram full of selfies. But anytime I posted a pic, I felt a gnawing discomfort, like I was wearing a costume that was too tight. After taking all those useless selfies, I began to realize how forced my smiles looked.

Next, I searched for someone else. Freddie Martinez wasn't on Instagram, but I found him on Twitter easily enough. His latest post was from half an hour before.

Film Forum playing one of my faves tonight for #MonthOfAThousandScares. #EvilDead2 lets go!

I smiled. So we also had horror films in common.

I put the bowl of popcorn on the end table, pure impulsiveness coursing through me. "I'm heading out."

"Where are you going?" Mom asked.

"Meeting a friend." I didn't love lying to my mom, but I knew she wouldn't stop me if there was a friend involved. And Freddie was a potential friend. Who I was technically going to meet for the first time. So, not really a lie at all.

GOING TO THE Film Forum in the hopes of bumping into Freddie may have sounded kind of stalkerish in theory, but I wasn't just going for him. *Evil Dead II* happens to be one of my favorite movies.

I found a spot close to the back and scanned the seats. There were already about ten people in the theater, but I didn't see any sign of Freddie. I started to think he wasn't going to show up, which I told myself was for the best. Because if he did show up, then I'd have to talk to him and I wasn't sure what I was going to say. Or actually, I did know; I just wasn't sure how to bring it up. How do you ask a boy why he pulled a prank like that? Did he know that Lux would freak out? Was he responsible for all the weird pranks at school that Saundra had described?

And most important, was he going to take the blame for the séance and get Lux off my back?

The house lights began to dim. He was a no-show.

And then suddenly he was walking down the aisle. I thought maybe he'd show up with some of the other Tisch Boys, or with a date, but the only thing accompanying him was a jumbo bag of popcorn.

I was sure he wouldn't notice me.

He spotted me immediately.

I snapped my attention to the screen. Freddie came into my row and sat one seat away from me.

"Hi," he whispered. When I glanced at him, I could only see his profile. His gaze stayed glued to the screen.

"Hello."

"You go to Manchester, right?"

"Hmm?"

"You're the new girl. The one who laughed at Lux."

My claim to fame. Of course that was why he recognized me.

On-screen a demon jumped out at Bruce Campbell and a chorus of muffled yelps rang out from all around us. Behind me a woman screamed so loud it almost made *me* jump. I turned around to see her clutching her date's arm and burying her head in his shoulder, yet she still kept watching the movie. I love that about horror: It's the only genre that aims to please while daring you to look away.

Neither Freddie nor I moved an inch.

I'd never met a single other person my age who'd pay to see *Evil Dead II* in the theater. By themselves. Freddie must've been thinking the same thing, because he leaned into the seat between us and whispered, "So, like, what are you doing here?"

The people around us gasped as if they were reacting to his question and not the movie.

It was a good question. What *was* I doing here? All I knew was that I couldn't stay at home trying not to obsessively check my phone. The great thing about a movie theater is that there's a rule about that sort of thing. But I took the coward's way out. "What are *you* doing here?"

Someone shushed us. Freddie twisted to give the guy a dirty look, but he went back to watching the movie, and so did I. Down in the third row, someone got so scared when an undead hand popped out of the floorboards that they flinched and tossed their popcorn in the air. This seemed to encourage Freddie to offer his own popcorn to me. I hesitated, but Freddie shook the bag, prompting me. So I dipped my fingers into the buttery kernels and smiled gratefully around a mouthful. Freddie smiled back. All around us the theater broke out in screams.

It was late when the movie was over. As Freddie and I walked to the exit together, I began to panic as I realized that soon we would have to start actually talking. I couldn't tell him that I had come here because I was stalking him on Twitter. And I definitely couldn't tell him that I knew he was probably the Infamous Manchester Prankster.

Fortunately, Freddie broke the ice. "This was very Donnie Darko of us."

I smirked. He was referring to the scene where Jake Gyllenhaal and that creepy-ass bunny sit together in a dark theater. "I'm not Frank, the bunny, in this scenario, am I?"

Now it was Freddie's turn to smirk, and suddenly we were two smirking idiots on a grimy New York City street, beaming with horror-movie afterglow. After all the confused looks from Saundra, this small exchange was enough to make my heart sing. Or scream, so to speak.

"I'm Freddie."

"Rachel."

"So, Rachel, you're an *Evil Dead II* fan?"

"Yeah," I said. "I can appreciate a good horror comedy."

"Have you watched *Shaun of the Dead*?"

"Of course. Though I'd say that that one's more of a comedy than a horror. *Slither*'s a better example of a pure horror comedy—oh—and *Ready or Not*, which was surprisingly fun. But Sam Raimi's still the reigning king of the genre as far as I'm concerned."

Usually when I talked to somebody (okay, my mom or Saundra) about horror movies, they'd stare at me blankly like I was speaking another language. Freddie was staring at me now too, but there was nothing blank about his expression.

He broke into a wide grin. "Nothing beats the unintentionally funny horror movie, though."

"Which one are you thinking about?"

"Saw."

"Are you serious?" I laughed.

Freddie nodded. "The bad guy's a Pinocchio-looking thing on a tricycle. How is that scary?"

"Well, is Damien scary in *The Omen*? He's a little boy!"

We both looked at each other for a beat, then mutually agreed that, yep, Damien was absolutely terrifying.

I had forgotten how nice it could be, finding someone to talk to about the things you love. It was like we already had a shorthand, and we'd barely just met.

Suddenly I wanted to talk about movies all night.

But we were the last ones left outside the theater and it put a point on the finite nature of the evening. I couldn't leave without asking Freddie the question I had come to ask him.

"It's actually funny that I bumped into you here because I wanted to talk to you about something," I said, keeping my tone casual. "It's about that abandoned-house party? The séance?"

"What about it?"

Maybe I was about to ruin the first real, genuine connection I'd made in a long time, but I had to risk it. The prank at the séance had kind of knocked my whole trying-to-fly-under-the-radar-as-a-normal-high-school-student thing out of whack and I needed his help.

"Well, I saw you with the speaker. You were the one playing buzzing noises. It was your prank."

My attempts at sounding casual now took on an accusatory edge. I'd come on too strong, and now I would probably scare Freddie away. I tried to reel it in some.

"It's just that Lux blames me for what happened," I said. "And I figure, if she's going to blame me then I guess I at least want to know what really happened."

Freddie had one of those faces that revealed every emotion he was feeling, and now his expression completely changed from the grinning, happy one he'd been sporting a few seconds ago to something more guarded. He pushed up his glasses, his thick eyebrows knitting together. "Did you come here tonight looking for me?"

He'd seen right through me.

"What?" I said, cheeks totally, immediately flushed. "No?"

"You did, didn't you?"

"I'm here because I love . . . *Evil Dead*. Look, it's cool, I'm not going to tell anyone it was you."

"I don't know what you're talking about."

He quickly averted his eyes, but the dude did not have much of a poker face. He wanted to keep it secret. That was fair. But I couldn't let it go. I'd found somebody who shared my interests: namely, horror movies, and a clear contempt of Lux McCray.

"I saw you with the speaker."

Freddie kept his eyes glued to the ground. "I didn't have anything to do with the séance. Someone else did."

"Oh yeah? Who?"

"Greta. She was clearly upset that we disturbed her."

I rolled my eyes, but when Freddie looked up, he seemed more amused than annoyed. I was glad I hadn't completely scared him away.

"Okay, hypothetically, say it *was* me," Freddie said. "You're accusing me of setting up an elaborate prank to scare people. Why would I do something like that?"

"Because you don't like those people. Because you're not like them and maybe they deserve it. Because you like scary movies and maybe you've seen it all before and none of it really frightens you anymore."

It was a lot. Too much to say to someone I had just met. And now that I'd said it I wondered if I was actually talking about him or me. But Freddie was smirking again. While I had found it kind of cute minutes before, it was completely aggravating now.

"You've been hanging around Saundra Clairmont too much, Rachel. There are no pranksters at our school. Do you really think all those millionaires would allow their kids to get terrorized?"

"How do you know I hang out with Saundra?"

"I've noticed you."

I'd noticed him too, although I never would have admitted it. But Freddie didn't look the least bit embarrassed, letting the words hang heavy between us.

But my mind snagged on something else he'd said. *There are no pranksters at our school.*

"You said 'pranksters.' Plural. Everyone else thinks it's only one person."

The impenetrable smirk faltered. It was nearly imperceptible, but I caught it.

"I'll see you around, Rachel."

When Freddie walked off, I didn't follow him.

Even though I wanted to.

PRANKSTERS. A GROUP of them.

I hadn't just imagined it—Freddie had slipped up. It seemed so obvious now. Of course he hadn't acted alone at the séance. He couldn't have pulled that off by himself.

I didn't know how big the group was or who the major players were, but I had a pretty good idea of who else was in on it. I'd been so focused on Freddie because he was the one in the shadows, controlling the buzzing with his portable speaker. But I'd totally neglected to consider the one person who hadn't lurked in the shadows but had been center stage.

Thayer Turner and I shared third-period Women in Literature. We were studying *Wuthering Heights*, and Ms. Liu was trying to convince us it was a good book despite how much she hated everyone in it. As she ranted, I watched Thayer. From Ms. Liu's perspective, it probably looked like he was taking copious notes, but from where I sat, one row over and one seat back, I could see that he was actually drawing an incredibly detailed face. It was grotesquely exaggerated, with dark, hollow eyes and crisscrossing scars.

"But why didn't he do that?" Ms. Liu asked. "Any opinion on the matter, Mr. Turner?"

Thayer's head snapped up. I had no idea what Ms. Liu was asking, and by the looks of it, Thayer didn't either. I watched as he put down his pencil, closed his notebook, and cleared his throat.

"Well, what I think you're really asking me, Ms. Liu, is why did he think he had the *right* to . . . do that? Why did he have the courage, the nerve, the *audacity* to . . . do the thing that he did that you were just talking about a second ago? And the answer, which I'm sure you'll agree with, is that it's because Heathcliff is a total babe."

"Okay, Thayer, thank you," Ms. Liu said loudly, trying to drown out the chuckles.

"What?" Thayer said. "All the descriptions in the book about him? Tall, dark, searing eyes warming Cath up on the moors. Break me off a piece of that Heath bar."

"I said *thank you*, Mr. Turner. Ms. Chavez, care to answer the question?"

She'd caught me off guard and I stared at Ms. Liu for a beat too long. "Sorry, what?"

"Your opinion on Heathcliff's desire for revenge."

"Oh. Um." My eyes danced over my notebook real quick. It was blank. "Revenge is bad."

Ms. Liu looked as though she was waiting for me to say more. The ensuing silence in the room was deafening. A girl in Thayer's row—one of Lux's friends—mouthed "loser" at me. Bram, sitting next to her, stared me down so hard I could feel myself wilting under his glare. From somewhere behind me, I distinctly heard the sound of an unimpressed snort.

The longer everybody looked at me, the more it felt like I had a bear trap around my neck. My mind went so blank that I couldn't even remember what book we were talking about, and I was pretty sure my mouth was making useless, halfhearted shapes.

But then the bell rang and everyone forgot I existed as they threw their stuff into their bags. I could breathe again.

Ms. Liu tried to feed us some last bits of information, but my focus was on Thayer. I channeled the adrenaline I was feeling into chasing after him.

As I ran out the door, I nearly collided with him. He was standing there, apparently waiting for me. "You were watching me in class."

"What?" I said. "No, I wasn't."

"I'm very observant. Don't try to lie."

"I'm not ly—"

"You followed me this morning, New Girl. Before first period and after second. I mean, I get it—I'm captivating. You can do whatever you want, but please try not to fall in love with me. It will only end in heartbreak."

"Uh." It was all I could manage.

But then he winked and bumped my elbow with his. It felt like an invitation to walk the hall with him. So I did.

"I saw your drawing," I said. "Nice shading of the, uh, scars."

"Thank you! Artists are rarely appreciated during their lifetimes."

"It was Leatherface, right? I love Leatherface."

Thayer served me a highly quirked brow. "Weird taste in guys, but who am I to judge?"

"I mean, he's my favorite movie bad guy of all time."

Thayer smiled but picked up the pace. "You're a horror fan."

"Yeah." I rushed to keep up. "I knew you were one too by the way you told that story at the séance. About Greta and Frank and the flies coming out Frank's mouth. You're a good storyteller."

"Well, aren't you full of compliments? I should let you follow me around all the time. But that story is completely true."

I let out a laugh and Thayer looked at me sideways.

"Come on, Thayer, I spoke to Freddie," I said.

"Freddie who?"

He was going to play dumb, just like Freddie had. Which meant I just had to cut to the chase. "Freddie Martinez. He told me about your group."

Thayer stopped walking again, and this time when he looked at me, it wasn't with skepticism or charm or humor, but alarm.

"Freddie would never tell," he whispered.

"So there *is* a group. I knew it."

"Shit," Thayer said. "Shit shit *shit*." He started walking again, faster than before, but I ran after him, compelled to find out more about this group. At first I'd only cared about the séance and clearing things up so I could get the target off my back. But I was fascinated by Freddie and Thayer, and I felt like they were part of something more. Something I wanted to be part of.

"Is it just about playing tricks on people?"

"No. Keep your voice down."

"Do you have to be a horror fan to join? How do you join?"

"Nobody gets into the club without an invitation, New Girl."

"So it's more than just a group. It's an actual club."

"Shit shit shit."

"Do you take minutes? Is there a treasurer?"

"Please stop talking to me now."

"I don't get the secrecy," I said. "What's the big deal?"

Thayer stopped and I almost bumped into him again. He was about to say something when a big guy walking with a trio of minions came up behind him. He rammed his bowling ball of a shoulder into Thayer's back, sending him stumbling toward me. The big guy leaned over to whisper something in Thayer's ear, laughing with his cronies before walking away. I didn't hear what he said, but reading his lips was easy enough.

"Did he just call you a . . ." I couldn't bring myself to say it.

"Ironic, isn't it?" Thayer said, rubbing his shoulder. "Especially since he's the one *whispering sweet nothings in my ear!*" That last part he shouted out, but only after the guy was far enough away to barely hear it.

"Trevor Driggs is an asshole." Thayer sighed.

"Hey!" I was already on the move. When I'd reached Trevor, I tapped him on the shoulder. "What the hell is your problem?"

He turned to me. "Excuse me?"

"What makes you think you can talk to people like that?"

It took him a minute, but then Trevor looked at me and at Thayer, who'd caught up to us. And he laughed.

"Getting the new girl to fight your battles for you, Thayer?" Trevor turned back to me. "What are you gonna do, rip my hair out?"

My face flushed. It was a stupid, uninventive jab, but it still got to me. My new reputation had caught like wildfire.

The late bell rang. Trevor and his band of morons snickered as they walked away and Thayer and I were left, watching them go.

"I can't believe he said that to you," I said. "Are you okay?"

Thayer shrugged. "Do you know what scares Trevor more than anything else in the world?"

I shook my head.

"Well, I do." Thayer hugged his books to his chest. "Thanks for trying to help. I like you, so I'm going to do you a favor. I'm gonna pretend we never talked. Nice knowing you, New Girl."

7

IT WAS OBVIOUS that Freddie and Thayer didn't want anything to do with me. So naturally, I couldn't stop thinking about them.

Later that day I was in Three-Dimensional Anatomy, my one art elective this semester. Every week we were tasked with rendering body parts out of different materials. Today it was clay, and I probably should've been paying more attention. At the very least I should've been watching out for Lux, who was in the class and had been shooting me daggers any chance she got. But my mind kept wandering to thoughts of Freddie and Thayer's club. While everyone else at my table was busy molding the gray lumps in front of them into hands or ears or noses, I rolled my clump absentmindedly on the table.

First Freddie had slipped up, and now Thayer. The

only facts I had were that they were part of a secret club that was up to no good. I'd already begun to think of them as puppet masters, the invisible hands behind all the strange and scary things that happened to the people at this school. It sounded kind of sinister. Bad. But I couldn't help thinking that it also sounded kind of . . . awesome.

At first it seemed like just pranks, but I was beginning to draw a connection. There had to be an element of horror in the club, too. I mean, the séance could've been a scene in a teen horror movie. And the rumors of past pranks all sounded kind of familiar. Like horror tropes, or urban legends.

I didn't even know the full purpose of the club yet, but I already knew I had to be a part of it. I wanted that same burst of adrenaline that I used to get from horror movies. The exhilaration of rubbing shoulders with fear and knowing it couldn't touch me.

Maybe these pranks could get me there.

"Rachel?" I jumped when Paul spoke. He was the art teacher, and he insisted that we call him by his first name. This, as he'd told us on the first day of class, was to let us know he wasn't like the other teachers around here. That and his hair, which was thin and long, just grazing his shoulders.

"Yes, Paul?"

"What are you making?"

I looked down at my three-dimensional human anatomy lump, which I had unwittingly rolled into a sad-looking phallus. I squished the clay between my fingers to destroy it immediately. "Still working on it."

Paul winced and pointed to the supply closet next to the window. "Maybe you need more clay."

"Great idea, Paul." I stood and walked to the closet, which was lined with shelves full of gray lumps in plastic wrap. I went to reach for one when another hand snatched it off the shelf. I turned to see who it was, annoyed.

"Ah, great," I muttered.

"Well, hello to you, too," Lux said. She stepped closer, forcing me to back into the closet. After I'd seen her at the start of class and she didn't immediately rush to kill, I'd figured I was safe, that maybe she'd calmed down some. Apparently not. I wanted to get back to my seat and out of her way. I reached for a different lump of clay, but Lux grabbed that one, too.

"Really?" I said.

"I've got a big art piece. The biggest."

"Congrats."

"You know, I've been thinking about you and what happened at the party."

"Look, I'm sorry about your exten—"

"Not that. I'm talking about that boy on your phone, Matthew Marshall?"

My breath caught. I'd thought for sure she'd forget his name.

"Matthew Marshall," Lux said again, watching me gleefully. She seemed to get some weird enjoyment out of saying his name. Or from watching my face as she said it.

"Don't say his name."

"Matthew Marshall Matthew Marshall Matthew Marshall. I knew you were a freak, but I didn't know how much of a freak until I looked him up." She tightened her grip on her clay, leaning into my personal space. "You're lusting over a dead boy."

Everything changed in a flash, dimmed just a little bit. And all the breath I was missing seemed to rush through me in a violent gust.

"Matthew Marshall Matthew Marshall," Lux kept chanting.

I was starting to feel hot, my starched uniform shirt taking on the texture of steel wool. Sometimes being reckless wasn't a choice. Sometimes it just happened

66

without me even thinking about it. I grabbed the first thing I saw on one of the shelves, only realizing it was a pair of scissors as I raised them over my head.

Everything went dark as I plunged the flashing blades toward her.

8

"**TELL ME AGAIN** what happened."

The only other time I'd been inside the assistant headmaster's office was on my first day, when he'd welcomed me to the school and told me that he was sure I'd make a fine addition to the "bright young minds" of Manchester Preparatory.

"She pulled scissors on me!" Lux said. The force of her words propelled her body forward so she was leaning halfway over AssHead's desk. "She was about to kill me!"

I sat across from AssHead (a nickname for assistant headmaster that I definitely hadn't come up with but that there was no way I wasn't going to use) and tried not to shrivel under his disapproving stare. I was trying not to do a lot of things. Trying not to look at Lux sitting beside me. Trying not to let my nerves take over my body. For now they only controlled my hands, which were starting to twitch as I picked at the edge of the armrest.

I was shaky with not only the realization of what I'd done to Lux, but also what I *could've* done to her. I'd imagined killing her. I'd seen it so clearly. It was only when Lux screamed and Paul ran into the supply closet to see what all the commotion was about that I dropped the scissors and realized what I had almost done.

"Settle down, Ms. McCray. Ms. Chavez, can you tell us your version of the events?"

My version of the events, as I remembered them, was as follows: I had white-knuckled a pair of scissors and held them between Lux and me, their double blades forming one sharp tip pointed right at her. I remembered the look on Lux's face, how her eyes went wide with terror. I remembered the long moment that passed between us. And I remembered that the only reason things didn't go completely to hell wasn't because I'd conjured up some self-control. It was because Paul had seen us in the closet and popped his head inside to see if we were finding things okay. If he hadn't done that, I honestly didn't know if we'd both be sitting here right now.

Hence the shaking hands. I hadn't just scared Lux. I'd scared myself.

But I didn't say any of this to AssHead. The deal I'd made with my mom—the one that kept my life devoid of more therapists and counseling and outside intervention—was that I keep my grades up and make friends. Getting expelled would effectively cancel out both of those things. So I shrugged. "I was getting a pair of scissors."

"To *kill* me with. She's a psycho. What is she even doing at this school, honestly, can you tell me?"

"Is it possible you got scared and only *thought* Rachel was threatening you?" AssHead asked.

"I'm not an idiot," Lux said. "I know what she was doing. She's come after me before."

AssHead's eyebrows quirked. "Oh?"

"At a party," Lux continued. "She pulled a prank on me and practically tore out my hair."

"I didn't touch your hair." But I said it in the low, sheepish voice of someone who sounded very guilty.

"It was your prank. Don't pretend it wasn't!" Lux said.

AssHead sighed. I didn't know him well enough to know what he was thinking. But whatever he was about to say next looked like it pained him. "You hear of these things happening in other schools in this city. But not here. We have a zero tolerance policy for any sort of violence."

Lux's entire posture changed and she looked at me

triumphantly. I had to admit, even when gloating, she was a Maybelline ad. It was deeply annoying.

"But," AssHead continued, "there is no evidence of actual violence here. Only the perceived threat of violence."

I let myself relax a little. I wouldn't get kicked out and this might not even affect my mom.

"*Perceived?*" Lux said.

"You say she threatened you with scissors; Ms. Chavez says she was just taking them off the shelf. Your art teacher says he didn't see anything but two students in the closet. It's your word against hers."

"I screamed," Lux said. "Why would I scream?"

"Because you hate me?" I suggested.

"I don't believe this," Lux said. "She's crazy. Ask her about the prank at the party. Ask her!"

AssHead humored Lux and looked at me. "Do you care to elaborate on this 'prank,' Ms. Chavez?"

The 'prank' was the reason for all of this. If I'd never gone to that stupid party, I never would've bumped into Lux in the first place. If I hadn't laughed at her, the whispers about me, the posts, never would've started.

I swallowed hard. I knew who was really behind that prank. I could've told her right then that there was a club at this school and she'd gotten caught up in their fun. I could've really blown it for them with just one word, taken the heat off me and delivered a true, clearer target.

But I either cared about this group too much or I didn't care about myself at all, because I said, "It was me."

Lux was not expecting that. AssHead seemed surprised, too.

"You see?" Lux said. "So are you going to expel her or what?"

"Well, no. Since the prank didn't happen on school grounds, there's not really anything we can do about it. But, Rachel, I think you owe Lux an apology."

"I'm sorry, Lux." And I meant it. I had nothing against her except for the fact that she seemed to hate my guts. I didn't know what had come over me in the supply closet, but I had to make sure I never felt that way again. I couldn't risk what happened last year happening here.

Lux paused at my apology, and I felt a flare of hope. Maybe that was all she needed to hear. Maybe she would finally take me out of her cross hair(extension)s and we could put this behind us. But Lux's expression did not change. She was still tense in her seat, still staring at me like I'd just tried to kill her. Which was fair, I guess.

"That's an admission of guilt," Lux said, glaring

at AssHead. "I know how this works, my father's an attorney." I knew as much from Saundra, who'd told me that even though Lux's dad made about a million bucks an hour and her mom traded money on Wall Street, Lux resented her parents for having boring jobs instead of working as editorial directors or celebrity stylists or some other position with cultural cache.

"I'm bringing suit," Lux said, shooting up from her seat.

"Okay, okay, no suing anyone in my office," Ass-Head said. But Lux ignored him, grabbing her tiny leather backpack and heading out the door.

"I don't think she was being serious," AssHead said, turning to me, though he didn't look so sure.

"She can do whatever she wants." I stood up to leave, but AssHead stopped me at the door.

"The school is aware of your past trauma, Ms. Chavez."

"My past trauma," I repeated slowly.

"Yes, your mother let us know what happened to you last year and we're here to support you. It can't have been easy to survive something like that. Just . . . I don't want to hear about any more pranks, all right?"

I avoided looking into his eyes, hoping he wouldn't see how hot my face was getting. I only nodded and slipped past him.

9

IT WAS A LONG way back to Brooklyn. On the subway, I practiced what I was going to say, going over my options on the 6, then settling on my defense on the L, perfecting it all on the walk home, and ultimately blanking on the climb to our third-floor walkup. The door had three locks on it, per my own request, and before I got to the second one, the door swung open. My mom stood on the other side with a scowl on her face.

"You're home early," I said.

"Mr. Braulio stopped by my class," she said.

It took me a minute to remember that this was Ass-Head's actual name. "Oh."

My mom stepped aside and I came in. Our place in Greenpoint was an adjustment from our old house on Long Island. It was about thirteen hundred square feet smaller, there was only one bathroom, and our downstairs neighbors played classic rock so loud that the floors vibrated. But I liked it here. I actually liked the fact that we were sandwiched between apartments and that there were people and noise at all hours of the night and that when I opened my window, I could smell the Polish food from the restaurant on the corner.

But right now, standing before my mom, I wanted to be anywhere but here.

"When I said you should get more involved in school, I meant join the field hockey team. Not get into lawsuits."

"Mom, please. I would never join the field hockey team."

"This isn't a joke, Rachel. You know, I was worried you weren't making friends. I didn't know I had to worry about you making enemies."

"Can I get something to eat first?" I shuffled past her to the kitchen. I stuck my head in the refrigerator in a futile attempt to avoid having this conversation. It'd been stupid of me, confessing to that prank. I still didn't know why I'd done it. It wasn't like I wanted credit for it. And I wasn't trying to protect a club that I didn't have anything to do with and that wanted nothing to do with me. But maybe a part of me just wished I *had* pulled that prank. Because Lux deserved it.

"I'll never make friends at that school," I said into the fridge. "The kids at Manchester are different."

"Different how?"

I grabbed a bottle of water and closed the door. "For starters, some of the senior girls are already on the hunt for their perfect debutante gowns and we have Craigslist furniture."

"I thought you liked that nightstand we repainted."

"I do," I said. I shook my head, trying to come up with a better example for my mom. "Some of my classmates still have nannies, Mom."

"They have housekeepers."

"If your housekeeper walks you to school every morning and hands you your lunch, I'm sorry, but you officially have a nanny. It's like I'm at school with a bunch of aliens. Actually, no, it's like *I'm* the alien."

"I know you feel that way now, Rachel, but every teenager feels that way, too."

"You don't get it." I tried to walk away, but you couldn't get very far in this apartment. I thought about escaping to my room, but I know my mom would have just followed me.

I flopped down on the couch. My mom sat next to me, forcing herself into my line of vision. "Okay, I don't get it. So tell me."

There was so much I wanted to say. The words filled my mouth like spit that I couldn't swallow, threatening to spill through my clenched teeth. But I didn't know how to say what was wrong. I didn't know how to say that I didn't feel like myself.

Not since what happened last year.

I couldn't tell my mother that ever since what Ass-Head called my "past trauma," it was like there were two sides of me at war with each other. I was either a regular teenager or I was a monster, and the one that I should've been—the normal, happy-go-lucky girl—felt like an imposter.

I was trying to do all the things I was supposed to. I was forcing myself to go to parties and meet people and gossip with Saundra in our corner of the lunchroom. And maybe it would've worked at a different school, but at Manchester, I stuck out. I couldn't blend in in a place where everyone was a perfect specimen, carefully curated to belong like priceless museum pieces. After the attack, I had been labeled a freak at my old school, and now it was following me here.

But I couldn't tell my mom any of that. Instead, what came out was, "You don't get how alone I feel."

With those words, I felt the mask I'd chosen to wear to survive Manchester—to make my mother think that everything was okay—starting to slip. I could feel it coming down with the tears. I wiped my cheek quickly before my mom could see. But my voice betrayed me.

"Mom, what happened last year . . . it changed me. It turned me into . . ."

My throat tightened before I could finish. And there was no point hiding the tears anymore either. Mom cupped my no-doubt blotchy, red face in her hands.

"You went through something that no one should ever have to go through," my mom said. "There is *nothing* wrong with you."

I bit my lip to try to stop the tears from coming and nodded.

But there *was* something wrong with me. It clawed at my insides, desperate to get out. Like the chestbuster from *Alien*. It hadn't burst out of my rib cage yet, but people could tell. No matter how well I wore the mask, people saw it. Lux saw it better than anyone.

"I know starting at a new school is hard," Mom said. "But it's going to get better. You just can't go picking fights."

"I know, I'm sorry." When my mom hugged me, I leaned into it. She smoothed my hair with her hand and it instantly made me feel better.

"My little Jamonada." She sighed. "Wanna watch a scary movie?"

I smiled into her shoulder.

10

THE NEXT DAY at school was a nightmare.

When I walked into a room, people did one of two things: They either started talking about me among themselves, or they stopped talking altogether. It was one thing to choose not to associate with people and another thing to have them actively shun you. The dominoes had been set up in AssHead's office and Lux's penny loafers had kicked them all down.

I got to Women in Literature early and took the corner seat in the back. I watched as my classmates filed in, all of them spotting me, all of them electing to sit in the seats farthest away from me. Even Thayer, the only person I'd actually had a conversation with, steered clear of my shame corner. I was an island, and the longer the desk next to mine stayed empty, the more it seemed to glow with glaring obviousness.

Class had already started and Ms. Liu was writing

something on the board when Bram walked in late. I watched as he saw the empty seat next to me and searched the room for another. But there wasn't one. He walked over to me with a resigned expression.

As he sat down, I got a whiff of pine and lime. His shampoo. Against my best efforts, the scent brought our kiss back to the forefront of my mind. If I could've cast the memory out of me with holy water, I would have, if only so that Bram couldn't see how fiercely it was making me blush. I wondered if he could tell what I was thinking about and began blushing. Then I wondered if he ever thought about it, even by accident, and blushed even harder.

No, he probably never thought about our kiss. Which was a good thing, because it almost meant that he hadn't told Lux about it either. For that, I was grateful.

"Term paper time!" Ms. Liu announced. "Your topic is: female authors and their male protagonists."

Thayer Turner's hand immediately shot up. "Can we have partners?"

Ms. Liu sighed. "Fine, you can partner up with the person sitting next to you."

I ducked my head down, face burning. The only way this day could get any better was if the ceiling crashed on top of me. I expected Bram to beg the person on his left to partner up with him, or to raise his hand and tell Ms. Liu he was in the wrong seat today. But out of the corner of my eye, I could see Bram staring straight ahead as if he hadn't heard Ms. Liu. It seemed like he wasn't going to put up a fight.

The guy sitting in front of me glanced back at us and snorted. Apparently, he found it hilarious that I had to partner with the boyfriend of the girl I'd allegedly tried to stab in the art-supply closet. Like Bram, I stared straight ahead and tried to ignore him, but I was relieved Bram hadn't made a scene. By the time the bell rang, I had finally worked up the nerve to speak to him. I turned to Bram, but he spoke first.

"I'll write the paper," he said. His voice was deeper than I expected, the low rumble of a train over tracks. It was weird, having kissed him without ever having heard him speak.

"Shouldn't I help?"

He swept the books off his desk and stood. "No."

By lunchtime, my phone was blowing up with new memes about me. Only this time, instead of me snatching Lux's hair out, these memes depicted me as a raging maniac with a pair of scissors. In one of the memes someone had placed a picture of my face over that of Lupita Nyong'o from *Us*, sporting golden shears. I had to give them credit for good taste.

I shoved my phone into my pocket and tried to feel grateful that at least no one was making fun of me to my face. I could deal with memes. Until I got to the lunch line in the cafeteria.

"Murderer."

My blood went cold, and I looked up to see who'd said it. It was the girl behind me on line. I spotted her micro bangs and remembered I'd seen her at the abandoned-house party. She'd been sitting out on the stoop, reading a book. There was an odd expression on her face now, almost like admiration.

"Excuse me?" I said.

"You murdered Lux McCray."

She spoke so calmly that it was unnerving. "I didn't—" My voice cracked, and I had to start again. "I didn't kill anyone."

"Not literally," the girl continued. "Just her image. With a pair of scissors, right?" She laughed and it sounded strange coming out of her mouth. "You're the Arts and Crafts Killer of Manchester. Kudos."

"Don't call me that," I said, but she didn't seem to hear me.

"Move it along, girls," one of the lunch ladies behind the counter said.

"I don't pay you to *rush* me," the girl growled at her.

I paid for my food and got as far away from the

girl as I could, but her words followed me like a dark shadow. I could feel panic start to set in. It made my tray quiver as I tried to unclench my hands. I didn't even bother to wait for Saundra at our usual table, just headed straight to the back. I didn't want to wonder whether she'd suck it up and sit with me or just avoid me like everyone else. I would make the decision for her. I picked a new table, the one adjacent to the door that opened to the back alley, where all the garbage got taken out. No one ever sat there. It was perfect.

I took out my phone and tried to steady my breathing. I could've distracted myself in a million different ways, so of course I went to Matthew's Instagram. My fingers typed his name in automatically, like they'd done a million times before. I tapped on the soccer picture again, the last one he'd ever posted. It wasn't just his smile, or how happy he seemed. I liked to see if there were any new comments. His friends had left all their goodbye messages in the post. They'd stopped a while ago, but sometimes a new message popped up. Nothing today.

"He's cute." Saundra peered over my shoulder, getting an eyeful of Matthew. "Is he from your old school?"

I startled and rushed to put my phone away. "Do you mind?"

The wounded look on Saundra's face made me instantly feel like crap.

"I'm sorry for snapping at you," I said quickly. "You just scared me."

"Geez, you're jumpy. Anyways, why are you sitting all the way over here?"

"You don't have to sit with me," I said. "You must've heard what Lux's been saying about me."

"What, that you pulled that prank on her at the séance? Please. No offense, Rachel, but I really don't think you have the energy to come up with something so elaborate. Also, I was the one who dragged you to that party. Lux is a known liar who, coincidentally, does not deserve that sweet baby angel boyfriend of hers, but that's beside the point."

Saundra either had the attention span of a gnat or she was kinder than I deserved, because she set her tray next to mine and sat down like the whole thing—my pariah status, the snapping—was already forgotten.

I felt my insides twist. Saundra still wanted to sit with me. Even though I sucked. She pitied me, which made me pity myself. I needed to put an end to this pity party before things got even more pathetic.

"I'm serious, you don't have to sit here. You should leave before someone else sees you talking to me."

Saundra looked at me, confused and maybe a little hurt. "Rachel—"

I stood. "It's fine, I'll go."

I was already on my way, palms pushing against the exit door. No alarm sounded and nobody stopped me.

Manchester wanted me there about as much as I wanted to be there.

I didn't go far. Central Park was across the street and it was a nice day. I planned to take one of my usual aimless, lazy strolls to forget about how shitty everything was. But before I did that, I stopped at one of the hot dog carts at the entrance. I'd never gotten around to eating lunch.

"Two hot dogs, please." Someone ordered from behind me. I spun around to tell off whoever had cut in front of me.

"Do you want yours with ketchup?" Freddie asked.

It took me a beat to answer. "And mustard."

He made a face but it faded quickly. "One with ketchup and one with ketchup and mustard, please," he told the vendor.

"What are you doing here?"

"I saw you leave the lunchroom. Got curious."

"So you decided to ditch, too?"

"Mhmm." Freddie handed the vendor a couple bucks and accepted the dogs wrapped in foil. He opened one up, saw the mustard, and handed it to me.

"Thank you," I said as I took it.

"You're welcome."

We walked farther into the park. I ate my hot dog silently as I tried to figure out Freddie's deal. Not just his motives for being here right now, but also the super-secret club he was a part of. The guy was kind of an enigma.

There was a dichotomy in everything about Freddie. He was slim but not scrawny. Sinewy, maybe. But if he were on a football field, he'd get plowed, easy. His hair was close-cropped and tidy on the sides, but the top was loose and messy and fell over his eyes. His eyes were nice. Deep brown and shrouded with so many lashes it looked like he wore liner. But his glasses threw enough of a glare to obscure them most of the time. It was like he was almost complete, but not quite. Almost put together. Almost perfect.

"So why'd you run off?" Freddie asked.

"Why'd you come after me?"

"I told you. Curious. Your turn."

I took another bite of my hot dog. "Isn't it obvious? I wanted to get away from there."

Freddie's mouth was full but he nodded. "Yeah, Manchester's a trip at first, but you get used to it."

"How did you get used to it?"

"I figured out a way to game the system. You have no idea how much those people will pay for a halfway decent book report." Freddie devoured his last bite of hot dog, leaving a small smear of ketchup in the corner of his lip.

I remembered what Saundra had said, about Freddie's illicit yet lucrative extracurricular hustle. "I don't think I can game my way out of this one."

"Rachel, I know Lux blames you for what happened at the séance. I'm sorry if that has made things tough for you at school. But it'll blow over. Something new will happen that'll have everyone talking and they'll move on."

"Will you and your mysterious club be responsible for this *something new*, by any chance?"

"Maybe." His eyes shone behind his glasses and his lips quirked, but I couldn't take him seriously with that bit of ketchup still on his face.

"You've got some . . ." I gestured at my own lip, and he swiped his hand over his mouth. "So if I ask you what you guys have planned, will you tell me?"

"Sorry, I can't."

I tore a bite off my hot dog and began walking ahead, forcing Freddie to catch up.

"Why do you want in so bad?" Freddie asked. "You don't even know what we do."

"I think I'd like it."

"You might hate it."

"I think I need it."

It sounded weird when I said it like that. Desperate. Kind of vulnerable. But it was out now and I couldn't take it back. "Did you hear that I almost killed Lux McCray with a pair of scissors?"

"Yeah," Freddie snorted. "She makes up all kinds of stuff."

"It's true." I stopped walking and turned to face him. He was taller than me, and I had to tilt my head slightly to look him in the eye. "I mean . . . I wasn't going to kill her, obviously. But I did attack her with the scissors. That part is all true."

Any trace of laughter left Freddie's face, but he didn't look at me like the rest of the school did, like I was a freak. "Did she threaten you?"

"Not exactly. I just lost my cool."

"We all do."

"Yeah, but I thought I could deal with it. Lately, though, everything I've been doing isn't cutting it anymore. I just need to find something that'll make me *not* lose my cool. Like . . . an outlet."

"And you think my club will do that for you?"

"I'm willing to try it."

I thought about what Saundra had said to me that night at the party: I just needed to find my people and everything else would fall into place. Maybe Freddie and Thayer and their club were my people.

As Freddie watched me, I wondered if this conversation would end like the last one we had, with him walking away and leaving me wanting. But this time felt different.

"What's your number?" he asked.

11

I CHECKED THE time on my phone, then the street signs again.

A few hours after I gave Freddie my number, a cryptic text had popped up on my phone.

Midnight at the corner of Camp Crystal Lake's killer and when Cillian Murphy finally wakes up from his coma.

I had figured out the references pretty quickly, but had no clue how to meet someone at the corner of Jason Voorhees and *28 Days Later*. Then I'd figured "28" must relate to a street, someplace in Kips Bay or Chelsea in Manhattan. But there weren't any streets named Jason on Google Maps. Finally, I'd searched for Voorhees, which also was not a street, road, boulevard, or avenue in Manhattan. But then Google asked if I meant *Voorhies* Avenue.

Bingo.

Voorhies Avenue intersected with East 28th Street all the way at the southern edge of Brooklyn, close to the beach. I couldn't imagine anyone from Manchester even knowing this place existed, let alone setting foot there. But it was the only place that fit the clue.

Unless there was another Voorhies Avenue—one that wasn't misspelled—up in Westchester or something. But if I had to take the Metro North to get there, I was out. Sneaking out of the apartment without waking my mom was one thing; trekking to the suburbs was another. That was a different level of scary.

As I stood there watching the minutes go by on my phone, I wondered if I'd made a terrible mistake. Getting lured to a faraway spot, when no one knew where you were, to go meet some strangers felt increasingly sketchy. It was too quiet here among the crammed-together houses. I hated quiet streets. They reminded me of Long Island.

The only noise came from the beating of my heart, getting louder in my ears and quickening with every passing minute. Soon, it was drowned out by the sound of a car engine. Far, but getting closer.

I could see a white van coming down the block, the only vehicle that had been on the street for the last fifteen minutes. When it slowed down in front of me, I noticed the lettering on the side: ROPA VIEJA CATERING, with a fading photo of what looked like chicken and rice underneath.

Was this my ride? Confusion set in, which only made my heart beat faster. I tried to peer through the window, but it was opaque.

"Hello?" At the sound of my voice, the side door slammed open.

Two figures jumped out so fast they were nothing more than a blur. Before I could scream, everything went black, as if I'd been knocked out.

But I was still awake, still breathing. I realized a hood had been pulled over my head.

I began yelling and my hands went immediately to tear the hood off, but someone yanked my arms down. I kicked but my boots cut through wide-open air. I continued shouting as they lifted me, as my knees hit a hard surface, as hands gripped my shoulders and forced me into a sitting position. The engine started up again, and I jostled with the sudden movement.

I couldn't see anything beyond the hood, but my breathing grew more and more rapid as images of the attack flashed before me, when I was held down on the kitchen floor, my arms pinned just like they were now.

I screamed. The sound that tore out of me was

primal, a sound I didn't recognize. But a voice cut through it.

"Hey, it's okay." In the complete darkness, the voice rang clearly in my ears.

"Freddie?"

"I'm sorry, Rachel," Freddie said. "Hey, pull over."

"No stopping now. This is how we do things," someone else said.

The club. I took a deep breath and tried to calm down. My heart was still beating at a breakneck pace, but now as much from adrenaline as from fear. It was almost exactly like the feeling I used to get from watching horror movies, but tenfold. One hundredfold. Adrenaline didn't always have to mean fight or flight, did it? What if sometimes it meant stay and see what happens? Adrenaline for the reckless.

"If she scares this easy, maybe we *should* let her go," another voice said. This time, it was a girl's.

"No," I said quickly. I'd gotten this far. "I'm fine."

"Good," Freddie whispered close to me, his voice like a calming balm. "We're almost there."

A new sensation broke through the darkness: a hand gently encircling mine. I squeezed Freddie's hand back, grateful.

The ride felt quick, like it hadn't lasted more than five minutes. But maybe that was just because everything inside me was racing. The van came to a stop, and two hands took me by my arms and hoisted me to a stand. We walked for a few minutes, and then I could tell we'd gone indoors when the salty smell of sand and ocean changed instantly to the canned smell of a damp room. I heard keys or a chain jingling, the wail of a metal door opening.

"Watch your step," someone told me. I lifted my knees high with caution. Freddie, who was still holding my hand, guided me carefully.

At last we stopped walking. There was a tug at the back of my head and the hood slid off my face.

I blinked quickly, letting my eyes adjust to the darkness. I was in front of a wall. A lumpy gray wall. After a few more blinks, I saw that the lumps were actually pieces of skeleton. Skulls, ribs, and hands were suspended in motion and reaching out to me, like they were trying to break free from the cement. I stumbled backward, my feet catching on a long metal rail on the floor that curved into the darkness.

"Easy," Freddie said, grabbing me before I fell.

I spun around and saw that he was standing next to three other people. There was Thayer; the girl I remembered from the abandoned-house party—the same one who'd called me a murderer on the lunch line; and then there was Bram Wilding. Lux McCray–dating, object-of-Saundra's-affections, reluctant-term-paper-partner Bram Wilding.

"You've got to be kidding."

"Only a little!" Thayer said. He wore a long red robe, or maybe it was a cloak. "We are always kidding, but only a little."

I struggled to understand what I was seeing. I was pretty sure I'd never once seen this mix of people together in school. I took in my current surroundings, a dark, low-ceilinged Halloween-looking bonanza, with ghouls up on the walls and weird train tracks along the floor.

And then there was Bram. Out of everything, he was the thing that made the least sense. I was beginning to wonder if this was some sort of murder club and I'd been incredibly stupid to let them take me to a second location. But as the minutes passed, none of them brandished any weapons.

Finally, Thayer edged forward, and I reflexively took a step back and tugged on the edges of my sleeves.

"So you like scary movies," he said.

Not what I was expecting him to say. "Uh, yeah."

Felicity fixed me with a brittle stare, but Thayer's face had broken into a grin. "What kinds?"

"Kinds?"

"Kinds of scary movies," Thayer said.

"Oh. Well, I like it when scary movies are atmospheric? I also like slashers."

"My favorite, too!" Thayer said. He was practically giddy now, which only seemed to make Felicity scowl more deeply. I avoided looking at Bram.

"Hey, quick lightning round for a minute: Who was the killer in *Halloween*?"

Was he kidding? "Michael Myers."

"Correct! And in *Prom Night*?"

"Would you lay off her, Thayer?" Freddie said. "Sorry," he said to me. "Thayer likes to get ahead of himself sometimes. I know this is probably really confusing."

"Yes," Thayer said. "You're probably asking yourself, 'Why is Thayer the only one who bothered to dress up for this momentous occasion?' The answer is, I tried to get everyone else on board with the Skull and Bones robes—you know, proper attire, but as usual, I was the only one who bothered to follow the dress code for the initiation ceremony." He flicked imaginary dirt off his velvety shoulder.

"Initiation ceremony?" I looked at the others, searching their faces for clues. Felicity looked kind of ticked off. Bram looked the way he always looked: borderline bored. But Freddie smiled, and I couldn't help but smile back, reassured in spite of the incredibly bizarre situation.

"Have you ever heard of Mary Shelley?" Freddie asked.

The question was so random it temporarily stumped me. Felicity pounced. "She doesn't even know who Mary Shelley is."

I could hear the derision in her voice, and even though these people had just kidnapped me, I still wanted to belong. To have my shot. Or at least to hear what their ridiculous supersecret weird-as-fuck club was about.

"I know who Mary Shelley is," I said. "She wrote *Frankenstein*, right?"

"Do you know the story of how she came up with the idea for *Frankenstein*?" Freddie asked.

I hated to admit it in front of Felicity, who seemed to be looking for any chance to crucify me, but I shook my head.

"Oh, but it's such a good story," Thayer said. He took a step toward me, his robe billowing behind him. I sensed a dramatization coming, like we were back in Ms. Liu's class. Felicity rolled her eyes.

"Mary Shelley and her boo, Percy—he was, like, *full* married by the way, quite the scandal—went on vacation to a villa in Italy—"

"—Switzerland," Felicity said.

"That's what I said, Switzerland. Anyway, they were

there to stalk Lord Byron, who was the first real celebrity of the modern era, not to mention a pansexual literary Adonis who was also—spoiler alert—screwing his half sister, in case you didn't know. Another scandal that people like to gloss over."

"Would you please get on with it?" Felicity said.

"*Chill*," Thayer said. "Fine, I'll just skip all the lessers who were there and get to the good part. Anyway, they were crazy mofos ready to paint the town red, but they couldn't because: rain."

Freddie leaned against the wall as Thayer talked, right beneath what appeared to be a neon zombie. He caught my glance and gave me a subtle nod, as if telling me that we should let Thayer have his storytelling moment and that he'd be getting to the point eventually.

"It was the worst summer ever," Thayer went on. "Like, on record. History-making, biblical proportions bad. It rained so much that the whole crew had to stay cooped up for their entire trip and they had no internet so they were super bored, obviously. And then Lord Byron was like, 'Here's a thought! Let's see who can come up with the scariest story ever.' Lord Byron thought he was going to win 'cause he was a lord or whatever, but nope, it was the godqueen of modern horror herself, Mary Shelley."

"She came up with the idea for *Frankenstein* as a result," Freddie said.

"And that's where we get our name," Thayer said, spreading his arms. "The Mary Shelley Club."

"So you guys are . . . *Frankenstein* fans?" I asked.

"Not just *Frankenstein. Horror*," Felicity said.

"So what do you do in this club?" My gaze flicked over to Bram, who seemed to be more interested in the chipping paint on the Lizard Man hanging above him. Thayer and Freddie and Felicity—they seemed more like the type: misfits with eccentric interests. But Bram, the most popular guy in school, the rich lacrosse jock? Why was he here?

"Did you miss the part about how Mary Shelley came up with *Frankenstein*?" Felicity said. "We create scary stories."

I snorted. "That's an interesting way of pronouncing 'pranks.'"

An instant uproar ensued, with Felicity, Thayer, and Freddie talking over each other to set the record straight.

"We're not *twelve-year-olds*."

"We don't like the word 'prank' or even 'pranksters'— that's a misconception."

"It's not *just* that. There's also rigorous movie-watching practices."

Whatever they wanted to call it, it didn't matter. Because now all I could think about was Bram's involvement in the séance prank. Had he willingly put his own girlfriend through that? I thought about when I'd first seen him that night: upstairs, having what sounded like a fight with Lux. Maybe he'd been trying to warn her to leave before the séance happened. Maybe he underestimated how it would affect her. Or maybe that fight sent him over the edge and he went after her on purpose.

Then, I thought about how Lux had made my life miserable for the last two weeks and how he had done nothing to stop her. Maybe they deserved each other.

Freddie and Thayer and Felicity were speaking so quickly now that their voices muddled together and canceled each other out. But then one line stuck out, clear as a bell over the rest. "*The game is a lot more nuanced than that.*"

"What game?" I asked.

"Enough," Bram said, tired of the arguing kids. "No more info until we know you're in."

The power that came with being the most popular boy in school seemed to extend beyond campus. I wondered if anyone had ever refused Bram anything before.

While Thayer and especially Freddie seemed happy to have me there, Felicity and Bram were ambivalent, even a little hostile. Even though they'd gone to the trouble of getting me to this weird place—wherever we were—I could tell from the look of Bram and the way he spoke that he wanted me gone. The expression on his face remained the same as it had been all night: mild disinterest.

I lifted my chin. "I'm in," I said.

Thayer pumped his fist in the dark air. "A new member is born! As formal invitations go, I think we pretty much nailed it."

"Yes, thanks so much for the ride. Very thoughtful. So can we get out of here yet?" I asked.

"There's just one more thing," Freddie said.

A devious grin formed on Felicity's face. "Initiation," she said.

12

I **SAT ON** the concrete floor in the dark. Felicity, sitting with the others a few feet before me, shined a flashlight on me. It felt like an intimidation tactic, because the beam of light was so bright that it prevented me from looking directly at her, or at any of them.

As I waited for whatever they had in store for me, I went over the facts I knew:

The Mary Shelley Club was small.

It was exclusive.

They occasionally watched movies together.

They pulled off what they refused to call, but clearly were, pranks—scenarios of their own making in which they elaborately planned and executed pranks that seemed to be inspired by horror tropes.

And there was a game. But I wouldn't know more about that until after the initiation.

I squinted against the glare from the flashlight. I

wasn't too excited about the shades of frat-bro hazing. I only hoped it was worth it.

"Tell us what your greatest fear is," Bram demanded.

I thought about whether to laugh or to take the question seriously. It was hard to tell what the right thing was, being that they weren't much more than shadowy figures. Literally. Also, one of them was in full-on cosplay robe.

"Um." I cleared my throat. "I'm afraid of spiders."

More silence. I imagined them turning toward each other, already regretting their decision to invite me here, and a small panic settled over me. After all this, I might have just messed up my one shot.

"Try again," Bram said. "And don't waste our time."

The panic mixed with relief, both emotions tingling through me. I could've said anything. I had the same universal fears that most people had. I was afraid of something happening to my mom. I was afraid of losing everything I had. But in the end, there was one thing that weighed heavier than everything else. The thing I thought about all the time.

"I'm afraid of myself." I blurted. "I'm afraid that I'm a monster."

After another moment of silence, Thayer quietly asked, "Why do you feel like that?"

I'd thought if I gave them something real, they'd lay

off me. If I'd known there would be follow-up questions, I would've stuck to spiders. Felicity's beam of light shone higher up on my face and I flinched away.

"I don't know, I just . . . I feel like, what if I'm not normal? What if I'm capable of doing really bad things and that's the real me?"

I tried to keep it vague, turn my confession into a more common fear, something less uncomfortable. It didn't work.

"Tell us about Matthew Marshall," Felicity said.

Hearing his name made my blood run cold. "How do you know about that?"

"We know everything," Felicity said.

I stammered, "Those records are—are sealed. I'm a minor."

"My dad's the state's attorney," Thayer said, actually sounding vaguely apologetic. "It wasn't that hard to find out."

My heart pounded against my ribs like it was begging to be let out. I couldn't say anything. I could hardly breathe.

"Rachel, you don't have to tell us anything," Freddie said. "But we can't let you in unless you give us something real. It isn't supposed to be easy. But it'll prove something to us. And hopefully we can prove something to you."

"Yeah, you don't have to tell us," Felicity chimed in, less kindly. "But we already know."

"You can tell us," Freddie said softly. "We won't judge you."

I'd taken so much care to hide this part of myself. To leave my life on Long Island behind and start anew. But here was this group of people who wanted to hear it out loud. Now it felt like a challenge. They were daring me to talk about it. And I wanted to challenge them back. Dare them to hear it.

"Last year my house got broken into while I was home," I said, my voice steadying. "A guy with a mask chased me. Attacked me in my kitchen. His name was Matthew Marshall."

Something about the fact that I couldn't see their faces made the words come more easily.

"I tried to fight him off, but he grabbed me, and he was strong. We both fell. He pinned me to the floor. And I just remember how cold the tile was." I took a deep breath as I felt it now, clear as if I was back there, helpless. It was like the flashlight beam was a tunnel leading straight to that moment.

"I was kicking my legs and fighting as hard as I could, but I . . ." The memories were coming fast, but instead of squeezing my eyes shut and trying to keep my mind blank, I kept going. It was getting harder to talk, like hands were encircling my throat and tightening their grip.

"He had a knife . . ."

I was getting to the hardest part, the part that I'd only spoken about to my mom, the police, and my therapist before I had refused to go back. But I had come this far. I could either swallow the words or spit them out. "I fought to point it away from me. We both fought. He slipped and . . ."

I scratched at my arms even though nothing itched. Actually, I couldn't feel anything at all. I scratched harder and harder, unable to stop myself, waiting to feel something hurt. "The knife went in him. And he died."

The words sounded inadequate once spoken. But they contained within them an entire history. Of who I was. Of what I'd done.

Of whose life I'd cut short.

I did not say the words *I killed him.* Even though that's what I did. I couldn't say it, even now as I tried to free myself from the truth of it. I didn't think I'd ever be able to.

This was the part I hadn't been able to stop thinking about for a year. The ghost that haunted me.

"He was just a senior in high school. He'd been accepted to Brown." I'd memorized the facts of his life like sports fans memorize stats. I was a masochist for it, hungry, devouring all of these details, all his social media, until it made me sick.

"He was a middle child with two sisters. He was on the soccer team. He had a girlfriend named Ally. His favorite food was peanut butter and jelly sandwiches, but only with apricot jelly. He loved anime and books by James Patterson. He was . . ."

I closed my eyes, trying to suppress the flow of tears. I'd torn my heart open admitting the worst thing I'd ever done—the worst thing that *anybody* could ever do. I felt hollow.

"It was self-defense," I said in a small voice.

Felicity's flashlight beam dipped, spilling over the dirty floor. Without the light shining in my face, I could make out the forms of the people in front of me again. I could not yet tell if they were full of judgment or disgust. Probably both.

I was officially out of my daze and crashing back to the now, realizing with searing clarity that I'd just shared my darkest secret with four strangers. No, worse: with four kids from Manchester Prep.

But then out of the darkness came Freddie's voice. "Thank you for sharing that." And then, "We accept you. If you'll have us."

I blinked. It took me a minute to process what he had said. No judgment. No disgust. As I wiped the tears from my cheeks, I realized I felt different. Lighter.

"Uh, yeah," I said. "Yeah, okay."

"This is still strictly probationary," Felicity said. "Until such time as we deem it *unprobationary*."

They rose to their feet. Apparently, the initiation was over and I had passed. I stood too, wiping the back of my jeans. Someone opened the door, and the room was flooded with moonlight. They filed out and I followed, weaving through clunky cars sitting on the weird railroad tracks I hadn't been able to identify before. We were surrounded by boarded-up game booths and derelict amusement park rides, the peaks and valleys of a log flume rising up in the distance like a mountain. When I looked up over the entryway of the building we'd just left I saw the words SPOOK-A-RAMA.

All the emotions I'd been holding back—the fear, the tension, the desperation—came bursting out in a laugh. It was just a silly, stupid haunted house. Not so scary after all.

Freddie hung back and waited for me.

"I've never been to Coney Island before," I said.

"Well, how's this for a first impression?"

"How'd you get the keys to this place anyway?"

Freddie pointed his chin to the rest of the club up ahead. "You can get the keys to anything if you can pay."

Made sense.

"What you talked about in there," Freddie said. He pushed up his glasses. "I'm sorry that happened to you."

There was so much he could've said, but I was so grateful he'd chosen that. He sounded like he really meant it.

"Welcome to the Mary Shelley Club," he said.

13

BY THE TIME I arrived at school the next morning, everything that had happened the night before felt like a dream.

Because A) it'd been incredibly weird. All of it—the hood, the abduction, Coney Island. It got even weirder the more I thought about it.

And B) no one in the Mary Shelley Club said a word to me. No more texts from Freddie with further instructions, not even a glance from Bram when I passed him in the hall. Though that might've been because he was with Lux, who would probably burn the school to the ground if I dared make eye contact with her.

But for once, I wasn't worrying about Lux or that everyone else at Manchester thought I was a freak, because right now, there was space in my mind only for the Mary Shelley Club. I was still trying to figure out why they were all in the club. Was it just to create havoc? Or maybe this was simply the way bored rich kids had a good time. But that didn't explain the game, something that required skill, strategy, and some kind of scoring system. It was shrouded in an element of horror, but it sounded kind of innocent. Kids play games.

Apparently, I was in the club, but I had no idea when the game would begin. I guess I shouldn't have expected an orientation packet and a syllabus, but still, they were being kind of over the top with the secrecy thing. By the time my first morning class let out, I felt like I was going to burst out of my skin with impatience.

I spotted Felicity at her locker after second period and sped up. She was stashing her books like they were a body she was desperate to bury. A Stephen King paperback fell out. I bent down to pick it up for her.

"*Doctor Sleep*," I said cheerfully. "Haven't read this one yet."

Felicity cast me a look very much in the family of the stink eye and snatched the book out of my hand. She slammed her locker door shut and skulked away without a word.

"It's bad form to talk about the club in school," Thayer said. I jumped. He was suddenly next to me, but just as quickly as he'd appeared, he was on his way again. I chased after him.

111

"I wasn't," I said quickly.

"It's an unwritten rule. No fraternization in public. It avoids suspicion."

"Got it." I didn't point out that talking and walking down the hall together might be misconstrued as fraternization to the objective observer. "Does Felicity hate me for some reason?"

"Of course not. Maybe. Probably. Felicity's the devil," Thayer said casually. "You look terrible, by the way."

"Uh, thanks. I didn't get a lot of sleep last night."

"Why not?"

Was he serious? "I was kidnapped by a band of psychotic assholes in a catering van."

"Well, aren't you kinky."

"*Look*, I know we're not supposed to be talking about it, but when do I hear more about the club?"

"Sorry, New Girl, can't share anything yet, but soon," he whispered. "My Fear Test's in two days. Lots to do. Exciting stuff."

"Fear Test?" The words sent a sudden thrill through me. But Thayer didn't answer. Instead he walked into Ms. Liu's class and took his seat, which left me to look for mine. Bram was in the back. After the weirdness with Felicity and Thayer, I wasn't sure how to greet him, or even if I should. I decided to follow Bram's lead of continuing to ignore each other's existence.

Which was fine until Ms. Liu started going around the class asking who we'd chosen to write our term papers on.

"Patricia Highsm—" Bram started to answer.

I cut in. "Mary Shelley."

Across the room, Thayer howled. Bram's nostrils flared. And Ms. Liu told us we'd chosen wonderfully.

At lunch I decided to scour social media looking for more info on the Mary Shelley Club members. Felicity didn't appear to have Insta. Bram's was private, but he was all over Lux's grid posing behind flattering filters, nuzzling her neck, and occasionally pulling silly faces. It wasn't a side of him I'd ever seen.

Someone cleared their throat dramatically behind me.

"Saundra! Hi." I quickly shoved my phone into my book bag.

She sat down next to me pointedly, tore into her slice of sourdough pointedly, and chewed. Pointedly. The point clearly being that she wasn't talking to me. Which I fully deserved.

"I'm sorry about the way I acted yesterday," I said. "I was a jerk. A really awful, big, obnoxious jerk."

"I'm listening," Saundra said.

"I'm just going through some weird stuff. Everyone

at school thinks I'm a lunatic and Lux McCray wants me dead and I'm pretty sure I flunked my bio quiz."

"Go on . . ."

"I'm sorry I freaked. I can't believe you still want to sit next to me after the way I acted. I'm lucky to have you as a friend."

I could tell Saundra was softening because when she sipped her kombucha through her stainless-steel straw, it was decidedly unpointedly. But to make sure I was fully back on her good side, I cleared my throat and nodded at the popular lunch table.

"Bram looks . . . nice today." The truth was, Bram didn't look any different than he normally did, but this was my olive branch.

Just like that, Saundra's face lit up and any awkwardness was swept away. It was the regularly scheduled Bram News Network, where Saundra was both the anchor and the pundit, delivering the latest breaking news. Right now she was reflecting on what his best feature was, but as I glanced over, all I could focus on was Bram's imperfections. A slight gap between his front teeth. Eyes darker than an abyss. The kind of shiny chestnut hair that belonged in a barbershop window display. Okay, I guess some people might find those faults charming. He looked up, sensing my gaze, and I quickly dropped my eyes to my sandwich.

Saundra droned on, and much like with cable news, I sat and absorbed all of it without really knowing why. As my brain turned numb, I knew I had to do something before I face-planted into my grilled cheese.

"We're kind of partners on a school project," I blurted.

Saundra's eyes bugged out of her head. "You're *what*?"

"Yeah. So that's gonna be fun."

"Why do you say it like that?"

"Like what?"

"Like it's *not* going to be fun?"

"Because Bram is . . ." I glanced at his table. "He's, like, impenetrable. He doesn't say much and he sort of looks angry all the time."

"Bram's a sweetheart."

"Okay, there's gotta be a reason you keep saying that about him."

"There is." Saundra leaned back in her seat and lifted her eyes dreamily toward the fluorescent lights above us, already lost in a memory. "It happened on an Upper Lower School class trip to the Empire State Building."

"Upper Lower?"

"The two highest grades in the Lower School got to go. We were in fifth grade. Anyway, we got up to the

Observation Deck and I got really dizzy. Right when I thought I was going to throw up or pass out or pee myself, Bram appeared next to me. I was so embarrassed that he was seeing me at my worst."

"Sounds awful."

"It was amazing," Saundra continued. "Bram took me to a quiet corner and held my gross, sweaty hand, and told me to look at him and keep breathing. *Fifth-grade Bram* did that. He was so composed and mature, even back then. He didn't let go of my hand the entire time, not until Mr. Porsif told us it was time to go. I still hate heights, but I'd go back to the top floor of the Empire State Building if Bram asked me to."

I tried to reconcile fifth-grade Bram with the Bram I knew. But the truth was, I really didn't know too much about him. Just one of his secrets. But we all had secrets.

"What do you know about Felicity Chu?" I asked. While I had Saundra's encyclopedic knowledge at my disposal, I might as well use it. Anything to keep her from going on about Bram.

"Felicity Chu?" Saundra looked behind her, as though Felicity was lurking somewhere close by, a vampire ready to strike. But as far as I could tell, Felicity wasn't in the cafeteria.

"She's freaky," Saundra said. "Why do you want to know about her?"

"Just curious. Her locker's close to mine. What's so freaky about her?"

Saundra fixed me with a wide-eyed look, like the answer was obvious. "Black lipstick."

I rolled my eyes, but Saundra didn't let up. "I'm serious. That is a *choice* when her mom is the CFO of Isee Cosmetics—she can have all the lipstick shades she wants. It's a real shame we're not friends."

"Anything else?"

"Okay, how about the fact that she hates everybody? And she's got a weird crush on Stephen King. Who has crushes on authors? *Old* authors."

"She reads a lot. Doesn't mean she has a crush on the author."

"She has a black-and-white picture of him hanging in her locker."

"Oh."

"Plus, I think all those horror novels are going to her head. Giving her ideas."

I kept my voice casual. "What do you mean?"

"She got suspended last year for kicking Alexandra Turbinado in the crotch during Pottery elective. And then again for doing the same thing to Reggie Held.

Which is extra weird because everyone takes Pottery to, like, relax, or fall in love, or whatever, but it just made Felicity super aggressive."

Definitely not something I would've found on Felicity's Instagram. Being friends with Saundra was proving beneficial. "Thayer Turner?"

Saundra looked at me funny and I realized that to her, it just seemed like I was rattling off a random list of Manhattan Prep weirdos. "Um, just curious because he seems nice. He let me borrow his notes."

"I wouldn't use those. All he does is goof off in class. Just another boy who thinks he's a lot funnier than he actually is. He's only still here because of his parents."

"Really? He seems like a normal kid to me."

"That's all part of the media-ready package," Saundra said, taking a sip of her kombucha. "Thayer's dad made him get a *normal* job at a movie theater so he can tell everyone his son is just like any other teenager. I assume Thayer goes along with it for the free popcorn. Who keeps texting you?"

I hadn't even realized that my phone had been buzzing in my backpack. Nothing got past Saundra. I fished it out.

Meeting at this address tonight. 9pm. Freddie.

"Who's it from?" Saundra prodded. "Some sort of emergency?"

I didn't want to lie to her, but I was bound to a secret now. "No, just a friend from back home."

My phone vibrated again. I quickly peeked down, avoiding Saundra's searching gaze.

Don't worry. No kidnapping this time. ;-)

14

IT WAS RAINING, and as I stood under my umbrella, looking up at the building at the address from Freddie's text, I felt like I was about to enter the mansion in *The Rocky Horror Picture Show*.

I was on the Upper East Side, just a few blocks from Manchester. The closer you got to Central Park, the nicer the buildings became, with elegant awnings and doormen in gold-trimmed uniforms poised just beyond glass doors. But the buildings that were even fancier than that didn't have doormen or lobbies. Some of them were small museums or the headquarters of societies, with crests next to their imposing double doors and ivy crawling up their walls; others were beautiful private residences. This place didn't have any gold plaques, and I was pretty sure it wasn't a museum. But it was still a beautiful limestone townhouse that probably cost more than my life.

I'd tried asking Freddie more questions by text, about who lived here and what we'd be doing tonight, but he'd remained evasive. So I rang the bell and waited.

Bram opened the door, looming large in the frame.

His usual oxford shirt and tie had been replaced by sweats and a black T-shirt with a skull snapping back its jaw. My brain seemed to glitch whenever I was alone with Bram and the first thing I said was "Is this your house?"

"Yes."

If Saundra only knew I was here right now. She'd freak.

"Are you going to come inside?" Bram said. "You're letting in the rain."

I stepped over the threshold, shaking droplets off my umbrella.

"I'll take it," Bram said. He dropped it in a pewter bin next to the door and then held out his hand. I hesitated until I realized that he was reaching for my jacket. The whole exchange stretched on for an impossibly long and silent minute, with the only sound in the grand entryway the shuffle of my wet raincoat slipping off my shoulders and the clinking of hangers in the coat closet.

And all the while, I could smell the pine-and-lime scent of his shampoo.

"H   ogize," I said. "For
what   Williamsburg?"

W   n Williamsburg was
my w   *myself on you like a
creep.*   the burning in my
cheeks. "I was drunk and I thought you were somebody
else, obviously. I know you're with . . . with someone,
and it was wrong and I feel horrible about it and it was
a mistake."

As I talked, Bram watched me with the dis-
interested look of a DMV employee, though the color
in his cheeks seemed to deepen. Maybe it was a trick
of the light.

"So, yeah," I said finally. "Sorry."

When Bram did speak, it was only to say, "Okay."

It wasn't much, but I took it as a sign that we could
finally put that mortifying episode behind us. And
maybe this quasi truce would extend to Lux. Maybe if
Bram and I could be cool, then Lux and I could be civil
toward each other.

Never had so much hope been squeezed out of a
tiny "okay."

"Everyone else is already in the study," he said.

I nodded like all of this was normal. The conversation we'd just had. That this place had a *study*.

"Um, which way do I go?" Bram's townhouse was

huge, and as I glanced around I realized that the Wildings were rich. Like *rich* rich. This place must've been two townhouses put together. There were an impossible number of doorways, all leading to high-ceilinged rooms filled with oil paintings and lavish furniture. I could see myself quickly getting lost, and I didn't want to be late for my first club meeting.

Bram gestured toward a winding grand staircase that sprouted from the foyer. As I started to climb it, I remembered the last night I'd spent at my friend Amy's house back on Long Island, over a year before. I'd decided to walk the five blocks home, and the entire time I could've sworn someone was following me. On that quiet night with no cars on the street or people on the sidewalks, all I could sense was my pulse pounding in my ears and what I was sure was someone's eyes boring into my back.

I felt that way now, the difference being that I wasn't imagining someone behind me. I could feel Bram's gaze like a hand brushing the back of my neck.

When we got to the second floor, we walked toward a light at the end of the hallway. The study was lit with warm lamplight and wall sconces and smelled faintly of the leather-bound books that crammed the bookcases along the walls. There were priceless accoutrements adorning the shelves—a Grecian urn glazed in turquoise, a charcoal sketch of an abstract nude figure, a brass ballerina being used as a bookend. I spotted a small painting of a blocky lady. I took a second to wonder if it was a Picasso before I realized that of *course* it was. You probably couldn't own a place like this if you didn't have a Picasso.

It turned out my mom had been right when she'd said private school would expand my world. Normally, I would have to go to the Met to see the things that Bram's family used as paperweights.

There was a large rosewood desk in front of casement doors that opened onto a balcony, and in the center of the room were a couch, a chair, and a chaise longue. Freddie, Felicity, and Thayer were spread amongst the furniture, limbs splayed with the kind of informal ease that comes from being deeply familiar with a place. Like animals in their natural habitat.

"Hiya, New Girl," Thayer said.

"You made it," Freddie said, flashing me a smile from the chesterfield sofa. He patted the space beside him, but under Bram's scrutiny, I suddenly felt shy and sat at the other end of it, leaving a gulf of chocolate-brown leather between us. Felicity didn't say anything at all.

At last, Bram sat in a tufted armchair. He may have been wearing sweats, but he still looked filthy rich and aloof in the big, throne-like chair. I couldn't help but think: *Bram, in the study, with the candlestick.*

"Let's get started." He reached for a remote on the side table and clicked a button.

A projection screen lowered in front of the built-in bookcase and Felicity stood up to hit the lights.

Freddie leaned over. "We like to begin our meetings with a scary movie," he said.

"Pick one," Bram said, nodding at me. He grabbed a keyboard and balanced it on his knees, his fingers poised, waiting for my cue. It felt like a challenge, one that he wanted me to fail.

As I held his gaze, my mind began to race. Was this another test? Like Thayer's twenty questions at the haunted house? For all I knew this club was all about trashy B movies or torture porn. What if they only liked highbrow stuff—the Oscar-nominated shininess of *Get Out* or *The Silence of the Lambs*? If I picked a classic, would that make me boring? *The Exorcist* was my favorite horror film, but they'd probably seen it a million times. What if I picked something none of them found particularly scary? Some people considered *Gremlins* for kids, but those little monsters were pretty traumatizing. I could go obscure and pick something none of them had heard of, but would that make me a pretentious try-hard? If I picked *Friday the 13th Part VIII: Jason*

Takes Manhattan would they just kick me out of the club immediately?

Who was I kidding? I would never in good conscience pick *Jason Takes Manhattan.*

And now I was taking too long. The room was all piercing stares, and I was the pincushion. I decided to go with something that covered all my bases. A B-movie classic.

"*Black Christmas.*"

"Original, remake, or remake of the remake?" Felicity asked.

"Don't insult the girl," Freddie said, his voice laced with amusement.

"Original," I said.

Bram's fingers danced over the keyboard, and on the screen, one file opened after another until a list of scary movies appeared.

"Behold, Bram's Ultimate Collection of Horror," Thayer announced. "True story: His parents once stumbled upon this hallowed list while curled up on the couch looking for *Sister Act 2: Back in the Habit.* So horrified were they by the disturbing array showing their golden boy's pent-up aggression that they proposed sending our dear Bram for psychoanalysis."

"And what happened?" I couldn't tell if Thayer was joking.

"He talked his way out of it, of course!" Thayer said.

"Champion of the debate team!" Freddie said.

"Voted most likely to host a talk show!" Felicity added.

"Guinness World Record-holder for biggest talker ever!" Thayer said.

They were obviously ribbing him, but Bram seemed to enjoy it because he did something I hadn't ever seen him do. He smiled. Then he clicked play and the words *Black Christmas* appeared on the screen in gothic white outline.

Thayer rubbed his hands together and grinned with excited anticipation. "Holiday movies always give me the warm fuzzies."

An hour and a half later and Thayer's warm fuzzies were still intact. He sighed, deeply satisfied. "Awesome."

Just one word, but it filled me with the confidence that I'd made the right choice. I fought to keep from beaming.

"You think every horror film is awesome," Freddie said.

Confidence gone.

"It's only awesome if you enjoy the voyeurism of tormenting a houseful of nubile young girls," Felicity said.

I shot Felicity an incredulous look. *Voyeurism?* Well,

yeah, but 80 percent of all horror was voyeuristic. Also, *nubile?* That word had the biggest ick factor. But I didn't say any of that. I was new to this group. I needed to tread carefully.

"Not to mention the misogyny," Felicity went on.

Screw it. Careful treading was for wimps. "You could look at it like that," I said, "Or you could say that slashers actually give the Final Girl the kind of agency that women in other film genres never experience."

There was a moment of silence as the others turned to look at me. I sank into my corner of the chesterfield a little, wondering if I'd spoken out of turn. But Felicity actually looked thrilled, like a stray cat presented with a bowl of fresh milk.

"Yeah, at the end," Felicity said. "Until then, it's just an hour of sorority girls running around naked—"

"—not in this movie."

"—or waiting by the phone," Felicity continued. "Such a tired sexist trope."

"This is the first major introduction to the call-coming-from-inside-the-house plot twist," I said. "It should be given credit for that."

Felicity rolled her eyes. "*When a Stranger Calls* did it better."

"You're missing the point. In a movie like this, the female lead takes control of her life."

"She gets *rescued*," Felicity said. "I'd hardly call that taking control."

"Okay, but Jess survives. We have to get through the early—yes, inherent—misogyny in order to show the protagonist breaking free of its trappings. It's character development. It's reflective of real life."

"Yeah, *Black Christmas* is totally relatable," Felicity said, rolling her eyes.

Sarcasm aside, I found myself leaning forward eagerly. I was actually having a conversation about horror theory with someone. Like Thayer had said: awesome. I could've gone on like that all night, and the way Felicity was sitting, fingernails clawed into the edges of her seat, poised to pounce, it looked like she could've, too. Maybe this was how to get Felicity to not hate me. Maybe this was the way to win them all over.

But then Freddie switched the lights back on and the spell was broken.

"Down with the patriarchy," he said, raising a fist in solidarity. This time, both Felicity and I rolled our eyes.

"But this is the portion of the evening where we answer some of your questions," he continued.

"You probably have so many!" Thayer said. He bounced up, suddenly determined to make use of every inch of the study as he took on the role of emcee for my benefit. He spun a copper-colored world globe and Bram promptly put a hand on it to stop it.

"Firstly, what is it that we do here at the Mary Shelley Club?" Thayer pontificated. "The simple answer is that we are horror aficionados. Appreciators of the technique of terror. Experts in the field of fear."

"As I said way more succinctly: We like horror," Felicity said.

"How long has the club been around?"

"A while," Freddie said. "But no one is really sure how long. Bram and I both joined as freshmen. Thayer and Felicity came on as sophomores last year, when other members graduated."

"You could say the objective of the club is to answer a simple question," Thayer continued. "What scares people the most?"

"Which brings us to the contest," Freddie said, casting me a secret smile.

I sat up straighter. If I'd had a notebook with me, I would've been taking notes.

Thayer cleared his throat. "To prove who amongst us is the most well-versed in the ways of fright, and to see which method of horror evokes the biggest reaction, we stage what we've come to call Fear Tests."

"Fear Tests?"

"Each of us comes up with a horror scenario," Felicity said. "It could be something original or a classic horror trope, maybe something you saw in a movie. And then we bring it to life." She smiled with her lips closed but stretched wide enough to crinkle the corners of her eyes. If she'd been going for a diabolical look, it was working.

"We're used to reading horror stories or hearing them around campfires or seeing them play out on a screen," Freddie said, "but the only way to truly feel fear is to experience it, to make it three-dimensional."

"Do horror movie tropes even work in real life?" I asked.

"That's part of the challenge," Freddie said. "Are all the things we see in horror films scary only because we're trained to see them that way? The shrieking violins, the angles of the shots? The anticipated jump scares? Or can we elicit real fear when we strip all the extra stuff away? No music. No perfectly framed scenes. Just you and what scares you the most."

I could feel goosebumps rising on my arms, but not from fear or anxiety. These were the excited kind. An electric thrill.

"We all get to direct our own Fear Tests," Felicity said. "And everyone plays a part."

"Kind of like being actors in a play," Thayer said. "A scary play."

"After your Fear Test is complete, we rate it," Felicity added.

"Kind of like being in the Olympics," Thayer said. "A scary Olympics."

"It's more like an exam," Freddie said. "Like in school, your highest grade can be a hundred. We each grade you, then tally up the scores to find the average. We evaluate your technique—"

"Your panache!" Thayer cut in, plopping down next to me on the couch.

"—ingenuity. Basically we're looking for something that makes your test stand out. Whoever has the highest rating wins."

"Wins what?" I asked. I thought it was a pretty reasonable question, but it was met with silence. Felicity in particular looked at me like I was definitely not worthy of being there.

"Bragging rights," Thayer said finally.

No cash prize. Nothing shiny to display on a shelf. I guess it made sense. What could you give to kids who already had everything?

"So the séance at the abandoned-house party . . . that was a Fear Test?" I asked. "Whose was it?"

"We all did that one together," Freddie said. "Kind of like a kickoff to the contest. A warm-up."

"All right, enough pleasantries," Bram said. "Time for the rules."

He stood. He'd hardly said anything the entire night, so now we were all hanging on his every word.

"We don't talk about the Mary Shelley Club," he said.

Thayer leaned close to whisper: "We've all heard the *Fight Club* jokes."

Bram cleared his throat and proceeded with the rules. They were as follows:

- The Mary Shelley Club is a secret.
- Everyone gets one Fear Test that all members must help execute. You must perform the task that the leader of the Fear Test assigns to you.
- You must pick your target before the test starts. That's your eight ball. You may scare everyone else in the room, but if you don't sink your eight ball, you've failed the test.
- The game isn't over until everyone's had their turn.
- Judging is left up to the other players' discretion.
- A member of the club may never be a target.
- If you break any of these rules, your game is over.
- A Fear Test ends when your target screams.

I tried absorbing it all, but even as I nodded along, I knew I wouldn't have a full grasp of everything until I actually played. Which meant I had only one more question.

"When do we start?"

15

TWO NIGHTS LATER, I stood in a dim alleyway in the East Village, facing a clown.

"Red or blue?" I asked, holding up the face paint palette. I was helping Freddie with his finishing touches.

"Red."

The party at Trevor Driggs's house had been going for an hour, and the rest of the club members were already in place for Thayer's Fear Test. Freddie's role wouldn't take more than ten seconds, but he was going all out anyway. I knew they all really got into the club, but this still felt a little excessive.

The face-painting kit we'd bought at Abracadabra came in a cheap plastic molding, but it had all the primary colors. It also came with a little makeup wand, but after coating Freddie's face in white, the little foam applicator was totally spent. My fingers would have to do.

I dipped the tip of my pointer into the red. I tried to keep my hand steady. I couldn't tell if my nerves were from my usual social anxiety or the fact that I was about to participate in my first Fear Test. I hesitated, my finger hovering over Freddie's face as our eyes locked. Or maybe it wasn't either of those things.

"This is deeply weird," I said.

"What? All clubs require participation."

"Yeah? You do this for Film Club, too?"

"Have you seen the Film Club? Clowns, all of them."

I smiled. "You mean the Tisch Boys?"

Freddie's face fell. "Is *that* what they call us?"

"Yes." I tried not to crack up at the look on his face.

"*No*. No. Please tell me you are joking."

"I would, but I cannot lie to you, Freddie."

He pretended to gag and I laughed.

"Film Club is like the bizarro version of the Mary Shelley Club," Freddie said. "Whenever we watch a movie it's usually something by Wes Anderson. He's Scott Tisch's favorite. We gotta kick him out of the club."

Talking to Freddie was so easy that it could make me forget my nervousness about the Fear Test. Almost.

"I don't want to mess this up," I said, raising my paint-smeared finger. "Hold still."

"It doesn't have to be a Warhol," Freddie said. "Actually, wait, go Warhol, give me the full Marilyn."

I grinned and lightly touched the spot above his eyebrow with the red paint, then gently worked my way down, reapplying more paint to cover his whole eye socket.

"I didn't just mean your face," I said. "I don't want to mess anything up."

I tried to focus on just painting his skin, but it was kind of hard to do while I was standing so close to him. Touching him.

"You'll be great," Freddie said. He held his glasses in his hand, but the way he looked at me, it was like he saw perfectly clear.

"I don't know what I'm doing."

"None of us do. It's mostly improv."

If I stopped to really think about what the club was doing, tonight and in general, it was supremely screwed up. But maybe this was just the evolution of fun for rich kids. Everyone else seemed to be partying or having sex or on xannies. Maybe scaring people was just the next level up.

But I wasn't rich. What if I wasn't cut out for this?

I held up the paint palette for Freddie to choose his next color. "Green," he said.

"Close your eyes." I used my middle finger this

time and started on his left eye. He kept it shut while I painted his lid, but his other eye squinted open, watching me through a wink.

"I don't think I'm good at thinking on the spot," I said. "I hate improv."

"Did I just uncover Rachel Chavez's secret fear?" Freddie's cheeks, now painted creamy white, expanded with his smile. "Improv?"

I wiggled my red and green fingers in front of his face. "Careful, I wield the face paint."

Freddie made a show of clamping his lips shut and I continued tidying up the oval outline around his eye. A moment of quiet settled between us and I decided to ask what was really weighing on my mind.

"Can I ask why you're in the club? Why you're so invested in pulling this prank?"

Freddie's eyebrows knitted together. "It's not a prank."

I could tell he had too much pride in what the club did—in the club itself—to call it just a prank, and maybe he was right. What we were about to do would amount to a lot more than *just* a prank.

"Okay, not a prank. But you're all putting a huge amount of time and energy into messing with someone. Scaring them." I lowered my hand, leaving Freddie's face half painted as he dwelled on my question. "Why?"

"Well, tonight, Thayer's getting back at somebody who's been making his life hell since fifth grade," Freddie replied. "Vigilante justice is pretty sweet."

"Is that why Thayer's in the club?" I asked. "To get back at the people who've wronged him?"

"You want my honest opinion about why Thayer and Felicity and Bram are in the club?"

I nodded.

"They live stable lives. Boring lives. They want for nothing. They go to sleep at night knowing they'll wake up to breakfast, their clothes ironed and hung up, and their maids at the door with their favorite snacks ready. They're practically toddlers. They'll probably stay toddlers their whole lives."

He said this all plainly, as if just stating the obvious. I could tell he didn't mean it in a disparaging way. I knew he would say it to their faces. And probably had.

"The truth is," Freddie continued, "they crave chaos."

I smiled. It felt like by grouping Thayer and Bram and Felicity together, Freddie had grouped us up together, too. We were separate from them. We weren't the gilded elite. I guess that made us sort of a team.

"Okay, but you still haven't answered my question. Why do you do it?" I asked.

"I, too, crave chaos," Freddie said, pairing his faux

tony accent with a devilish grin. "The way I look at it is as a great social experiment. What does fear do to a person? How can we control it?"

"Control it?"

"Yeah. We can work with fear, like a sculptor works with clay. It's art."

My mouth twisted into a dubious smile as I looked at his crudely painted skin. What I'd done to his face was definitely not art. "That's kind of a stretch."

"Well, I don't know." But his tone said he did know. Freddie had obviously thought a lot about this; I could tell by the way his eyes lit up behind his glasses. "Art is all about drawing an emotion out of someone, right? A beautiful painting could make you feel wonder. A song could make you cry. A movie could make you laugh. Evoking an explosive, immediate reaction out of someone? There's nothing more visceral than being scared. It's why some people love watching scary movies. I love being scared."

"Yeah, but we're not doing all this in the hopes that Trevor will love it. We want him scared. We want him to suffer."

Hearing myself say that out loud made a shiver go down my spine. Was I getting in over my head?

"Trevor's entire existence is based around the idea that he's better than everyone else," Freddie said. "Fear strips that away. It's the great equalizer. And when you're truly scared, there's nowhere to hide—no private school, no popularity, no trust fund. It's just you and your most base emotion. Fear is where the truth lies."

I thought about my own fears—how my skin vibrated whenever I was panicked, like a monster was trying to get out. I didn't let myself dwell on the thought.

But Freddie's ideas were big, and they filled up the small alleyway.

"You're really passionate about this stuff," I said. I could tell that if Freddie's cheeks weren't covered in white, they'd be blooming pink, as though he thought he'd said too much.

"I'm just trying to say that fear is kind of this important thing in our lives," Freddie said. "It'll always be there. And if you let it, fear will hold you back."

I thought of the ways my own fear could take over sometimes and leave me paralyzed, how anxiety crawled out of my mind and became something physical, ruling my body and pulling all the strings.

"With the Mary Shelley Club, we're taking the fear back," Freddie said. "Once you take control of it, it gives you back your power. You can let go. It's freedom."

"Seems reckless."

Freddie tilted his face back. "Freedom?"

"Letting go." I had a flash of Lux in the art closet, the scissors in my hand. I was afraid of that part of myself. And I could feel that fear coursing through me, trying to take control, trying to talk me out of doing this Fear Test. But if Freddie was right, then maybe what we did tonight really would give me some power back.

"What if I suck at improv and things go haywire?" I asked. "Is there, like, a safe word to stop the Fear Test?"

Freddie thought for a moment. "Sure, we can have a safe word. Pick one."

"Armadillo," I blurted. It was the first thing that came to mind, and it made a smile crawl onto Freddie's face.

"Okay, I like that. If anything goes wrong—if you feel uncomfortable at any point and want to bail, just say 'armadillo.' This doesn't have to be scary." He paused, then shook his head, laughing. "I mean, yes, making it scary is kind of the objective, but it isn't supposed to be scary for *us*. For us it's gonna be fun."

"That a promise?"

"Absolutely," Freddie said. It was his smile—like a little kid's—that convinced me. He was about to play his favorite game, and he had a new friend to share it with. I smiled back, feeling the excitement rising in my own chest.

"Okay, I'm done." I stepped back to examine my creation. "Have you considered that you might be *too* dedicated to this club?"

"Dedication is the only way to win, Rachel." Freddie put the blue, frizzy wig on his head and smiled, his mouth a garish red. "As reigning champion, I should know."

16

TREVOR DRIGGS

WHEN TREVOR DRIGGS answered the door, he found the third nobody of the night standing on the other side. A short girl with short hair, looking way too angry to be at a party.

"Who are you?" he asked.

"Felicity Chu."

"Do I know you, Felicity Chu?"

The girl brushed her fingers over her little bangs and peered past his shoulder, into the party. There was a boy trying to do a handstand on a coffee table. But a girl jabbed him in the gut and he crumpled into a drunken heap.

"We go to school together," Felicity said. "I'm in three of your classes."

Trevor was still drawing a blank.

"I let you cheat off my physics test last week."

Nope. Still couldn't place her. And anyway, he'd cheated off a lot of people last week. Trevor didn't want to be an asshole, but . . . "You sure you're at the right house?"

A hand snaked onto Trevor's shoulder and squeezed. Trevor turned to find Bram standing there, drink in hand and with a smile that said he was three-quarters of the way to lit.

"Let her in, man," Bram said. "The more the merrier, right?"

Trevor didn't know who this happy-go-lucky Bram was or what he'd done with the real Bram, who would never let some rando in. But as he paused, the short girl, whose name Trevor had already forgotten, slipped by him and immediately disappeared into the crowd.

"Dude, we just letting anybody in tonight?"

Bram just shrugged and steered Trevor away from the door, his touch sure enough to lead anyone to a chiller plane of existence.

"Do you want to spend the whole night playing bodyguard?" Bram asked. "Or do you want to finally make a move on Lucia?"

Trevor followed Bram's eyes to Lucia Trujillo, who sat at the edge of the couch talking to Lux and Juliet. He'd been crushing on Lucia like crazy since school started again, when she'd come back from a summer in South America all different. She was tanner, for one thing, and she'd dyed her hair to look like honey, which suited her real nice. And her body. Her body . . . Basically, the girl had come back grown.

He'd never really considered her an option before but tonight, he was going to let her know. She was def on the menu and he was starving.

"And all you have to do," Bram said, shoving his drink into Trevor's hand, "is *relax*. Talk to her. Be the Man."

Trevor had meant to take a sip, but that wasn't enough for a Man so he gulped down the whole thing. Vodka, straight. He winced as the alcohol shredded his esophagus. "I'm the Man."

The guys went to join the girls on the couch, their empty seats awaiting their return. No one was dumb enough to take them.

Trevor liked that. He also liked that when he and Bram sat down, the girls' attentions swung back to them. Lux slid onto Bram's lap and Lucia got up from the armrest to sit next to Trevor. She sat so close now that her thigh touched his thigh and there was nothing but two thin pieces of denim between them. Trevor liked that, too.

"Hi," she said.

Usually when a pretty girl was talking to him, Trevor's responses came in slo-mo. First he smiled. Forgot himself. Then, way too late, he'd respond.

Same thing always happened on the field. Nerves made everything slo-mo. Coach had to psych him up pregame to keep him on track.

"So, Driggy," Lux said. "Rumor has it you still don't have a date for the winter dance."

"That's, like, two months away."

"A month and a half," Lux said quickly. "If you don't ask someone soon, the perfect girl just might get snapped up."

The girl could multitask. She shared a look with Lucia while still concentrating on Bram's ear, gently pulling at his lobe. And then her mouth came down on it. Trevor watched, transfixed by the movement of her lips.

The slo-mo caught up with him and Trevor reminded himself that Lux was his best friend's girl. But her mouth. He caught a glimpse of tongue.

Trevor licked his own lips. But then he noticed that Bram was looking at *him*. With his girl's teeth still tugging on his ear, Bram stared. It wasn't even a mean stare either. It was more of an *I get it* stare. Lux was hot, and Bram was generous. *It's okay, you can look.*

But now Trevor felt sorta dirty. He quickly looked

away, his eyes landing instead on Lucia, who caught his gaze eagerly, like she'd been waiting with a net. A good sign. She was obviously interested, but no way was he going to ask her to a dance that was happening a month and a half from now, like a loser—especially in front of all these people.

"This song is dope," he said instead.

"Yeah," Lucia said. "I love Chance."

It was Kendrick, but whatever. The conversation stalled before it could start. When Trevor didn't know what to do on the field, he looked around for cues. His eyes darted around the room now, searching. Maybe there'd be somebody doing something stupid, somebody he could make fun of to get a laugh out of Lucia.

That's when he saw it.

"What?" Trevor sat up. There was a red balloon animal on the credenza. A dog standing on its hind legs like it was begging for a treat.

"I said, wanna share?"

"Huh?" He looked at Lucia, who was holding out a cup. *Focus, Driggy.* He took a swig of her drink. More vodka.

When Trevor looked at the credenza again, the balloon dog was gone. But then Trevor saw something else. He fumbled the cup, nearly dropping it. He blinked once, then again, wondering if he should slow down on the drinking because he was definitely seeing things that weren't real.

There was a girl standing in the corner of the living room with a red, round clown nose on her face.

"What the hell?"

"Excuse me?" Lucia said.

"Wait here."

As soon as Trevor got up from the couch, the girl with the red nose turned away. He walked toward her but she walked faster, joining the crowd of people. He shoved through them, pushing people out of his way.

"Hey!" He grabbed the girl's shoulder and spun her around.

The girl glared at him. Had he seen her before? She was kinda cute with lots of freckles and a pissed-off look on her face. But no red nose.

He was definitely seeing things. It hit him then, who she was. "You tried to kill Lux."

She began to walk away. "Blow me."

"How did you get in here?" He grabbed her elbow and noticed that her fingertips were stained red and green.

"Let go of me." She wrenched out of his grip.

"Get out of my house."

"Gladly."

Even after she'd left, the door slamming behind

her, Trevor stayed standing in his foyer numbly, still thinking about the red nose and that balloon animal. A familiar knot formed between his shoulder blades, an annoying feeling that he couldn't shake. He opened the door again to make sure the girl was gone, but then stumbled back when he saw what was waiting on the other side.

A clown. A frizzy blue wig, a painted grin, and his finger hovering over the doorbell. He was even holding balloons. "Birthday gram!" The clown giggled.

"NOPE!" Trevor slammed the door shut. Now he was breathing hard and the only thing he was capable of doing was leaning against the closed door with all of his strength. He tried to catch his breath.

Trevor *hated* clowns.

When he was seven years old his parents had hired a clown for his birthday party. They'd made Trevor sit on the clown's lap for pictures. And Trevor had had an accident. Right there on the clown's lap.

That clown—who smelled of face paint and body odor (Trevor would never forget it)—started cursing like crazy when he felt the wet mess. Trevor had never heard bad words spoken out loud by a grown-up before, and it freaked him out. Not least because the ugly words had come pouring out of a mouth that was red like a gash. The expression on the clown's face still haunted

Trevor, morphing into something monstrous as he picked Trevor up by the armpits, yelling, "He pissed on me!" Trevor shuddered as he pictured the guy's painted purple eyebrows, his white makeup caked into pitted skin, flaking off in some parts.

But that had been a long time ago, and this was a mistake. He needed to relax, go back to his friends, and chill the hell out.

Back at the couch, Bram and Lux were glued together. His hands to her hips, her hands to his hair. And their lips. Anyone watching might wonder if they were trying to get unstuck or sink into each other. It was kissing quicksand.

Trevor sat down next to Lucia. He was still the Man. Still time to make the Move. "So I was thinking . . ." He trailed off, but it wasn't the slo-mo this time. There was music coming from somewhere, fighting the party playlist. It burrowed in his ear like a nasty fly and he couldn't do or think of anything else until it stopped. He fished his phone out of his pocket, but that wasn't it.

"Somewhere you have to be?" Lucia asked, her tone light, but she was def getting annoyed. Trevor put his phone away and shook his head. "I'm staying right here."

But he couldn't be the only one who heard the music. Tinny, way too jolly-sounding. It was an itch in his brain. "Yo, does anyone else hear that?"

"Hear what?" Bram said, coming up for air.

"I think it's coming from upstairs. I *told* people the second floor was off-limits." He was starting to get up when Bram's hand pushed him back down.

"You stay, I'll go." Then, in a low voice in Trevor's ear, he added, "*Be the Man.*"

Bram was probably just going to scope out a room for him and Lux, Trevor thought, but whatever. Back to the matter at hand. Lucia was looking extra eager tonight. But then Lux leaned over and she and Lucia started whispering like Trevor wasn't even there.

His pocket buzzed and he took out his phone. A text from Bram.

Something weird up here.

"I'll be right back," Trevor told the girls, who continued ignoring him.

He had to sidestep around Jamie Powells, who had his tongue shoved down George Chen's throat, then nearly crashed into a girl as she flew down the stairs. Felicity Something. Her eyes were wild.

"What were you doing upstairs?"

But she didn't answer. As he watched her run off he noticed a blue smear on her sleeve. *Makeup?* It reminded him of the awful face paint that clowns used. He turned back to the stairs. He hesitated. Something weird was going on. Trevor bounced on the balls of his feet, just like he did before a game, pumping himself up. Nothing to be scared of.

When he got upstairs, he didn't see Bram. But he also didn't hear any trace of the strange, tinny music that had made the hairs on the back of his neck stand up. It was almost too quiet. The noise from downstairs felt muted, like someone had put pillows over his ears. "Bram?"

Trevor's phone buzzed. A text from Bram.

Bram can't help you.

"What? Bram, where you at, man?" he muttered.

That music again. Now Trevor could make out what it was. He'd heard that song before. It was the exact same song that had been playing at his seventh birthday party.

The music was coming from down the hall. From Trevor's own bedroom. His door was open, and then, in an instant, a light switched on inside. His bedside lamp.

Trevor was drawn to it like a moth. He treaded slowly. That knot between his shoulder blades was back, his whole body stiffening with dread. He felt like he was being watched.

"Bram?"

No one was there.

But then he saw feet sticking out from under the other side of the bed. Trevor rushed over and now he could see it all. "Bram!"

Bram was facedown on the floor in a pool of blood.

Trevor was about to reach for him when he noticed something by the blood. Red, too, and sticky. A footprint, but way too big.

Trevor's breathing grew shallow when he saw the smiley face embossed on the sole of the imprint. Then Trevor noticed more footprints. A trail of them, all leading one by one to the closet door.

He should've run. He should've called for help, done something. But that delayed response again.

A buzz.

Another text. From Bram.

HAPPY BIRTHDAY

HAPPY BIRTHDAY

HAPPY BIRTHDAY

And then, a giggle. A maniacal, cloying, disgusting giggle, getting louder and louder.

"What the hell?" Trevor yelled, backing up.

The closet door banged open and out lunged a clown, swinging a knife. He let out a cackle and this time there was no delayed response. This time Trevor ran like he was on the field—no, like he was seven years old and a killer clown was out to murder him.

He ran downstairs, nearly tripping over his own feet. The crowd parted and someone cut the music. Trevor stood there in silence, his chest heaving for air. They were all staring at him, some of them even taking out their phones to film him. When he looked down, he could see why. There was a wet stain down the front of his pants.

17

WE RAN, SHOES thwacking pavement, my hair whipping my cheeks, the wind swooshing by my ears. All of it colored by the sound of my breathing—hard and electrified.

Our rendezvous point had been decided beforehand: Tompkins Square Park, seven blocks from Trevor's duplex, a five-minute breakneck run from the scene of the crime. Some of us could have left for the park once we finished our roles in the Fear Test, but we'd wanted to stick around, to see Trevor get his.

Felicity could've run track, she was going so fast. I, on the other hand, was out of breath by the second block, but the buzz of what we'd just pulled off kept my legs pumping. Freddie's wig was off, but he was still in costume a few paces ahead of me. He turned and reached back for me and for five blocks we ran together, hand in hand, through the black-paved streets and past the twinkling buildings.

The running, getting away with it, the feeling of Freddie's fingers interlocked with mine—it turned all of Manhattan into a blur. I squeezed his hand and he squeezed back, both of us grinning like, well, clowns.

We burst into the park. Felicity was already waiting there, palms on knees, gulping air. A minute later, Bram showed up. Half of his long-sleeved tee was dyed red, his cheek and jaw streaked with it, too. It looked real, though we all knew it would never congeal and turn brown like real blood would. He rubbed a towel into his damp hair, making it stick up in clumps. He wasn't out of breath, though.

"Took an Uber," he said. "I told everybody I tripped and hit my head."

"They believed you?" I asked, my breath ragged.

"Head wounds are gushers." Bram ruffled the towel around his head. "Where's Thayer?"

We looked around, waiting. The longer the minutes stretched, the more our buoyancy began to char at the edges. And then Thayer barged in through the shadows. I'd never been more thrilled to see a knife-wielding clown in a park.

"HE PISSED HIS PANTS!" Thayer yelled to the sky.

I looked over at Freddie, and his expression matched mine. He was the first to start laughing. And like water on high heat, we all started bubbling with it. Bram's shoulders shook, Freddie down on his knees, weak. It may have been Thayer's Fear Test, but it was a team effort. Us against the world, wrapped up in a weird bubble that nobody could pop right now.

"Technically, you didn't make him scream," Felicity said. But even she wasn't immune to this jubilant feeling. Her usual scowl had lifted and was on the verge of breaking into a runaway smile.

Thayer shook his head. "I'd take piss over a scream any day. BEAT THAT, MOFOS!"

"How did you know he was afraid of clowns?" Freddie asked, clapping Thayer on the back.

"The greatest trick the devil ever pulled was making us forget he pissed himself in front of a clown before. His seventh birthday party. I was there. It's one of my fondest memories."

"You're lucky Trevor is so damn afraid of clowns," Bram teased, "because those bloody clown shoe prints were cheesy as fuck."

"It got the job done, didn't it?" Thayer said.

"Just saying." Bram shrugged. "I was about to break character."

"What are you going to say to Trevor?" I asked Bram. "He's going to know someone was messing with him. And that you were a part of it."

"All Trevor knows is that he was drunk. No one else saw a killer clown."

I watched Bram, took in how easy it was for him to lie. This all boiled down to a prank, but it was designed to be cruel—Thayer's revenge for Trevor's years of bullying. Although I thought Trevor deserved it, I still wondered how Bram could do that to his friend.

"But I wanted them to see me," Thayer said.

"Yeah, why didn't you come down to the party?" Freddie asked.

And now I remembered that that had been part of Thayer's original plan. He was going to come down the stairs and run around scaring everyone else at the party for some "extra credit," as he'd put it.

"Players who don't finish their tests get an incomplete," Felicity said.

"Where is that in the rules?" Thayer said. "Going down the stairs was just garnish. I still served a delicious freaking meal."

"Why didn't you go down the stairs?" Freddie asked again.

"Okay, I was going to, all right? But I tripped. Someone pushed me."

"You tripped or someone pushed you?" I said.

"I don't know. I almost fell down the stairs but I caught myself. I lost the momentum, though. Decided to go out the window instead." He was still breathing too hard for me to tell whether this rattled him, the fact that there was a hitch in his test. But with his next deep breath came a change in subject.

"I was on fire, man. I killed it. I put Trevor in his place!" He bounced up and down like a spring, all energy and excitement. "I finally put that asshole in his place."

Whatever thoughts any of us had about the hiccup in Thayer's plot were already being erased by the realization of what we'd just done. The memory was so fresh I could practically smell it, breathe it in, feel it tingling my skin.

"He was so scared," Thayer said. "He was scared shitless."

"He was," I said, smiling. "We all saw it."

"But not all of it," Freddie said, whirling around. "Bram. You were in the room. Did Trevor lose it?"

Bram took a moment and settled into his regular posture: broad shoulders slightly hunched, head bent.

When he looked up, his lips stretched so slowly that it took a minute before I realized he was smiling. "He lost it."

Thayer let out a delighted whoop.

We noticed two men coming into the park from the west side. They were about ten yards away. We froze. So did they. The men took us in, turned around immediately, and got the hell out of there.

Freddie cracked up, pointing at Thayer in his ridiculous clown costume, and then at Bram, covered in blood. Bram looked down at himself, messy with the red goo, and started to laugh, too. In seconds, we were all reduced to giggles again, Thayer practically squirming on the ground.

Anxiety and exhilaration were two sides of the same coin; both made you lose your breath, made your skin vibrate so strong your teeth could chatter. But on one side it felt like torture, and on the other it was elation. Enlightenment. Nirvana. It was the crystal-clear sense of the whistling trees all around you and the dark green grass tickling your cheeks. It was going dizzy but not feeling like you were about to faint. Feeling, actually, like you could float.

It was this, right now. And it was perfect.

Who knew that scaring someone could feel like this? I touched my humming lips, trying to make this emotion tangible. But what I felt was power. A sensation that had eluded me since the previous year.

Our laughter died down. On one side of me, Freddie readjusted his glasses, looking up at the black sky. On the other side of me was Bram. Tonight's Fear Test had thawed the icy layer that had always seemed to stand between us. And for the first time Bram smiled at me. I smiled back.

If I was a monster, then so was everyone else in this club. And for once I didn't feel like such a freak.

We could be monsters together.

18

FREDDIE HAD BEEN right when he'd told me that pretty soon, everyone would move on from my drama with Lux.

The morning after Trevor's birthday, no one looked at me funny as I passed them in the hall, I didn't hear the words "Arts and Crafts Killer" whispered under anyone's breath, and there weren't any memes about me floating around. All anyone could talk about was what had happened at Trevor's party. Well, not what had happened at the party so much as what had happened to Trevor (and his pants). Khakis are a *choice* on any occasion, but a particularly bad one for Trevor last night, given how obviously it darkens when wet. But hey, hindsight.

Trevor did the smart thing this morning and stayed home. But his friends still had his back, spinning the story so that the Infamous Manchester Prankster was to blame, spilling water down the front of Trevor's pants. Some people began to doubt the photos and videos of the event, attributing the dark spot on Trevor's pants to a shadow. But I didn't mind all the stories coming out of the rumor mill. Even if nobody knew that it was the Mary Shelley Club who'd brought Trevor Driggs to his knees, we knew it. We were the mysterious prankster. We were the bogeyman. I grinned just thinking about it.

When a guy bumped into me in the hall and didn't bother to apologize, I realized I could just make him the target of my Fear Test if I wanted to. The club was a game changer. The club was a *mood*.

And I knew I wasn't the only one enjoying this.

I saw Felicity walking down the hall with her head held high, switching up her regular floor-gazing skulk. I passed Freddie too, who was huddled with his Film Club friends. We shared a secret smile over their heads, no words needed.

But the biggest change came from Thayer. In Women in Literature, Ms. Liu was comparing Carson McCullers to Alexandre Dumas, so the Dumb Ass jokes practically made themselves. But Thayer didn't make a peep. Even Ms. Liu seemed surprised, occasionally sneaking looks his way when she said Dumas's name. Thayer just sat back, all dreamy eyes and perma-smile. He didn't need to clown around today. He'd done enough of that for a lifetime.

If Bram felt bad about what had happened to his supposed best friend, he didn't show it. He came up to me after class and handed me a book. "This is my favorite Mary Shelley biography," he said. It was a thick paperback, with yellowed pages and curled edges. "It could help with the term paper research."

I thanked him, and as he walked away he didn't shoot me a withering stare. So: progress.

Apparently, I learned at lunch, I was changed, too. At least according to Saundra, her eyes narrowing suspiciously as she sipped celery juice from a thermos. "What's the deal with you? You've been, like, smiling all day."

"I smile."

"Not really."

"Occasionally."

"Rarely."

"Stop it." I laughed, which just proved her point.

"You've got a secret," Saundra said definitively.

I shook my head. I couldn't tell her about the Mary Shelley Club. But it also wasn't just the club. The truth was, I didn't know exactly why I was feeling so good.

But for the first time in a long time, I was just happy. Chill. Content. And when that's not your usual state of being, you tend to want to hold on to it, no questions asked.

I popped a french fry into my mouth and shrugged. "Still thinking about Trevor's pee party, I guess. The guy got what he deserved."

"I know! Trevor Driggs is such a douche canoe. I wish I was there to see it in person."

"Mhmm." I didn't say anything, but it was like Saundra could read my mind.

"You weren't there," Saundra said skeptically. I kept chewing to avoid answering, but I was a crystal ball and Saundra was a fortune-teller. She nearly sprayed celery juice out of her nose. "You were *there*?"

We had tried to be discreet, but judging by how many selfies were being taken at Trevor's house, I was sure I'd unintentionally photobombed someone's Insta by now. There was no point in lying about not being there. Saundra would find out.

"Yeah. I just heard about it and went."

"What the hell?" Saundra said. "And Trevor just let you in?"

I nodded. "He was distracted. Obviously."

"Well, why didn't you tell me? I would've gone with you!"

"You specifically told me on Friday afternoon that you were looking forward to bingeing *Gilmore Girls*."

"That's just something people *say*, Rachel; nobody actually means it!"

"Okay, I'm sorry. Next time Trevor throws a party, we'll go together."

Saundra scoffed and looked across the lunchroom at the popular table. "As if Trevor's going to be throwing any more parties in this lifetime."

The kids at Trevor's usual table—Lux, Bram, and the other shiny, pretty people—were consorting like normal, as if there wasn't a gaping six-foot-lacrosse-defender-shaped hole there. Saundra leaned toward me, pushing aside her plaid Williams Sonoma thermos. "Tell me everything. Did you actually see him pee himself? I heard he was crying. Was he crying *and* peeing? Like, at the same time? Can Trevor multitask?"

"He ran down the stairs crying that a clown was out to get him," I said. "And his pants were wet."

"Holy crap."

"I think he was pretty drunk."

A peal of laughter left Saundra's lips. "Beautiful," she said. "If anyone deserves public humiliation, it's Trevor Driggs."

I munched on another fry, if only to try to keep my grin from being too obvious.

* * *

My mom noticed a change in me, too. Our normal dinner conversation was sprinkled with inquisitive looks in my direction.

"You're in a good mood," she said. "Meeting new people at school?"

This was her not-so-subtle way of asking if I was sharing my toys and making friends. "Mhmm," I said through a mouthful of the Neapolitan ice cream we were having for dessert.

"Oh, really? Did you join a club, like I suggested?"

I let the ice cream melt on my tongue. "Mhmm."

"Which one?"

I swallowed. I needed to think quickly. "Knitting."

"Knitting."

I shoveled another spoonful of dessert into my mouth. "Mhmm."

"I didn't know there was a knitting club at school."

Neither did I, but now there would have to be. I was mentally kicking myself; I'd probably have to buy some knitting needles and yarn just to keep up with the lie. Which would mean that I would need money. Which reminded me that I needed a job.

"Does the club need an advisor? I took a few knitting lessons once. I could probably—"

"It's a secret knitting club," I said too quickly. "So please forget I said anything."

My mom licked her spoon. "I was only kidding," she said finally. "Could you imagine me advising a club you were in?"

No. No, I could not.

"I'm glad you're getting along better with the other students. I just heard about a student who isn't so lucky. Do you know a boy named Trevor Driggs?"

I swallowed. "I know Trevor. Why?"

"I heard he relieved himself at a party?"

I hadn't realized the story of a seventeen-year-old boy peeing his pants would reach the teachers' lounge. "Yeah, I heard that, too. I think he just drank too much."

The look on my mom's face was equal parts sad and confused. "It's not one of those social media challenges? Like for YouTube?"

"No, Mom, definitely not that."

That sad look was still on Mom's face. She picked up her glass of iced tea but stopped short of drinking it.

"That poor boy," Mom said. "How awful."

"He's a jerk, Mom."

"Rachel, have some compassion."

I continued eating, but couldn't taste much anymore. My mom's words reverberated in my head, gnawing at that happy feeling I had had just a few hours earlier. Maybe it was true that what we'd done to Trevor was awful, but it was also true that he deserved it. Thayer had suffered daily torment at Trevor's hands, and we'd helped Thayer level the playing field. I put a terrible person in his place. I wasn't about to feel bad about it.

I served myself more ice cream and ate it up.

19

THE NEXT NIGHT, Mom shook an already-nuked bag of microwave popcorn in one hand and held up the TV remote in the other. "Wanna watch something?" she asked. "I think a new Gut Stab movie just came out On Demand. *Gut Stab Six*, I want to say."

"Sorry," I said. She'd stopped me on my way out, and I grabbed my jacket off the hook by the door. "I've got plans."

Mom dropped her hands, the popcorn and remote flopping against her pajama pants. "Where are you going?"

"Just seeing some people." Then I added, haltingly, "Friends."

"Oh," Mom said, breaking into a smile. "Saundra?"

"No." Saundra had been begging me to go on a shopping spree with her, and although holding her bags while she wore down the chip on her credit card sounded great, Madison Avenue would have to wait. "Other people."

"On a school night?"

"It's a good thing you don't care about that kind of thing!" I turned the doorknob. "The Gut Stab movies suck anyway."

"*Gut Stab Six*!" Thayer bellowed. Behind him the projection screen in the Wilding study lowered slowly. "We are about to embark on what is sure to be a perfectly mediocre addition to the horror canon. New Girl, tell me you haven't seen this one yet."

"I haven't seen this one yet."

"Yes!" Thayer pumped his fist in the air and held it for a moment like he was frozen in the end credits of an '80s film.

"None of us have seen this one," Freddie said. "It's kind of a special occasion." He sat next to me on the couch and passed me a bowl of fresh popcorn, stopping to look at me for a long moment. "You look different."

There wasn't anything different about me. Except the lip gloss I'd applied on the subway on the way here. Saundra had given it to me one day after I complimented her on it. She'd said boys like gloss more than lipstick. I looked the tube up online and saw that it cost sixty-five dollars. It was almost too expensive to wear. I didn't know why I was wearing it now. Or maybe I did. Maybe it had something to do with the way Freddie was looking at me.

But now I felt self-conscious. I pressed my lips together, trying to subtly smudge away sixty-five dollars. "Different?"

Freddie shook his head. "Not, like, different," he said, flustered. "Good. Not like . . ." He pushed his glasses up. "You look nice."

I smiled, and the gloss stayed put. "So what happens when none of you have seen a movie before?"

Felicity strolled over to where I was sitting and dug into my bowl. "We draw a lottery and stone the winner to death." She took a seat on the carpet, close to Bram's chair, and munched on her fistful of popcorn.

"Felicity!" Thayer hissed. "Hush. You'll scare the poor girl."

"We play a game," Bram said distractedly. Something on his phone had his full attention and he reached over to Felicity, tapping her on the shoulder to show her whatever it was. She leaned back, her head resting on the edge of Bram's knee so she could see what was on his screen. And then she did something I'd never seen her do before. She giggled. She stuck her tongue out at Bram, a giant pink slug breaking through two black lips. And Bram, amazingly, stuck his own tongue out at her.

The whole exchange fascinated me. I wanted to know what was on Bram's phone, what kind of sorcery he'd just conjured to get Felicity to laugh. But mostly I wanted to know who those two people were, because I'd never met them before. Maybe that meant that one day, Bram might share a joke with me. I imagined the two of us laughing together and felt a pang of something I was too proud to call jealousy.

"We like games," Freddie whispered, snapping me out of my reverie. "I wasn't sure if you could tell."

"Oh, I got it," I whispered back.

"It's a senior citizen's idea of fun," Bram said.

Thayer pulled a stack of papers out of his backpack and began to hand them out. "Bingo!"

Like, literal bingo. It looked like something Thayer had made using Microsoft Word. It was possibly the dorkiest thing I'd ever seen, and I was totally there for it. There was a five-by-five grid with each box labeled. I looked over my sheet and read them all quickly.

- Villain's not really dead
- Hero falls while being chased in woods
- "Let's split up!"
- No phone signal
- Running upstairs???
- Hiding under bed / in closet

Some boxes just had a single word, like:

- *SEX.*

And some boxes came with little questions at the top that I had to fill in myself, like *Who will die first?* and *Body count?*, which was the middle square.

"How am I supposed to know who dies first?" I whispered to Freddie.

He held up his own sheet, which he had already started filling in. "You just guess."

For who would die first he'd simply written *The Custodian.* I pulled a pen out of my bag and wrote in my own answer: *The Childhood Friend.*

"Rules are simple," Thayer said as he killed the lights. "Circle a box when it happens on-screen, yell bingo when you get a line, celebrate your superiority over the rest of us, et cetera, et cetera."

"Ready?" Bram asked the room. He clicked on the keyboard and *Gut Stab Six* began.

The bingo game made *Gut Stab Six* a lot more enjoyable than it otherwise would've been. But so did the fact that I was seeing it with a group of people who felt exactly the same way about it. Which was to say, we all hated it because it was trash (lousy dialogue, bad acting, every horror cliché known to man), but we also watched every minute devoutly because we loved it.

I circled one of my boxes every time there was a corresponding scene in the movie. Thayer giggled and let out a *whoop!* every time he circled a new box. But Freddie kept missing his. He was distracted.

It reminded me of when we'd first watched a movie together, back at the Film Forum, when we were keenly aware of each other and made sure to keep our eyes glued to the screen. But this time I kept catching Freddie sneaking glances at me.

I checked my bingo sheet, then looked up. Freddie quickly looked down at his own sheet, pretending he hadn't just been looking at me.

"*Creepy Kid,*" I whispered.

"Huh?" Freddie said.

I tapped my pen against his paper. "A creepy kid just appeared."

"Oh." His glasses reflected the pale blue glow of the movie, hiding his eyes. He pushed them up as he circled the box on his sheet.

"Thank you," he whispered.

I reached for some popcorn from the bowl sitting between us just as Freddie did the same. Our fingers touched, and we both jerked our hands back as though we'd touched something hot.

"Sorry," I said quickly, and Freddie said it, too. On the floor in front of us, Felicity whipped around to shush us.

I turned back to the movie, but was distracted by Freddie. I wanted more popcorn, but I was waiting for him to go for it so I would know when the coast was clear. Out of the corner of my eye, I could tell that he was doing the same thing. He watched the movie, then watched me, then grabbed a single piece of popcorn and popped it into his mouth. He ate slowly, his razor-sharp jawline tightening as he chewed. He swallowed, which I took as my signal to take a piece of popcorn. It felt like we were on a seesaw, picking up popcorn and chewing, picking up popcorn and chewing.

We had the whole routine down pat without missing a beat, even when Thayer erupted with a new *whoop*! But somewhere along the line, when I dipped my fingers into the bowl, they found Freddie's fingers again. This time, our fingers stayed put, like they had minds of their own. Freddie's fingers were soft and slightly slick with butter. On-screen, the blond girl and the brown-haired guy whose names no longer mattered began to take each other's clothes off.

"Have sex?" Freddie asked.

I tore my eyes from the two gyrating figures on screen and turned to Freddie. "Like . . . now?"

He pulled his buttery fingers from mine and pointed down at my sheet. "Like there."

"Oh!" I nearly choked, and I wasn't even eating popcorn. I circled the SEX box, hoping he couldn't see how warm my cheeks were.

"Bingo," Freddie prompted.

"Bingo!" I said a little too loudly.

"Bingo?" Thayer asked. I showed him my sheet and he waved it around, happier for me than I was for myself. "We have a bingo here! You know what that means."

Felicity whipped her head around, looking uncharacteristically thrilled. Thayer grabbed a handful of his popcorn and flicked it at me. Bram, weirdly, did it, too, a small smile fighting its way onto his face. Freddie laughed and half-heartedly tossed some bits of popcorn on me, too.

Then I learned why Felicity was so happy. She took her full bowl in both hands, walked right up to me, and dumped it over my head.

"It's tradition," she announced with a self-satisfied grin.

20

I MAY HAVE just joined the Mary Shelley Club but already I was devoted.

I'd found a pack of weirdos who liked the same things I did, and we shared a secret, which made every minute we spent together feel heightened—alive. We were doing something bad and it felt so *good*.

In fact, ever since the Mary Shelley Club had come into my life, I'd noticed I didn't feel as anxious as I normally did. Memories from that terrible night on Long Island stopped storming into my mind unbidden. A club about fear was helping to rid me of mine.

All I wanted to do every day was leave the world of Manchester behind so I could hang out with the club, where we could shed our itchy wools and stiff button-downs to slip into our real clothes and be our real selves. Occasionally some of us even slipped into something more extravagant, like when it was Thayer's turn to pick a movie to watch and he chose *Re-Animator*. He said it was to honor Mary Shelley with "hands down the best modern reimagining of *Frankenstein*." But I think it was so he could show up at Bram's in a green surgical gown and skeleton mask split in half in homage to his favorite scene in the movie.

The meetings were frequent, happening twice, sometimes three times, a week. The club had its own set of routines. Some, like the impromptu debates, were easy enough to grasp. There were times when I found myself in heated discussions with them about things like who was the worst Bad Guy, Jason Voorhees or Michael Myers.

"Michael Myers hands down," Felicity said. "He's a dog killer!"

"Jason killed a dog, too," Freddie reminded her.

"Kill all the humans, if you ask me, but dog deaths have no place in horror movies," Thayer said. "I'll start the petition on change dot org."

"There's no way Jason even ranks as a good villain," I said. "He was just a socially awkward loser who couldn't swim."

"Wait, does being a good Bad Guy mean you're nice deep down or that you're perfectly evil?" Bram asked. "And does being a bad Bad Guy mean you're not evil enough?"

These were the kind of deep, existential questions all teenagers ask themselves.

At first, I felt a bit daunted by their closeness. They had rituals, habits, and inside jokes that had been built up over time. But I soon found my rhythm. When we watched *Hellraiser* (Freddie's choice), anytime one of the characters disparaged Brooklyn the club would throw popcorn at the screen and cry, "Anything's better than Brooklyn!" And when we watched *The Birds* (Bram's pick), everyone in the group mimicked Tippi Hedren's over-the-top pose as the birds attacked, her arm arched all the way over her head so as not to block the view of her beautiful face. From that scene forward, we all kept our arms at that ridiculous angle for as long as we could until Felicity was the only one left with her elbow in the air. As the credits rolled, she bent at the waist and took a bow to mark her triumph.

The club's brand of fandom was wrapped around a healthy dollop of ridicule, the understanding being that we had the right to make fun of our favorite things because we loved them so much. It was something I understood innately, one of the moments when I felt seamlessly a part of the group. I'd never thought a feeling of kinship with a group of people could be so overwhelming.

Just the same, there were times when I was glad I

hadn't been there very long, because some of their rituals were hard-core. The night we watched *Us*, Thayer involuntarily yelped when one of the doppelgängers showed up. Bram barked a laugh and smashed the space bar on his keyboard. The screen froze, Freddie and Felicity leaped up, and Thayer instantly buried his head in his hands and moaned.

"Thayer, your time has finally come!" Bram said.

"What's going on?" I asked.

"Come on, Thayer," Freddie said. "Show Rachel what happens when a club member gets scared during a movie."

"But it's cold," Thayer whined.

"Rules are rules," Felicity said.

The next thing I knew, four of us were standing on the balcony and one of us was in the street in his underwear, holding his clothes bunched over his crotch.

"This is cruel and unusual punishment!" Thayer yelled.

"Quiet," Bram said, having way too much fun, "you'll wake the neighbors. Now get on with it."

Thayer let out a final annoyed grunt, then dropped his clothes, threw his hands up in the air, and ran down the block making as much noise as a pack of cans rattling off a newlywed's car. We watched him go and doubled over the stone railing of the balcony, filling the crisp air with the wispy plumes of our laughter. We laughed until we were dizzy, losing our equilibrium.

After that, I learned never to get scared during movie night. And over the course of several movie nights, I learned something new about each of the members.

Thayer loved gore, the more gratuitous the better, but he was also a sweetheart. When I mentioned I was looking for an after-school job, he hooked me up at the movie theater where he worked, a tiny cinema with two screens. The two of us worked weekends, him at the concession stand and me as a ticket taker. When there were no more tickets to take, I'd join him behind the counter and we'd talk and eat free popcorn all night.

I learned that even Felicity, Mistress of the Dark, was capable of deep, silly, unconditional love. Just not toward humans. We walked to her place after a club meeting one night so I could borrow her Chem notes. (Felicity was a meticulous note taker.) As soon as we entered her apartment, two German shepherd puppies named Hitchcock and Häxan jumped on her and licked her, pawing at her clothes. She pretended to be annoyed, but as I headed toward the bathroom, I turned back and saw her get down on all fours and roll around with the dogs, digging her face into their fur and talking in a baby voice.

But the person I got to know the most about was probably Freddie, just by virtue of the fact that we actually hung out together outside of club meetings. Whenever he decided to skip Film Club, we'd meet up after school to walk to the subway together, where he'd take the train uptown and I'd board the one going down. For the half hour between the double doors of Manchester and the automatic doors of the 6 train, we talked about everything. We theorized about Felicity's core damage (there had to be something), found common ground that we didn't talk to anyone else about (we were both Latinos but his Spanish was way better than mine), and argued about movies (he was a purist and a fan of the classics, while I was willing to give reboots and new movies a chance).

As we grew more comfortable with each other, we got into animated discussions. Our most intense argument was about when a scary movie was most appreciated.

"It's in the moment," Freddie said.

"No, it's after the fact."

"What are you talking about? *Life* is about living in the moment. And there's nothing more *in the moment* than being scared—than being alone, out-of-your-mind-with-fear, really sitting with it as the scene is playing out."

"Yes, that's good horror," I said. "But really good horror happens when the movie's over. If it sticks with you. If, long after you've stopped watching, you're still looking over your shoulder. Then you know you're really scared."

We couldn't come to an agreement on that one, but it was still fun discussing it. But probably my favorite thing I learned about Freddie was that, sometimes, all I needed to do was look at him for a beat too long to draw out the color in his cheeks.

I even discovered something new about Bram. He had an encyclopedic knowledge of horror. He was like Freddie in that way, but while Freddie could tell you how many frames there were in the shower scene in *Psycho*, Bram could probably tell you what kind of sandwich Janet Leigh ate on set before filming it. If he liked a movie, he'd find its script and commit every word to memory. And if he *really* liked a movie, he'd even recite the lines as he watched, which I discovered—to my immense amusement—one night when we all sat down to watch *I Know What You Did Last Summer* and I spied him silently shouting along with Jennifer Love Hewitt, daring the killer to come and find her.

And during the most recent club meeting, I had also learned that Bram had a little sister. She showed up unannounced in the study while we were in the middle of *The Omen*, with the same slope to her nose and the same shade of brown hair as Bram. She couldn't have been more than ten.

Bram paused the movie, which was good because we were at the scene right before little Damien knocks his mother over the banister.

"Where's Celia?" he asked.

"I don't need a babysitter."

"Millie." Bram's voice instantly took on a parental tone and I hid a surprised smile behind a fistful of popcorn.

"She fell asleep on the couch," Millie said. "Can I watch, too?"

"It'll give you nightmares."

"I don't get nightmares anymore."

"We all get nightmares." Bram got up. "Let's go."

As Bram and Millie headed upstairs, Freddie stood up, too. "Snack break," he said.

Freddie and Thayer went down to the kitchen for refreshment refills. I got up to go to the bathroom, but Felicity slipped inside before I could, shutting the door in my face.

So I headed upstairs. I'd never been to the third floor of Bram's townhouse but figured there must be another bathroom there. I heard voices as I walked down the hall and realized I must be near Millie's room.

I peeked inside. Bram was sitting on the edge of Millie's bed and pulling the blanket up to her chin.

In school, Bram was the popular kid. In the club he was just as big a geek as the rest of us. At home he was apparently a sweet big brother. He wore a different mask depending on who he was with.

Bram looked up and caught my gaze. I immediately ducked out and kept walking, but Bram was right behind me.

"What are you doing up here?" All traces of loving big brother were gone.

"I was looking for a bathroom."

"Downstairs."

"Taken," I said.

Bram just gave me a look and the awkwardness nearly pushed me down the stairs. He knew I had been lurking.

"Um, I also wanted to talk to you about our paper," I said.

Given the subtle furrow in Bram's brow, he clearly didn't believe me.

"We could set up a time to exchange notes, narrow down the topics we want to include," I suggested.

"You want to talk about our paper? Right now?" Bram asked.

I was starting to get less intimidated and more annoyed. "Okay, Bram, good talk." I skipped down the rest of the stairs, Bram right behind me the whole way.

"Wait," Bram said finally. "Come by after school tomorrow. We can work on it then."

No club meeting. Just me and Bram alone for the first time. I was already regretting bringing the paper up at all.

"Looking forward to it," I said.

21

WE DECIDED TO work in the dining room.

Bram sat at the head of the table and I sat to his left,
the silence stiffly squeezing itself between us now that
we didn't have other people as a buffer. The only other
signs of life were outside the room: A woman who was
not Bram's mother was prepping dinner in the kitchen,
and Millie and her babysitter were rushing between
after-school programs and lessons.

When my phone buzzed with a new text, I picked
it up with relief.

Updates!!!

I never should have told Saundra about this study
session. I knew that I would have to tell her everything.
Not the important things, like how awkward it was to
sit here with Bram, but the little things, like what he
was wearing.

What is he wearing? came Saundra's next message.

And then, immediately after that: *What is his mouth doing right now??*

I made a face at my phone. I glanced at Bram, who was reading something on his laptop. His lips were parted slightly, and I could see the small gap between his front teeth.

Bram reads with his mouth open, I texted, and then instantly deleted every word. I looked back at Bram. He must've been concentrating hard because now he was biting his bottom lip. I bit my own lip, an involuntary response. His eyes flicked toward mine and I clamped my lips shut and put down my phone. I would not be answering any more of Saundra's questions.

And I would not look at Bram's lips again.

Right. Back to Mary Shelley.

"Here, I started typing up her bio," Bram slid his laptop over to me.

I quickly scanned what he'd written. Mary Shelley was the daughter of a radical anarchist father and a feminist mother. She'd run away from her father's house with her married lover when she was just a teenager, and written *Frankenstein* when she was a teenager, too.

"Are you going to mention her marriage to Percy Bysshe Shelley?" I asked.

"He's a footnote," Bram said.

"He was an important part of her life. We have to at least mention him."

"We can mention him, but there's no reason for him to take up so much space in our paper. He's not the focus here."

"He rounds out her story."

"Not the focus."

"I don't get why you're dismissing him so much."

"I don't get why you're defending him so much." There was a slight narrowing of Bram's eyes. He managed to deliver the statement with so much judgment even without raising his voice a single octave. It was a talent.

"I'm not defending him," I said, "but he was present for Mary's formative years. She wrote *Frankenstein* while she was with him—"

"You're giving him too much credit."

"And you're trying to erase him from her story."

"Maybe he should be erased. He was an asshole."

I'd never seen Bram this combative. I mean, he kind of always was, beneath the surface, but while everything about his body language was as cool as ever—the way he slouched against the antique dining chair, the way he barely bothered to look at me as he spoke—he was more riled up than I'd ever seen him. I watched as he took a golden Zippo lighter out of his pocket and repeatedly flicked it open, the movement small but fiercely methodical.

"I had no idea you had such strong feelings about a Romantic poet."

Bram actually rolled his eyes. "*Romantic*. He repeatedly threatened to kill himself if Mary didn't love him back. He manipulated her into liking hi—"

"Now who's giving him too much credit?"

Bram let out a bitter laugh. "I guess I shouldn't be surprised you like Percy."

I sat back, mouth slack. It sounded like an insult—it definitely had to be. "What is that supposed to mean?"

"Forget it." He pushed his chair back and stood, heading directly for the bar cart that seemed to be in every room of his house.

"Isn't it too early to drink?" I muttered as Bram grabbed a bottle.

"It's club soda, if that's okay with you."

I looked down at my paper, which was filled mostly with useless notes and a whole bunch of nothing. We weren't getting anywhere, and to top it all off this was just as uncomfortable as I'd been dreading. But the worst part—the part that I *hated*—was that I knew Bram was right about Percy. The guy didn't sound that great, but at this point I was in too deep. We were at an impasse, and I wasn't about to be the first one to lay my sword down.

So basically we were going to fail this assignment.

Damn Percy Shelley and damn Bram.

I grabbed my phone off the table and typed out a quick message to Freddie. *This study session is a disaster.*

Sounds about right, he wrote back.

Is Bram even human? I typed.

"I'm half vampire," Bram said, suddenly peering over my shoulder. I dropped my phone and it bounced on my thigh before clattering to the floor. By the time I sat back up, face bright red, Bram was back in his seat. He didn't seem the least bit bothered by my text.

"You and Freddie seem . . . close."

Of all the things that could've come out of Bram's mouth right then.

"We're not . . ." I wasn't sure what to say. "We're not—"

But it didn't matter what I said—or tried to say—because Bram kept talking. "You sure that's a good idea?" he asked.

"I said we're not . . ." I trailed off, becoming less concerned with forming a complete sentence than with the fact that Bram was trying to dictate how I should live my life. "Why is it any of your business?"

Bram shrugged vaguely, and my annoyance grew

exponentially. Were club members not allowed to be *close*? Was this another version of the unspoken no-fraternization rule or one of Bram's personal hang-ups?

"Freddie's been nothing but nice to me since I met him," I said. "You, on the other hand, have been kind of a dick."

His expression soured and I was glad I'd finally drawn a stronger reaction than a furrowed brow or a smirk.

"I'm just saying," Bram began, "it's not healthy. All your downtime, all your friendships, all your *relationships* shouldn't revolve around the Mary Shelley Club."

"I have a life outside the club," I said, indignant but also a bit humiliated at even having to point that out. "I have other friends."

"Who?"

"Saundra Clairmont." He seemed to consider the name, as though he hadn't been in school with my lone friend since kindergarten, which incensed me further.

"Look, I don't need your advice on how to live my life. Or your warnings about getting too close to people. I've been through enough stuff in my life. I know how to take care of myself."

"Your attack."

The words hit me like cold water on my face, and I

felt the fresh prick of tears in my eyes. I didn't understand why he'd bring up that awful part of my past.
The one I'd told him about—been forced to tell him
about—in confidence.

If he'd been trying to shock me, give me some sort
of jolt to throw me off-balance, it had worked. But I
didn't have to stick around for this. I flipped my notebook closed and started gathering my pens into my
book bag.

"Rachel."

"Why would you—" I took in a shaky breath, surprised to find I was winded. I stood and swung my book
bag strap over my shoulder. "You don't—you don't know
how you'd react if two people broke into your house.
And you were alone. And—" I stopped talking. I didn't
like the way my voice sounded, didn't like that I was still
standing there, in front of him. My face felt hot and
unshed tears blurred my vision. At least I wouldn't have
to look at Bram as I shoved past him.

I made it to the foyer and the foot of the grand
staircase before Bram caught up to me. His fingers
closed around my arm and it was like I was back in my
old house on Long Island, Matthew Marshall's gloved
hand pulling me down.

I froze.

"I'm sorry," Bram said, standing in front of me. By then I'd managed to blink back any wetness in my eyes. I could see Bram clearly. He seemed serious.

"I didn't mean anything by that," he said.

"You meant to make me feel weak," I said carefully.

Bram shook his head, opened his mouth to say something, but then seemed to think of something else. "Did you say it was two people who broke into your house?"

"Yes, what does it matter?"

"You didn't mentioned that before."

I didn't know why I hadn't mentioned it at the initiation. But I knew I didn't want to give Bram anything more. Not another bit of info, not another minute of time.

Except I didn't move, and neither did he.

"My intention was not to make you feel weak," Bram said. "It was exactly the opposite."

The part of my arm that Bram was holding on to— *still* holding on to—hummed, but no longer with the memory of Matthew Marshall's grip. I was hyperaware of the feel of Bram's fingers, the pressure of them. We hadn't stood this close, or touched, since that night outside the abandoned-house party. Just like then, he was close enough for me to smell the pine and lime in his hair. Close enough that neither of us heard the doorbell ring, the maid open the door, or even the sound of someone heading our way.

Not until Lux spoke.

"What is this?" she said.

Bram dropped his hand and I almost whipped around to ask what she was doing there before I remembered myself. It made sense that she'd show up. Bram spent so much time with the Mary Shelley Club it was easy to forget that he probably spent the rest of his nights with his girlfriend.

"We're working on a school project," Bram explained.

"With *her*?" Lux asked. "Why didn't you tell me that?"

Bram glanced my way. "Didn't seem worth mentioning."

I looped my arm through my book bag's other strap.

"See you in school," I said to neither of them in particular. They didn't seem to notice as I left.

22

I WAS AT work, manning the ticket line. The last of the night's movies had already started playing, but I had to wait for any final stragglers. Saundra sat perched on my stool. She'd bought a ticket for the movie even though I would've just let her in for free. But she didn't seem the least bit interested in seeing it. I was both jealous of all the money she had to burn and also kind of touched that she'd burn it just to hang out with me.

"I can't believe you work with Thayer Turner. Is he as annoying as he is in class?"

I glanced back to see Thayer behind the counter. "I barely know him."

Saundra shrugged and launched into something about one of the girls in her Calculus class. But I was only half listening, still thinking of my study session with Bram the previous night. Thinking of what I'd told him about the break-in. Thinking of his vague warnings about Freddie. And what had it meant that he ran after me? Why did that moment feel just as charged as that time we'd kissed?

"Do you have a massive crush on someone?" Saundra asked.

"What? No." The idea that thinking of Bram registered in any way as full-crush mode made my stomach turn.

"So just a minor crush, then?"

I picked up one of the ticket stubs from the discard box and tore it into smaller bits. "Where is this coming from?"

"You have this look on your face. And you've been acting a certain kind of way, that's all."

"What kind of way?"

Saundra slurped her jumbo Diet Coke. "Like you're hiding something."

This was the only downside to the club. While I liked the secret aspect to it, I hated having to lie to Saundra. It was only a matter of time before she figured out that something was up. Saundra, who had her finger on the pulse of all things Manchester Prep—who wasn't happy unless she knew every secret of every person in the school—was on to me. And I wasn't sure my poker face could combat her discerning gossip radar.

"I don't know what you're talking about." I continued

to tear more stubs into careful, tiny pieces while avoiding her eyes.

"Why were you talking to Felicity Chu earlier?"

Damn it. Felicity had slipped up this morning by talking to me in the hallway. We were both taking books out of our lockers at the same time. She wanted to confirm our plans for tomorrow night, when we were going to work on her upcoming Fear Test. The whole exchange must've lasted less than thirty seconds. It was so short that I'd forgotten about it. But Saundra hadn't.

"She told me I had something in my teeth."

"Felicity Chu?" Saundra said. "Doing something nice?"

Damn it again. I might as well have said she had stopped to give me a birthday present. Saundra was only going to keep digging deeper and deeper until she hit bone. I was about to come up with another lie, but Saundra spoke up.

"You know what, she probably said that just to embarrass you. Felicity probably loves pointing out food in people's teeth."

I glommed onto the idea. "Yeah, she's the worst. Anyways, what's going on with you?"

"I wanna try this new Jack Dewey smoky-eye tutorial," Saundra said. "Do you want to come over tomorrow? I'm gonna need help because I never get those right."

As I looked at Saundra's hopeful expression, I realized I wanted to. Not because I could help perfect a smoky eye (I couldn't), but because I genuinely missed hanging with Saundra. So having to turn her down made me feel terrible. "I can't tomorrow. Sorry."

"You've got other plans?" Saundra sounded deflated.

"Yeah." I hoped it was enough of an answer because I didn't want to actually lie to her.

"They don't involve your nonexistent crush, do they?"

I looked her in the eye this time because this definitely wasn't a lie. "No."

"No plans with Felicity Chu either?" Saundra teased.

I blinked and began tearing up a new stub. "Definitely not."

After school the next day, Felicity and I met on the steps of the Met. It had been her idea, so we could blend into the crowd. There must've been hundreds of tourists there, but I was pretty sure we both still stood out in our matching uniforms. Felicity in particular looked like an undercover PI in her trench coat. I had no idea what she had planned for us, but I was pleasantly surprised that she'd asked me to go on this top secret mission with her. She wasn't exactly my favorite person, but it was still nice to feel wanted.

"So where are we going?" I asked.

"Meatpacking District."

I checked my subway app to figure out the fastest way to get there. "We could take a bus and transfer to the West Side, or we could walk across the park."

Felicity looked at me long and hard. After a few seconds she started down the stairs, without any indication that I should follow her.

My cautious excitement started to ebb as I realized I didn't even know why we were going to the Meatpacking District to begin with. My mind filled with visions of a frozen locker filled with raw cow carcasses. And me in the middle of it. Alone. With Felicity. Maybe she'd asked everyone else in the club to help her with this. Maybe I'd been the only one stupid enough to say yes.

But this was part of the club rules. Felicity's Fear Test was coming up, so she got to assign roles and tasks. I had to trust that Felicity had a plan for me that didn't involve locking me in a meat locker, and in the meantime, I was taking notes for how to do things when it came to my own Fear Test. I followed Felicity down the stone steps, and by the time we got to the curb, a black town car with tinted windows had pulled up.

The driver got out and opened the back door for us. Felicity ducked inside without a word, but I hesitated.

The last time I'd gotten into a vehicle with tinted windows, I'd had a hood yanked over my head.

"Get in!" Felicity barked.

I sighed and scrambled inside. The driver closed the door behind me.

As we drove through the park, Felicity made it very clear that she wasn't in the talking mood. She pulled a worn paperback copy of *Misery* from her backpack.

"Stephen King is cool," I offered.

"He's the greatest living American writer," Felicity corrected me. "Also, there's the hotness factor."

"The what?"

"Don't pretend he's not good-looking." She flipped to the author photo on the back and looked at me expectantly. It was clear to me that I would have to choose my words carefully here, so I thought my best option was to just smile and nod appreciatively. Felicity turned back to her book.

"So, where are we going?" I asked. I had no idea if this was even Felicity's car. Did she have a personal driver, or was there an app like Uber but for rich people who only wanted to ride around in huge town cars?

"I told you, the Meatpacking District, are you slow?" Felicity did not look up from her book as she said this.

"I mean, like, for what purpose?"

203

"Supplies."

"Okay, and what do you need my help with?"

"Talking."

"Talking to who?"

"People! Just people, Rachel!" She took a deep breath and composed herself. "I'm not great at . . . talking to people."

"No kidding," I muttered. Any excitement about doing something secret, maybe even dangerous, was all but gone. Now I was really regretting not taking Saundra up on her smoky-eye adventure.

Felicity dropped the book on her lap, let her head roll back, and let out a guttural sigh. "Okay, fine. I, like, snapped at you," she said. It wasn't exactly an apology, but it was probably as good as I was going to get.

"We could try again," she said.

I was confused. "Try again?" Then I got it. "To have a conversation?"

Felicity nodded but also kind of squirmed in place.

"We really don't have to," I said. As awkward as this car ride was, we only had about fifteen minutes left and I was perfectly happy to spend them in silence. But Felicity was suddenly an open book.

"Ask me whatever you want," she said. "We can bond. Or whatever."

Okay. "Who's your target for your Fear Test?"

"Sim Smith."

I still wasn't familiar enough with every student at Manchester, so it took me a minute to place him. "That sophomore who's really into gold chains?"

Felicity gave a curt nod. "We dated at the end of last year. I was a sophomore and he was a freshman. You don't have to say it—I know it's embarrassing."

That he was a freshman? *Not* that he looked like he raided his mom's jewelry box?

"It's not embarrassing," I said. I tried picturing Felicity in a relationship, but all I could imagine was a praying mantis devouring her partner.

"Anyways, that little freshman turd cheated on me," Felicity said. "So now he has to die."

"What?"

"I'm joking," Felicity said. As if her joking tone wasn't exactly the same as her regular speaking tone. "I can't kill him. But I can scare him. And I'm going to *really* scare him."

"Great," I said in what I hoped was an encouraging-girlfriend tone. "That's really good for you."

"Did anyone ever cheat on you?"

I shook my head.

"Did anyone ever *date* you?" Felicity asked.

"Well, there was this guy in ninth grade," I said. "I was really into him and I was pretty sure he was into me. We flirted a lot, actually. He would write me these little notes in English class that were—"

"So you never dated anyone." Felicity's eyes roved over me. "Didn't think so."

The car came to a stop and the driver got out. He opened the door on Felicity's side and she stepped out while I quickly opened my own door. Felicity slipped on a pair of jet-black oversize shades that covered nearly the entire top half of her face.

With her shades and her Burberry trench, her gray school uniform was almost beside the point. Felicity tromped across the cobblestone streets like she owned them. I followed her past the Stella McCartney and Diane von Furstenberg storefronts all the way to the edge of the district, where the loading zones of factories butted up against the West Side Highway. There apparently were still meatpacking places in the Meatpacking District. My fear of being trapped in a meat locker with Felicity reappeared.

The farther we waded into the loading zone, the stronger the smell of thawing flesh got. The place was busy, with men in rubber boots climbing from the backs of open trucks to enter the cavernous warehouses. On the other side of us there was just a chain-link fence separating us from the highway traffic that whizzed past. There was grunting. Shouting. Anyplace I looked

I saw grime. The trucks, the workmen's clothes, their hands. Cow blood everywhere.

Felicity seemed to see none of it, though. She strutted through the loading zone like it was her living room.

There was a man with a dolly unloading a truck and Felicity walked right up to him. "I'm looking for Roger," she said.

"Who are you?" he asked.

"Just tell Roger that Dolores Claiborne is waiting for him," she snapped, then added reluctantly, "please."

The guy looked her over for a minute, but then went inside to get this mysterious Roger.

"Dolores Claiborne?" I hissed.

"One of Stephen's seminal works."

"You're on a first-name basis?"

"If you so much as—"

"What?" I said, fighting back a laugh as Felicity got riled up. "It's cute."

She looked like she wanted to kill me.

"What kind of supplies are we picking up here?" I asked.

But before Felicity could answer, another man came outside, wearing a rubber apron covered in questionable juices. It should've been gross, but Felicity and I exchanged glances—it'd make an amazing costume for a Fear Test.

He jumped off the loading dock and met us on the asphalt. "Dolores?"

Felicity raised one finger. "You got it?"

Roger looked to see if anyone was watching us. There were other men milling around the loading zone, but all of them seemed too busy carrying boxes, and in some cases, whole slabs of meat. He reached into a plastic bag and took out a hook.

A big hook. The kind you could stick in a pig and use to drag it across the ground. It looked like the same hook the fisherman in *I Know What You Did Last Summer* used to kill all those '90s heartthrobs. Except this one had a—

"Neon-orange rubber grip?" Felicity said. "We didn't agree on that. And it's not very sharp."

"This is a quality boning hook," Roger protested. "The handle is for your comfort."

"I don't want comfortable," Felicity said. "I want *menacing*. I want someone to see it and *pee their pants*. I want it sharp and without that ridiculous rubber grip. And I want it now."

There were no ifs or buts about it. While her obvious sense of privilege would normally make me roll my eyes, I had to admit that I kind of admired Felicity here. Not the brattiness, but the asking for what she wanted. Demanding it.

Roger opened his mouth to argue with her, then seemed to think better of it. He he let his shoulders slump and said, "Okay. But it's gonna cost you extra."

Felicity flicked her wrist dismissively. "Whatever."

"What does a nice girl like you need a boning hook for anyway?"

"Is this the *News at 5*? Just get me the hook."

Yeah, Felicity really wasn't good at talking to people. Roger plodded back into the plant and Felicity and I were left outside to wait.

"We came down here for a hook?" I said. "Couldn't you find one online?"

"What, and leave a paper trail? Naïvete is not cute, Rachel."

When Roger came back out, he pulled another hook out of the plastic bag. This hook didn't look new at all. There was no gleam to the steel. It was smudged and almost rusted in parts. But the sharp curve matched Felicity's smile perfectly.

"I'll take it," she said.

23

SIM SMITH

SIM SMITH'S STEPDAD was a used-car salesman but dressed like he operated a lot full of brand-new Porsches. Tie pin, bespoke suit, a fat gold Rolex on his wrist, which, according to him, was the only piece of jewelry a man should wear besides brass knuckles. Sim didn't agree with that.

Sim liked chains. Skinny chains, thick chains, gold, silver, whatever. Chains were hot. He had one necklace with a little vial that had a single grain of rice inside it with a single teeny word inscribed on it: "valor." It wasn't Sim's favorite chain but it looked good on him and he learned real early that girls dug it. So. He wore a necklace.

The necklace made Sim stand out, and so did the fact that his stepdad owned a car dealership. It wasn't the bougiest job, especially when compared to everyone else's parents at Manchester (there was a kid in Sim's grade—Steeper Carlyle—whose dad was a friggin' sportscaster), but Sim enjoyed the perks. It wasn't because he could have whatever car he wanted. No, the best perk about Sim's stepdad owning a used-car lot was the fact that Sim could take girls there.

There were so many cars—at least a hundred—but squeezed together, they looked like a sea of thousands. And you could just get in one and then lots of stuff could happen inside. Plus: reclining seats. The most beautiful two words in the English language. Hooking up with girls here was a total win-win. You had complete privacy and new(ly refurbished)-car smell, and all Sim had to do was wait 'til his stepdad was asleep and then swipe his work keys.

Sim had a name for this little spot on Flatlands Avenue where the lot was: Sim's Point. 'Cause he figured, all those old movies where the teenagers park their cars and make out? It was always at some scenic point. And there wasn't anything like that in Brooklyn. So. He made it happen.

It was kind of what he was known for at Manchester. If somebody at school wanted access to a car for fooling around, all they had to do was either pay up or do Sim's homework for a week. And nobody ever tried to steal the cars 'cause they knew if they did, Sim's step-dad would break their legs. So. Win-win-win.

The moral of the story was that Sim loved his step-dad, like, a lot. Just for making Sim's Point possible. And right at this moment, Jennifer Abrams seemed to love Sim a lot, too. She was hanging all over him as they walked among the cars. It was after eleven, and in this part of Brooklyn, that meant there was no one and nothing around to disrupt them, just the changing traffic lights and the B47 bus passing every twenty minutes beyond the chain-link fence.

Sim checked himself out in the darkened driver-side window of a Toyota Corolla. Hair was properly coifed with a good two inches of height. Supreme Playboy pocket tee hanging mostly loose, except for the strategic French tuck in the front of his Burberry slim fit jeans. His midnight-blue velvet bomber jacket by—

"Can we go?" Jennifer said, tugging him toward a cherry-red Jaguar. "Let's get in this one."

Sim pretended to consider it, tilting his head, cocking his eyebrows as he examined the car. It was nice, definitely, but . . . no reclining seats. So. "I got just the car for us, babe."

His turn to tug on Jennifer's arm now, but she stood her ground like a boulder. "This is a *Jaguar*." She said it like she was out of a Mary Poppins movie or something. *Jag-you-AHH*.

Sim huffed. There was one car out deep in the lot that he liked to use. It was just a 2004 Volvo. A junk-bomb. But there was room. No stick shift to poke him at the worst possible time, and the seats were worn polyester, which was really so much more comfortable than it sounded. Way more comfortable than the reupholstered stuff, which could be slippery and always squeaked. The 2004 Volvo was his lucky car. It got him lucky. The Jaguar was all wrong. So.

"This other car . . . ," Sim said, trying to think something up quick, "it's got a surprise for you."

Jennifer's lips turned up at the corners and her eyes sparkled behind her glasses. "What kind of surprise?"

"You'll see." Sim didn't know what it was about glasses, but he loved them. Anybody ever asked, he told them it was a librarian fetish or something, but he just liked that it made girls' eyes look big and bright. Any time there was a magazine lying around and he was bored, Sim would draw glasses on the girls in the pictures.

The last girl Sim had dated didn't wear glasses, but he liked that she had a temper. It was hot. He def/prob should've ended things with her before starting things up with Jennifer, but Sim wasn't smooth like that. Didn't know the proper formula for the how and when of sidepiece management. So instead of figuring it all out, Sim had bounced. It was like his stepdad always said: Don't fix your problems—dump 'em. And Felicity Chu was a problem.

Sim led Jennifer to the Volvo, which was surrounded by prettier cars like no one would notice the difference. Jennifer could tell, though. She didn't look impressed. "What's the surprise?"

"The car's name is Jennifer," Sim said. "I named her after you."

He waited. And then Jennifer jumped on him, her hands all over the sides of his face and her mouth all over his. Worked. Every. Time. They got in the car but—

Wait.

"Did you hear that?" Sim said, breaking their kiss.

"Hear what?"

"There was, like . . . a thud."

"That was my heart," Jennifer said.

Whatever, a girl was on top of him. Sim wasn't about to waste any more time. He peeled off his midnight-blue blue velvet Armani bomber jacket and focused on the important stuff. More lips. The two kept kissing, but then Sim heard it again. Not the exact same noise. A sort of scratching this time.

And it was closer. Right on top of them.

"You didn't hear that?"

"*Sim.*"

"No seriously, there was scratching on the roof. You didn't hear it?"

"All I hear is my doubt, telling me that maybe I shouldn't be in a car with a guy who is *making excuses* not to make out with me."

"But I heard—"

"You want to hear something so bad, fine!" Jennifer took out her phone and Lady Gaga's voice drifted into the Volvo, telling them they couldn't read her poker face.

Sim wasn't about to sit here with a totally hot girl and just listen to music all night. So. He flipped her over, reached to the side of Jennifer's seat, and pulled its lever. He hovered over her as she slowly reclined backward. He started kissing her again, proving how focused he was on nothing but her.

And the noise he'd heard. Yeah, he couldn't get it out of his mind, like, at all. Which made Sim keep his eyes open. Which was a weird way to kiss someone, but it allowed him to spot a shadow looming just beyond the rear window. And soon, there wasn't just a shadow, but movement. Something dark flashed outside the car. Sim's lips stopped moving. Had he closed the gate in the chain-link fence? But he always closed the gate. Did he forget to lock it, though?

"Why aren't you kissing me back?" Jennifer asked. "It's like I'm kissing a dead fish."

The closer the shadow got, the more it looked like a person. Someone must have snuck in. No telling if it was male or female, just someone wearing a thick black coat, a hoodie pulled so low it obscured their face.

Sim crouched over Jennifer, frozen, as she continued to paw at his clothing obliviously. The shadowy figure was ten paces away.

Five.

Jennifer let out the most vicious scream and Sim leaped back, smashing his head against the roof. "WHAT!"

"This is my favorite song!" Jennifer squealed.

"*That's* why you screamed?"

"Um, hello, they never play the Ruperts on the radio anymore."

Sim wasn't going to sit here any longer. And not just because the Ruperts sucked, but because there was definitely someone outside the car. Sim couldn't see them anymore, but that noise from earlier was back. On the roof again. Louder. And then the car shook.

"Was that you?" Jennifer whispered. For the first time, concern flashed on her face.

"Quiet, I think there's someone out there," Sim whispered, every inch of him tensed and waiting for the next noise. It came from the roof. The undeniable sound of shoes hitting metal. The roof dipped slightly, let out a low groan.

"Boo!"

Sim jumped but it was only Jennifer, giggling hysterically.

"Why would you say 'boo' right now?!" he hissed. "Like, why would you choose this moment of all moments to say 'boo'?!"

"Okay, you don't want to be my boo, I get it, gosh," Jennifer said. "What about sweetie? Sugar bear? Pookie?" Her hand caressed his shoulder. "Are we gonna screw?"

No. Not when there were freaking *footsteps* on the roof of the car! And not with a girl who couldn't hear anything but that awful Ruperts crap. Damn, Sim needed to seriously stop dating the worst girls.

"Let's go. Someone's playing a prank or something," Sim tried to open the door but it wouldn't budge. "Are the child locks on?"

Sim jumped again when he heard a tap on the window. But it wasn't the dull sound of knuckle on glass. No, this was sharper. Like metal on glass. When he looked up, Sim's heart almost stopped.

It was the Black Hoodie. Holding a big-ass hook.

"FuuuuuuUUUUUUUUUCKKKKKK." Sim kicked the door open, slamming it into the Black Hoodie, who went down with an *oomph*.

Sim ran, ignoring the sound of Jennifer calling after him.

But the rows of cars turned the place into a tight labyrinth, preventing Sim from making a clean run for it. He rounded trunks only to smack into bumpers. His hips thwacked against side-view mirrors, eventually tearing one clean off a convertible. His stepdad was going to kill him. But not if this Hoodie freak got to him first.

Sim nearly cried with relief when he saw that the gate was two car rows away. He'd be there soon.

But then the Black Hoodie popped up to block his way.

Sim stumbled back. How had he gotten there so quick? Sim had left the freak behind. Now this dude popped out of nowhere, looking even bigger than before. He was so close that Sim could now see his face. White. Stoic. Scars. It was a rubber mask.

The Black Hoodie pushed Sim hard and he pinballed between two car doors on his way to the concrete. The Black Hoodie was leaning over him, raising a knife in the air, when Sim kicked out. He'd been smart to wear his Acne Studios Jensen Grain boots tonight. They not only made him an inch taller, but also came to a fine, hard point at the toe. He slammed the tip of his boot into the Black Hoodie's side so hard Sim could feel ribs crunch.

The Black Hoodie let out a grunt and doubled over, holding their abdomen. It was Sim's only chance. He ran out the gate and didn't look back.

24

THE NEXT EVENING, we regrouped at Bram's house after Thayer and I were done with our shifts at the movie theater and Freddie had finished pitching in with his mom's catering business.

It was Felicity's turn to pick a movie. I had pegged her as a fan of black-and-white movies, like *Nosferatu*, or some weird Swedish silent film from the 1920s. But Felicity ended up going with *Urban Legend*. At first, I had no idea why, but then it became clear.

"If I could live during any era it would be the glorious—if brief—time in history when Joshua Jackson had his hair bleached," Felicity said. "*Urban Legend* and *Cruel Intentions*. Peak Joshua Jackson, if you ask me."

And there it was. Felicity: the Joshua Jackson superfan. She watched the screen with rapt abandon as Joshua Jackson tried to make a move in a parked car.

"Ew, no," Thayer said. "Peak Joshua Jackson was *The Mighty Ducks*. That movie was my sexual awakening."

"I can't believe we're talking about this," I said. "Peak Joshua Jackson is *The Affair*, obviously."

"You watched *The Affair*?" Freddie asked, eyebrow suggestively cocked. "Gotta say I'm more of a *Fringe* guy."

"Does no one here have any respect for Pacey Witter?" Bram said.

I was back in his house for the first time since our disasterous study session, and so far we'd successfully managed to avoid all interaction. Which was an arrangement we both seemed happy with.

"Okay, a compromise," Felicity said. "Peak Joshua Jackson is the Joshua in the one episode of *Dawson's* where he had frosted tips."

Felicity was in a surprisingly good mood. Maybe it was Joshua. Or maybe it was the fact that she'd gotten her cheating ex to go running scared into the night. We hadn't done much beyond dressing in incognito black and scraping a few twigs over the roof of a used car, and yet, I gotta say, it was deeply satisfying. Maybe now Sim Smith would think twice about taking girls to his stepdad's creepy car dealership.

"Now *this*," Thayer said, "this is a beautiful example of the parked-car trope. Take notes, Felicity."

On the screen, Joshua Jackson was dangling from a tree, his shoes scraping the top of his car.

Felicity scowled. "I don't need lessons on how to stage a Fear Test from the guy who sent an eight-year-old down the hall last year and called it a day."

"Thayer paid a girl from the Lower School to stand in the hallway before the final bell rang last year," Freddie whispered to me. "I think he was banking on the scary-sad-girl-with-long-hair factor, but it was broad daylight and nobody cared. One of the worst Fear Tests on record."

Thayer let out a gasp. Freddie's whisper had apparently not been low enough. "How dare you?" Thayer demanded. "It was a quality test. Way ahead of its time."

"It was garbage," Felicity said. She threw a handful of popcorn at him. Bram leaned over to pluck the kernels off the floor but as he stretched his arm out, he winced and grabbed his side. I seemed to be the only one to catch it.

"I still say I deserve a do-over," Felicity said.

"No do-overs," Freddie said. "That's against the rules."

"I was injured during my own test." Felicity held up her arm to punctuate the point, an Ace bandage encircling her wrist. According to Felicity, when Sim had popped open his car door he'd seriously injured her, but I was pretty sure the only bruising she'd experienced was to her ego. "I didn't get a chance to complete the rest of my test."

"*Rest of your test?*" Thayer said, tickled. "Girl, you weren't gonna do anything but chase him anyway."

"Personal injury is part of the risk," Bram piped in. "You have to come to terms with your test being a failure."

Felicity exhaled loudly through her nostrils. "It wasn't a failure. I scared him."

"Okay," Bram said. "But the biggest scream of the night came from Jennifer over a song."

"Screw you, Bram."

"Hey, it wasn't a failure," Freddie assured her. "You scared Sim."

"Yeah, but his girlfriend wasn't scared at all," I said.

"Um, who asked you?" Felicity said. "The target is the only person you have to scare."

"But when there are other people in the Fear Test, shouldn't their reactions count for your overall score?"

"New Girl makes a good point," Thayer said. "We should add that to the rules."

"No way," Felicity said. "The rules existed long before she joined the club."

But Freddie leaned toward me. "What would the terms be?"

"I think if you're going to do a Fear Test with a lot of people present, that's going to be a harder test to pull off. The more people to convince, the bigger the risk."

Felicity got up from the couch, blocking a shrieking Rebecca Gayheart on the screen. "So we're just going to take New Girl's advice on how to play this game?"

"It would make things more interesting," Freddie said.

"We know how you love to make things more interesting," Bram said. I didn't know what he meant, but Freddie didn't seem to take too kindly to the remark.

"This is ridiculous." Felicity pointed a finger at me. "The only reason you're in the club is because you found out too much about us."

Her words landed like a blow to my stomach.

"Felicity," Freddie said, his usual chill tone taking on an edge of warning.

But Felicity ignored him. "You were a threat to our ecosystem," she said to me. "You were getting too close to finding out about us. Nobody actually wanted you in this club."

"That isn't true," Freddie said quickly.

Thayer piped in. "We're always on the lookout for new recruits. You fit the bill."

We were sitting in our usual movie-watching spots but suddenly it felt crowded, with their gazes boring into me. Here was an opportunity for Bram to speak but he let it pass him by, his silence saying all I needed to hear.

Felicity turned back to the group. "The rules are bigger than any one of us. You can't just change them."

And with that, she was done, grabbing her coat and leaving.

Nobody said anything for a moment, and it felt like a curtain had been pulled back. Before, all I'd noticed were the great things about the club. I'd been naïve to the fact that there could be something ugly festering beneath the surface.

Thayer came to sit next to me, filling the space between Freddie and me.

"Felicity can be kind of dramatic," Thayer whispered. "She's upset because her test sucked, as her tests always inevitably do. Okay? We good?"

I nodded because it seemed like the response Thayer wanted, but I couldn't shake what Felicity had said. Did they really want me here? Suddenly I wasn't so sure, but I didn't budge and we continued with the movie. For the first time a Mary Shelley Club meeting didn't feel like the cozy blanket it usually was for me.

Freddie tried to catch my gaze, but I kept my eyes on the screen. The killer had finally caught up with Tara Reid and she let out a blood-curdling scream.

25

BY MONDAY MORNING everyone at school had heard about Sim and Jennifer's hookup from hell. In the People's Court of Manchester Prep, they were defendant and plaintiff, arguing two wildly different accounts of what had happened.

Jennifer told everyone that Sim had taken her to a sketch AF car dealership in bumblefuck Brooklyn to bone and then suddenly made up some story about a killer with, like, bait and tackle or something, and then Sim just ran away, leaving Jennifer to figure out where the heck she was—did she mention she was in bumblefuck Brooklyn? Alone? At *night*!—and Sim very obviously totally just couldn't get it up.

Sim told everyone that the Infamous Manchester Prankster had gotten him, threatened his life with a hook and then a knife, but then he'd beaten the prankster to a pulp with his bare hands and he was definitely *not* impotent. He had absolutely zero problems in that department. He had the opposite of that problem. He could prove it to any doubters.

Saundra was delighted with the new scandal.

"Prankster my *ass*!" she said, throwing her head back and laughing gleefully at lunch. "Obviously, I believe Jennifer," Saundra said.

"Why?"

"Because Sim can't get his story straight? First he sees a guy in a hoodie? Then the guy disappears. Then he sees him again with a hook. Then Sim apparently knocks him out when he opens his car door." Saundra had gathered every scrap of info from both parties, leaving nothing on the parking lot floor. "Then he runs but is stopped by the hooded man again and this time he has a knife? No hook anywhere in sight? And then Sim *beats him up*? That is highly unlikely, my friend. The only thing Sim has ever tried to beat is—we now know for sure—his nonfunctioning dick."

I nearly choked on my kale. "Saundra!"

"What? I never liked Jennifer Abrams, but I believe women."

Just as she said this, the lunchroom din was interrupted by the screeching of metal chair legs being dragged across the floor. Sim hopscotched from a chair to a table, getting everyone's attention.

"I am telling the truth!" he declared. The desperation in his voice was tinged with hoarseness, probably from denying his impotency all day. "I was attacked! That guy almost killed me!"

I spotted something white soaring in a soft arch toward him, landing at his feet. And then again. Napkins? Tissues? I followed Sim's confused gaze to see where the flurry of napkins was coming from. Felicity pinched a new napkin and threw it at him, like it was a rose and he was a performer. Except weirder, obviously.

"What are you doing?" he shrieked.

Felicity shrugged and said in her patented monotone: "Cry me a river."

Jennifer Abrams stood up then, too. She made a quick beeline toward Felicity, pinched a napkin from the stack in Felicity's hand and started flinging them at Sim, too. And then other people joined in. Tissues flew like feathers from a pillow fight, the laughter and mocking applause drowning out anything Sim was trying to say.

"This is ridiculous!" he said. "I did nothing wrong!"

I spotted my mom walking up to Sim and trying to get him to come down from the table, and then more teachers joined her. As Sim was being pulled off, he bellowed, "It was a big, scary dude in a hood! A big, scary-as-fuck dude in a scary-as-fuck mask!"

Everyone else laughed or jeered or continued to throw their napkins at him, but everything in me stopped.

Mask.

None of us had worn masks to Felicity's Fear Test.

I decided that Sim must've been mistaken. But that word stuck with me for the rest of the day, like a hot breath on the back of my neck.

It was the kitchen floor that came to me first. I could feel the familiar laminate, the coolness against the back of my head. My hands were preoccupied, fists clutching, fingers curled in black fabric as I tried to push him off me. But he was too strong. Every time I grabbed at a forearm, it'd slip out of my grasp. And there were his knees, locked on either side of me, pinning me down.

I reached up for his face, but the rubber mask of a muted monster stared down at me.

I woke up, skin clammy and breathing hard. I fought with my blanket as though I was still fighting for my life. It took a minute for my fingers to relax and unclench.

It also took me a minute to remember. Because it wasn't a nightmare. It was a memory.

I buried my face in my hands. I hadn't thought about that night in so long; I'd forced myself not to, but

230

something had unsettled me. Since joining the club I thought I'd buried that memory deep but it had found a way to come out, like a zombie's hand breaking through the surface of a fresh grave. I pressed my hands into my eye sockets until I felt pain. Until the blackness there burst with glowing shapes and patterns.

26

I COULD'VE TALKED to my mom about my nightmare. But I didn't want to worry her. So I was back on my old bullshit. The moment I started to feel a creeping sense of anxiety, I shut it down by doing something really stupid. Tonight's rendition of stupid was climbing down the fire escape outside my bedroom window, riding the subway into the city at two A.M., and not stopping until I was standing in front of a building in Washington Heights.

I held my phone in my hands, waiting for an answer to my text. I watched the screen, clicked it back on every time it went dark. Then three dots.

Be right down.

It was only then that it hit me just *how* stupid this was. But I couldn't turn back now. I was here because I had thought that by joining the Mary Shelley Club, I was beginning to push past everything I'd been through last year. And for a while it had worked—I wasn't rattled by fear, wasn't thinking about what had happened to me and what I'd done. But that nightmare shook me up. The rumor of the Masked Man had triggered something, and now I couldn't think about anything else. So I needed to stop thinking, period.

Freddie pulled open the door to his building. He wore black sliders over slouch socks, sweatpants, and an undershirt wrinkled by the sleep I'd just interrupted. He wasn't wearing his glasses and when he looked at me, it was through a squint.

"I'm sorry I woke you up."

"You can wake me up anytime. Want to come in?"

"Your family's probably sleeping," I said, though I remembered that he'd once told me his brother worked weeknights as a security guard.

"My brother's working and my mom's a deep sleeper. It's way too cold to be out here." His voice was soft but authoritative, like he wasn't going to take no for an answer. "Come in."

We walked through the lobby, which was a muted pink and smelled like vegetable soup. The elevator was small, only a few feet wide, and dipped slightly as we stepped inside. Freddie hit number twelve and we sputtered and lurched upward.

The ride was slow, but neither of us spoke. My

mind was still swampy with flashes of my nightmare. When we got out I followed Freddie to apartment 12C. The hallway light bathed a triangle of space inside the apartment, but when I closed the door behind me, it was pitch-black. I felt Freddie's fingers encircle mine and he led the way to his room.

Freddie switched on a lamp. There were posters all over the walls—*The Thing*, *The Evil Dead*, *Halloween*. Two twin beds rested against opposite walls, both unmade. I didn't know which one belonged to Freddie. There were two dressers, distressed from age, not by artistic choice. The furniture reminded me of my own.

In the world of Manchester, it was easy to forget that there were other people who lived like me. But then there was Freddie.

"So," he said, taking in a deep breath. "Do you need a cheat sheet or something?"

"I'm not here for your services," I said, then blushed. "I mean, I don't need your help with school. Well, maybe Earth Science."

"I got you," Freddie said. "But why are you really here?"

"I had a nightmare." I felt ridiculous saying it out loud, but Freddie deserved the truth of why I'd woken him up. "I couldn't go back to sleep and I needed to clear my head and you gave me your address once, to meet up for Thayer's test, remember? And I really wasn't thinking."

Freddie seemed unfazed by my rambling. "What was the nightmare about?"

"Just . . . it was more of a memory. I dreamed about what happened last year."

There was a look on his face like pity, which bothered me. I didn't need anyone feeling sorry for me. "It's fine. I'm fine."

"Do you want to talk about it?"

I shrugged. "I guess it was on my mind because of what Sim said about Felicity's Fear Test. That he saw a guy in a mask."

"I wouldn't really trust anything Sim says. He got scared and left his girl to fend for herself. Of course he's going to make up stories to maintain his cred."

He was probably right. Felicity had done a good job of hiding her face in that giant hoodie. Sim probably didn't know what he'd seen. Speaking of Felicity.

"Is what she said at the last meeting true? Did you only let me into the club because you were worried I was going to expose you?"

Freddie's face fell. "You know you belong in the club just as much as any of us."

I could tell he meant it, but no matter what he said,

Felicity's words had burrowed deep. "I just still feel like an outsider sometimes."

Freddie sat on his bed and scooted over to make space for me. I sat beside him. The lamp bathed the room in a warm glow.

"My mom used to work as a housekeeper for Bram's family," Freddie said. "Did you know that?"

I shook my head, but it made sense given their dynamic. There was a familiarity between Freddie and Bram, like two different species of fish that swam in the same bowl. I always attributed their dynamic to the club, but now I knew it was more than that.

"It's actually how I ended up at Manchester," Freddie continued. "Mrs. Wilding was kind of, like, my sponsor. She put in a good word for me. Anyway, sometimes after school I'd go over to their house and Bram was always there. I'm the one who got him into scary movies."

"Really?"

"Yeah. We'd watch them on his laptop every day after school until it was time for my mom to go home. The first time I ever watched *Amityville Horror* was at Bram's house. Coming from this tiny apartment, big mansions in scary movies didn't ever get to me. But at the Wilding place? We were, like, eleven, all the way up

236

in Bram's room, like three floors away from the rest of civilization. It was pouring out and we both thought we were going to die that night. It was amazing."

Freddie's eyes flashed with excitement and I understood exactly the feeling he was describing.

"That's what it's supposed to feel like," I said. "Nerve-racking, pit-in-your-stomach, shaky like someone's got you by the heart, squeezing it 'til you feel like you can't breathe and then . . . air. You know?"

"*Yeah,*" Freddie said, nodding emphatically. Somehow his hand found its way to my knee, but just as quickly he took it back again.

"You never told me how you got into scary movies," he said.

Right. My story wasn't as fun as Freddie's. "I only started getting into horror . . . after what happened. The break-in. I thought that maybe if I watched enough scary movies I could train myself to become numb to fear."

Freddie watched my face, his eyes searching mine. It made me realize how close we were sitting.

"Did it work?" he asked softly.

"At first, yeah," I said. "The club worked better, though. Or, I thought it did. But as much as I love being in the club, sometimes I feel out of place. Felicity and Bram—they're not the most welcoming people."

"Bram?" Freddie's eyebrows furrowed. "Did he say something to you?"

I thought of telling Freddie what Bram had said about him, his warnings about getting too close. But I didn't want to stir anything up. "Just his general attitude toward me," I said.

"Look," Freddie said, "I've been in this world for a while—the world of Bram Wilding, the Mary Shelley Club, Manchester—and I still feel like an outsider, too. I mean, look at where I live."

"I like your room. It looks like mine."

Freddie smiled like he didn't believe me. "I didn't invite you to join the club because I thought you were a threat to us. I invited you because I wanted you there."

I held on to the fact that he'd said "I" instead of "we." Even if it was just him who wanted me in the club, it was enough. It was everything.

"I'm sorry I woke you up," I said for what seemed like the millionth time. "I feel like I forced my way into your room."

"No, I've been meaning to get you in here." As soon as he said it, he lit up red like a siren. "I don't mean . . . not like that. There's something in my bedroom especially for you."

I bit the inside of my cheek to keep from grinning.

Maybe it was a trick of the light, but I could swear even the tops of Freddie's ears looked sunburned.

"You know what?" Freddie stammered. "I'm gonna stop talking now and just show you."

He crawled toward a clunky machine on the windowsill behind his headboard, his bed squeaking with the movement. I wondered what his mom might think if she heard the noise. She might think we were doing something bad, even though we weren't doing anything bad, but really, would it even be so bad? I let my mind wander, let my face get hot.

I stayed very still.

Finally, Freddie flipped a switch, sending lights dancing on my arm.

"Is that a film projector?" I whispered.

"Yeah."

Freddie took a sheet off the floor on his brother's side of the room and flung it over the closet door to create a makeshift projector screen. He turned off the lamp.

The film was black-and-white and there was no audio, but I recognized it instantly. The stark brightness pulled me in like a moth to a flame even if part of my shoulder and head blocked the projection.

"Old film reels and canisters are kind of, like, prized

possessions in Film Club," Freddie said. "One of the guys found this at a flea market. I traded him my reel of *Goldfinger* for it. But you've probably seen this one anyway."

I watched the scene play out on the wrinkled sheet. Something about how old it was, how silent, made it more magical. "*Bride of Frankenstein*."

It was the scene where the Monster walks into the laboratory to meet his mate. Freddie and I had to sit apart so the beam of light could pass between us, but we still caught parts of the images on our bodies, the lightning-streaked tips of the Bride's hair splayed on my sleeve, part of Dr. Frankenstein on Freddie's cheek.

I realized that being there with Freddie had helped me shake off the bad feelings from my nightmare. Now I was feeling something else, and I wanted to feel it even more.

Freddie turned to look at me, as if he could hear my thoughts. I didn't know what images were playing on my face but he couldn't seem to look away.

"¿Te puedo besar?" he asked.

He smiled, and on his face, Dr. Frankenstein let out a soundless cry. I grabbed him and the doctor both and pulled them toward me. Like Freddie had said, I'd seen this one anyway.

We kissed long enough for the Monster to feel

hope and love and rage, the scene playing out against our moving arms and faces, painting us in dramatic grays. Finally, the Monster met his bride for the first and last time, and their silent screams were awash on our skin.

27

"WHO ARE YOU TEXTING?" Mom asked. She plopped down next to me on the couch and tried to peek at my phone screen, but I held it out of reach.

"No one!"

"Is No One cute?"

I rolled my eyes. "Mom."

"What? I've noticed that your texting activity has skyrocketed exponentially all of a sudden. And I know it's not Saundra."

"How do you know?"

"Because you'd tell me if it was her."

She had me there. I didn't particularly want to tell her about Freddie, especially since I didn't know if there was anything to tell. We'd made out in his room. On his bed, to be exact. For a *while*. But that had been two days ago, and now it was the weekend, which meant that I didn't get to see him again in school, which meant any number of things could've happened. Like, he could've forgotten about me. Or changed his mind. Or had a long forty-eight-hour think about how much he really wasn't into my kissing style.

But at least we were texting. He sent me cute memes and asked about my plans for Halloween, and we chatted back and forth about a whole bunch of top-ics that were not about how we'd kissed. Hence, all my questions and doubts.

This was probably the kind of thing my mom could theoretically help me sort out. She *was* starting to ask a lot of questions about where I was running off to most nights. And I was pretty sure she wasn't buying my knitting club excuse. If I was going to keep lying about the club, I could at least be honest about who I was texting.

"Do you know Freddie Martinez?"

A slow smile crept onto Mom's face and I was already regretting my decision to tell her anything.

"I taught him last year," she said. "Are you guys . . . hanging out?"

"Kind of."

Mom tucked her lips between her teeth like she was biting back a grin, but a little squeal still managed to slip out.

"Mom!"

"I didn't say anything!"

"You were thinking it."

"So Freddie's the knitting club?"

"*Mom*." I grabbed a couch cushion and tried to fuse my face with it, still hearing my mom's giggles as I did. She pulled the pillow away. "I'm happy you're . . . making connections."

"This isn't, like, a Craigslist ad, Mom. We're just friends."

"Well, do you like him?"

I gave a noncommittal shrug. Which I knew my mom would know how to read. She confirmed that with another little squeal.

"You know, most parents would be wary of high school boys," I said.

"Well, I know Freddie. He's a very upstanding gentleman. And most parents don't have a daughter as *responsible* and *smart* and *not-quick-to-rush-into-things* as you." She squeezed a hug out of me and leaned her head on my shoulder. I let her because it felt nice, and because my mom deserved a normal moment with me. After last year, I guess this was like her hitting the Normal Teen Daughter jackpot.

"Are you two going out tonight?" Mom asked. "It's Halloween!"

That was actually what Freddie had just been texting me about. The Mary Shelley Club traditionally halted all proceedings on October 31, but there was a party that lots of people from Manchester were going to. I had my own Halloween tradition, though.

"Gonna watch *Halloween*," I said.

"Again?"

"They don't call it a classic for nothin'." Also, I needed inspiration for my upcoming Fear Test and I was hoping Michael Myers and Laurie Strode could provide some.

I was all ready and settled in. I had grabbed the big bowl of candy that Mom had prepared for any trick-or-treaters because I was pretty sure no costumed kids were going to show up at our door.

Actually, there had been one kid about half an hour earlier. A tiny Minion from down the hall, who was only allowed to collect goodies from floors two through four. I put a mini Twix in her plastic jack-o'-lantern and sent her on her way.

Just as I was about to hit play, there came a knock on the door. Mom snatched away the candy bowl and went to open it.

Catwoman walked into the apartment. Specifically,

Michelle Pfeiffer's Catwoman, complete with shiny black latex and white stitching. Behind the mask, Saundra winked and said, "I am Catwoman, hear me purr." And then she purred.

"Saundra!" Mom said. "You look great." Which she would still have said if Saundra had walked in wearing a potato sack.

"Thank you, Ms. Chavez!"

"What are you doing here?" I asked.

"Hello to you, too," she said, and twirled. "I came to get you for the party."

"I told you I wasn't going."

"Yeah, but you always say that."

"And I always mean it."

"And yet you always end up at a party."

"Only because you drag me."

"Exactly," Saundra said. She walked across the living room and back, as if determined to show just how far latex could stretch. Like, there was really no need for the leg lunges (in fact, they looked kind of dangerous in those stiletto boots), but Saundra went to town anyway. "This costume is too sweet not to be seen."

"The attention to detail is really something," Mom said. "Rachel, I think you should go!"

"I always knew I liked you, Ms. Chavez." Saundra pointed her toes and ran her hand up and down the length of herself like she was both the model and the prize on a game show. "So let's go find you a costume already!"

I almost twisted my ankle stepping out of the Lyft, which was majorly pathetic, as I was in kitten heels barely an inch off the ground. Saundra, surprisingly surefooted in her boots, helped steady me.

We stood in front of one of the many warehouses in Industry City, a part of Brooklyn I'd never even heard of that sat right next to the Gowanus Bay. Looking around, I saw there wasn't much to the so-called city, just rows upon rows of the same boxy buildings, packed neatly like extra-large shipping containers with walkways between them. Some of them were stores, others looked like office buildings. The one we were in front of had no signs of any kind. It could've been an abandoned loft where serial killers disposed of bodies. Which I guess made it the perfect place for rich kids to party.

At home, Saundra had rummaged through my closet, flinging clothing around until she declared everything basic. My mom offered up her closet, and that was where I found it. As soon as I saw the frilly periwinkle dress, the idea for the costume materialized in my head.

"It's hideous," Saundra had groaned.

"It's perfect."

My mom's beloved Cincinnati Reds baseball cap had been shoved into the corner of her closet, unworn since about 2016, but tonight it was coming out of retirement. I had the dress, I had the hat, all that I had left to do was plait my hair into two neat braids.

"What are you supposed to be?" Saundra had asked when I stepped out of the bathroom, ready to go.

"I'm P.J. Soles."

"You're BJ Souls? Is that, like, an appliance store? A law firm?"

"What? No, I'm *P.J. Soles*, the actress. You know, from *Carrie*? The mean girl who wears a baseball cap the entire movie? Even to prom?"

Saundra stared at me blankly. "*Carrie*? The movie?"

"Yes!"

"Never heard of it."

"Okay, let's just go."

At the warehouse, I couldn't stop fidgeting, but I didn't know if it was because my dress itched or because I was about to step into uncharted territory. I'd already been to a couple of parties this school year and it'd been weird, to say the least. I wasn't exactly looking forward to whatever fun surprises might jump out at me here. But there was no turning back now. Saundra had her claws in me—literally: Catwoman's black-polished nails were digging into my wrist. I had no choice but to follow.

It was dark inside the warehouse, and empty too, with peeling damp walls straight out of *Saw*. But we followed the sounds of booming bass to a stairwell at the back. The second floor was a totally different vibe, with bodies bathed in strobe lights, and house music that sounded like wild animals thrown into a ball pit. On a little platform was some kid whose ticket to this party seemed to be the fact that his parents had clearly paid for DJ lessons. He stood behind his equipment and bobbed his head while his Beats headphones rested uselessly around his neck.

But the cherry on top was that there were masks everywhere. The familiar tingling started crawling up my arms, my neck, my cheeks. Flashes of my night-mare from a few nights before pushed their way to the front of my mind. It was hot in here, too noisy, too many people. Now I was the one digging my nails into Saundra's wrist.

This happened to me sometimes in large crowds, the sense that the walls were closing in. But it was ten times worse with everyone wearing disguises. I could feel the panic coming. It threatened to swallow me up.

"Maybe this wasn't such a great idea," I said. But

of course it was too loud to hear anything well, and when Saundra turned to me, she just nodded enthusiastically.

"I know, right?!" she shouted over the noise.

We made our way through the throng and I tried again, louder this time. "Can we find a quiet corner or something?"

"Quiet corner," Saundra snorted. "Do you want people to start calling you Quiet-Corner Rachel? Because they will!"

I tugged at the hem of my frilly dress. What kind of unbreathable fabric was this, anyway? And then, a darker thought: What if I fainted? What if they didn't call me Quiet-Corner Rachel, but Faints-at-Parties Rachel? The corners of the room started to get hazy and white. The fear was settling in. "I need to go."

"What?" Saundra's voice came distant.

"I need to—"

There was a tap on my shoulder and the jolt was just the defibrillator I needed. I spun around, breathing hard and suddenly very alert, the edges of my vision crystallizing back into focus.

Felicity stared at me. "Excuse me," she said.

She wore a towel secured tightly under her armpits, the rest of her bare skin painted in various shades of gray. Her usual bob was tucked under a slick pixie wig. But the pièce de résistance was the shower curtain. She must've been wearing a harness beneath the towel that held the rod over her head, and the white curtain itself was spray-painted with the shape of a shadowy figure, knife in hand. She looked like she'd just walked out of a silver screen.

"*Psycho.*" If there was a touch of marvel in my voice, it had been fully earned. Felicity not only had the best costume here, she had figured out a way—thanks to that shower curtain—to kept people at arm's length. Everyone had to clear a path so she could pass by. It suited her. And it made me jealous.

"She didn't mean that," Saundra said quickly, misinterpreting what I'd said, but Felicity ignored her. Saundra and I both stepped back so that Felicity could get by. She looked me up and down before saying, "Nice costume." Then she was off, swallowed up by the crowd.

"That was mean," Saundra said. "There's no reason to be sarcastic."

"Who invited Norma Watson?" Thayer was suddenly beside me, looking approvingly at my outfit.

"Who's Norma?" Saundra said. "She's supposed to be somebody named Carrie. And who are you supposed to be? A toddler?"

Thayer's costume consisted of overalls, a rainbow-striped thermal shirt, a rubber butcher knife, and his hair sprayed with red dye. He was obviously Chucky, and I obviously needed to introduce Saundra to some horror classics.

Thayer shot Saundra a horrified look.

"I didn't know how badly you needed the club," he whispered in my ear, hand on my forearm. "But it's clear to me now."

I felt oddly defensive about Saundra. We may not have had anything in common, but she had stood by me even when Lux was breathing down my neck. And unlike the rest of the club, she actually spoke to me at school. I would've told him as much, but he was already on the move.

"Gotta go—my Bride of Chucky awaits." I watched Thayer walk toward a boy wearing a blond wig and a leather jacket over a white dress and realized I was smiling. And that was a pretty good sign that whatever panic and anxiety I'd been feeling before had subsided.

The masks around me weren't menacing. With a clearer head, I could see that there weren't that many masks anyway. Mostly face paint, headbands with animal ears, and the occasional glued-on open wound.

Nothing was out to get me except my own imagination.

I turned to Saundra. "So are we going to dance, or what?"

"Hell yeah!" Saundra giggled and jumped into my arms. Her delight was infectious.

28

SAUNDRA'S STILETTOS DID not impede her dancing at all, and I grabbed onto her just to stay afloat in the crowd. I let the music wash over me, let it fill my ears and head and stomach, feeling it thrum through my skin like I was a human speaker. Just as my feet were getting tired and I was running out of breath, I felt a tap on the shoulder for the second time tonight.

Freddie's grin was wide, and I could feel my cheeks stretching with my own smile. He wore a homemade costume, too: a fedora, a red-and-green-striped sweater, and a glove with plastic silver knives taped to the fingers. He also had a name tag, in case it wasn't obvious who he was.

HELLO my name is Krueger.

"Well if it isn't the man of my nightmares."

"My friends and I were supposed to dress up as famous directors but I was like, *nah!*" he said over the booming voice of Pitbull telling us to get wild. "Anyway, you came!"

I'd texted him from the Lyft to let him know I was on my way. It felt good, knowing he had been on the lookout for me. "Saundra needed me!"

"I'm glad! You look great! P.J. Soles?"

"See?" I said, rapping my fingers against Saundra's arm. "People get it!"

Saundra nodded, but she was distracted by trying to teach an astronaut how to dance.

I looked down at my outfit. "It was the best I could put together on short notice!"

"Maybe this tardy will burn out butter for two."

Huh? The bass had ticked up a decibel or four, and I couldn't make out what Freddie had said. I leaned in, positioning my ear closer to his mouth so he could repeat himself.

"Maybe this party will turn out better for you!" he said. Then he winced and rolled his eyes. "It was a *Carrie* reference. Sorry, that was lame!"

I laughed. "This party is slightly better than Carrie's prom! But only slightly."

"Quick, you wanna pour a bucket of pig's blood on someone's head? I'll be your John Travolta."

My lips curled. "You're the sweetest."

"GET A ROOM!"

Freddie and I both turned to Saundra, who was currently draped over the spaceman and had apparently heard every word of the too-obvious effort we were putting into our witty banter. But this was the first time Freddie and I had seen each other since the night in his room, and I couldn't be sure anymore if my skin was vibrating from the music or from being so close to him.

Saundra said something indecipherable but clearly inappropriate and began to slink away with the astronaut.

"Wanna dance?" Freddie asked. I nodded and pulled him into the crowd.

It was amazing how different I felt now compared to when I had first walked into this place, with my anxiety threatening to stifle me. Dancing with Saundra had taken my mind off things, allowed my thoughts to go blank, but dancing with Freddie—his uncoordinated jerking moves and carefree bobbing—made me want to stay in the moment.

I watched the way the strobe lights set the edge of Freddie's jaw ablaze with silver, could see the tip of his tongue as he parted his lips because the dancing was making him pant. I studied a bead of sweat forming above his top lip until it spilled over his Cupid's bow and disappeared into his smile.

The crowd made us occasionally bump into each other. His hip against mine, my elbow in his side. But I couldn't blame the others for the way my fingers reached for him. Clutching the stripes of his sweater. Grazing the belt loops of his pants. They were tiny touches of torture. A tease—a taste of what I wanted when I was dying of hunger.

"We probably shouldn't be dancing," I said, swallowing. "Fraternization rules."

"You're right." Freddie took my hand and led me away.

I'd found a quiet corner in this warehouse after all. My back was against the polished concrete wall and Freddie was against me, fraternization rules shattered. I gripped the back of his neck, my fingertips tangling in his hair. I guess he did like my kissing style, because his mouth lingered on mine, careful and urgent. I nipped his lips with my teeth. With my eyes closed, there was nothing but the feel of him and the muted, pulsing bass.

Making out with Freddie was like watching the best scary movie. Every nerve ending felt raw, exposed; my stomach flipped, shaky. He was both the thing seizing my heart and the air all at once. I put my palms against his chest and pushed him just far enough for me to catch my breath. I could feel Freddie's chest expanding beneath my touch.

"What happened to the unofficial no fraternization rule?" I said.

"'Unofficial' being the operative word." Freddie brought his index finger to my bottom lip, like even if he wasn't kissing it he still needed access. "And anyway, everyone breaks rules at parties. It's all about crossing social divides."

"And what social divides are we crossing?"

Freddie tilted his head from side to side, thinking. "The somewhat geeky but inherently suave guy dances with the mysterious, beautiful new girl."

I could feel a tingling in my cheeks. "Mysterious?"

Freddie leaned in again. "Not the operative word."

I would never again resist when Saundra suggested we go out. I would stay here all night.

But then a gaggle of wannabe film directors rushed toward us, all flanking Freddie. He tried to catch my eye over their heads but Scorsese (the costume was mostly eyebrows), Tarantino (chin), and Spielberg (*Jaws* shirt) all grabbed hold and more or less lifted him off the ground. Tisch Boys liked to go hard-core.

"We're going to finish this conversation later!" Freddie called, but the directors had already dragged him a significant distance, and he was too far now to hear my answer.

I grinned as I waved him off and began searching for Saundra. Maybe because I was actually enjoying myself for once, the universe chose to knock me down a peg. Out of the corner of my eye, I saw an actual ghoul coming my way.

Lux was dressed as some sort of sexy farm animal. Given the height of the ears on her headband, she could've been anything from a bunny to a jackass. It was anybody's guess. She approached like an unexpected gust of wind, ready to blow my candle out. I was as good as fizzle and smoke.

Lux flicked the bill of my red cap. "Trying to make Halloween great again?"

She was lucky there weren't any scissors within reach.

"You know, I almost forgot about you, freak. But then I remembered how much I hated you when I saw you sneaking around my boyfriend's house. So I did more research." She paused dramatically, savoring my reaction.

"We know Matthew Marshall is dead," she said, counting this point off on her finger. "And we know you're obsessed with him because you go instantly psycho at the mention of his name." She ticked this off on another finger. "But the details of his death are what's really interesting."

"Stop." I said, even though I knew my distress was her ammo, the lighter fluid to her raging flames.

"No," she said. "We're just getting to the good part. He was *stabbed* to death."

She would never stop. I understood that now.

"Did Bram tell you?" I blurted out.

Something in Lux changed, a minuscule flicker that made her go rigid.

"What does Bram have to do with this? You two have talked about this?"

I didn't know what she was playing at. What she and Bram were possibly playing at, but I didn't have to stay to hear it.

I turned to leave but Lux's viselike grip dug into my elbow. "Stay away from my boyfriend."

It wasn't clear if Lux knew everything, but she knew enough to concoct an epic rumor. And if she was worried about me and her boyfriend, I could count on it being the kind of rumor that would destroy me.

I yanked my elbow back, my walk turning into a brisk run. The claustrophobia was back, worse than before. There were too many bodies in my way. Ghosts and athletes and sexpot puppies, all gyrating to the music. I weaved around them but still bumped into most. I'd been in this world a minute ago and now nothing felt more incongruous than this party.

But then I stopped, frozen in place by what I saw. Amongst all the costumed partiers there was someone else. Another person in a costume but not like anyone else's. He was just standing there, watching me. All in black, and wearing a mask.

The same white mask from my nightmares.

The one from my past.

No. I was seeing things. It was my fear, my anxiety, my mind playing games. I was panicking and my mind was just taking the thing I was most afraid of—the thing that had crawled into my nightmares—and convincing me it was real.

But I needed out. I started moving again, but everywhere I turned, there he was, always just a few yards away, always still and watching me. The beating lights were knocking me off-balance. I blinked and whipped around, looking for the other lights, the ones that spelled out the exits, but soon everything was a dizzying display of flashing red.

I quickened my pace, but so did the masked figure. No matter how far from him I got, he got closer. Now I was pushing past people, arms knocking against shoulder blades, elbows in ribs. The guy in the mask, he moved faster, too. He shoved through the crowd just as I did, and everyone he pushed out of the way glared or shouted at him. Which meant they saw him, too.

Or was that just my mind again? All the faces around me began to morph together, ghosts and mummies and dirty looks from behind face paint bleeding together into the same rubbery white.

I was getting closer to the back of the warehouse, closer to where I thought the stairs were. But every time I turned my head, he was right behind me, three yards away, then one yard away. He swiped at me and missed.

I ran faster. My breathing hitched, coming shorter and shorter, the red flashing in my eyes. I reached the edge but there were no stairs, no exit, just a high gray wall. I spun, looking for a way out, kept spinning, searching, until someone grabbed my upper arms. I would've screamed but I was petrified.

It wasn't the masked figure, though.

The person steadying me was Jason.

As in Voorhees, the killer from *Friday the 13th*. I gulped in air, letting his mask consume my whole line of sight. The steadiness brought me back down, and when I looked around I didn't see the masked figure anywhere. Now that I'd stopped spinning, all the masks around me began to look like cheap plastic again. My breathing slowed, coming back to normal. Had there even been anyone chasing me in the first place?

The real Jason Voorhees didn't talk, but this one did. "Dance?"

It was the last thing I wanted to do. But it meant I wouldn't have to be alone, at least for this moment. I pulled him toward the center of the dance floor.

It was just as DJ Freshman decided to play the first slow song of the night. Well, as slow as an autotuned Miley Cyrus song could get. Jason and I challenged it, swaying even slower than the beat. He rested his hands on my hips and I let myself rest my head against his chest. I took in deep breaths, allowed myself to be engulfed by him, and by the weird song, the randomness of this moment. The fear was subsiding and I was getting my bearings again. I already knew that as soon as the song was over, I would go.

But I was so lost in the moment that I didn't even realize we had stopped swaying until Jason bent his head low. "Leave the club."

I pulled my head back. Did he mean this club—this warehouse? No, of course not.

I reached up and brushed the mask up over his face.

I should've recognized his voice. Low, like the rumble from subway tracks.

Bram's eyes were unwavering. I used both palms to push him away from me. This time when I looked for the signs for the exit, I found them. I left without looking back.

29

IT WAS MOVIE night the next evening. When I walked into Bram's study he acted like he always did. Like I was a barely registering blip on his radar. Like what had happened at the Halloween party hadn't happened at all.

But I knew that no matter how he acted I was very much still on his mind based on the movie he chose for us to watch.

"Tonight is one of my favorites," he announced. "*Funny Games.*"

He didn't look at me as he said it, which meant he missed seeing the color drain from my face. *Funny Games* was a movie about a family who are at their lake house when two young guys, as clean-cut as any of the boys at Manchester, show up at their door asking to borrow some eggs. When they enter, they hold the family hostage and torture them.

A home invasion movie. He picked the English-language version for my benefit, surely. This way there were no subtitles for me to ignore. Bram, who apparently still wanted me out of the club, was going to force me to watch and listen to this. And I would. I would be like Malcolm McDowell in *A Clockwork Orange*, my eyelids forcibly pulled back as I watched the horror unfold before me. I told myself I would do it to prove my standing in the club. For my sick, twisted exposure therapy. And for my own pettiness, so that Bram wouldn't intimidate me with this dick move.

I sat motionless, not letting any trembling fingers or nervous lip-biting betray me, but inside I was an earthquake. Freddie, sitting next to me on the sofa, must've felt the tremors because he slipped his hand into mine and made our fingers interlock.

Your breathing's different when you're conscious of it. When you have to remind yourself to do it. So you count your breaths, make sure you don't forget them, but they remain shallow. You breathe deep, trying to reel in a good one, but no matter how much you gulp it's never enough.

I made it as far as the scene where one of the home invaders uses a TV remote to disturbing effect before I flinched and turned away. As if on cue, Bram turned to look at me, his eyes daring me to say something. And

I realized in that moment that all the intensity I was feeling wasn't just due to the movie. A lot of it—the nausea, the revulsion—was due to *him*.

I didn't let my eyes waver. This dance of ours that started at the Halloween party continued here. As I watched Bram, I pictured the clamps from *A Clockwork Orange* on his own eyes, piercing beyond his eyelids, into his eyes themselves, making them bleed.

"Pause it." I said it in a low voice, like I was testing it out. But Bram, who had been watching me and clearly waiting for me to buckle, heard it. It was only when the screen froze that the rest of the club realized what had happened. "Are you scared?" Felicity asked, her grin spread so far back I could practically see her molars. "You know what happens when one of us gets scared."

Thayer looked at me with excitement, only to soften when he saw my expression. "This is obviously triggering for her," he whispered.

"I'm not scared," I said, standing up. I didn't want them to see the lie on my face. Even Freddie, who tilted his head, trying to catch my gaze. But I avoided looking at any of them. The movie had shaken me. "I'm just realizing the time. I have a test to prep for, and not just of the fear variety."

"You're scared," Felicity teased.

The words were Felicity's but Bram might as well

have been the one who'd spoken. I couldn't stomach the idea that he'd gotten to me. That his mind games were working. I grabbed my book bag and coat.

"Hey, you're not going anywhere," Felicity continued. "We follow rules here. You can't just duck out because you don't like the movie."

Was she serious right now? "You ran out of *Urban Legend*."

Felicity dwelled on this for a moment. "That was justified."

I was *this close* to going full Linda Blair on her.

"Lay off, Felicity," Freddie said, then got up as if to follow me, but I left the study quickly and then jogged down the stairs and out the front door without stopping. When I was on the street I heard Freddie shout my name. He chased me for nearly an entire block before I spun around to face him. We almost knocked into each other.

"What's going on?" he panted, catching his breath. "Why'd you take off like that?"

"Do you guys talk about the Mary Shelley Club outside of the club?" I asked.

"What? No. You know the rules."

"Bram does," I said. "Bram talks to Lux about it."

"He wouldn't."

I breathed in. Getting air was still hard, but the

swift shot of cold felt good. "Why would he choose that movie?"

Freddie exhaled in a puff of white and readjusted his glasses. "Bram likes art-house horror. But I don't think he picked *Funny Games* thinking it would get to you."

"Of course he did."

"It's just a movie, Rachel."

Freddie's words felt like a slap. No, like a pat on the head. Like I didn't understand the difference between fiction and reality; between monsters and boys. Like my feelings didn't matter. "I don't need you patronizing me—"

"I wasn't!" Freddie cut in, eyes wide.

"I'm not a toddler."

Freddie stepped back and dug his fingers beneath his glasses, rubbing his eyes. I already felt ostracized by Bram—by Thayer and Felicity, who never related to a horror movie. Freddie had come after me, but it seemed like every word we uttered was another brick thrown on the wall forming between us. Freddie didn't understand either.

But then he put down his hands. His eyes were filled with sympathy. "I'm sorry," he said. He closed the gap between us, and when he put his arms around me, I let him. "I'll talk to Bram if you want."

I shook my head against Freddie's chest. I wanted to put this night behind me. I didn't want to spend any more time thinking about Bram. I didn't want to think about *Funny Games*. And I especially didn't want to think about the fact that my fears weren't as gone as I'd thought they were.

30

THE NEXT TIME I saw anyone from the club was at the Shustrine when Thayer and I worked our weekend shift. Both screens at the theater were well into their showings, which meant I could leave my post at the door and join Thayer at the concession stand. Immediately he brought up the last club meeting.

"The Mary Shelley Club is fun," Thayer said. "But it isn't a perfect little oasis. Now you know that."

"I don't really want to talk about it." A part of me felt like I shouldn't have run out like I did. I'd let my emotions get to me. But the main reason I didn't want to revisit that night was because I didn't want to think about Bram. I went to the popcorn station and half-filled one of the small popcorn bags, keeping my hand on the butter pump for an unhealthy length of time.

Thayer was slumped over the candy counter staring at his phone. He'd designed his phone case himself. It had one of those Evolution of Man–type charts, but instead of sketches of a caveman and *Homo erectus*, it was called "The Evolution of Jason" and depicted the *Friday the 13th* killer in all his incarnations. There was Mutant Lake Child Jason, Pitchfork-Wielding Pillow-head Jason, and ultimately it evolved into Jason in Space with a fishbowl astronaut's helmet over the hockey mask.

Thayer was watching *Sleepaway Camp*, a remake of the movie that held the distinction of being both the worst '80s movie and the worst horror movie of all time. So of course, it'd been rebooted. Now it starred America's teen sweetheart, Ashley Woodstone.

"I heard she got a dialect coach to nail the Brooklyn accent," I said, hopping onto the stool next to Thayer and wiping butter off my chin.

"Real dedication, considering she barely has any speaking lines."

"Truly the Meryl Streep of our generation."

As far as weekend jobs went, this was a pretty sweet gig. All the movie-smell popcorn I could want and Thayer for company. Once the films got started and all the moviegoers had their fill of refreshments, we had the lobby to ourselves. (Rob, the Shustrine's manager, was manning the box office. He locked himself in there pretending to do work, but really he was gambling on his phone.)

"If there was a movie made about your life, who would you want to play you?" Thayer asked.

"Ashley Woodstone, obviously."

"Yeah, she'd probably grow some freckles just to look like you."

"I wouldn't doubt it."

"I want her to play me, too," Thayer said. He turned the movie off, which was a good thing because *Sleepaway Camp* was trudging toward its finale—one of the most mind-boggling endings of all time, and not in an *Inception* sort of way.

"So, any closer to finalizing your Fear Test, New Girl?"

I gave him the usual answer: "I don't know when I'm doing my Fear Test, I haven't chosen my target yet, and when are you going to stop calling me New Girl?"

"When are you going to realize that nicknames are a sign of endearment and intimate friendship?" He got back on topic. "Choosing your target is truly a sacred experience. Don't waste it like Felicity. She just goes after her latest loser ex. Next year it'll be whatever masochist dares to date her. But I've known Trevor would be my target since I joined the club. The only reason I didn't pick him last year was because I was a newbie. I needed to stretch my Fear Test muscles first, get the hang of things. Maybe you do, too."

"Yeah."

"Or you could just go after her already."

"I haven't picked anyone yet," I said innocently, popping a piece of popcorn into my mouth.

"Sure you haven't," Thayer said. "You haven't almost killed her with a pair of scissors either, and her name doesn't rhyme with Sucks."

I'd known he would come to this conclusion. Anyone would. But I told him the same thing I'd been telling myself since the moment I learned about the Fear Tests. "I can't go after Bram's girlfriend."

"That's nowhere in the rule book, but it sure is sweet." Thayer's voice lost its sarcasm but was still coated in something that pointed a big neon arrow at my naivete. It implied that I shouldn't extend a kindness to Bram that he would never reciprocate for me. And here I was, back to thinking about him. "Why's Bram such a dick?"

"Bram's not a dick, he's broody." Thayer's eyes narrowed and smoldered all at once, trying to make the word come alive. "That's his MO. Everything he does is to live up to it."

"He's broody *and* he's a dick. The two aren't mutually exclusive."

"He's weird. I mean, none of us are totally aces up here," Thayer said, pointing to his temple. "If we were normal, we wouldn't be playing this game."

"Ahem."

Thayer and I both turned at the sound of a pointed cough. A guy stood across the counter, tapping the edge of his credit card on the glass surface in slow, annoying clicks.

"Can you not see we're talking here?" Thayer said. "What do you want?"

"Uh, some Twizzlers?"

Thayer rolled his eyes. "Of course you do."

He hopped off his stool and bent to get the rubbery vines. I brought up the text app on my phone. Thayer was right. I'd known who my target would be all along. And if Bram wanted to mess with me, then I could mess with him back. I sent out the message quick, before I could change my mind.

My turn to play.

31

I SAT STILL on a swing in a dark, quiet playground. My Fear Test was about to begin, and sitting on the swing beside mine was my target's boyfriend.

Suffice to say that it was awkward. Well, more awkward than my usual laugh-a-minute experiences with Bram. But since I'd sent out the text, I'd planned my Fear Test meticulously, worked out every possible angle, and this was the way it had to be.

After a gabfest with Saundra where I'd subtly inched toward the topic of Lux and what she did with her free time, I discovered that Lux had a regular weekly babysitting gig in the Ditmas Park neighborhood in Brooklyn. I was surprised she'd come this far out on the Q line, but Saundra informed me that lots of interesting people (the list began and ended with a couple of actors and a rock band) lived in Ditmas Park. Looking around at the grand manors here, I understood why.

The neighborhood was famous for its old Victorian houses, enormous and beautiful with their roof turrets and wraparound porches that didn't seem to belong in New York City. TV shows filmed here whenever they needed to pretend they were out in the suburbs. Some people had chicken coops in their backyards. The place was a surreal oasis plunked in a gritty city, and that was exactly the vibe I was going for.

The fact that Lux had a regular babysitting gig was almost too perfect. I drew from my favorite kind of horror: psychological. The kind that made you feel dread and unease even though nothing graphic or violent was happening. The kind that messed with your head, the way Lux liked to mess with mine.

We would wait until the kid was asleep and then we would start. Thayer's role was that of Ambience Manipulator (a title he'd chosen for himself.) He'd subtly change things around the house, just a tiny bit, to get Lux to doubt everything she was seeing. Turn over pictures, manipulate dolls and action figures. Make the inanimate unsettling.

To get Lux on edge, I also put Felicity on door and window duty. She was tasked with tapping windows and turning doorknobs, creating phantom sounds to make Lux think she wasn't alone.

The whole while, Freddie would be upstairs, where

all he had to do was identify the squeakiest parts of the floors and make heavy, slow footsteps.

If Lux still wasn't freaked out by then, Freddie would get louder. He'd run and stomp and slam the back door on his way out. But that was our backup plan. If Lux could get scared at the mere sound of buzzing flies, then I was pretty sure I could get her to at least scream at the sound of an abruptly slammed door.

Then, Thayer, Felicity, and Freddie would rendezvous at the outdoor benches of the Top of the Muffin café three blocks away.

Which left Bram and me.

We were staked out at the playground across the street, an optimal vantage point for us to watch the house, and for me to watch Bram watch his girlfriend get scared.

It was twisted and wrong, what I was doing—what I was forcing Bram to do—but it was the nature of this game. My Fear Test made this mean streak in me acceptable—expected, even—and I was going to embrace it.

But sitting together in silence wasn't making this easy. I knew, though, that a part of me must've craved this tension, where the only sound between us was the straining squeal of the swing chains. I wanted to force this moment between Bram and me. We needed to have some words. I decided they were going to be on my terms.

Except neither of us said anything. Our silence was accentuated by the sounds around us. The distant patter of boots on pavement from beyond the playground gates, a car stopping at a traffic light, the swing chains with their piercing rhythmic screeches.

Bram sat cozy in the chunkiest cable-knit sweater I'd ever seen. With the sleeves pooling over his knuckles and his hair flopping over his eyes, he looked like a kid. An intimidating one. The longer we went without speaking, the stronger the sheet of ice between us became. I needed to crack it.

"Why do you want me out of the club?"

Bram had been expecting the question. He planted his feet in the ground and pushed off, swinging just slightly more than he had been before. "Is this why you assigned me this role? So we could chat?"

"You want me out of the club because you knew I'd go after Lux. Right?"

Bram's legs quit pumping and he eventually slowed to a full stop. When he looked at me he leaned his cheek against the swing's chain, which tugged down his skin, revealing the pink under his eyelid. His face morphed into something ugly. "I want you out of the club because you don't belong."

The bluntness of his statement, said without irony or shame, struck me hard. Did I not belong because I was a freak? Because we weren't of the same class? If I'd had any doubt before that Bram hated me, I was clear on it now. "You're a prick."

His mouth twisted in a rueful smirk. "I'm sorry if that hurt your feelings, but what do you expect? You're about to scare my girlfriend."

"She's my target. You, on the other hand, can walk away if you want to. No one's twisting your arm to be here, Bram."

"I have to be here. Those are the rules."

I had hoped that talking to him would bring some clarity, peel back one of his masks so I could understand him better. But all he was doing was layering them on now. I was more lost than ever. "What kind of monster does this to his own girlfriend?"

"You don't know anything about me."

"This isn't the first time you're doing this to her either," I continued. "The séance Fear Test at the abandoned house—Lux was scared the most."

"She wasn't supposed to be at that party," Bram said, and I thought I heard remorse trickling into his voice. "It wasn't her scene."

"You still went through with it."

"I tried to get her to leave." He pinched his sleeves

between his fingers, the wool looking like the hand wraps boxers use. "We fought about it at the party."

I remembered hearing them arguing in one of the rooms upstairs. He looked at me, his gaze sharp enough to cut. "Lux and I have our problems. We fight and we break up and we get back together. But I care about her."

"You might care about her, but you don't love her. Not really," I said. "You wouldn't be doing this if you did."

"You really want to talk about monsters?" Bram said. He dug his shoulder into the chain and leaned toward me so that we were inches apart. My first instinct was to look away, cross my arms. But I couldn't break eye contact. He wasn't looking at me but through me. Like he saw in me what I spent every moment trying to hide.

"I find it really interesting that you chose this for your Fear Test. Not Lux—anyone could've guessed you were always going to choose Lux. But the fact that we're staging it as a home invasion."

"This isn't a home invasion," I corrected him. "No one's going to be seen—"

"You went through something awful on a quiet night in a quiet house," Bram cut me off. "And now you're going to put someone else through that. So yeah, let's talk about monsters, Rachel. Let's talk about how fucked up this is."

I was the one who'd wanted to talk, to air things out,

to take the gloves off. And now it felt like I was backed up against the ropes. Guilt tugged at my edges, making my fingers twitch, making me want to reach for my phone and call the whole test off. Was I going too far? Was this still just a game?

But I knew why I'd chosen this for my Fear Test. A part of me wanted to have all this play out—the girl in a big, scary house—and be on the other side of it. I needed to look at what had happened to me from a different angle. I had the chance to be the puppet master this time, to change the outcome, to have everything come out safe and okay. This was catharsis.

"Lux may toy with people sometimes," Bram continued. "But don't act like that's not exactly what you're doing right now."

He finally tore his gaze away and looked straight ahead at the house where his girlfriend was moments away from being scared out of her mind. Hopefully.

"I'm nothing like Lux. Or you," I said finally. "I would never put a game before someone I cared about."

"Which is exactly why you don't belong in the club."

My fingers stopped twitching. I no longer wanted to reach for my phone. There was a reason why Bram and I never talked, and as much fun as this was, I was ready to start my Fear Test.

"When she calls you," I said, "tell her she's just

imagining things. Make her think everything's going to be all right."

Giving instructions felt good. And Bram, who cared so much about this game, would have to comply. He checked his watch. Like, an actual timepiece and not something that told him now many steps he'd taken today. He stood up and walked away, leaving his swing squeaking in the wind.

32

LUX McCRAY

LUX McCRAY DIDN'T like babysitting, and she certainly didn't need the money. But being Wyatt Salgado-Hydesmuirre's nanny was a coveted position that she couldn't pass up. And not because she loved Wyatt. He was a cute kid, but Lux mostly cared about his dad. Not in a gross babysitter fantasy way. Ew.

She cared because Henry Hydesmuirre was a bigwig at Condé Nast. Lux wasn't sure what his position was exactly (COO, CFO, VP—she knew it was a combination of any of those letters). But the details didn't matter. What mattered was that if she got along with Henry's son, then she was good as golden to get an internship at *Vogue* before senior year. There were at least two other people from her school who'd interviewed for the babysitting job, but Lux had beaten them out.

The Salgado-Hydesmuirres required her services on their weekly date night, which could be anything from a movie, to a fundraiser, to a white-tie eight-course dinner gala. All Lux had to do was show up and spend about an hour with the six-year-old before putting him to bed. It'd been the same routine for the last five months: play with Wyatt and his always-new, always-expensive toys, make sure he brushed his teeth, give Sugar a chew toy to gnaw in her doggy bed, put the kid to sleep, and then, finally, text Bram to let him know the coast was clear.

She would usually wait a half hour before texting Bram. She killed the time by kicking back on the deep brown leather sofa in the living room and scrolling through IG. She spent a few seconds looking at each post, double-tapping as she went. She got to a photo of Lucia, head tilted and lips pursed. Poor filter choice, yet again, and when would this girl learn her angles? When Lux zoomed in, she could see a blazing zit that did not have enough concealer on it on the underside of Lucia's jaw. Lux wrinkled her nose and scrolled past the post without double-tapping.

After a couple more minutes of this, she looked up

and found Wyatt standing in the room. She gasped so loud that Sugar, on the doggy bed at her feet, jumped. "What are you doing here?"

"I can't sleep," Wyatt said.

Now the dog was out of bed too, and scampered to Wyatt's bare feet. Soon they'd be playing together. Soon they'd be hyper. This was not good.

"Just close your eyes," Lux said. "You'll fall asleep before you know it."

She prided herself on how tough she was with kids, that she wasn't a pushover. She knew instinctively that babying Wyatt—scratching his back like he always requested, and sitting with him until his eyes fluttered shut—was the wrong approach. He was way too old for that stuff, and anyway, if she started that precedent, then she'd have to do it every time she came over. No. Tough love was the way to go. None of this coddling bullshit. No one at her house had ever given her attention when she cried. Toughness, she knew, had to be instilled at a young age.

Wyatt's parents were always shocked when they came home and learned that the boy had gone to sleep without putting up a fight. To them, Lux was a miracle worker. She tried ever so subtly to hint that she could also work miracles fetching lattes for editors or assisting at photo shoots. But so far, no internship offer. Yet.

"It doesn't matter if I close my eyes," Wyatt said. "I keep hearing noises."

"What kind of noises?"

"It sounds like someone's tapping on my window."

The Salgado-Hydesmuirres lived in a huge house in a neighborhood full of huge houses that looked nice, but inside they were crap.

"It's just the cold, Wyatt." The houses here lived and breathed, but seemed to perpetually suffer from pneumonia. Always drafty, always leaky; you couldn't take a step without the floors moaning.

"The cold doesn't make noise."

"It does in this house. Now go to bed."

Wyatt sighed and marched back upstairs in his too-small spaceship pj's, muttering about climate change and how it wasn't that cold out tonight anyway.

Lux went back to her phone, but it was only a couple of minutes until Wyatt showed up again. The whole thing was legit getting old.

"Can you stay in my room until I fall asleep?" he asked. All her tough love crap went out the window. Now it was just about expediency. The faster he went to sleep, the faster she could text Bram, and she really needed to text Bram.

He always came over after Wyatt was asleep, but

she still wasn't sure if he would tonight. They'd had a fight.

Lux couldn't even remember about what, just that Bram had been acting weird and then she'd said something she probably shouldn't have and he said some things he definitely should *wish* he hadn't and the whole thing had blown up.

They hadn't spoken a word to each other at school earlier. Yeah, they'd sat at the same table for lunch like always, but they couldn't help that. Lux and Bram were practically doing the whole cafeteria a favor just by sitting there so that people could ogle them. But although they'd had conversations with everyone around them, Lux and Bram hadn't directly spoken. She hoped no one had noticed.

The sooner she texted Bram, the sooner their fight would be over. Hopefully.

"Okay, let's go," Lux told Wyatt.

She tucked the kid in again but his eyes stayed open, two giant pools of concern. "Can you check the window? Just to make sure?"

Lux forced a smile. This bedtime routine was dragging. She was going to ask for a raise. She went and pulled back the curtain. "See? Nothing there." No one anywhere near the window, no one in the trees, no one on the sidewalk. She did spot someone in the playground, though, sitting on the swings.

Perv.

She didn't care how nice this neighborhood was or how much yard space this house had—you couldn't pay her to live this close to a playground. A million rugrats running around by day and the skeeviest people at night.

"Can you just stay until I fall asleep?"

Lux rolled her eyes but figured she could text Bram from here as soon as Wyatt nodded off. She took a seat in the rocking chair in the corner of Wyatt's room. Her hand buzzed and she looked at the screen. Her heart did a little skip when she saw that it was a text from Bram. He was ready to make up, too.

Kid asleep?

Not yet. He hears monsters.

She watched the ellipses blinking.

So you told him about me? Devil emoji.

Lux grinned. It'd probably be healthier if they talked about their fight, maybe tried to work it out so it didn't happen again. But this—pretending nothing had happened at all and sweeping it under the rug—was a million times easier. Lux was about to text back when the furious barking started. Lux groaned.

"Sugar!" Wyatt said, springing up in bed. "We left Sugar downstairs!"

"Sugar's fine." But even as Lux tried to get Wyatt to lie back down, Sugar wouldn't stop whining. Eventually, she was screeching and Lux could hear the dog's little nails pawing at the bottom of the stairs.

"You have to get her," Wyatt said.

"Fine," she said. "Stay in bed."

Lux stepped into the hallway; the dog's barks were louder there. The weird thing was, along with the barks, Lux thought she heard shushing. Like someone was trying to calm Sugar down.

When she got downstairs, Sugar was busy chewing on her toy. Lux swooped the puppy up, ready to take Sugar upstairs, but something caught her eye. She stared at Wyatt's *Star Wars* action figures on the living room floor, trying to figure out why they looked so . . . off. And then she realized the oddest thing. Instead of lying in a heap like always, the toys were all upright, standing in a circle.

Lux kicked her foot out and the figures toppled over, some spilling far across the hardwood. Usually she hated how much noise this house made, but now she stood frozen in place, listening. For once, the creaking old house was silent.

Unease settled over Lux's skin like a dusting of fresh

290

snow. She had the unshakable feeling that someone was here with her. But when she looked around—through doorways and behind club chairs—there was no one.

A moment later came the noise from upstairs. Footsteps over her head. "I told you to stay in bed," she muttered. She raced up to Wyatt's room, secretly glad to get out of the living room. But Wyatt was in bed, sound asleep.

Lux stood in the doorway, trying to reconcile this peaceful image of him with the footsteps she'd just heard. She held Sugar closer to her chest and struggled to remember the sound exactly. Finally she convinced herself that she'd misheard it, that it must've been the pipes.

She closed the door to Wyatt's room and went back downstairs. She sat on the couch with Sugar, stroking the puppy's puffy white fur. She felt like a movie villain, but having what amounted to a breathing lump of cotton candy lying across your lap was a pretty good thing in a very old house when it was this late at night.

Then Lux heard it. The tapping noise Wyatt had described.

It wasn't just her imagination, because Sugar perked up suddenly, her little body totally stiff, ear flaps up.

Only now, the tapping was on the living room window.

It wasn't a knock, more of a *plink*, like a long finger-nail was rapping slowly on the glass. Or a pebble. Was it Bram? Could he be chucking stones at the window in a warped attempt at romance? Lux went to the window and pulled back the curtain in one swift *swoosh*.

There was no one there.

It must have been the wind.

Throwing pebbles at the glass.

There was a new tapping, now at the door.

She swiped at her phone screen and pulled up her message thread with Bram. *Was that you at the window? Are you at the door now?* But when she read what she'd written, she held her thumb down to delete it all.

She sounded crazy. As much as she wished she could, Lux couldn't sink into the couch. And she couldn't ignore the persistent noise, which grew louder with every passing moment. She untangled her legs, placing her feet silently on the floor, and clutched Sugar. She made her way to the foyer. There couldn't be anyone at the door.

But there *was* someone at the door.

Lux saw it now, the doorknob twisting first to the left, then, slowly, to the right.

"Bram?" she whispered. She got closer. "Bram?" she said more insistently, her cheek pressing against the wood. Lux wrapped her fingers around the knob. There was no resistance. She swung the door open.

No one.

She shut the door quickly, hugging Sugar to her chest. She was imagining things—this old house was *making* her imagine things. Like the noise she now heard above her.

Pipes. The old pipes.

But Lux was lying to herself. Anyone could tell the difference between the clanks of pipes and the groan of hundred-year-old original wood floorboards. Wyatt was asleep in his room and there was no one at the door and she was holding the only other living thing in the house. But someone was upstairs.

Lux didn't move; she didn't even breathe.

The noise she was hearing was footsteps again. She counted them. First four. Then two. And, after a long pause—one.

Her phone buzzed and she jumped, dropping the puppy, who let out a pitiful whimper as she scampered away, her little nails clacking on the hardwood. It was a text from Bram.

Be there soon.

How soon? She texted quickly, trying to stay calm.

Few blocks away.

I think there's someone in here, she typed.

She waited for Bram to reply, but a new text never came and she was getting anxious.

Hurry. I keep hearing all these noises, she texted again.

Another beat that stretched excruciatingly long. She saw the dancing ellipses pop up, but then they disappeared. Her brow crinkled as she watched the screen. Finally Bram wrote back.

You're imagining things.

Even though it was what she wanted to hear—that it was nothing—it still felt crummy to have her fears invalidated. She clenched her jaw. *Just get here.*

There was a broom closet between the living room and the kitchen that the family mostly kept all their untidy crap in, and Lux went to it. There was enough room inside for her to stand. She wedged herself in the dark, cramped space and listened.

After a moment, she could hear the front door opening. She strained to hear more, hoping for the sound of Bram's voice. Maybe he'd call to her, or maybe he'd announce himself and scare off whoever was upstairs.

She shook her head. *There is no one upstairs*, she reminded herself. But as she listened for a sign—for *something*—all she heard was footsteps slowly going up the stairs.

"Bram?" she whispered. She wrapped her fingers

around the doorknob, turning it slowly so that it did not make a single sound. She pushed the door open a sliver, only enough for her to peek through. She had a straight line of sight to the staircase.

There was no one there. But it must've been Bram. He'd gone up to check that the coast was clear, which it obviously was. She wasn't going to stay locked in a closet. There was no order to that, no control. She pushed the door open farther and slipped out. Her socked feet padded up the staircase. Lux didn't stop until she got to the second floor. Wyatt's room was down the hall to the right. She knew Bram would have checked there first. She turned left and walked to the end of the hall, where the Salgado-Hydesmuirres' master bedroom was.

When she got there, she saw a man standing with his back toward her and nearly collapsed with relief. It was Mr. Hydesmuirre. She recognized his London Fog coat. He must have come home early.

"Mr. Hydesmuirre, I'm so sorry, I didn't—"

But when he turned around, the face she saw was not Mr. Hydesmuirre's. It wasn't even human. It was white, rubbery, covered in ugly scars. A mask.

Lux's scream was so loud and so forceful it propelled her out of the room like a bottle rocket. She ran down the hall, but the man in the mask came after her.

She couldn't let him catch her. She didn't slow down when she got to the stairs. She continued to pump her legs, to sprint, but he was right behind her. She could feel him like she could feel the hairs rising on the back of her neck. And then she could feel two firm hands pushing into her shoulder blades.

As Lux fell the rest of the fourteen steps and crashed to the bottom of the staircase—a scream stuck in her throat—the last thing she saw was that monster's face.

33

LUX SPENT THE night in the hospital with a broken arm and six stitches in the back of her head. Bram sent out a text saying he'd found her unconscious at the bottom of the stairs. But when Lux woke up, she had a story. One that was different from the one I had intended to tell.

According to Bram, Lux said there was a man in a mask. And he'd tried to kill her.

There was a flurry of texts from the rest of us, wanting more details and asking more questions. But the texts from Bram stopped coming.

The next day it seemed like the whole school had as much information as I did. The rumor mill of Manchester was spinning on overdrive, pouring with sympathy for Lux, exalting Bram for rushing to her rescue. It wasn't like when Sim had declared that a masked man was after him and no one believed him. Everyone believed Lux. It was like a trend. Largely ignored but as soon as the most popular girl in school christened it acceptable, it was all anyone wanted to talk about. The Masked Man was a thing now—as exciting as a new handbag or the latest pointless game app. An instant legend, on everybody's lips.

The news was of such mythic proportions that Saundra couldn't even wait for lunch to talk about it. She cornered me at my locker after homeroom, breathless with excitement. "Someone attacked Lux! Someone in a *mask*!"

I shut my locker a little too forcefully. I felt bad when Saundra jumped, but this whole thing had me on edge. It'd been my Fear Test and it'd gone all wrong. Someone had gotten seriously hurt and I was responsible. Indirectly or not, I had put Lux in harm's way.

And there was the issue of this mask. There wasn't supposed to be a mask in my Fear Test.

"Can we not talk about it?" I started walking to my next class, but Saundra followed, incredulous.

"Are you kidding me? Your nemesis got taken out and you don't want to talk about it?"

"She's not my nemesis," I hissed, looking around to make sure that no one was listening.

"What, are you scared that someone's going to think you did it?" Saundra asked, her words colored with a sprinkling of laughter. My cheeks colored red.

"Oh my gosh, I'm *kidding*! What if there *is* a prankster after all? What if the mask is, like, his calling card? Ooh, what if he's hot?"

I stopped walking and now it was my turn to be incredulous. "Lux was *hurt*, Saundra."

Saying it out loud—hearing it all over school—made it more real. It made my involvement in it more real. My pulse was already at a quick pace and getting quicker; my cheeks tingled, my teeth were on the cusp of chattering. My whole body was acting like it couldn't hold up the anvil of guilt bearing down on me.

"Yeah," Saundra said. "Hence, I'm a fan."

My phone buzzed in my hand—a text from Felicity. *Emergency meeting on roof. Now.*

"I gotta go," I told Saundra.

The roof was a recreation space surrounded on all sides by chain-link fence, but no one ever came up there. Thayer, Felicity, and Freddie were all huddled together.

"What's going on?" I asked when I got there. Nobody answered. They were looking behind me at Bram, who'd just shown up.

"Bram, I'm sorry," I started. But Bram stalked right past me, to Freddie. He rushed him, grabbing two fistfuls of his blazer and pushing him against the bulkhead door.

"It was you," he said. "You did this."

Felicity watched with unabashed interest while Thayer stumbled back, out of the way. But I tried to put myself between the two boys.

"What is wrong with you?" I pushed my palms on both their chests and when Bram finally noticed me, he let go of Freddie.

"What the hell was that?" he asked me. "Were you in on it? Was a masked man part of your Fear Test?"

"*No*," I said. "I don't know how Lux got hurt. I'm sorry, Bram, the test was only supposed to rattle her."

"How convenient for you," Bram said. "The person you hate the most almost got killed."

His words were like a hot knife gliding slowly through my middle. I already felt guilty, but hearing it out loud from him compounded the guilt. It was heavy, crushing me. And I couldn't even defend myself.

"Hey, Rachel told us all her plan," Thayer said. "We all stuck to it."

"I want to know what you're accusing me of," Freddie said to Bram over my head. He was a lot calmer than I'd thought he'd be, given that Bram looked like he wanted to murder Freddie.

Bram bit down, his jaw tightening. He breathed in, as if trying to regain some chill, but it came off more like a bull huffing through flared nostrils, ready to charge. "Lux said there was someone in a mask on the second floor. And since you, Freddie, were the only one who was supposed to be up there, it was obviously you."

Freddie shook his head. "I left through the backyard. Like Rachel told me to."

"Stop lying!" Bram roared. He was nearly on Freddie again, raising a pointed finger at his face like a loaded gun. "You put on a mask. You chased after Lux."

"Bram, why would Freddie do that?" I asked.

"He was at the rendezvous with us," Thayer said. "We were waiting for you."

"Freddie only left the house after Lux fell down the stairs," Bram said. But it sounded like he was trying to convince himself.

"Did you see the person in the mask?" Felicity asked Bram. "When you showed up and found Lux, did you see anyone?"

Bram took a breath. He looked like someone trying desperately to calm himself down, to not say something out of line that he would regret. He shook his head. Then he turned to me with the same intense focus he always had. The force of his gaze made me take a step back, sticking close to Thayer. But Bram's eyes followed me. It was like we were the only ones up on the roof, and the rest of the members of the club fell away. "You didn't plan for this to happen? You didn't tell Freddie to chase Lux?"

"No," I said. It was a small, simple word, but I hoped it was big enough to convey that I meant it. It looked like Bram believed me because he turned to Freddie next.

"You're too obsessed with this game," Bram spat. "You took it too far this time."

"No, I didn't," Freddie said. His voice was just as even as Bram's, but with much less venom. He didn't seem intimidated at all. "I get that you're mad. Your girlfriend got hurt and the Fear Test didn't go as planned and Lux should have run out of the house."

"What?" Bram said.

"You have to admit she fell into the trope where the babysitter stays inside. Classic mista—"

Bram lunged for him again, and this time I wasn't quick enough to get between them. Bram's fist crashed against Freddie's lip, splitting the bottom one. Behind me I could hear Felicity squeak with surprise and Thayer shout something unintelligible.

"This isn't a fucking game," Bram said.

Freddie touched his lip and looked at the red stain left on his fingers like it was nothing more than war paint. "Yes, it is."

A moment passed where Bram seemed to collect

himself, breathing in, setting his features back to their normal passive calm. But everything felt like it had changed, like we'd crossed a line as a club that we wouldn't be able to get back behind. Bram walked through the stairwell door without another word.

Thayer and Felicity looked at Freddie, maybe hoping for some clarity about what to do next. Freddie always seemed to know what to do next. But all he did was shrug. "He'll cool off," he said. "Just give him a while."

And with that, Thayer and Felicity left the roof, too. But I hung back.

"Did you wear a mask last night?" I asked quietly.

When it'd been Bram asking the questions, Freddie stood his ground, cool under the threat of Bram's wrath. But now that I was the one asking, he looked like he'd just taken a second punch. Shocked. Exasperated. Wounded.

"You think I messed with your Fear Test?"

"I think Lux really saw someone wearing a mask. I don't know why she would lie about that."

"I don't know either," Freddie said. It suddenly felt like that night when he'd shown me *Bride of Frankenstein* had happened forever ago. When he took a step toward me, I took a step back. The hurt in Freddie's eyes was magnified by his glasses.

"Do you believe Bram?" he asked. "Do you think I went behind your back and put on a mask and actually tried to hurt Lux?"

I didn't want to.

But. "You were the only one upstairs."

"Rachel, I left. I followed your instructions and left to meet everyone at the rendezvous point."

This time, when I didn't say anything, it was Freddie who pulled back, shaking his head. I hadn't outright accused him of anything, but there'd been enough said between the lines to sever something between us.

He headed for the door, but when his hand was on the knob, he took a deep breath. "I can't believe you think I'd do something like this."

"Freddie—"

"If there was someone else up there last night, it wasn't me."

He left, leaving me alone on the roof.

34

IT HAD BEEN a week since my Fear Test and I was still trying to make sense of how it had gone wrong.

It could only have been one of three things.

A) Freddie had put on a mask for some reason. Maybe he'd thought it'd be a good idea, help my test. Maybe something went wrong and Lux's fall down the stairs was just an accident. Maybe Freddie didn't want to take the blame for what had happened to her.

B) Lux was lying. She didn't actually see anything. She fell down the stairs on her own, and to make the whole story a little

less embarrassing—and maybe get herself more attention—she glommed onto
something she'd heard Sim say. A prankster wearing a mask.

C) There was someone in a mask, and
they were messing with our Fear Tests.

I pushed option C out of my mind as soon as I thought it. It was the least likely thing, and the one I refused to accept. Because a rando in a mask was way too similar to what had happened to me last year. And what happened last year needed to stay in the past.

But the thing about the past was that there were other people who lived it, too. Mainly my mom. And all she apparently wanted to do was talk about it.

"How are you doing?" she asked, leaning over to grab a handful of popcorn from my bowl.

It was a weird question to ask in the middle of *Hereditary*.

"I'm fine," I said without taking my eyes off the TV. "Why?"

"I heard about what happened to Lux McCray."

I swallowed and watched as Toni Collette worked on her miniature art project. "What's that got to do with me?" I asked, and then wondered if that sounded too defensive.

"I'm just wondering if it brought anything back up for you."

On-screen, Toni Collette broke one of the tiny pieces of furniture she was working on. I watched her fly into a rage and destroy the entire display.

"I haven't given it much thought at all," I said calmly.

I didn't turn to see my mother's face but I could picture it. Concerned. Slightly disappointed that I was not being honest. And finally, open, beseeching, hoping that I'd say something.

"Do you know anything about what happened?" I asked. Maybe the teachers had been briefed about Lux's trauma, just as AssHead had been briefed on mine. Maybe my mom knew a detail that none of the students knew, something that would help me cross out one of the possibilities on my short list.

"Just that Lux was alone in a house and there was a man in a mask who attacked her." My mom shuddered. "It hit so close to home when I heard it."

Too close.

I grabbed the remote and clicked the stop button.

"I've seen this one already," I said. "And I'm kind of tired."

It was early but I retreated to my room. The idea of a masked man was my worst nightmare, and he wasn't confined to my dreams or memories anymore.

The *dream*—no—nightmare. Again.

The same figure, the same black clothes. The mask. He was on top of me, just as he was every time, but now he was holding a knife. I knew this was a dream. And yet, fear still gripped me so hard I couldn't budge. My hands reached for whatever they could, scrambling all over the cold kitchen tile, but the only thing I could grab was fistfuls of bedsheets.

I watched as the figure lowered the fist-clenched knife almost in slow motion, the gleaming blade inching closer to my chest.

I sat up in bed. A thin film of sweat dotted my hairline, my eyebrows. I gulped for air.

Even out of the nightmare all I could see was the mask. The white, old-man face with thin lips and sunken cheeks. The same face Sim and Lux had claimed to see. The face that had chased me around at the Halloween party.

The face I'd left behind on Long Island. Or thought I had.

35

FREDDIE AND I hadn't talked since the emergency meeting on the roof, almost two weeks before. Not that I blamed him. I'd accused him of doing something terrible—something I wasn't even sure he'd really done. There were so many times when I wrote him an apology text, but I always deleted it before I hit send. There was no way he wanted to hear from me.

The worst part of it all was that I missed him. Freddie was the only person I wanted to talk to after my latest nightmare. And after school I still caught myself waiting for him so we could walk to the subway together, even though we hadn't done that in a while. I wanted to talk about our favorite movies, tease him about all his wrong opinions, say something to make him laugh.

The hard truth was that either Freddie had done

something bad, or he hadn't and I was needlessly punishing him. Either reality sucked.

And Bram wasn't talking to anyone in the club at all. Which meant no more club meetings in his study. It was like I'd traveled back in time to those first few weeks of school, when I knew him only from the whispers that trailed him wherever he went. These days, he was constantly at Lux's side when she wasn't in class. I saw her in art class, where we dutifully avoided each other. She wore a gray-and-pink ski cap to cover up her stitches, the dress code having been waived especially for her.

Felicity was back to her normal self, which mainly meant ignoring me when we were at our lockers getting our books. I still had Thayer, though. Weekends at the Shustrine were my lifeline to the club.

When our shift wound down and the concession stand was quiet with just the hum of the popcorn machine, I asked him if he knew what the hell was going on.

"About the Masked Man?" Thayer asked. He had a *People* magazine open on the counter, flipping through it absentmindedly. "No clue. But I figure Lux is lying."

"Why?"

He shrugged. "She's a liar. End of."

"That's it? *Lux is a liar?*"

"You know that better than anyone. She told the whole school you tried to kill her with a pair of scissors."

I glanced at his magazine to avoid looking at him. "Right," I muttered.

"Or maybe she's not lying," Thayer said. "Maybe she got scared because your test was so good and she fell down the stairs and she *thinks* she saw someone in a mask because she heard Sim talking about it in school and mass hysteria is real and all that jazz. The point is, you shouldn't feel bad about it."

Feeling bad wasn't the issue. I wanted answers. Everything felt so up in the air right now. Lux. Freddie. The club.

"Bram punched Freddie," I said. "How are they gonna come back from that?"

Thayer slid the magazine aside. "New Girl, you don't know this because—as your name implies—you're brand-spankin'-new. But Bram and Freddie have been known to have their little tiffs from time to time."

I inched closer on my stool. "Really? Like physical fights?"

Thayer waved his hand dismissively, neither confirming nor denying my question. "All I'm saying is there's been plenty of drama between members before. And it's always been resolved. In due time. Bram's just gotta cool down, put on the ol' ice mask, and do some stomach crunches in his underwear while listening to Huey Lewis and the News. Then he'll let us know when he wants to do his Fear Test and the game'll continue like normal."

"Freddie said the same thing on the roof. That the game will just keep going. The game feels pretty much over, don't you think?"

"The game isn't over until everyone's played." Thayer flipped another page of his magazine. The article, a puff piece about some reality show contestant, stole his attention away.

The sudden absence of the club in my life made me realize how heavily I had relied on it as my main social outlet. I still had Saundra, of course. Now that I had more time on my hands, we hung out after school. I invited her over to the apartment in an attempt to recreate the club's horror movie nights. I started off with a sure bet: *Scream*. A perennial fave. But to my horror Saundra showed up at my apartment with her tablet loaded with the MTV series based on the movies. When I told her, very gently, that I would rather tear my skin off than watch that abomination, she laughed and hit play.

So that was the end of movie nights with Saundra. We still had lunch, though, with her regularly scheduled Bram show. She spoke of his hair (shinier than ever), and his heroism (sticking by Lux's side through this traumatizing ordeal), and his hotness (scorching and getting hotter), her words mixing all together in a Bram lexicon blender.

I watched him at the center of the room. It was ridiculous that he was always around—in my lunchroom, in my classes, in my thoughts—and I couldn't just go over and talk to him. I wanted to know what Lux had told him about her accident. If he was ever going to host another club meeting. If he had completely shut us out forever.

From the pulsing static of Saundra's words, two broke through.

". . . breaking up."

"Huh?" I said.

"Marcela Armagnac told me that Bram and Lux are on the verge of breaking up," Saundra repeated.

"But you just called him heroic for . . . basically sitting next to her at lunch."

"Exactly," Saundra said. "The rumor is that he doesn't want to be with her anymore, but he can't break up with her *now* because it'd make him look like an asshole, or like he didn't want to be with her because she has an ugly scar on the back of her head."

Lux hadn't parted from her ski caps yet and there

was rampant speculation that it was because her scar was unsightly. I wanted to groan but it would have been the loudest groan in the world and I really didn't want to draw attention to myself.

"I hear Lux is still really shook and she just wants to move on from everything, including maybe Bram, and now she's desperate to see other people and maybe so is he, but they want to wait until after the ski trip."

The ski trip. I'd first heard about it from Thayer a few weeks before, and the closer we got to it, the more it was brought up. It wasn't a school-sanctioned trip, but it was tradition. The juniors and seniors organized it themselves, and headed up to Hunter Mountain for a day of skiing and a night of cabin debauchery. According to Saundra, it was the "highlight of the winter season."

"And you believe all this?" I asked. I was never convinced of Bram's feelings for Lux, but I knew that Lux held on to her relationship with Bram with an iron fist. She wouldn't let anything come between them.

"Oh definitely. Have you noticed how they don't laugh together anymore?"

Anymore? I'd never seen Lux crack a smile, let alone laugh. And the only time Bram let out a chuckle was when he was doing something bad.

"Once you stop laughing with your partner, your relationship takes a nosedive. It's irreversibly damaged."

Saundra may have never been in a relationship, but she had stored away enough online relationship-quiz wisdom to date an army. "The boy is obviously just biding his time until it's socially acceptable for him to leave."

"I think he cares about her," I said, careful not to use the word "love." I didn't know why I was defending Bram, but Saundra's gossiping was getting to me.

"How would you know?"

"I know him better than you do."

Saundra stopped eating and I did too, horrified that I had let the words slip out.

"How would you know him better than I do?"

I thought quickly. "We're working on a paper together, remember?"

It was due in a couple of days, and the club being over (or on hiatus) didn't mean our grades had to suffer. Plus, it gave me an excuse to finally confront him.

I stood up. "In fact, be right back."

I left the table, leaving my ramen to grow cold. Saundra called my name, but once she saw that I was heading toward the definitive center of the room, she stopped.

When I reached their table, it was Lux who looked up at me first.

"Can I help you with something?" she said in a tone that was the farthest thing from helpful.

"We need to talk," I said to Bram, ignoring her.

No matter what Saundra thought, Bram definitely wasn't the laughing type. The way he was looking at me made me forget whether he'd ever laughed before.

"What do you want with Bram?" Lux said.

"I need to talk to him about our project."

He pushed away from the table and stood up, towering over me. "I'll be right back," he said to Lux.

"Bram," Lux said. "Seriously?"

But Bram was already walking away and I was following him. I didn't *not* notice the tension between him and Lux. Maybe there was something to those breakup rumors.

We didn't stop walking until we were in front of his locker, which he proceeded to unlock. "Bold of you. Coming up to me in the caf."

"You're not untouchable, Bram. And I really do need to ask you about the paper."

Bram pulled a stapled report out of his locker and handed it to me, the words MARY SHELLEY AND HER MONSTER in bold on the cover page. Below it were both of our names.

"We were supposed to write it together."

"You can read it to make sure it's to your liking. I'm sure it will be." He shut his locker and started to walk, but I called out after him, "What did you mean on the roof?"

Bram turned back to me. "What?"

"When you said Freddie takes things too far. What did you mean by that?"

Bram hesitated, as if he could see that I was willing to hear him, but what he said next was still tinged with skepticism. "You can't see Freddie for who he really is because you're blinded by love."

A sputtering laugh came out of me, and the sound ricocheted too loudly in the locker bay. "I'm not in love with him."

"You're in something," Bram said. "He was the only one upstairs. The obvious answer is usually the right one."

"You're the only one in the club who thinks he did it," I said.

Bram checked his watch, bored, ready to go. "Is it really so hard to believe that someone who takes this game too seriously—who is desperate to win it—would do something crazy to sabotage it?"

"Love isn't the only thing that blinds you," I said. "Fear makes you blind, too. I don't know why, but something about me scares you. Has since I joined the club."

I knew I was right, but something in Bram's expression made me doubt myself. He started to walk away again. "Good talk."

I read the term paper that night, lingering on the last few lines.

Mary Shelley writes of two men. One, an intellectual capable of creating life from death. The other, a grotesque creature made of human body parts and covered in scars. But it isn't the obvious monster that we have to be afraid of. It's the one that looks like us and acts like us.

Mary Shelley's message was clear: Real monsters aren't the ones created by man. The real monster is man himself.

36

SAUNDRA CONVINCED ME to go on the ski trip.

To be fair, I gave in pretty easily. My friends weren't talking to me, my nightmares were fiercer and more frequent, my grades were in the crapper, and I didn't have Freddie. I would endure a day on the bunny slopes if it was a distraction from my life.

Saundra even managed to find a spot for me in Lawrence Pinsky's uncle's cabin. According to Saundra, Lawrence Pinsky's uncle had gotten rich after suing the city when a cop car ran over his foot. He'd bought the place near Hunter Mountain with part of the settlement money and let Lawrence borrow it for the trip. Saundra and I paused at the door, listening to the sounds of way too many people already inside. It took a minute for Lawrence to open the door, and when he did, he looked none too pleased to see me.

"I don't know you," he said, his eyes roaming from

my blue-and-orange Islanders ski cap down to my lace-up boots.

"Lawrence, this is the friend I told you about. Rachel Chavez."

"I don't remember you telling me about a friend."

Saundra rolled her eyes but kept smiling like this was a typical exchange of pleasantries. "Omigawd I legit told you about Rachel."

Lawrence pulled out his phone, making quick work of producing the text Saundra had sent him the previous night in which she had very clearly written: *Thanks for letting me crash! Can't wait to see you! This trip is going to be awesome!*—in which she very clearly neglected to mention me.

The duffel bag in my arms was starting to get heavy, and my Doc Martens, which were apparently not equipped to handle the mountain snow, were getting soggy. I stood there wondering if I'd have to catch a bus back home and how Saundra, who liked to talk so much, could be so bad at communicating.

"Oh," Saundra said. "Okay, my bad, but Rachel has nowhere to go. You have to let her stay."

"Can't she go to one of the other cabins?"

"No, of course not, she doesn't know anyone at the other cabins."

Lawrence looked me over again. "You go to our school?"

Sometimes being the mysterious new girl really bit me in the ass.

"Forget about it." I fumbled with my duffel as I looked for my phone. "I'll just text someone else and see if they—"

"Lawrence, don't be a dick," Saundra said. "I mean, I'm joking—I'm not calling you a dick—but seriously, don't be a dick."

"Fine. But you'll have to share a bed," Lawrence said. "We're swamped in here."

"No worries!" Saundra said.

Finally Lawrence stepped aside to let us through. Someone called his name and he disappeared deep into the house.

"This place is huge!" Saundra spread her arms wide, her overnight bag swinging on its strap and bouncing against her hip.

She was right. This mansion in the woods was big enough to get lost in. Maybe Lawrence really was being a dick. We were only a foot inside but the vastness of it was something I had forgotten existed, living in the city. The living room was actually split into three spaces all separated by sectioned-off couches and coffee tables.

I could've fit my whole 650-square-foot apartment in the living room. And the ceiling went beyond the main staircase, up to a second floor, opening up to a skylight. A fire was already roaring in the fireplace, and people lounged on the long couches and the fuzzy rugs on the floor.

Freddie was one of them. We locked eyes at the same time, but I was the first to look away.

"Nothing is going to beat this trip," Saundra said.

"Totally," I said, and hoped I sounded convincing. So much for a distraction.

All it took was a quick circle around the room for me to realize what kind of people were mooching off Lawrence Pinsky. The misfits. The kids who didn't really belong to any cliques, either by circumstance or design. Which explained Saundra. And Freddie, too. When even Lawrence Pinsky—infamous for sobbing in class every single time he got a grade lower than a B—couldn't recognize you, you knew you were a nobody.

I sat on one of the couches, waiting for Saundra to get back from the kitchen, and scrolled through my phone. Or pretended to. I couldn't get any service here, but staring at my screen beat trying to make conversation with the people around me. As much as the Mary Shelley Club had helped buff the edges of my social anxiety, that discomfort still thrived within me. Plus, I was doing my best to avoid talking to Freddie. My feelings for him jumbled into something I couldn't make sense of. Bram's words had gotten under my skin, but I still missed him. He was the only one I wanted to talk all this stuff through with.

But when I glanced up, I spotted Freddie looking at me. He had a drink in hand, and I thought for a moment that he'd come over and say something. But after a beat that stretched too long, he headed in the direction of his Film Club friends, who were sitting on the floor, hunched over a board game called 13 Dead End Drive.

Saundra plopped down beside me on the couch and handed me a beer.

"So what's the deal with you two?" Saundra took a long sip from her Solo cup.

"What?"

"I was just in the kitchen with Freddie. He was asking about you."

I sat up straighter. "What did he say?"

"He was surprised to see you here. He seems sad. And you seem kind of sad. So, naturally, I assume something must be up with you two."

"Nothing," I said. "Nothing's up." I hadn't expected the pang of guilt that bloomed in my chest. I'd thought it'd get easier to lie to Saundra, but it was only getting harder.

"You sure?" She looked at me suspiciously. "Sometimes I think you're an open book, but then sometimes . . . like when I see you exchanging super-loaded looks with Freddie Martinez, or when you suddenly walk up to Bram out of the blue in the lunchroom, I don't know. You're hiding something."

There were two sides to me—one that was desperate to confess all to Saundra, and another that needed to keep things under wraps, afraid that if I told one secret, they'd all come spilling out. Both sides were playing tug-of-war, pulling so tight I might snap in half.

I hadn't really told Saundra anything about me and Freddie, trying to keep my Mary Shelley Club life apart from my regular life. But now I wondered why. I needed someone to talk to, and even if I couldn't tell Saundra everything, I could still tell her *something*. "Freddie and I kinda had a thing . . ." Reacting to her scandalized look, I quickly amended the statement. "For like a minute. Really, barely worth mentioning. And now—" I shrugged, waved my hand vaguely. "I dunno. Things are weird."

Saundra pushed out her bottom lip in full sympathy. "Why weird?"

"I just don't know if he's the guy I thought he was. Someone told me I couldn't trust him."

Saundra snuggled in next to me until we were both perfectly ensconced in the corner of the couch. I didn't know what she was drinking, but it must've been good because she looked relaxed and peaceful and like she didn't want to be anywhere but here. Weirdly, I began to relax, too.

Maybe it was the warmth of the fireplace, or the negligible traces of cheap booze coursing through me. But Saundra's head on my shoulder actually felt kind of natural. Her being this close—it was the tangible feeling of real, pure friendship.

"As the resident gossip maven of Manchester Prep, I'm better at dispensing advice on the contents of someone's character than some random person who wants to keep you and Freddie apart. So here's my two cents, for free: Is Freddie an outsider at our school? Def. Is he a criminal who makes quick cash by cheating for the highest bidder? Absolutely. Does that make him a bad person, though? Not necessarily. From what I know about the guy, he seems nice. And I know you like nice guys."

"You do?"

"Yes," she said. "You're smart and pretty and you've

got a good head on your shoulders. You'd never go for the asshole."

I smiled, partly because of what she'd said about Freddie, but mostly because I'd finally told her something real about my life, and it felt good.

"Speaking of nice guys . . ." Saundra looked across the room and I followed her gaze. I thought she was searching for Freddie, but she was zeroing in on a guy named Aldie Something. He was talking a mile a minute with two other guys, also talking a mile a minute.

"He's cute, right?" Saundra sighed and laid her head on my shoulder. Tentatively, I laid my cheek against her head, her hair soft against my skin. She didn't make a move to shake me off and so there we stayed; two buzzed, lazy, warm girls, giggling over a boy across the room. It felt nice having a best friend.

So, was Aldie cute? He was tall. And big. And he seemed to like talking, so that was a plus as far as Saundra was concerned. Not my type, but, "Yeah, he's cute."

"I should hook up with him tonight."

"That's bold."

"We're unsupervised in the woods. It's a bold kind of night."

My phone buzzed in my back pocket and I fished it out.

A group text from Bram to all of us in the Mary Shelley Club.

My turn, it said simply, followed by instructions on where to meet. I felt a chill run down my spine and couldn't tell if it was from fear or excitement.

Two guys thundered down the main stairway suddenly, and I snapped my head up from my phone. They jumped over coffee tables and bumped into unsuspecting people, hooting and hollering. And they wore white masks.

LED facial masks that they'd probably stolen from some girls' suitcases, but it was obvious what they were doing.

My heartbeat quickened as I watched them blaze through the cabin and everyone exploded in a mixed chorus of laughter and complaint.

"It's the Masked Man!" someone shouted gleefully. "The Masked *Men*!"

Saundra seemed to enjoy it, sitting up with an open-mouthed grin on her face. I turned toward Freddie. Our eyes locked and he looked as unamused as I felt.

37

I DIDN'T WAIT for Freddie, even though it would've been easier to find this place together. But I didn't want the awkwardness between us inside the cabin to follow us out here. Thankfully there was the occasional streetlight along the road or I might have accidentally trekked into the woods by now.

The snow crunched under my boots. I didn't like this. Normally I'd be pumped on the eve of a Fear Test, but something about this felt all wrong. I didn't even know what Bram had planned yet, but the fact that he was just springing this on us, in an unfamiliar setting, when the club was this fractured, set off all my alarm bells.

Now, with the darkness pressing all around me, I knew that I wasn't excited—I was nervous. And as I walked, every shape around me seemed to take on the form of a masked man.

But a noise stopped me. It came from behind. I turned around but saw no one. I started walking again. There was only the sound the snow made as it flattened beneath the soles of my now completely drenched Docs, but I couldn't shake the sense of someone else being behind me. It stuck to me like a shadow.

I spun around, shining my phone's flashlight through the space around me. The beam shone on a pair of black boots. I gasped, jumping back, and raised the light, my fingers trembling. Felicity's face stared back at me. She put her arm up to block the glare like a vampire caught in daylight.

"What the—!" I took a moment to catch the bit of breath she'd managed to snatch out of me. "Why were you following me!"

"Because I was trying to scare you," Felicity said as though it was obvious. "Scaring people is what we do."

Ugh, Felicity. As much as I didn't want to talk to her right now, she seemed confident of the direction we were going, so I walked in step.

"Ready for tonight?" she asked.

I shook my head. "No prep, no instructions, no assigned roles. What happened to the usual protocol?"

"Bram wants to flex," Felicity said. "Or he's lazy. Whatever, I'm just hungry for another test."

Yep, definite vampire vibes. "You sound excited."

"Fear Tests are the whole point of the club. Of course I'm excited. Why aren't you?"

I let her words linger and the silence stretched its long fingers and pointed them at me. Felicity watched me out of the sides of her eyes, her face turning into a giant snarky snarl. "Maybe you're not such a fan of Fear Tests after failing yours?"

"I didn't fail mine. Lux screamed."

"Right, because of the Masked Man. Which you didn't plan. Or did you?"

"I just want to get this over with."

"It almost is." It wasn't Felicity who said it but Bram, his voice rumbling toward us from up ahead. The rest of the Mary Shelley Club—including Freddie—were huddled together behind the general store, which stood as quiet and empty as an old shoebox.

"What took you so long?" Thayer asked, bouncing on his feet, trying to shake off the cold.

"Rachel was slowing me down," Felicity said.

"Let's cut to the chase," Bram said. "We're going to Pinsky's cabin."

"A cabin-in-the-woods trope?" Thayer said. "Gotta say, I expected more from you, Bram."

"Not a cabin in the woods," Bram said. "More of a home invasion."

Flashes of *Funny Games* came back to me. I should've known he'd do something like this.

"Your tasks are simple," he continued. "Create chaos."

"Who's the target?" Felicity asked.

Bram looked straight at me when he said it. "Saundra Clairmont."

I froze, and it wasn't from the cold. Bram knew what he was doing but still acted like it was nothing. I guess to him it was.

"No way," I protested. "She's my friend."

"That didn't seem to matter when you guys targeted my best friend and my girlfriend."

"Revenge Fear Tests," Thayer said. "A fun new twist."

Bram reached inside a large backpack and tossed something soft and bulky to me and Felicity. "Put this on."

The Black hoodies. I hadn't noticed before, but the guys were already wearing theirs, all dressed identically. "And this." The next thing he handed out was white with a rubbery texture. I dropped the mask as soon as I realized what it was.

The mask. From Sim's and Lux's tests, from my own home invasion. "Why?"

"Because masks are all the rage. And this is my Fear Test." Bram slipped his mask over his face, and I couldn't look at him anymore.

Felicity slipped her mask over her face like she was slipping on the perfect prom dress. Thayer seemed to examine his for a minute, but ultimately put it on. Then it was just Freddie left. He seemed to catch my eye for the millionth time that night, but he didn't say anything to me. Instead, he said something to Bram. "What are you doing, man?"

"I don't have to explain anything to you," Bram said, his tone a warning.

"I'm not putting it on," I said.

"Rule number two," Felicity said, the mask barely muffling her glee. "You must perform the task assigned."

Freddie, a stickler for the rules, finally succumbed. "The faster we do it, the faster it's over," he whispered.

"No," I shot back. "I'm not playing anymore. I quit."

"The game isn't over until everyone plays," Thayer said, echoing almost exactly what he'd said at the movie theater.

"Bram, how can you play?" I said, desperate to drill some sense into him, into *someone*. "Your girlfriend got hurt and we still don't even know why."

"You can't quit," Felicity said simply.

"Watch me," I said.

"You can't quit," she said again. "Because if you do, we'll tell the whole school that you killed a boy in your own house last year."

My breath caught in my throat. I felt like I was choking. Worse, choking in front of an audience of pale-faced monsters. "What?"

But Felicity didn't repeat herself. She knew I'd heard her perfectly. I looked around, trying to appeal to at least one of them. Freddie looked up at the sky, like he couldn't bear to face me, even from behind the mask.

I turned to Thayer. Thayer couldn't actually buy into this.

"We have to stick together," he said in a voice so low it came out borderline meek. "This ensures that we stick together. That we're a team, through the good and the bad."

"Are you serious?" My own voice sounded foreign to me, thick with unshed tears.

Bram stepped toward me but I stepped back, wincing. He slipped his mask up so it rested over his forehead. He whispered so only I could hear.

"You heard Felicity," he said. "I don't want to do this any more than you do. But we all had initiations, Rachel. Not just you. We all have secrets that could destroy us."

He bent down and picked up the mask that I'd

discarded. He pressed it into my hands and all I felt was the cold pressure of his gloved knuckles mingling with the horrid rubber.

"Did you choose Saundra because I chose Lux?" I asked him. "Because I'm sorry. I'm sorry about what happened to her." I meant every word, but Bram acted like he didn't hear any of it.

He slipped the mask back over his face. "If you want this to be over, just make sure she screams."

38

SAUNDRA CLAIRMONT

SAUNDRA SPIT BLACK sludge into the sink. The gunk made an angry, crumbly splash on the pristine porcelain as it oozed its way toward the drain. Bits of it dribbled down her chin, spilling over her blackened lips. The slits between her teeth were stained with the stuff. When she looked into the mirror she found the picture of death smiling back at her. Not just death, but hundred-year-old-, marinating-in-death-juice-beneath-the-earth kind of death. But it was worth it. She'd been using this charcoal toothpaste every day for the past month and it'd been making her pearlies the whitest ever.

She did one more round with the toothbrush, then rinsed until the black goo was gone. She shut off the bathroom light and headed back toward her room.

She wanted to look her extra best because tonight was special.

Saundra hadn't expected the night to go like this. The most she'd hoped to get out of this ski trip was some good intel on all the random hookups that were bound to go down. But to her surprise, she—for once!—was going to have a random hookup of her own.

Rachel had been acting super sus lately, which at first kind of bothered Saundra because, hello, they were friends and they were supposed to tell each other everything. But tonight Rachel had snuck off somewhere and it turned out to be for the best because Saundra needed her privacy right now.

When Rachel had started at Manchester, she'd been like a bird with a broken wing. A tiny, little, clueless hummingbird, totally lost and shivering because her heart was beating a million times a minute. Saundra's parents had instilled a sense of charity and hospitality in her, and when Saundra had seen Rachel she felt it was her duty to fill the poor girl in on how the school operated. Then she surprised herself by actually really liking the weirdo. Saundra knew that she (sometimes) talked a lot, and some people never wanted to stay and listen. But Rachel always did.

Still, sometimes a girl had to strike out on her own. And tonight was one of those nights. With Rachel gone, Saundra had the bedroom to herself, at least for a little while. Which meant the clock was ticking. As soon as Rachel left the cabin, Saundra had downed the rest of her mixed drink and set her sights on Aldie Kirkba. She walked over to him, tapped him on the shoulder, and without saying a word, led him away from one of his dumb board games and up the stairs.

As random hookups went, this was Saundra's best. Also her first, but that was a minor detail. She and Aldie lay in bed together, on top of the covers (for now), fully dressed (reluctantly), and making out (sloppily). But Saundra didn't mind the slobberiness. It meant Aldie was excited, which reinforced how much he was into her. He wasn't the coolest guy in school (hi, they were staying in Pinsky's cabin), or the smartest (3.1 GPA— he'd have to work on that), or even one of the richest (his parents, Alicia and Baz Kirkba, owned their own party supply company, but Middletons they were not). Aldie, though, was a good'un. And cute.

The thing was, Saundra was having trouble focusing on his parents' jobs, or his GPA, or anything about the boy because the only thing that was consuming her thoughts right now was his hair. As she ran her fingers through it, she could feel every single strand pricking her skin. "Did you just get a haircut?" she breathed.

"What?" came Aldie's muffled response.

"Your hair feels . . . alive."

"What?" he said again. Aldie was having his own trouble focusing, trying to both swirl his tongue around in Saundra's mouth and unhook her bra at the same time.

"It keeps poking me," Saundra said.

"What's poking you? Your bra?" Aldie asked, his tongue still in her mouth. Then he stopped, took his tongue out of Saundra's mouth, and looked her in the eye. "My dick?"

"Your hair."

She couldn't help the marvel in her voice. Hair—a *boy's* hair—had never felt this glorious before.

"That's not gonna be the only thing poking you tonight," Aldie said.

"What?"

Aldie stopped fiddling with Saundra's bra and unglued himself from her lips. "Was that stupid? Am I making too many references to my dick?" He waited for Saundra's answer, but only for a split second before cursing under his breath. "That was so stupid. I'm so stupid."

"Noooo," Saundra cooed, trying to sound as soothing as possible. As soothing as his hair felt as she rubbed it like a genie's lamp. "Yes to poking. I love your hair."

Maybe it was the endorphins of making out with a cute, super-heavy guy, but his hair actually looked like it shimmered. Like someone had spilled glitter all over it.

Aldie smiled and went back to kissing Saundra with verve. His lips felt kind of rubbery, but, Saundra thought, maybe that's what lips feel like when you're falling in love. As they kissed, Saundra decided that from this moment on she'd call him by his given name. Aldous. If he was going to be her boyfriend, he'd have to upgrade to his proper government name.

As he returned to swirling his tongue in Saundra's mouth, there came a crash from downstairs.

"What was that?" Aldous asked.

"Jenga," Saundra said, pulling him back to her mouth. Even though she was sure it sounded like something shattering and not a pile of tiny wooden bricks toppling over. But, details! This counter-clockwise tongue thing was interesting and she wanted more of it. She held her hand to the back of Aldous's neck, both to make this makeout sexier and also to keep him in place. But Aldous pulled his head back, distracted.

"I don't think that was Jenga," he said. "Someone would've come to get me if they were playing Jenga. Avery and Donavan *know* Jenga's my jam."

"Forget Avery and Donavan!"

"Yeah. Okay. But they're my best friends—"

"You're lying on top of a girl here!" Saundra said. "In a bed. Alone. And there are stars everywhere!"

Stars and hearts and butterflies. Saundra definitely saw butterflies.

Aldous's tongue twister of a mouth quirked up into a sly smile. "Right."

This time when Saundra put her hand on the back of his neck and pulled, he obliged.

Except there was more noise then. Loud, terrible sounds from the first floor, rising up the stairs. She knew Aldous heard it too, because his lips stiffened and paused against hers.

"So much Jenga," Saundra mumbled about the definitely-not-Jenga noises. The sounds only grew louder, accompanied by yelling and screaming. It was coming closer, and then the bedroom door banged open.

Both Aldous and Saundra jolted up when a masked figure skidded to a stop before them.

"Oh not this again," Saundra said. "Don't you knock?!"

Aldous's reaction was a little different. He sprang out of bed like he'd just been stuck in the ass with a cattle prod. "What the hell!" he yelped.

"It's just a loser in a mask," Saundra said. But the

longer the person in the mask stayed in the room, saying nothing, the more he gave Saundra the heebie-jeebies.

"Get out of here!" She tried to stare the masked monster down, but his edges became hazy. Blurred. It almost looked like two masked people standing one in front of the other. Now she was starting to freak out.

"Don't just stand there, Aldous! Protect me!"

"Aldous?" Aldous repeated, confused.

"Fine—*Aldie*, whatever, just do something!"

The person in the mask jumped Aldous and the two fell, thrashing on the floor, all limbs and backs, looking like they were melding together. Saundra knelt on the corner of the bed, making herself as small as possible as she watched the commotion. And then it occurred to her that this was exactly what had happened to Lux and Bram. A masked madman had also come after them. She and Aldous and Lux and Bram were sharing the same experience. They were practically the *same*. Maybe, Saundra thought, she could talk to Bram about it. Maybe she'd get invited to sit at their table and compare notes on whoever this ridiculous prankster was.

But as she thought about this, Saundra noticed that the masked person wasn't even interested in Aldous. No, he was fighting back Aldous, reaching for *her*.

Yeah, she was nope-ing the hell out of here.

Saundra scurried off the bed, skipping over the tangle of Aldous and the Masked Man and running out of the room. The living room, formerly bumping with life, was eerily quiet now, engulfed in darkness and disarray. Ceramic shards on the carpet, food on the rugs. Where had everyone gone?

Saundra turned and saw a group huddled together behind the couch: Avery, Donavan, and Julie, the people Aldous had been playing with. Their eyes widened in terror at something behind Saundra and she whipped her head back.

And then, suddenly, there was the masked person again. But he didn't come from upstairs. He came from the kitchen. Saundra squeezed her eyes shut and then opened them again. Was she seeing double? Or had this guy chased her downstairs? Things that were supposed to make sense became muddled in her mind.

This Masked Man saw her—*watched* her—and Saundra's first instinct was to point to the huddled, snively guys in the corner. "*They're the ones you want!*"

But the Masked Man barely glanced in their direction. He still wanted *her*. It was just her luck that so many guys wanted her tonight and none of it was going her way.

Saundra ran. She ran through the kitchen and the Masked Man chased her. She was the mouse now and he was the cat and she did not like those odds. She ran out of the kitchen and back to the living room and this time Saundra had the wherewithal to grab a heavy bookend off a shelf. She spun around, knowing the masked guy would be right behind her and she wasn't sure if he ran into the bookend or if she really crashed it into his head, but either way the guy went down in an explosion of a million glittery shards.

She'd done it. She'd defeated him.

Saundra took a moment to catch her breath, wiping sweat from her forehead. The first floor took on its eerie new quietness again. But out of the corner of her eye she saw a flash of black cross the hall.

Saundra needed to get the hell out of there. She ran for the front door. But as soon as she got there another masked figure popped up in front of her.

"Why are there so many of you!" she shrieked. She must've been imagining things. There were too many of them, it was all in her mind. She blinked over and over again but the new masked person didn't go away. She'd always hated whack-a-mole.

Saundra turned back and flew through the living room and up the stairs. Her plan now was to get back to the room, find a closet, and lock herself in there. Aldous would be there—he would know what to do. But when she got there, Aldous was gone. Instead, there was a masked figure. *Another* one, or the same one from before, idling like they were waiting for a party to start. "Are you freaking kidding me?"

Saundra fell to her knees, tired, confused, dizzy. She'd once seen on an episode of *Grey's Anatomy* that when someone threatened to kill you, you were supposed to tell them your life story in order to gain sympathy. Luckily for her, if there was one thing she was good at it was talking about herself.

"I was born three weeks early in the middle of one of the hottest summers on record on the island of St. Croix. It ruined my parents' fourth-anniversary trip—" She would've gone on, but the Masked Man interrupted her.

"Scream," he said.

Except it wasn't a he. The voice was female. Actually, the voice was familiar. It sounded echoey and distant, but Saundra *knew* that voice. She'd heard it often enough, every day at lunch.

"Rachel?"

A heavy pause filled the room as the two looked at each other, Saundra from her knees and the person through the mask. And then they—Rachel—spoke again. "Just scream!"

Rachel or not, Saundra didn't have to be told a third time. She angled her head back and let one rip, her scream shrill enough to shake the house. Or at least that was what it felt like.

Saundra caught her breath and the Masked Man . . . woman . . . (Rachel?) . . . stood there a moment longer, then fled.

39

THERE HAD BEEN a time not so long before when the anticipation leading up to a Fear Test felt kind of delicious. Like the blood in my veins was spiked with something sweet and bubbling—a high no drug could possibly touch. And the moments after a Fear Test— the comedown, when the worry of being caught mingled perfectly with the elation of pulling it off—were the best part.

Now I ran down the stairs as fast as I could, my palm slick with sweat as it slid down the banister. It was just one flight but the stairs were steep and I worried about tripping. My head vibrated with the sound of my breathing, coming fast, and the guilt of what I'd just done.

This game used to be candy. A sugary, addictive treat. Now there was only the sour aftertaste and the seeping knowledge of just how bad for you it was. The excitement that'd eclipsed everything before was eroding, eaten away by the harsh truth of what we were doing. It was a game of terror, but all we were doing was terrorizing people.

When I reached the bottom of the stairs I looked back, expecting Saundra to be right behind me, demanding answers. She wasn't there, but somebody else was. Standing on the second-floor landing was one of my own, a monster in a mask.

"It's over!" I shouted. My voice was hot and half muted by the rubber over my face. I didn't sound like myself, and the longer I wore the mask, the more the guilt and disgust ate away at me. "She screamed!"

I tried to make out which of us it was, but we were all in the same uniform—the black hoodie, white mask. From this strange angle, staring up at them, the person looked both dwarfed and menacingly large. They were little more than a dim shadow, with only the mask truly noticeable, its whiteness a ghostly beacon in the darkness. Whoever it was stood still for a moment. A statue. Like they were listening, considering what I'd just said.

"What are you doing?" I demanded. "Let's go!"

They finally moved, but instead of following me down, they turned into the hallway and out of my view.

There was no time for this. I had to find the rendezvous and a safe place to pull off my mask. I briskly walked down a hallway but then a closet door swung open, nearly crashing into me. A hand reached out of the darkness and grabbed mine, pulling me in.

"What the hell?" I shouted. The door closed behind us, squeezing us into the tight space. I was crammed between swinging coats, some thick enough to be smothered by. My first reflex was to swing but my hand was caught midway, followed by a "Shh."

"Freddie?" The only light in the closet came from the crack in the doorframe. Not enough to illuminate him, but I knew instantly that it was him by his scent.

"What are you—" I stopped to jerk my mask off my head. "What are you doing?"

Outside the door there was the sound of someone running past. "Anyone could've seen you," Freddie whispered.

I yanked off the hoodie, my elbows knocking into Freddie and the coats. A few weeks ago I might've been thrilled to be in a closet with Freddie, shedding layers of clothes. So much had changed.

The hoodie was off, but it wasn't enough. I could feel the familiar dread crawling up my skin like fire ants, my arms feeling weak and heavy, and all I could think to do was to reach out. My fingers felt for Freddie, searching for purchase, winding into his sweatshirt.

"She knew it was me," I muttered, my voice hitching

with panic. "She knew it was me under the mask, she's going to figure it all out—the Mary Shelley Club, she already thinks I'm keeping secrets—"

Freddie pulled me into him, wrapping his arms around me quickly.

"It's okay," he said. "It's over. I heard her scream."

"She's going to hate me."

"She'll be confused like everyone else. I'll give you an alibi, okay? You can tell her you were in a closet with me, making out all night."

It was hard to tell if it was meant as a joke, considering that in another timeline, we might have been doing exactly that. It put the spotlight on the awkward way we'd left things, and how we'd never actually sat down to talk everything through. Maybe this was the universe sending me a sign that we were meant to hash things out.

Freddie seemed to think so.

"Do you still think it was me?" he said. "What Bram accused me of, hurting Lux. You still believe that?"

I didn't know anymore. I didn't want to.

"Compromising the club would be the *last* thing I would ever want to do. Not only because I love the club, but because you know what would happen if we got caught. Bram, Thayer, Felicity—they'd be okay. But you and me? We don't have a safety net. We don't have family lawyers to bail us out of any binds. We can't mess up."

I nodded fervently.

"If you don't want to be with me, that's fine," Freddie said. "But I can't stand back and let Bram convince you that I'm some monster. He's the one who made us wear masks tonight. He chose Saundra to get back at you. *He's* the one who's acting like a lunatic, Rachel."

It was dark but I could feel his face close to mine, his warm breath. He wanted nothing more than for me to trust him. The truth was, I wanted that, too.

"Freddie, I—"

We jumped at the sound of a crash. It was so loud I could feel it in my bones—loud like the whole cabin was coming down.

Freddie and I didn't need to say anything. The intensity of our conversation evaporated instantly, replaced by something graver. He reached for the door-knob first and we both ran out of the closet.

There was a group of people huddled in the grand foyer, looking down at something. I thought it was strange that they were looking down because all I saw was the gaping hole up above. The skylight was gone, with nothing left but shards of glass still dangling from the frame.

"There was somebody up there!" a boy cried. "I saw someone up there!"

But the rest of the crowd was strangely quiet. A tense quiet, like people gathered around a torched house or a car wreck. I broke through the crowd until I could see what they were looking at.

I recognized her hair first before I saw her face. She lay in the middle of the floor, too still. Her eyes stared up at me. I couldn't remember what I said or sobbed in those moments. Just that my eyes instantly flooded, while Saundra's stayed lifeless.

40

"WHAT HAPPENED?" I asked. My voice didn't sound like my voice. It was dazed and hoarse, and I didn't know if it was from crying or screaming or both.

I also didn't know how I'd gotten to the rendezvous point, behind the empty general store, standing with the Mary Shelley Club again. We were not the stoic, sober ghosts from earlier in the night. We were disheveled and rambling. This time everything was completely fucked.

The last thing I remembered seeing was Saundra's face, frozen in fear. It was the last thing, the first thing, the only thing I could think of.

Everything else fused together: the dark woods, the endless snow, the medley of rushed voices. Felicity was loud—jarringly, unexpectedly loud, asking where we all were when it happened.

There was Thayer. His face was blank but wet with tears.

Bram was the last to join us. He emerged from the dark edges of the woods, silent and stumbling like some kind of Frankenstein.

Somebody was letting out ragged sobs and it took me a moment to realize it was me. "Can somebody please tell me what happened?" I asked again.

Freddie's hands were ice-cold when he cupped my face. "Are you okay?" he asked.

I stared back at him, not understanding the question, but he kept asking it. The words eventually rearranged from "Are you okay?" to "You are okay." Over and over again until I could finally breathe.

"We need a plan," Felicity said. "The cops are going to come and they're going to be asking questions."

"That's what you're focusing on now?" I nearly screamed.

"Rachel's right. We need to slow down. We still don't know what happened," Freddie said.

Something caught my eye, a flash of dark red. The stuff was smeared on Bram's fingers. Some of it on his cheek, his hair. The sight of it made my mind short-circuit, go back to the spot on the floor where Saundra lay, surrounded by the pool of blood that had been seeping out of her.

"Whose blood is that?" I asked. But nobody heard me.

Bram caught me looking, though. He wiped his hand on his hip and the red disappeared just like that, soaked up by the black material.

"We don't say anything," Felicity said, pulling me back into the moment. She was pacing. I didn't know if she was talking to me or to us or to herself. A part of me wanted to laugh. This was what the club was really about. Not fun movie watching, not debates about horror.

"We don't say anything," I said, mimicking her, my words spilling over clumsily.

"She's in shock," Freddie was saying. "I think she's in shock."

"Forget about her. We need to get our stories straight!" Felicity said. "We can't expose the club."

The club. Really? I leaned my head back and this time I let a laugh ring out. They stared, but I didn't care. I laughed so much that my teeth chattered. I laughed so much I shivered. And as they stared at me, watching me shake, I said, "Saundra is dead."

Everyone stopped. Felicity stopped talking and Bram stopped pacing and Thayer stopped crying and Freddie stopped looking at me like I was a fragile thing. I wasn't sure why that had commanded their attention. All of us had known she was gone. I only said it because nobody else had yet. And it felt like something that needed to be said. Maybe if I said it more it would sink in. Feel real. Because it didn't yet. "She died."

"Is this Captain Obvious story hour?" Felicity asked.

"Shut it, Felicity," came Bram's voice, dark and thundering.

Saying the words out loud didn't make me stop, though. It actually felt like everything in me started moving again. My heart started pumping so hard I could feel it down to my toes. The numbness all around me washed away. There was a scream inside me and it filled my head, so loud that it shook me.

"Saundra jumped through the skylight," Felicity said. "She killed herself."

I was on my feet in an instant, rushing toward Felicity. "She didn't kill herself!" I yelled in her face. Felicity was only an inch away from me, but I couldn't see her clearly through my tears. "She wouldn't do that!"

Saundra had fallen.

Or she'd been pushed.

And as soon as I thought that, I felt in my bones that it was true. There was that masked figure on the landing. The memory came fast and burning, like taking a bitter shot of straight alcohol. I'd seen someone at the top of the stairs right before I went into the closet with Freddie. I remembered how the person had just stood there when I tried to talk to them. How uneasy

I'd felt. How every hair on my body had stood up like a warning flag.

"We were running around with masks on trying to scare her," I said. Whoever pushed Saundra had been wearing a mask too, which meant we were responsible. *I* was responsible. That burning feeling from before turned into a sticky roiling in the pit of my stomach. I was nauseous suddenly. Sick.

"Yeah, if anyone asks, how about we don't fucking say that," Felicity said.

"We all tossed our masks, right?" Freddie asked.

There were grumbles and nods. Thayer, who'd been holding his mask in a white-knuckled fist this whole time seemed to suddenly realize it. He hurled it into the woods like it was a live grenade.

"Bram, give me your lighter," Felicity said. She kicked at the ground where she stood, spattering snow and clumps of dead grass like she was a dog trying to bury a bone. She dropped her mask into the newly made hole. Bram fished a gold Zippo out of his pocket and passed it to Felicity, but he was still holding his own mask. He examined it, and from three yards away I did, too. There was blood on it, standing out against the monster's white face. Bram shoved the mask into the front pocket of his hoodie. I squeezed my eyes shut and shook my head. There were too many things being hidden away, too many secrets.

"We have to tell someone what we did."

"We didn't do anything," Thayer said. He said it over and over again, trying to make it more true.

"Someone died. Saundra *died*," I said. "We have to tell them what we were doing."

I could hear sirens in the background, getting closer, and it was all too obvious who I meant by "them."

"Was I not clear before, Rachel?" Felicity said. She was in my face suddenly, pointing a finger at me like it was a knife. "You want to confess to a crime that doesn't even exist? You'll be the only one, because none of us will back you on that. You go against the club, and we go against you."

"Are you seriously threatening her right now?" Freddie said.

"*Guys*," Thayer cried.

But neither of them contradicted Felicity. Not Thayer, and not Freddie.

I looked at Bram. Just the sight of him was enough to strike up rage in me, pounding in my head. It tried to burst through me, break through my skin with its ugly talons and be unleashed. It was his fault that this had happened. He was the one who'd made us put on the masks.

I imagined *his* lifeless body on the floor instead of Saundra's. My pounding head was filled with the dark fantasy that he'd been killed instead of her.

"Enough." Felicity flicked Bram's lighter open and a flame sparked to life. She dumped it in the hole she'd kicked into the ground. It landed on her mask and a small fire roared to life. The smell of burning rubber was instant. I looked down at the mask, the hideous, shriveled white face staring up. But soon the whole thing was ablaze, curling and bubbling.

The sirens were so close now it was like they were inside my head. The cold scratched at my cheeks, tickling them raw. I was dizzy. I felt so utterly powerless. Who knew the game would end up like this? I looked around to see if anyone else was feeling this awful, too. But all I saw were monsters.

I bent over and vomited into the snow.

41

I WAS BACK in my old house, in the same kitchen, in the same nightmare. He was there. We thrashed on the floor but no matter how hard I fought, we always ended up in the same position: with me on my back and the masked figure on top of me, his knees pinning me in place, one hand busy restraining my arms, the other pointing the knife at me.

The dream had always been the same but this time was different. This time, I stopped struggling. And when his knife came down, I let it pierce my chest. He put his whole weight into it, leaned down to meet me, his rubber face only inches from mine. But no matter how deep the knife went, I felt nothing. He was the one letting out the guttural moans. Blood seeped first from between his waxy white lips, then poured freely from his eyes, dripping onto my face.

I woke up with my sheets tangled around my legs

and my face wet. When I brought my hands to my cheeks, I was sure they'd come away red. But it was only sweat. Or tears.

I took a deep breath, but it caught in my throat when I looked at the foot of my bed. Standing there was Matthew Marshall. And next to him was Saundra.

The two stood side by side, staring at me like the world's most screwed-up wedding cake topper. The only movement came from the blood that oozed out of them, trickling at first, then in waterfalls.

"Scream," Saundra said.

She placed one knee on the bed and then the other, moving toward me while dripping blood on my blanket. She crawled until she reached me, her eyes bugging out of her face, her smile wide, teeth stained red.

"Just . . . SCREAM."

So I did.

I screamed so loud my mother came into the room to stop me. She grabbed my shoulders and shook me. Or maybe I shook of my own accord. I wasn't sure. I didn't know if I had been dreaming or if they were ghosts or if I'd died and gone to hell. I wasn't sure of anything except that when I looked toward the foot of my bed, Matthew and Saundra were gone.

"It's my fault," I said, my words waterlogged with

tears and snot. My mother searched my face, concern and confusion coloring hers.

I needed to be clearer. She needed to understand. "It's my fault they're dead!"

"Oh, honey, no."

"Yes, it is. First Matthew, now Saundra. Saundra died because of me. Saundra died—"

Mom's tight embrace cut me off in midsentence. She shushed me and pushed my hair back and whispered words of comfort in my ear.

But she didn't understand.

In a cruel twist of fate, Saundra got what she'd always wanted: She was the hottest topic of conversation at school. A few people speculated that she was high (because why else would she be up on the roof?) and that she must've tripped and fallen. Some suggested that she had flung herself through the skylight in some, I don't know, final act of dramatic anguish. But most people believed something else. That there was a person in a white rubber mask on that roof with her. That they pushed her.

There were a lot of people in masks that night. Everybody had seen them. But some people swore that when Saundra landed in the middle of the grand foyer, they'd looked up and seen a ghostly, unmoving face staring down at them.

I believed all and none of it, picturing every possible way Saundra could've fallen until I couldn't think of anything else. I was physically at school, but walked the halls like something out of a Romero movie, my zombie shuffle on point without even trying.

We were called into an assembly to discuss what had happened to Saundra. It wouldn't be the only one. Before he took the stage, AssHead pulled me aside and said there would be another assembly for Saundra, a proper memorial, and that if I wanted to speak at it I should.

"I know how close you two were," he said, frowning.

I must've vaguely nodded because AssHead answered with "Great," and then took to the stage to talk about Manchester losing one of its "brightest lights" in a tragic accident.

My phone buzzed in the front pocket of my bag and I bent down to take it out. Another text from Freddie, asking how I was doing and if I wanted to talk. It was the latest in a string of texts he'd sent me, all of which I'd left unanswered. I couldn't deal with him or anyone else in the club. Any last remnants of the Mary Shelley Club's fun and playfulness had died with Saundra. If it'd ever really been fun or playful to begin with.

* * *

I slogged through my classes, wondering if I should've taken my mom's advice to stay home. In art, our teacher, Paul, said we should let out whatever emotions we might be feeling today in whatever expression and medium we wanted. To my left, a girl who hadn't stopped crying since the beginning of class was cutting a broken heart out of construction paper. To my right a boy was drawing Deadpool.

I went to the supply closet pretending to get materials, but mostly looking for a quiet place where I didn't need to do anything. Not be brave or sad. I stared at the shelves in front of me, numb with guilt and grief.

It was a while before someone walked in. Of course, it was Lux.

"Oh," she said. "You."

"Oh," I said flatly. "Me."

I expected her to say something mean. Like how my freckles were *too much*, on account of how pale I probably looked. Or how my uniform somehow looked like it was still crumpled on my bedroom floor. But Lux only tugged on her ski cap, fixing it so it was perfectly centered over her forehead. Her mandatory accessory only made me feel guiltier.

"I'm sorry about what happened to you," I said. It was the best I could come up with, short of admitting that I was pretty much responsible for her accident. Lux could be mean, but she hadn't deserved to get hurt. Saundra hadn't deserved to die. And I didn't deserve to stand in the middle of this mess and remain unscathed.

Lux looked surprised by my statement. And she surprised me with her response. "Just FYI, I wasn't, like, going to tell anybody about that boy you knew. Who died."

It was like I had entered a different universe, or at least a different art supply closet. Because the last time we'd been here our conversation was kind of the exact opposite of this one. Last time Lux had chanted his name, taunted me. Now she avoided saying it. Maybe the accident had made her realize some things.

Or maybe I had Lux all wrong. She wasn't the typical horror archetype. Not the Babysitter, not the Victim, not the Bitch. Just Lux. Mean one day, not so mean the next.

"And I'm sorry about your friend, too," Lux added.

My first instinct was to say, *Don't be sorry*, but that felt wrong. *Thank you* didn't feel any better. Didn't matter: Lux went on talking.

"It must be traumatic for you. I know what that's like. I went through a trauma, too. That stuff stays with you." She gestured toward her cap. "Like, I'm glad I survived, but now I have to wear this stupid thing until my hair grows out."

I sighed. Even when she was trying to be sympathetic, she still found a way to make it all about herself. Plus, the cap looked amazing on her. I had already spotted several other girls wearing ones like it.

Lux cleared her throat. "When you go through a traumatic experience, it's important that you have someone to talk to. Which is why I'm talking to you right now. In case you were wondering."

Watching Lux attempt to be nice was like watching a baby giraffe attempt to walk for the first time. Still, I had to give her points for trying.

"Yeah, trauma sucks," I said. "At least you have Bram by your side."

"Is that a joke?" Lux said, her eyes narrowing, instantly looking more like her normal self.

"What?"

"Bram and I broke up."

"You did?" I'd had no idea, but then why would I? Bram wasn't exactly an open book. More like an old, thousand-pound tome that came with an ancient lock. "Why?"

"Um, that's none of your business?" But then Lux looked over her shoulder to see if anyone was near the closet and turned back to face me. "But between you and me? Everyone thinks he's some big hero and that he saved me the night the Masked Man attacked me. But he didn't. Like, at all."

Oh. Was that really enough to break up over? I wasn't one to judge, but I guess to Lux, if you couldn't run into a house and KO the madman, you weren't worthy of her love.

"He doesn't deserve the blame for what happened to you, though," I said. "No one could have gotten there quick enough."

"No, that's what I'm saying. He *was* there quick. Almost too quick. Why?"

I stared at her blankly. "I don't kn—"

"One minute there was some masked freak trying to kill me and I bump my head and black out. The next minute I wake up and Bram's right there, with a mask and a coat tossed off to the side?"

I could feel my forehead crease, hear my heartbeat loud as an analog clock. Because I wasn't sure I was actually hearing what Lux was telling me or, more accurately, what she was trying to tell me about her once-loving and now ex-boyfriend Bram.

"You think he was the one wearing that mask and coat?"

Lux looked at me for a moment, the seconds ticking by slowly. "I didn't say that."

"So what *do* you mean?"

Lux seemed to suddenly find it very important to study the tins of colored pencils and charcoal. She shuffled materials around like it was her duty to tidy up.

"Nothing. It just freaked me out," she said. "One minute there was a masked man and the next minute there was Bram. It was not a good association."

I swallowed. Why was Lux confiding in me? I was a nobody who she'd hated for months now. Then I realized that this was probably why she felt comfortable talking to me in the first place. Who would believe me?

42

I WASN'T A zombie anymore. My brain had been fully resurrected and was working overtime, going through every detail Lux had shared with me. She must've realized she'd said too much—said something bad—about Bram. It fired me up that I wasn't alone in suspecting Bram anymore. That Lux, the person who knew him best, seemed to think he may have been capable of hurting her. *If* that was what Lux had been hinting at.

Either way, I had a mission. I needed to get to the bottom of this.

At lunch I took my tray and avoided my usual table, with Saundra's empty seat. I walked until I was standing in front of Sim Smith.

"Hi," I said. "Can I sit here?"

He was sitting alone, but I wasn't sure if it was because lunch had only just started or because he still couldn't live down his breakdown. He nodded, eying me suspiciously. I sat.

Sim was the only other person I knew who had seen someone in a mask. This was recon. I needed to gather more info before I could just start accusing Bram. "Can I ask you something?"

Sim nodded again, though he looked like he was still afraid I'd start throwing napkins at him. Felicity had unfortunately started a trend.

"What happened to you that night you saw the guy in the mask?" Sim made a sound, something between a sigh and a groan. "I believe you," I said quickly.

"You do?" He watched me like he was a bird and I was holding out a handful of crumbs. He wanted a nibble, but he also could've taken flight at any moment.

I nodded. "I know you saw someone in a mask. I was just wondering if you saw something else, something *specific* that you could tell me about?"

Sim thought for a moment, then shook his head and gave a half-hearted shrug. "Just a guy in a mask. He chased me. But I fought him off."

"You fought him?"

"Yeah. He tried to kill me but I fought back."

I deflated a little. He meant when he'd pushed open

the car door—the move that had knocked Felicity to the ground. Maybe he did like to exaggerate after all.

"I did three years of karate in elementary school," Sim continued. "I only got to orange belt but—" He curled his arm and flexed, as though there was some sort of evidence of his training in his bicep. There wasn't. "Well. It was technically three summers, not three years, but the body never forgets. I kicked that sucker hard enough to knock him on his ass."

A kick? "Where?"

"In my stepdad's car dealer—"

"Where on his body, Sim?"

"Oh. In the ribs. The right side of his ribs."

A memory came back to me, hard as a lightning bolt. "Thanks, Sim, gotta go."

I found Freddie just as lunch was coming to an end. The cafeteria was thinning out, but there were still too many people around. I led him to the first private place I could find.

The janitor's closet was filled with bottles and mops and the antiseptic stench of bleach. My head was starting to spin, but it wasn't from the toxic fumes in this airless space. Being in a closet with Freddie teleported me back to that night in the cabin. Which was exactly what I wanted to forget and what I needed to talk to him about.

"Are you okay?" Freddie asked, but didn't wait for me to answer. "Why aren't you answering your texts? We can talk—I want you to talk to me. Is that why you brought me in here?"

"Saundra didn't fall. And she didn't jump either."

The first bell rang out through the halls, triggering a speedy trample of feet beyond the closet door. But neither of us made a move to head to class.

"What are you talking about?"

"Bram pushed her." As I said the words I felt a weird sensation of relief. It had been Bram, and now that I knew that, I could handle him. Face him. Take him down.

"What?" Freddie leaned back against a metal shelf overflowing with rolls of toilet paper. Some of the rolls wobbled, threatening to spill over the edge.

There was hardly room to pace, but I needed to expel all the energy I had pent up. I clenched and unclenched my fists while trying to put my thoughts in order.

"The night after Felicity's Fear Test—the one with Sim Smith—I saw Bram trying to pick popcorn up off the floor."

"Okay," Freddie said slowly. "What about it?"

"He had to stretch to reach the popcorn and when he did, I saw him wince. Like he was in pain. He even held his side for a second."

Freddie's eyes clouded over with confusion, and it frustrated me that I couldn't get this all out fast enough. "I just talked to Sim. He said that when he saw the Masked Man at the car dealership, he fought him off by kicking him in the ribs."

The second bell rang out but we still didn't move. I let my words sit there, searching Freddie's face to see if they would sink in. I needed him to see that this wasn't just a conspiracy theory. The rib thing was the most damning piece of evidence, but it wasn't the only one— Bram had been shady since this all had started, even going so far as to point fingers at Freddie, probably to deflect suspicion from himself.

"Even Lux thinks he might've been the one to attack her."

"What?"

I nodded vigorously, pleased that this seemed to shake Freddie. "How did Bram get to Lux so quickly after the attack and not see anyone running off?"

"You're saying Bram got to that house early, put on a mask, and tried to attack his own girlfriend?"

"Yes."

"Why?"

"To mess with us. To mess with me. But it tracks, Freddie."

"I'm not sure that it does."

I didn't get it. It wasn't like they were best friends. In fact, Bram never had anything good to say about Freddie. He'd pretty much told me to stay away from him.

"Why are you defending him?"

"I'm not defending him," Freddie said. "Actually, I'm relieved you no longer think I was the one messing with Lux. But we can't just go accusing Bram of murder."

I leaned on the shelves and this time a roll of toilet paper did tumble down. I kicked it across the tiny room.

"Bram has blood on his hands." I meant it figuratively, but then I remembered that it worked literally, too. "When we all met up behind the general store, after the cabin—Bram had blood on him."

Freddie straightened, pushing himself off the shelves slowly. "I didn't see any blood."

"It was on his fingers and mask."

"Why didn't you say anything?"

"I don't know, there was a lot going on—I wasn't thinking straight." My urgency made me push off the shelves too, cutting the space between Freddie and me in half. "But there—that's evidence. That's forensic evidence."

"It might not have been Saundra's blood," Freddie

said. "And he would've had his maid wash all his clothes by now."

"But not the mask," I said quickly. "He didn't throw it away in the woods. I think he kept it."

"Yeah, but he would've cleaned it himself."

"Maybe," I said. "But there could be traces of something."

Freddie had an answer for everything I was throwing at him, but not for this. My words filled the small closet, charging the air around us with an electric energy.

"We'll have to find it," Freddie said.

My heartbeat quickened at the sound of "we." It reminded me of that night in his room when we talked about how different we were from the rest of the club. I felt like we were a team back then. I felt that way again now.

"How?" I asked.

"It'll be hard. But I think I know where to start."

43

WE HAD TO wait a week, but the perfect opportunity finally arose.

Tonight, our uniform was a white shirt and black slacks. Freddie squirmed in his, hooking his finger into the collar as if he could stretch it wider by sheer force of will. It didn't take a genius to understand why he was uncomfortable. Freddie had started going to Bram's house as the housekeeper's son, eventually graduated to being a guest, and then, ultimately, to being Bram's friend. Tonight, things had come full circle and he was relegated to being the help once again.

It was Bram's birthday, and even though he was turning seventeen and getting too old for this, his parents still threw him a party every year. Freddie's mom always catered it, and when Freddie and I offered up our free services as cater waiters, she was all too happy to accept.

Hence the two of us standing in Bram's kitchen.

Since the Mary Shelley Club wasn't exactly having any more meetings, Freddie thought the best way for us to get back into the Wilding house to hunt for evidence was to do it during Bram's birthday party, where there would be enough people present that nobody would notice if we slipped away.

Which was as far as our plan went. It wasn't the most thought out, but it was the best we could do on short notice. I had to find dirt on Bram, and being in his house was my best shot. I was grateful that Freddie was there. I could tell he hated the idea of serving Bram's friends—our classmates—but he didn't bail.

"Hey." I faced him and pinched the tips of his collar. Even after everything that had happened, I still gravitated toward him. My fingers found excuses to touch him, as they did now, smoothing down the fabric on his shoulders. "Thanks for doing this with me."

The squirming stopped beneath my touch and I could feel Freddie's chest rise and fall with a deep breath. The intensity that had nipped his features slackened enough for him to smile. "This? This is nothing."

"It's not nothing. It means a lot to me," I said, giving his shoulders one more squeeze. Bram's kitchen was all white, gleaming marble, and at the moment it was overflowing with food and activity as we rushed to prepare the hors d'oeuvres for the guests. Every inch of the sparkling surface was covered with trays, themselves covered with a variety of tasteful finger foods. Bram's mother stepped into the kitchen for a final look, and Mrs. Martinez rushed over.

I'd never seen Bram's mother before tonight. I'd known she was a model when she was younger, but she could've still been one if she wanted to. Her skin was flawless, her hair shinier than most people's half her age. Her clothing reflected the décor of the house in that it was elegant and chic, but even without all of that, I would've been able to tell that she was rich. There was something about her posture, the way she tilted her head and bent her wrist. She carried herself like a person who moved freely in a world that was wide open to her. A customer of life. Bram carried himself the same way.

"Do either of you know how to pour?" Freddie's brother, Dan, appeared before us. Freddie and I were just moonlighting as cater waiters, but this was Dan's regular job on the weekends. Tonight he was in charge of showing us the ropes, which, judging by his scowl, really seemed to piss him off.

He had the same light brown coloring as Freddie, and his features were similar too, but it was like someone had assembled him all wrong. The eyes that were soft behind Freddie's glasses and framed with long lashes were too close together on Dan's long face. The bottom lip—pillowy on Freddie—was set in a constant frown. But the biggest difference between the brothers was their hair. Freddie had fantastic hair, thick for the grabbing. Dan's hair was black and slicked back, like he'd gotten his fashion sense from the Sopranos. "Pouring drinks?" Freddie asked. "Uh, no, Dan, I've never poured a drink in my life."

"These people like their drinks poured a certain way," Dan whispered, even though Mrs. Wilding was definitely not listening. He lifted his left forearm, on which a neatly folded cloth napkin hung. He positioned the neck of a closed bottle of wine over it and demonstrated the pouring motion, his thumb jammed up the bottle's indented bottom. "Do you think you can handle that?"

Freddie and I exchanged a look. There was no way I was pouring anyone's drink like that.

"Mom, where's my brown sweater?" Bram bounded through the swinging kitchen door in slacks and a crisp white shirt. He stopped in his tracks when he saw Freddie and me. "What are you two doing here?"

"Isn't it great?" Mrs. Wilding said. She came up behind us and placed a hand on Freddie's shoulder. "Freddie's helping out Maria tonight. You kids grow up so fast. It feels like yesterday when you two were playing video games together."

"Yeah, it does." Bram fixed his gaze on me. "You work for Maria now, too?"

Mrs. Wilding turned her attention to me. Curiosity flitted over her face, but she never dropped the delighted lilt in her voice. "You know Bram?"

"I go to Manchester, too."

"Oh wow. Bram, why didn't you invite your friends to the party?"

"Freddie said he was busy," Bram said smoothly.

"Mom really needed all the help she could get tonight," Freddie said.

"Well, look, if you two get a chance to get away from the kitchen for a bit, we'd love to have you join us," Mrs. Wilding said.

"Thank you," I said. We both knew we were most definitely not to join.

Mrs. Wilding's smile was bright and magnanimous, and just like that, the awkward blurring of friends and domestics was neatly dealt with. She let go of Freddie's shoulder and turned back to her son. "No sweater tonight, sweetie. You're wearing the tie I laid out for you."

Bram gave us a cold look, then headed back upstairs with his orders as his mother swept out of the kitchen.

"Guests are starting to arrive!" Dan said. "You, go greet them and offer drinks." He carefully placed a tray of tumblers on my upturned palms and pointed toward the door.

In the grand foyer Mrs. Wilding was greeting the guests. There was a handsome couple of about Mrs. Wilding's age who obviously were not there for Bram. But they had brought their teenage son with them.

"New Girl?" Thayer asked.

Had I missed something? Were Bram and Thayer publicly friends now?

"What are you doing here?" I whispered.

He slipped off his peacoat, revealing a fitted black suit, black shirt, and black tie underneath—a color I'd never seen Thayer embrace so fully before. He handed his coat to the waiting maid like it was something he did every day. The gesture was small, inconsequential, but it reminded me that for all the time he spent slumming it with me at the theater, Thayer still belonged to this gilded world.

"Haven't you heard we're the new Obamas?" Thayer said. "We're invited to everything." I watched his parents, still busy chatting with Mrs. Wilding. So here was the state attorney father on the senatorial track. Thayer plucked one of the tumblers off my tray and downed its contents. When his glass was empty, he grabbed another.

"I'm only supposed to be serving these to the adults."

Thayer laughed, maybe for the first time since the night at the cabin. It sounded like an imitation of happiness. "You've never been to one of these parties before, have you? Just keep the drinks coming."

Bram came down the steps with a smile affixed to his face like his tie was secured to his collar: all stiff and unwanted.

It looked like it wasn't just Freddie and me wearing costumes tonight.

Bram stopped beside me and leaned in. "I don't know what you're doing here tonight, but if I could give you one suggestion: don't."

He picked up a drink and gulped it down before leaving the empty glass on my tray. If I hadn't thought he was hiding something before, I knew he was now.

44

THERE WERE WAY too many old people here for a seventeen-year-old's birthday party.

The first floor of the Wilding townhouse was made up of high-ceilinged entertaining areas. In every corner, there were sparkly people holding out similarly sparkly tumblers, waiting for me to fill them. Dan had been wrong about the whole pouring thing—people didn't care how you poured their drinks, they just wanted the booze. And I was there to provide a constant flow.

Though I'd interacted with nearly every person there, I had never felt so invisible in my entire life. The black-and-white drabness of the cater waiter uniform rendered me, essentially, part of the background. I was a moving piece of furniture. So, it was just like my regular MO at parties, only now I came with drinks.

It was a lot like a high school party where people got together to get loose and talk over each other, except here, I waded through murmurs of societal gossip, insane real estate talk, and even some business networking. All boring stuff because practically everyone at this party was an Old. I felt sort of bad for Bram. The party was extravagant, and I could only imagine what the presents would be, but there were only about twenty or so people here who were our age.

Thayer wasn't hanging out with any of them, though.

Along with my mission to get into Bram's room, I had a new side mission: to keep an eye on Thayer. I hadn't served him any more drinks but someone else must have, because he was teetering. As the night wore on, his demeanor changed: limbs getting looser, laughs coming faster. It took guts to get drunk at the same party your parents were at, but this house was big enough to keep Mr. and Mrs. Turner blissfully oblivious.

Right as I was about to offer Thayer a glass of water, something dragged my attention away. Bram's clique was there, with Lux notably absent. Trevor, Lucia, and a dickwad named Tanner were holding court by the Steinway in the living room. They were so much younger than the adult guests, but they already resembled them, playing dress-up in their suits and couture gowns—a dress rehearsal for the next generation of masters of the universe.

Freddie tried to pass by them quickly, but Tanner stepped in front of him, picked lint off Freddie's shirt, and proceeded to laugh about something. This exact moment was what Freddie had been dreading. It wasn't the uniform or that he'd never done this before; it was that no matter how well he could blend in at Manchester, in the real world, they were the ones in suits and he was the one in a uniform. Freddie's biggest fear was being realized tonight. And he was doing this just to help me.

I made a beeline for the group. "Hey, someone was asking for more canapés in the . . . I want to say music room?" Freddie didn't look like he knew what a music room was, but he gave me a grateful look before disappearing. By now Bram's circle was, mercifully, too engrossed in conversation with an older guest to even notice me.

"There's rumors, but nobody knows who he is," Lucia was saying.

"Do you think it's someone from your school?" the older man asked. Instead of a suit or dress shirt, he wore a beaten leather vest over a threadbare shirt that looked like it was out of a value bin but probably cost more than my wardrobe. If I'd had to guess, I'd have said he was one of the writers from Mr. Wilding's publishing house. "It would make for a great book." Definitely a writer.

"No way," Trevor said. "No one at Manchester is capable of that."

"They're calling him the Masked Madman at school," Lucia said.

I'd been about to keep circling but that glued me in place. I grabbed the glass out of Trevor's hand even though he hadn't asked for a refill and poured as slowly as humanly possible, my ears perked.

"I quite like the alliteration," the writer said. "The Masked Madman of Manhattan's Manchester Academy."

"Prep," Lucia corrected.

"It'd need to be changed for publication."

Lucia's eyes sparkled as she inched closer to the writer. "Can I be in it?"

The writer gave her a roguish grin and I almost threw up in my mouth.

"So this Masked Madman has been terrorizing students?" the writer asked.

"Some people think it's a prankster," Tanner said.

"It's more than just a prankster," Lucia said.

"*Some* people who were at that loser Pinsky's cabin claimed they saw a bunch of people in masks," Trevor said. "But I heard there were drugs there that night, so who even knows."

"So did that girl kill herself," the writer asked, "or do you think the Masked Madman pushed her?"

"Killed herself," Trevor said. "Saundra was probably on drugs, too."

"Saundra was not on drugs."

The whole group got quiet and turned to look at me. I'd pierced their bubble, disrupted their willful ignorance of those meant to be neither seen nor heard. I was the ottoman who'd just spoken English.

A blush rapidly rose up my cheeks, but I couldn't let them talk about Saundra that way. She had worshipped these people, and this was how they remembered her? They were discussing murder theories like they were golf stats. Saundra didn't die so a bunch of rich jerks could use her name as cocktail party fodder.

Tanner picked up the conversation a little too loudly, eager to pretend I didn't exist.

"My money's on Gunnar Lundgarten being the Masked Madman," Tanner said. "That dweeb has anger issues."

"What about Thayer Turner?" Lucia said. "He's always pulling pranks in class. Look at him now. What is he even doing?"

We all swiveled to see Thayer across the room, laughing at something so hard that he was resting his forehead on a woman's shoulder. When she moved away uncomfortably, he nearly toppled over. I left Bram's group and hurriedly cut across the room. I sidled up to Thayer, catching the tail end of his conversation.

"Such a tragedy, what happened," one of the men said. "A life cut so short."

Talk of what had happened to Saundra was catching like fire. Now that everyone was well and boozed up, the boring subjects of business and board associations had been replaced by the much more exciting world of teenage death.

"It was officially ruled an accident," Thayer said.

"I heard there were kids running around that night wearing masks," another man said. "There are rumors—"

"Officially ruled an accident by the police!" Thayer said, and laughed. "So they can't pin anything on us. The club's untouchable!"

I nearly dropped my tray, but it wobbled enough to send its lone remaining tumbler to the floor. The splintering crash silenced everyone around us.

"Oooh, butterfingers," Thayer said. A laugh bubbled out of his mouth. "Butter fingers. But her fingers. Butt fingers."

He was long gone. The broken glass would have to wait. I clamped the tray under one arm and grabbed Thayer's elbow with the other. I ignored Dan's murderous stare and didn't stop walking until I'd taken Thayer all the way up the stairs to the study. I pushed him onto the couch.

"Frisky," Thayer said.

"What the hell was that out there?"

"What? I was making conversation."

The door swung open, revealing Freddie balancing a tray in one hand. He quickly closed the door behind him. "What's going on? I saw you guys heading up here."

"Thayer's drunk and talking about the club."

"It's called a *recruitment strategy*. You're welcome."

Freddie shoved his tray at Thayer. It was half-empty but still had plenty of little canapés. "Eat those and sober up." He was already across the room, unscrewing one of the water bottles on the bar cart. He came back and handed that to Thayer, too.

The door swung open again and Dan poked his head inside. "What are you guys doing in here? People are *parched*! And I had to clean up a broken glass."

"I'll be down in a sec," I said.

Dan huffed and began muttering in Spanish to Freddie, but I could only understand a few words. Something about how he was going to dock our pay.

"Yeah, that only works when we're actually getting paid." Freddie went over to the doorway and forced his brother's head out so he could close the door. But just as soon as Dan was gone, I opened it and gestured for Freddie to follow me outside so Thayer couldn't hear.

"I'm going to stay," I whispered. "I'm worried about him."

"I'll stay with you."

"Dan might lose it if one of us isn't down there feeding the animals."

Freddie nodded. "Okay. Come find me afterward."

I watched him jog down the stairs. But when I returned, Thayer wasn't on the couch. A chill blew through the room and I saw that the balcony door was open. Fear seized me as my mind went to the worst place, reeling with visions of Thayer splayed out on the pavement. I rushed to the balcony.

Thayer was standing there, looking out at the street.

When he turned around, I realized he wasn't as drunk as I'd thought. Or maybe he'd sobered up quickly, because the looseness and laughter were gone. His features had settled in straight, somber lines. I remembered the last time I'd stood there with the rest of the club, trying to catch my breath from laughing so hard at his antics on the street. Now I caught my breath with relief.

I approached Thayer slowly and it made his eyebrows knit together. "Why are you acting like I'm about to jump?" he asked.

Because you spent the night getting drunk and blabbing

our secrets and you haven't been the same since the night at the cabin and I'm worried about you. But I didn't say any of those things. "Just, please don't stand so close to the edge."

But he didn't budge. In fact, he bent at the waist, hanging over the railing and letting his arms dangle in the air. "It's one story high, Rachel."

I was beside him now and peeked over the balcony myself. He was right; we were only on the second floor. If he did go over, he'd barely break an arm, let alone his neck. I squeezed my eyes shut, trying to avoid thoughts of Saundra. The way her eyes had stared as she lay on the bed of shattered glass.

I snapped my eyes open to get the picture out of my head. As I looked at Thayer swaying slightly, something occurred to me. "You called me Rachel."

Thayer had no response. No wisecrack. No smile. He just continued to look out, eyes roving the buildings across the street, the park on the left, the twinkling traffic on the right, but seeing nothing. All I wanted was for him to call me New Girl again.

"Do you know what ended up happening to the first Mary Shelley Club?" he asked. "I mean, the originals, the ones at the villa in Switzerland."

I shook my head.

"Lord Byron made it to thirty-six. He died fighting a war for Greece. He did better than Percy Shelley, though. He drowned before he even turned thirty. At least they both made it farther than Polidori—who was obviously in love with Byron, by the way. He wrote the seminal vampire book way before Stoker did. He was talented. But he killed himself at twenty-five. Mary made it pretty far. She died in her fifties. But one person from their circle survived them all, living way into her eighties. She kept to herself. Never married. Took jobs as a caretaker and teacher. She was also the only one among them without a creative bone in her body. I doubt she even participated in the game that night."

"Claire Clairmont." Mary's stepsister; lover to Lord Byron and mother of his daughter; and somewhat in love with Mary's husband, Percy, too. She played a vital role in Mary's life. But when I'd first read up on her, she was memorable only because she coincidently shared a last name with my best friend. Saundra.

"The Final Girl," Thayer said. He placed his hand on the stone balcony and I noticed that his fingernails were pale purple. It brought me back to the present, to this freezing balcony and the party blazing underneath us.

"Why are you telling me this?"

He shrugged. "Just thinking of our group. Which of us is gonna go first. When. How."

"Thayer."

"The police are calling it 'death by misadventure,'" he said.

"People say they saw someone with a mask up there."

Thayer shot me an unreadable look. "Something was going on with Saundra that night—something was off. I'm going to find out what."

"Thayer, that's what I'm trying to do, too," I said eagerly. "We can help each other." But when I took a step toward him he shrank away from my touch.

"I'm not some fragile—" he began. "It's normal, okay? When someone you know dies it's normal to think about this stuff."

"I know."

"I'm taking this seriously, all right?"

"I am, too."

"Look at where we are." He spread out his arms, gesturing at both the street and the party. "I'm in a suit at a stupid party like a girl didn't just *die*. We're monsters."

Thayer shook his head, roughly sweeping a hand over his short hair like he wanted to tear it off his scalp. "I shouldn't be here right now. And neither should you."

"I'm only here to check on Bram. I think he had something to do with all of this."

Thayer looked like he was on the verge of laughing at something that wasn't funny. "Good luck with that."

He stepped past me, back into the study, and didn't stop until he was out the door.

It was now or never. I had to get to Bram's room and find evidence, a clue, *something* that would confirm my suspicions about him. But when I left the study, someone was standing in my path.

"What are you doing here?" Bram asked.

"Nothing. I was just leaving."

"No, stay." His tone was less than welcoming, but then he continued. "Really. You wanted to step into my world tonight. You haven't seen anything until you've been to the after-party."

It felt more like a threat than an invitation. But there was no way I was going to turn it down.

45

IT WAS WEIRD, how smoothly the transition went. Bram's adult-approved birthday party finished at a respectable and firm eleven P.M. People left as if on a schedule, ushered out gently by smiling members of the waitstaff. But the young people lingered. All of the kids from the popular tables at school said goodbye to their parents and began slinking away upstairs, faint laughter trailing them like rising champagne bubbles.

"Bram's parents are leaving, too?" I asked Freddie. He and I were in the foyer, handing back coats to the last remaining guests and watching Mr. and Mrs. Wilding leave with Millie in tow.

"His parents aren't going to stick around for the after-party." Freddie said it like it should've been obvious, which, yes. But Bram's own parents having to leave their own house?

"Why are rich people so weird?"

Freddie shrugged. "Letting Bram have his little after-party is their tradition. They let them go wild and act out, but the Wildings are only going two blocks away, to Bram's grandparents' house. They're letting Bram have fun on a very tight leash."

"So Bram's and everyone else's parents are okay with a houseful of teenagers drinking?"

"It's like a warped version of the parents who let their kids drink at home instead of drinking outside the home. Here, the party is confined to the study," Freddie said. "And it's a lot more than just drinking."

Well, that sounded ominous. "Have you been to his after-party?"

"Once. A long time ago. It was ridiculous."

Vague. Guess I was just going to have to see it for myself. "Can't wait."

"What?"

"Bram invited me." The surprise on Freddie's face rubbed me the wrong way. Was it that hard to believe that Bram could invite me to his after-party? Or maybe Freddie suspected, as I did, that Bram's invitation wasn't extended in the spirit of friendship.

"Look, I came here to find something on Bram," I continued. "If he's going to be acting drunk and stupid at this party, then his guard will be down and I'll have a better shot at nailing him."

Freddie's eyebrows dropped and I realized I probably could've chosen a better phrase. "Bram's after-party is not your scene," Freddie said. "Trust me, Rachel."

I wasn't there to party. I was there for Saundra. And I was getting really tired of boys telling me which other boys I should or should not be hanging out with.

"I'm going," I said.

This time, Freddie didn't try to argue.

The Mary Shelley Club's regular meeting space had been transformed. The study, which usually felt so cozy with its dark walls and leather surfaces, felt stuffy now, crammed with bodies and booming music, the air oppressively hazy with a mix of vape and cigar smoke. The kids who I only knew as background actors at the central cafeteria tables wafted through the room, the girls' perfectly contoured faces shiny with highlighter and the glow of overheated abandon, the boys' mouths cracked open too wide, showing too many gleaming white teeth. When I saw them every day, under the fluorescence of school light bulbs, of course I noticed the glimmer of privilege. But now it was like they were on fire.

The after-party was where all the tensions of the night's earlier stuffy conversations and constricting blazers and ties seemed to boil over. Here kids foamed at the mouth like rabid drunkards, bubbly liquids dribbling down chins and Adam's apples, seeping into the buttoned crevices of the chesterfield sofa I'd sat on every movie night. It obviously wasn't just drinks, though. Little baggies and vials were passed around like party favors, and there was no way Bram's parents could've been okay with this. Or maybe they were. I realized that I really didn't know how Bram's world worked.

Everyone laughed, wild and shrill like hyenas. It was maniacal, almost, and definitely powered by something other than pure delight. They tossed handfuls of canapés at each other—the same ones Mrs. Martinez had so painstakingly constructed and that Freddie had carefully laid out in neat rows on slate trays. And the only thing I could think about was how someone was going to have to clean this all up. A faceless servant that none of these people would have to think about or see.

They drank money. Not literally, but a few them huddled together to have a chugging contest with a Dalmore 64. I only knew what it was called because people would point it out at every opportunity, an edge of crazy awe in their voices. I finally broke my loner streak and asked the person beside me what a Dalmore 64 was. The girl only looked at me, standing there in my waiter uniform, like I was an idiot, and said, "A one-hundred-and-sixty-thousand-dollar bottle of whiskey."

I felt simultaneously sick and thirsty.

"More drinks now!" a boy shouted in my ear. This boy, TJ Epps, was in art class with me. The only things he drew, painted, or sculpted were boobs.

"I'll give you one hundred dollars if you go get me a drink right now." He choked on his own chuckle. "Okay, five hundred dollars." He didn't even give me the opportunity to turn him down or accept. A part of me hated myself for wanting to skip to it and fetch him a bottle. "Okay, fine," he continued. "I'll give you one thousand dollars if you get me a drink and let me lick it off your—"

I didn't let him finish, just ground my heel into his foot and moved to another corner of the party, where it was only a matter of time before someone else propositioned me for a drink.

Despite all the monsters I'd seen in horror movies, nothing compared to this. Freddie had been right. This was ridiculous. I didn't belong here. I probably should have left, but I was transfixed. It felt like I was watching a movie. It felt like *The Purge*.

Was Bram as disgusted by all of this as I was? He couldn't be—this was his own party. These were his rules. He was easy enough to spot—whichever corner of the party he visited livened up. People clinked their glasses against his, boys pounded him on the back, girls squeaked and got on their tippy-toes to drunkenly wrap their arms around his neck.

The tie Bram's mother had laid out for him was no longer around his neck. His top two buttons were undone, collar up, shirttails out. His hair stood up in clumps and his cheeks were beet red. Like a gentleman, he sauntered over to the girls who had cigars and offered to light them with his golden Zippo. He chatted, flirted, threw back his head and laughed with everyone, pulling them in for hugs.

But it was just another mask.

No one else could see it because this was the only Bram they knew, but it was so clear to me. The Bram that I'd gotten to know would rather listen than talk. He was a neat freak who picked up every last piece of popcorn that fell on this floor. Even now, when he saw a boy drunkenly reaching for a girl, Bram would distract him and pull him into his orbit without the guy even knowing that Bram had interfered. And when he thought no one was looking, Bram would glance at his wristwatch. I'd seen him do that before. It always meant he wanted to leave.

But apparently not before the night's main event got underway.

There was a couple making out on the big desk in front of the balcony doors, but Bram swept them off in one clean motion, which was met with a chorus of laughter, even from the two girls he'd just ousted. He climbed on top of the desk.

"I want to express my deepest thanks." Bram placed his hand over his heart and bowed his head. "It is an honor to spend my birthday with my closest friends. Even if you are all a bunch of assholes."

The truest thing he'd ever said. And while he'd just insulted his "closest friends," they ate it up. This was Charismatic Bram. Charming, Top Dog Bram. King of Manchester Bram. He radiated it. And it was, admittedly, difficult not to buy into it.

"Seventeen," he continued. "Soon we'll officially be adults." A mix of *boo*s and *woo*s. "And we'll have *responsibilities* and *expectations* and the weight of the *entire fucking world on our shoulders*. Who am I kidding—we already have all that. So live it up tonight!" Cheers. "Let's get off our fucking faces!" More cheers. "And give me my fucking birthday presents or get the fuck out!"

Bram hopped off and sat in his throne-like

armchair, having practically been carried there by the cheers. Around me everyone held their glasses up high and chanted one word over and over.

"Presents! Presents! Presents!"

Had Bram actually been serious? Were people going to line up and give him big gift-wrapped boxes? Was this another party ritual?

"All right, people, who's up first?" Trevor Driggs said. His eyes roamed the room, searching for volunteers. Plenty of people squealed or raised their hands, but then someone pointed at me and shouted, "The waitress!"

"The waitress!" Trevor said excitedly, coming over to clap a hand over my shoulder. This would be the third time we'd ever talked face-to-face and he still didn't have any idea who I was.

"I didn't bring anything," I began, but somehow I ended up standing in front of Bram in his chair. This was stupid. But I could feel everyone's gazes burning holes into me, including Bram's. I refused to let them see me sweat.

I patted down my clothes. All I had on me were my keys, my phone, and a MetroCard. I took out my keys, attached to my favorite key chain. It was a red key fob for Room 237 at the Overlook Hotel. I worked the keys off the ring and handed the keychain to Bram. "Happy birthday."

Bram looked it over, and when our eyes met, I thought he was going to speak, but the only noise came from something shattering in the back of the room. I flinched. Bram didn't.

Trevor swooped in and snatched the key fob out of Bram's hand. "What the fuck is this?" He pinched it between his fingers. "Why do you think Bram would want this?"

Because Bram loved Stanley Kubrick. And he knew every word of *The Shining*. And he'd once gotten into an argument with Felicity about it, saying it was one of the only movies that improved upon the book. And he actually did killer Jack Nicholson *and* Shelley Duvall impressions.

But Trevor didn't know any of that. "Wait." He squinted. "Did the waitress just give Bram the key to her hotel room? Holy shit!"

Trevor laughed and threw the key fob back at Bram and the room rang out in whistles and hollers. I slunk back, trying to get lost in the crowd to hide my burning face, and the party continued as it had before.

Bram remained in his seat, receiving his gifts. I watched as Sebastian Santamaria pulled Bram's chin down and plunked a yellow tablet on his tongue. Seth

Gebahard shoved a wad of hundred-dollar bills into Bram's hands. Lucia Trujillo and Emily Vilford came up to Bram as a package deal and began to make out in front of him.

Yeah, I'd definitely given Bram the wrong gift. It was time for me to get out of here.

"Where do you think you're going?" A boy stepped in front of me, Pete Something or Other. I took a step to the side and he did the same, blocking me. He was slow—definitely high on something—and he had his shirt off. "You're the only girl in here not wearing a dress, you know that?"

"As riveting as this conversation is, I'm leaving, so if you could—"

"A challenge," Pete said. "But we can work around it." He cupped my breast. I reacted without thinking. Reckless. I grabbed his hand and bent it back and I wasn't going to stop until I heard a snap.

Pete was on his knees in an instant, then on his stomach as I held his arm behind his back while he screamed. "Stop! Stop! Get off me!" he yelled.

His words shook me from my blind rage, and the realization of what I was doing—what I had been about to do—made me stumble back. Three girls in gowns who had watched the entire thing unfold before them put their cigars in their mouths long enough to nod their heads approvingly and golf-clap in my direction.

"I'm—I'm sorry," I stammered. "But you shouldn't have—"

"You nearly broke my arm!" Pete yelled. Every feature on his face was contorted, his eyes wide, his teeth bared. He was a savage animal about to bite, his hand reaching for my ankle.

"Are you fighting a girl?" Trevor Driggs said gleefully, suddenly hovering over us. Pete laughed too, an ugly sound. Then he scrambled to his feet and lunged for me.

"Hey!" Suddenly Bram was there, and he tackled Pete back to the floor. Trevor kept laughing, practically wheezing, even as Bram and Pete wrestled at his feet. Pete pushed Bram into the bookshelves so hard that a couple of books fell onto their heads. And all around me people were chanting for the fight to keep escalating like it was a birthday song.

I watched the fight, watched the people all around me, and my stomach turned. Their stupid little party—so elitist and exclusive—was a nightmarescape of base impulses and worst instincts. I didn't want to be a part of their rituals and games. I was over it.

I was over all rituals and games. Mary Shelley Club included.

I left the study. I had been temporarily blinded by the glitz, but now my focus was clear. I had a mission. Instead of going downstairs and out the front door, I headed for the third floor. Bram's bedroom was there, and I was determined to find what I had come for.

46

BRAM'S BEDROOM DIDN'T look like a typical teen boy's. The walls were a deep hunter green, illuminated with warm light from sconces and library lamps. The walnut furniture looked straight out of a Restoration Hardware catalog, topped with graceful touches that seemed more to a designer's liking than to Bram's. The carpet practically looked freshly mowed. Everything was tidy and not a single thing was out of place, like a cleaning lady lived in the closet.

But there was something that screamed Bram. A collection of gigantic horror movie posters from the 1920s and '30s, all professionally framed, lining the walls. The Wolf Man, Dracula, and of course Frankenstein stared back at me menacingly from radioactive-green backgrounds, their names big and sharp-edged. I stopped to admire them, but only briefly. I had work to do.

My first stop was the closet. Movies and TV told me that was where people generally hid their secrets. The rest of Bram's bedroom might have been pristine, but his closet proved he was a typical red-blooded teen. It spilled over with clothing and sports equipment, his lacrosse stick thingy nearly hitting me in the face before I dodged it. There were three boxes on the top shelf. Perfectly sized to hide a mask. I brought down the first box. It was full of cables and old electronics. The second box had an assortment of caps and hats that I'd never seen him wear. The third box was the messiest, with notebooks and loose pieces of paper. I rummaged through it all, but still no mask.

I searched the rest of the room, peeking under the bed (nothing) and inside his desk (papers and pens). All that was left was Bram's laptop, placed at the center of his desk as if waiting for me. It wasn't the mask, but maybe there'd be something on there that I could use. But when I tickled the keyboard, the screen came to life, requiring a password.

In desperation, I typed out anything that came to mind. "Password" didn't work. Neither did "123abc." I typed in today's date—his birthday—but nothing. "Lux" didn't work either. No, Bram would pick something personal to him. A favorite movie, maybe. But "FunnyGames" was a bust. I glanced around the room, searching for a clue, muttering his name under my breath like an incantation. What did Bram like? What did Bram hold more dear than anything else?

My eyes caught on the vintage *Dracula* poster and it hit me. He cared mostly about himself. My fingers punched in *Stoker*. And just like that I had access.

His documents folder. I remembered how Bram had buried his movie collection seven folders deep. Maybe he buried other things. I searched the names of the files, looking for something that was innocuous yet telling. It didn't take me long to find a folder named *MSC*.

Mary Shelley Club.

It had to be. Inside the folder was another folder, labeled *Chaps*.

There was a noise in the hall; someone was coming. I closed the file and quickly ducked into the closet. Through the small crack, I watched Bram walk into the room and nearly gasped. There was blood spilling from his eyebrow, down his cheek, his jaw, onto his clothes. His features were pained, angry, and he tore off his shirt, bunching it up in his hands to wipe his face.

I watched as he stood there, holding his bloody shirt, breathing hard enough to make his bare chest heave. I wanted so badly to know what he was thinking. Was he upset that he'd been in a fight? Was he upset by his own party?

For the longest time I'd wanted to see Bram just like this. I'd seen glimpses of him before, as the caring older brother, the popular jock, the horror geek, the messed-up boyfriend, but I'd always wondered who he was when he was alone. Was he a killer?

I waited for him to show himself. To let out a guttural scream and knock over all his bookshelves and act out in a violent rage. But all he did was sink onto the edge of his bed and slump forward, his head bent. He emptied his pants pockets, tossing cash and pills on the bed behind him, until he was left holding my key fob.

He looked at it for a long minute, and he might have kept looking for even longer, but I accidentally nudged the closet door. I froze, but Bram's head snapped up. His eyes zeroed in on the crack in the doorframe, and if he thought there was a monster in here, he wasn't afraid. He stood and approached me, but I swung the door open before he could get to it.

He didn't seem all that surprised to see me, but maybe he was keeping his emotions in check.

"I should be mad that you're in here."

Yeah, I thought. *You just found me snooping in your room. Get mad. Show me who you really are.* But all he did was go to one of his dressers and pull out a plain white T-shirt, slipping it over his head.

"But I get it," Bram continued. "Your friend just

died. You're distraught. You want answers. What I don't understand is why you're so attached to the idea that I'm the bad guy."

Was he serious? From the beginning Bram had been cold to me. He had never wanted me in the club—he'd told me as much. Saundra had ended up dead in *his* Fear Test. Bram could say he wasn't a bad guy, but he'd barely shown me a sliver of good.

"The Upper Lower School trip."

"What?"

"Fifth grade. You went to the Empire State Building. Saundra was scared, but you calmed her down. You held her hand until it was time to leave."

Bram looked at me blankly. "Saundra was afraid of heights," I said. I could feel my voice starting to quiver, but I had to go on. "The only way she ever would have gotten on that roof was if you were there with her."

"What are you talking about?"

I swiped at a tear. "She told me that herself. Don't you even remember?"

"Rachel." Bram said my name like he felt sorry for me.

"Freddie was with me when Saundra died," I said. "But I have no idea where you were or what you were doing. I'm trying to find out what happened. That's why

I'm at your party, that's why I'm in your room—I need to know."

It was my voice that betrayed me. The sound of it ragged, desperate. It was all I could do not to break down in front of this boy who didn't care about anything or anyone except himself. And the worst part was that his eyes wouldn't meet mine. Even in this moment, when I felt scraped bare.

"Look at me, Bram." To my surprise my voice didn't sound angry. It sounded tired. "Why don't you ever look at me?"

Bram did look at me then. And for the first time, the mask that he'd worn since the moment I'd met him fell away and I glimpsed something real in him. The look in his eyes was different. Softer, somehow. For once, he didn't look like he hated me. He actually looked like someone capable of empathy. He walked over to his bed and lifted the corner of the mattress. Underneath was the mask. He came back to me. "Is this what you came here for?"

I didn't need to fight him for it; he placed it in my hands. It was wiped clean, but part of the fabric, where it had touched the monster's rubber forehead, was stained dark. Bram saw the spot that I was fixated on.

"Blood," he said. "But it's not Saundra's. It's mine."

He pushed back the hair that swooshed over his forehead, revealing a cut close to his hairline. It wasn't like the fresh cut in his eyebrow. This one was healed but was still tinged with pink. "Saundra smashed a bookend over my head. Knocked me out cold. I deserved it."

I stepped closer, my fingers reaching to touch this damage that Saundra had done. It was so recent, indelible; it was like she was still there. I dropped my hand when I realized what I was doing, shifting my gaze from the scar to his eyes. "What are you saying?"

"I didn't come to until she'd already fallen," Bram said. "I'm truly sorry for what happened to her, Rachel. But it wasn't me."

I couldn't accept that. New tears sprang to my eyes, unbidden. Saundra was dead and it was somebody's fault. "It was you."

"No."

"Then why were you hurt the night after Felicity's Fear Test?"

"What?"

"I saw you grab your ribs and wince. Sim told me he kicked the masked guy in the ribs. So why were you hurt that night?" I made sure to keep my voice steady and calm, clear as a bell.

"I don't know what you're talking about."

He was lying. I could hear it in his voice, see it in his

eyes. All of him suddenly, subtly, dimmed. And he knew I could tell, because he came closer, like he needed to contain the situation, contain me.

"You're a liar," I said.

"Rachel, don't believe me about anything else, fine, but believe me about Saundra. Whatever you think of me, you know I didn't do anything to her."

I shook my head. "I don't know that."

"You do know that. Deep down you know it. You want me to be the bad guy because it means you can ignore the truth."

I shook my head, shaking the tears loose from my eyes. It had to be Bram. All signs pointed to him—*it had to be*. Putting all the blame on Bram was easy, because it meant that I didn't have to take any of it for myself. But more than that, it meant I didn't have to acknowledge the truth locked away in a dark corner of my mind. The truth about who the Masked Man really was.

I was taking bigger and bigger gulps of air, but I still felt like I was suffocating. Bram was so close I could feel the heat from beneath his fresh shirt, could smell the infuriatingly intoxicating scent of pine and lime in his hair. I realized suddenly that his arms were around me, and my arms were around him, too. I didn't know why we were hugging—*if* we were hugging. It felt more like he was holding me up.

Without my realizing it, his finger was under my chin, gentle as it tilted my face up. "You know the truth, Rachel. You've known all along."

He was so close that the line between hate and heat blurred. His touch on my skin felt electric. The air felt combustible.

I blinked. Stepped back. Immediately, whatever spell we'd unwittingly found ourselves under broke. I walked out of the room and didn't stop until I'd left the party. I didn't look back.

47

I COULDN'T STOP thinking about what Bram had said.

Deep down you know it.

Ever since Sim had said he'd seen a masked man, I'd wondered, *What if?* And when he'd appeared at the Halloween party, I convinced myself it was just my imagination, but the logical part of my brain still wondered: *What if?* And since Lux had said she'd seen him, the words pounded in my head like a mantra.

What if? What if? What if?

And now with Saundra, it seemed so obvious.

It was him.

The second person from my home invasion. Because Matthew Marshall hadn't worked alone. There had been two people wearing masks that night, and while one of them stayed, one of them got away.

What if the person who'd fled from my house that night was back?

What if he was infiltrating the Mary Shelley Club's Fear Tests, trying to send a message?

What if he was after me?

So what does a person do when they're fairly convinced there is a masked killer out to get them? They go back to high school Monday morning.

It wasn't like I could stay home—it was the day of Saundra's memorial, and I'd promised AssHead I'd say a few words. I sat in the auditorium doing a fairly good impression of a normal girl whose life wasn't being threatened by a masked madman. I held a sheet of loose-leaf paper, my speech for Saundra. The scribbled handwriting was nearly illegible, even for me. The glee club was onstage finishing some song about grace. Behind them hung a sheet obscuring some big surprise AssHead was going to tell us about. I could only assume it was a giant plaque honoring Saundra's memory. I wondered whether Saundra would've loved having her name permanently engraved on a shiny gold surface or if she would've hated being associated with this school forever. I hated myself for not knowing for sure.

When the glee club was done, AssHead walked on the stage to usher them off. He led us all in a round of applause. I joined in too late and stopped too late too, only lowering my hands when AssHead looked at me pointedly.

"And now, a word from one of Saundra's friends," AssHead said. "Rachel Chavez."

I stood and climbed the three short steps to the stage, taking my place behind the podium. I let the seconds pass as I smoothed my page. My hands were shaking and my skin was starting to itch under my collar. The lights seemed extra bright, like they could probably wash me away.

I suddenly hated AssHead and everyone in this auditorium for making me do this. But then I found my mom in the crowd. She was standing in the back with the rest of the teachers. She was already crying and I hadn't even started yet. And then I found Freddie. He nodded encouragingly when our eyes locked.

My skin felt less itchy. The lights no longer seemed that bright. I looked down at my paper and began to read.

"When I knew that I'd be up here to talk about Saundra, I tried to think about what to say to honor her. Because she'd want something great. She deserves that. I tried to think of all the best things about her. Like that she was generous. She was happy to help anyone, in any way she could. And she was bold. She could introduce herself to people like it wasn't the hardest thing in the world to do. And she hated scary movies." My voice caught on a sad, wet laugh, and for a moment I looked up from my paper. There was a somber smile on Freddie's lips.

"But in the end, the reason I loved her most is selfish. I loved Saundra because she was my friend." I took a deep breath, heard it crackle over the microphone. I read the next line silently to myself before saying it out loud, the ink going blurry behind my tears. "She was my friend when no one else wanted to be. And she didn't deserve what happened to her."

I tried to find the club members in the crowd. Felicity was looking up at the ceiling lights, bored. Thayer didn't seem to be listening either, slumped in his chair, listless as a corpse. Bram watched me, though, his eyes locked with mine. There was a little bit more left to my speech but I couldn't really see it through my tears. I decided that Saundra wouldn't want me to be a big, sloppy mess up there. "So yeah. To Saundra."

The Manchester student body clapped and Ass-Head came to join me at the podium. I was about to head back to my seat but he stopped me.

"Would you help me unveil this?" he said, gesturing to the big white sheet behind us.

I went to stand on one side of it while he stood at the other.

"What happened to Saundra Clairmont was a

tragedy," AssHead boomed into the microphone at the podium. "She was beloved by all, a friend to all, and she certainly will be missed by all. But she will not be forgotten. Behind me is something that will be mounted in the lunchroom. A plaque that won't only honor Saundra, but will also be honoring the beneficiaries of the Saundra Clairmont Fund, which her parents have generously set up. Students who receive the scholarship will have their names permanently added to the plaque."

AssHead tugged on his side of the sheet and I tugged down on mine. The revelation was met with gasps. I started clapping because it seemed like the thing to do, but the gasps just grew louder and turned into shocked murmurs and whispers.

I twisted to look at the plaque properly. I stopped clapping.

The plaque was covered in red spray paint. I had to step back to read what the paint spelled out.

Freddie Martinez

Felicity Chu

Thayer Turner

Bram Wilding

Then I saw my own name, police-siren red.

AssHead was saying something into the microphone, but his voice fizzled in my ears, words losing all meaning and fusing into incomprehensible static. I searched for the club members. We looked at each other, uncomprehending.

The thing was, everyone else in the auditorium was looking at us, too.

48

THE FIVE OF us were crammed into AssHead's office, trying to make ourselves smaller under his glare. It was weird, standing shoulder to shoulder after taking so much care to not be seen together. But there was no separating us now. We had been named.

"What is the meaning of this?" AssHead asked.

Of course none of us said anything. We didn't know what to say.

"Somebody had better start talking," AssHead said. "Why were all of your names spray-painted on the plaque?"

Because we're part of a secret society responsible for Saundra's death. I wondered which of us would talk. But we all remained silent, staring at our shoes with sudden interest. Anyway, AssHead had asked the wrong question. He should've asked *who* had written all of our names on the plaque. But if I told him it was the Masked Man, he might have given me detention for being a smartass.

"One of you'd better—"

"I don't know," Felicity said. "I don't have anything to do with these people."

I had to give it to her—she was good at lying. She actually looked like she was disgusted to be associated with us, and appalled to even be called in here. Maybe because she didn't need to act very hard.

"Who vandalized the plaque?"

"I. Don't. Know," Felicity said again.

"I'm not looking for attitude, young lady. You were all on that list and there must be a reason. Miss Chavez?"

My head snapped up, my body suddenly alive with nerves.

"I told you the last time you were in my office that I didn't want to hear anything more about you and pranks."

I didn't know what to say. How could I begin to explain this? My head spun with all the various ways I was about to blow it for myself and the rest of the club, just by merely hesitating right now. But Freddie saved me.

"Mr. Braulio," he said, "clearly, none of us knows what this is about. And none of us would disrespect Saundra's memory like this. I mean, why would any of us put our names up there? It's like asking to get kicked out of school."

"So if you don't know anything about this, then you don't know anything about a game either, I take it?" AssHead searched each of our faces, and if there was ever a good moment to develop a poker face, it was then.

How had he known about the game?

He picked up a piece of notebook paper and held it up. "This was taped to the back of the plaque," AssHead said, and then he read it: "*Finish the game.*" Any idea what that could mean?"

He put the paper down on his desk again. I didn't dare look at anyone else and give anything away, but I could feel a wave of panic pumping through us, a collective heart about to burst in the silence that followed.

"I will find out why you were all listed on Saundra's plaque, and I will find out what this game is," AssHead said.

We continued to stand there like we didn't know each other. But as I glanced at the others, I knew the club well enough to know that they were scared. So was I.

Bram sent out a group text after school. He was holding a meeting in his study. There had been a time when I couldn't wait to go to the Wilding study, would drop everything, lie to my Mom and Saundra, just to be there. Now I dreaded it.

But we needed to figure out what the hell was going on.

"Someone is after us." Thayer stood in the center of the room. The harsh light of day came through the glass terrace doors and washed Thayer in pale tones. "Someone is after us and they're trying to expose us."

"You sound paranoid," Felicity said.

"Our names are spray-painted on a golden fucking plaque, Felicity!" Thayer yelled.

"Calm down," Freddie said.

"Oh, calm down?" Thayer said. "Yeah, oh, uh, how about *fuck you!*"

"Okay," Freddie said, standing. He didn't seem upset or defensive. Bram was the natural leader of this group, but Freddie was the one who always stayed levelheaded whenever shit went down. He did the same now.

"We can't point fingers at each other," Freddie said. "We're supposed to be a team. Now, someone put us on a list, which means that someone is after us."

Bram spoke up. "What we need to do is stop playing."

Felicity shot him an appalled look. "Listen to yourself. The game isn't over until we've all played."

"This has gone on long enough," Bram said.

"You read the note," Felicity said. "We need to finish the game."

"We need to figure out who wrote that note," Freddie said.

I thought again of what Bram had told me: *You know the truth, Rachel. You've known all along.*

"I know who it is."

The club turned to look at me, watching me expectantly.

"In my initiation, when I told you guys what happened when I was attacked. I left something out. I told you there was one person there. Matthew Marshall. But there was someone else. Another person in a mask."

Their faces colored with varying degrees of shock, except for Bram, who knew all of this already. Felicity leaned forward, eyes sharp. "That's quite the omission."

"Who was he?" Freddie asked. If he was hurt that I hadn't shared this with him, he didn't show it.

"I don't know. He ran off. He never came forward after what happened to Matthew. The police had no leads." I swallowed and picked at the cuticle of my left thumb. I only looked up again after a few moments passed, afraid of what the club's reaction would be. "What if he's back?"

"Why would he . . . ?" Thayer started.

425

"To get back at me," I said. "Revenge for killing his friend?"

"So let me get this straight," Felicity said. "Some guy from your past is tormenting us by threatening to further expose our whole deal unless we finish the contest where he'll probably kill us?"

When Felicity said it, it sounded ridiculous, but, "Yeah." I stood up. I couldn't just keep sitting there, doing nothing. "You don't have to worry. It's me he wants."

"So what now?" Thayer asked.

"We have to finish the game," I said. I never thought Felicity and I would agree on something so preposterous, but she was right. If I wanted to put an end to this, we would have to put an end to the game.

"Wait, hold up." Freddie stood up, too. "We don't know that it's this guy you're talking about."

"Who else would toy with us like this?" I asked.

"Whoever it is, we can't just follow his commands," Freddie said. "He wants to finish the game so he can lure us into a trap."

"No," I said. "We're going to be the ones to lure *him*."

I was making the plan up on the fly, but as soon as I said it, I knew it was the only way to make this stop.

"Look, if this guy followed me here, then he's determined," I reasoned. "And if he showed up at all the other Fear Tests, then he's going to show up at the final Fear Test, too."

They watched me, their collective stares *Children of the Corn*-icy. I felt awful for bringing them into my nightmare, but there was nothing I could do about it now. Except get them on board. "Now that we know he'll be there, we can level the playing field," I said. "We can smoke him out. Put an end to this."

I didn't yet know what that meant, or what I'd be willing to do for us to come out on top. All I knew was that the only way out of this fucked-up game was through it.

I had to face the monster.

That night, I dreamed we were in the kitchen. Again. Our designated battleground. Like always, the tile floor was cool under my head. I couldn't see anything behind his mask, no eyes behind the eyeholes. He was calm. Ready. But this time so was I.

This time, I was the one holding the knife.

I plunged it into him.

49

THE NIGHT CALLED for fear. It was close to two in the morning and quiet on the Upper West Side. Well, quieter than usual for New York. The only people still outside, lurking in the streets, were looking either for fun or for trouble. So here I was. I was playing a game, but it'd stopped being fun a long time ago.

I walked alongside the waist-high stone barrier that surrounded Central Park. It was snowing and the wisps of white filled the air, like the sky was a down pillow slashed through the middle. Its beauty did not escape me. And to think that if I'd been in bed right then, I'd have missed it. My mom hadn't caught me all the other times I'd snuck out, and tonight had been no different. Sneaking into Central Park was another story. I'd never been to the park this late, but I knew it'd been closed for an hour. I'd actually googled it. Would there be guards at the entrances? Gates closed? Would they cart me off to jail if they caught me?

I should've been scared because I was walking into the belly of the beast. The Masked Figure was out to get us—*me*—and I was heading straight for him. But I felt calmer than I had in a year. This time I wasn't going to let him hide in the shadows. I was ready to confront him, find out who he was. Stop him.

There was a lone figure standing like a statue at the Eighty-First Street park entrance, his shoulders and head frosted with snow. A pit of dread formed in my stomach and grew bigger and bigger as I drew closer, until finally, the shadowed features of his face assembled into someone I recognized.

"Thayer?"

He blinked like I'd startled him, even though he'd been watching me approach. "Hey," he said.

"You want to go in together?"

"Yeah." He stuffed his fists into the pockets of his thick Canada Goose jacket. "Let's get this over with."

It turned out there were no guards blocking our way, none of those blue wooden NYPD sawhorses to weave around. We walked through the open entrance and into Central Park like we were taking a stroll at noon.

Usually grass and a network of trails and pathways

could be seen, but all of it lay buried under an expanse of white. Only the lamps, glowing like little moons in the night, demarcated the pathways.

Freddie's instructions for his Fear Test had been simple: Meet at the Delacorte Theater.

It was an open-air amphitheater that overlooked the stony turrets of Belvedere Castle. That section of the park was ensconced in trees and follies and reservoirs like it was straight out of a Grimms' fairy tale.

I'd been there only once before, two summers earlier, when Mom had gotten us tickets for Shakespeare in the Park and we drove in from Long Island. Even then, with the lamps on, park maps, and packs of people all there to see the show, Mom and I had still gotten lost, meandering through the lawns and winding roads. Now I started typing into Google Maps, but my hands must've been numb from the cold, because my phone slipped out of my grasp and made an indelicate belly flop into the snow. I picked up the phone and tried to wipe it down, but Thayer was already on the move and I couldn't lose him. I pocketed the phone and caught up.

The park was so different at night. When it gleamed in daylight, Central Park was the city's beating heart. There could've been a million people inside, but it always felt like it could expand endlessly to make room for more. But at two in the morning, there were no joggers or cyclists. No park attendants in their green golf carts. No street vendors selling ice cream and over-priced bottles of water. At nighttime, the city's beating heart was a black hole.

"Is Freddie here yet?" I asked.

"I don't know."

"Do you know what he's going to do for his Fear Test?"

Thayer shook his head, and the silence that elapsed was so deep I could hear the snowflakes landing on our jackets. Minutes passed like strange whispers in the dark. We'd been inside the park only a few minutes, but already it felt like we were in another world, the city falling away, blurred out. It was like we were inside a snow globe; the edges of everything seemed to fade into nothingness.

I felt stiff fingers sharply graze my arm. I jumped, but there was only a tree, its low-hanging branches reaching to scratch me. I tried to steady my breath, but my heartbeat was revving like a chain saw. That was how I knew I was scared—*had been* scared since we'd gotten here: when the most mundane things took on a sinister vibe. It was just a tree, and it was just the park, but all of it was giving me the creeps. If this was a Grimms' fairy tale, we were at the part where the decep-tive whimsy of the story gave way to the unexpected gruesomeness hidden within it.

Thayer's silence wasn't helping. I wanted more than anything for him to go back to being the guy I'd known, cracking obscene jokes just to make me laugh. The guy who'd existed before Saundra died. I had the distinct feeling that I was walking with someone I knew and yet didn't really know at all.

At first, I noted with relief that our steps were so clearly imprinted in the snow, because it meant somebody could potentially find us if the Fear Test went sideways. Then, I realized that it also meant that these tracks could lead someone directly to us. It was like the scene with the hedge maze in *The Shining*. I was Danny and somewhere out there was Jack Nicholson with an ax.

Some people would probably find this setting serene. A calm, black-and-white contrast to the bustling city beyond the borders. But I couldn't shake the feeling that something seemed *off*. I looked behind me and found darkness. More darkness in front of me, but in the distance I could swear the darkness took form.

I stopped in my tracks.

"Do you see that?" I asked. "Up ahead, it looks like there's someone there."

"I don't see anything." But Thayer didn't even look in the direction I was pointing. And anyway, what I thought I'd seen must've slunk away or evaporated, because the view was back to formless black.

Still, the uneasiness stayed with me. With every step we took, I had the sinking feeling that Thayer knew something I didn't. That my friend, a person I should trust, was actually leading me somewhere I shouldn't be going.

"Thayer, what's up?"

He didn't even try to answer this time. A twig snapped but I forced myself not to react. I put my hand on his forearm and he finally stopped, looking me in the eye for the first time tonight.

"You don't have to be scared," I said. "If the Masked Man is here, he's only after me."

Thayer looked down at the ground but I bent my knees, forcing our eyes to meet.

"I'm ready for him. Whatever happens tonight, we're going to stop all this."

When Thayer did look up, it was with glassiness in his eyes. "Was Saundra into drugs?"

"What?" I said.

"Hard drugs."

The randomness of the question made me laugh, a short, sudden burst. "No. Never."

Thayer nodded, like he knew just as well as I did that the suggestion was ridiculous.

"I got her autopsy report," Thayer said.

My ears perked up. I knew he had access to this

stuff through his father, even if his father didn't realize it.

"She had LSD in her system. A lot of it. Someone drugged her."

"What?"

"She was tripping," Thayer said. He was looking down as he spoke, his chin tucked into his neck but I could hear the tears in his voice. "She was seeing things."

"Tell me everything, Thayer. What did you find out?"

"You can really hurt yourself when you have a bad trip. When you have that much acid in your system and you have a bad trip, you could do really dangerous things. And Saundra was having a really bad trip—"

He was starting to repeat himself, the words coming faster and faster, so I stopped him, got to the point. "How do you know? You couldn't tell she was having a bad trip from an autopsy."

Thayer finally picked his head up and looked at me, almost like he was surprised I hadn't caught up yet. "I was on the roof with her."

There was a sound, a rushing in my ears. It felt like all the air was gone, and no matter how much I tried to gulp it in, I got nothing. I must've been breathing, though, because I was still standing there. My heart was still beating. "What—what are you talking about?"

"It isn't anyone from your past, Rachel."

I felt the hairs on my arm rise. I got the sense that there was someone else close by, watching us. Stalking us. Another twig snapped, even though Thayer and I were standing still. I looked around, but Thayer's words had me dizzy, like I was the one who'd been drugged.

"Did you—did you push Saundra?"

"No!" He was adamant, frustrated, but he was having trouble saying everything he wanted to say. As if there was too much of it. "I didn't—this is much bigger than me. It's bigger than our game."

The noise wasn't restricted to my mind anymore; it was getting louder, coming closer.

"We aren't the only ones playing—"

"Thayer, watch out!"

The noise in the woods became a person in a mask, upon us as though out of thin air. He held a knife up and slashed it downward. One swift motion that stopped with an ugly squelch in the middle of Thayer's back.

Thayer's mouth, open in midsentence, stayed gaping, silently howling as he sank to the ground.

50

MY HANDS CAME up to cover my own slack mouth, tears pricking my eyes. In the seconds that I stayed shell-shocked, the masked figure ripped the knife out of Thayer and came after me.

I tried to run, but I wasn't quick enough. He slammed into me, bringing us both down to the ground. I twisted around so I could see him, anticipate any sudden moves. Flashes of my kitchen on Long Island came flooding back to me. The icy snow on the back of my neck seamlessly transformed into cold tile, and this person's grip became Matthew's, his knees digging painfully into my hips.

It was like the memory infused me with adrenaline. As if the nightmares had been rehearsals for this very moment. He gripped the knife in both hands and raised it above his head, but but I blocked him with my forearm. With my free hand, I felt around, shoving through the wet powder until I found a rock. Big as a heart. I grabbed it and swung.

The rock made a dull thump as I crashed it into the Masked Man's temple. Fear and adrenaline had made me strong—stronger than him, at least—and it was enough to knock him out. He collapsed on top of me, lifeless.

I kicked him until he was completely off of me and I could scurry out from under him, kicking the knife away. I sat up, gulping in ragged breaths. A few feet away, Thayer was facedown on the ground. I crawled to him, the snow turning slick under my palms and seeping through the fabric of my jeans. I flipped him over and searched for the wound, patting him down—searched for a pulse too, but my hands were too shaky to be of any use.

I dug into my pockets, my fingers scrambling for my phone. When I finally yanked it out and tried to thumb it on, the screen stayed black. The surface of it was streaked with moisture—residual droplets from when it had fallen it in the snow earlier. I shook the phone, smacked it against my thigh, nearly broke my finger slamming it down on the power button again and again. Nothing.

No phone, no help, and the Masked Man was lying right there.

I had to go get someone. I had to help Thayer. But even though I knew I should be running, my body seemed to move of its own accord toward the Masked Man.

I approached him slowly until I was hunched over him, my fingers reaching out to touch him. I turned him onto his back. He seemed lighter now. Smaller. I curled my fingers under the edge of the mask and yanked it off in one quick motion. It was Felicity.

51

I RAN.

I could see one of the castle towers that poked up behind the Delacorte. It was my North Star. Freddie must be there by now, I thought, and even if he wasn't, there must be a patrol cop around the premises, someone I could flag down for help.

But when I got to the theater, there was no one. I skirted the perimeter, stopping at every ticket window to slam my fists against the closed wooden slats, hoping someone would come, but it was boarded up for the winter. It wasn't 'til I reached the entrance at the side that the door gave way when I pushed it. I ran down the aisle, passing rows of seats, working my way to the grand circular stage. The place was cavernous, empty except for a lone figure.

I nearly sobbed with relief when I saw Freddie standing in the center of the platform, his back toward me. I could only make out his silhouette, but I knew it was him.

"Freddie!" I called as I ran to him, racing up the steps. He heard me coming and turned around and I didn't stop until I was practically on him, my body colliding into his. He gripped me by the shoulders, holding me up as my knees buckled.

"Rachel, what's wrong?"

"It's Felicity." I was trying to catch my breath and get everything out at the same time. "Felicity's the one who's been doing this to us. She's the Masked Man."

"What are you talking about?"

"I pulled the mask off her myself. She attacked Thayer."

"What?"

"Just now. She stabbed him. He needs help."

Freddie pulled me in, enveloping me in tight arms.

"It's okay." He whispered it into my hair. And then he asked, "Are you scared?"

"Yes," I said, trembling.

"Good."

"What?" I pulled back, searching Freddie's face. All I saw there was a smile.

He took something out of his pocket and slipped it over his head. The white rubber mask stared back at me. Freddie wore it like a blue ribbon.

"That isn't funny, Freddie."

"The test is almost finished, Rachel." From his other pocket, he drew out a switchblade, expertly flicking open the blade. "All you have to do . . . is scream."

52

I TURNED TO run, but Freddie's fingers were already clenched around my wrist, the tip of his blade suddenly against my sternum. I tried to grab it with my free hand, but Freddie pressed the blade harder, shaking his head.

This boy holding a knife to my chest couldn't have been Freddie. I didn't recognize him. I'd wandered into the uncanny valley somehow, and I wanted out.

"The rules," I said frantically. Rules were the only thing that made sense right now, and, something told me, the only thing that Freddie would adhere to. "A member of the Mary Shelley Club can never be a target."

Not me. It couldn't be me. I'd just asked Thayer who the target was tonight. I realized slowly that when he didn't answer, it wasn't because he didn't know. It was because he *did*.

"You're still probationary, remember?" Freddie said.

"You were never a member of the Mary Shelley Club. My Fear Test began the moment I met you. Before you even knew what the Mary Shelley Club was."

He didn't need the knife; his words were a stab to the heart. Was this a nightmare? Was I asleep? I told myself to wake up, dug my fingernails into the meaty parts of my palms, hard enough to draw blood. But nothing roused me. Not even the knife still pointed at my heart.

"The rest of the club didn't think I'd be able to pull it off. Especially Bram. They thought I'd slip up or you'd catch on, so they let me go with it. I guess they thought it'd improve their own chances of winning."

Freddie's voice, muffled behind the mask, took on an anecdotal quality, the way it did whenever he talked horror trivia with me. It was a punch to the gut, remembering moments like those, where we could happily waste so much time discussing the minute details of our favorite slashers.

All of it had been a lie. I'd opened up to him and he'd used it all against me.

"Do you get it now?" he said. More urgency in his voice, more pressure behind the knife. "Felicity, Bram, even sweet Thayer. They were all lying to you. When you were trying to figure out who the Masked Man was? We all knew. We all put on the mask, we all twisted the knife. Can you just appreciate that? How long it all took? The buildup? I served a five-course meal, Rachel—just for you."

He pulled off the mask and showed it to me, as if I was seeing it for the first time. "Didn't you ever notice the face? Long. Sunken cheeks. Scars everywhere. It's Frankenstein, painted white."

Of course it was. Mary Shelley's monster had been staring me in the face all this time and I couldn't see it. Only someone who had an obsession with horror movies would take a cue from the *Halloween* mask: repurpose a recognizable, innocuous face by turning it into something horrible. Freddie was probably really proud of that one.

"So tell me," he said, "how'd I do?"

I tried to push him off me but Freddie's grip was too strong. I'd never seen him this way. In all our time together—as friends walking to the subway, when I was kissing him in dark corners—I'd never seen just how intimidating he could be. How menacing his smile actually was. It was like watching a performance, but I couldn't follow the plot.

"This isn't you," I said. "You're good." It wasn't just a tactic, an attempt to appeal to his compassion. I meant what I said. "I know you didn't kill Saundra."

"Why? Because I was with you when she died?"

444

"Because Thayer told me," I said. My teeth were starting to chatter, but it had nothing to do with the cold. "Before Felicity stabbed him, he told me he was on the roof."

Freddie sighed and shut his eyes, annoyed. "See, this is why he had to go. He was blabbing to everybody. You know he was going to confess to knowing what happened to Saundra. That he'd been up there when she got spooked. That I drugged her."

"You what?"

"He didn't tell you that part?" Freddie said. "Saundra *fell*, Rachel. Thayer chased her all the way up to the roof—she basically led him there herself—and she got scared. She tripped over herself and fell through the skylight. Thayer actually tried to catch her but . . . well, you know."

It made sense now why Thayer had done a complete one-eighty after Saundra's death. He blamed himself.

"She was never supposed to die," Freddie said. He almost seemed to feel bad.

"You drugged her."

"Only to make things more interesting."

I crave chaos. He'd told me that a long time ago and I was only starting to understand how seriously I should've taken him.

"Thayer couldn't leave well enough alone. He had

to go digging. He grew a conscience. I couldn't let him talk."

"So you unleashed Felicity on him?"

"If he confessed to the Saundra thing, then he'd confess to the game, and to the club. Felicity understands that."

I hated how clinical he sounded, talking about violence and death and betrayal like they were predetermined answers on one of his cheat sheets.

"Under*stood*," I spat. "I bashed her head in."

Freddie watched me carefully. "You're bluffing," he said.

"I'm not."

He must've heard something in my voice or seen something in my face, because his expression changed, almost like he was amused.

"You think I'm bad. But of the two of us"—he poked me with the knife—"only you've killed somebody."

Despite everything—despite the feel of his knife as it threatened to break through my coat—I longed for another way out. I receded inside myself, searching for a glimmer of hope, for something that would take me out of this situation. A magic word that would make all of this stop.

"Armadillo."

My voice was so small I doubted if Freddie fully

heard me. I could barely hear myself. At first he seemed confused, but then his eyes dimmed, a black flicker of recognition dawning on him. We were back in that alleyway, before Thayer's Fear Test, when I'd painted his face with my fingers and we'd discussed safe words, never thinking I'd ever need to use one with him. Back in a time before I really knew how screwed up this game could be.

I let out a shaky sigh as I felt the pressure of Freddie's knife lessen, his hand dropping slightly. But then something hardened in his eyes. "I'm sorry, Rachel, I can't break the rules. I can't let you go."

That wasn't good enough.

Maybe my mom was right. Maybe I should join the field hockey team, because I kneed Freddie in the groin so hard that he groaned and dropped his knife. He stumbled, reached for the blade, but I got to it first. I grabbed it and swung, knocking its hilt into the bridge of his nose, which exploded with a satisfying crunch. It was enough to knock him onto his back.

I took off.

I hoped the trees and the darkness were enough cover. After everything, after the truth, after seeing who was really behind the mask, I kept coming back to the fact that all of this was just a childish game. Not just the club itself, but even this very moment, when I was at once running for my life, panting for breath, and basically playing a fucking game of tag. Only, if I was caught, I was dead.

My warring thoughts, my racing heart, the darkness of the park—it was all closing in on me, and before I realized it was there, I'd slammed into something. No, someone. I bounced back, expecting Freddie and already swinging my arms, but it was Bram.

I recoiled but then I remembered I didn't have to be scared. I was still gripping the knife in my hand. I held it up over my head like Norman Bates had taught me.

"Rachel, wait." Bram took a step back, his hands out, showing me that they were empty.

"I know everything!" I barked, my voice shredded. "I know I'm the target!"

"Rachel, I'm on your side."

"Bullshit!" Of course he would say that. I aimed the knife at his lying mouth. "I don't believe you."

"You shouldn't!" Freddie called, walking through the trees to us, a hand clamped over his bleeding nose. "Bram was in on it the whole time. He's the Stu to my Billy Loomis!"

Freddie walked up next to Bram and I swung the knife between the two boys to keep them back. It felt as useless as swinging a twig between two approaching lions. Both of these assholes were dangerous and I didn't trust either of them. But there was something I could do—a last-ditch effort to see if Bram was lying.

"Thayer told me we aren't the only ones playing. What did he mean?"

"I'll tell you everything," Bram said, but before he could say anything more, Freddie tackled me. The next thing I knew my mouth was shoveling snow and the knife had flown out of my hand. I scrambled up, searching for it, but by then, the knife was back in Freddie's hands like it'd never left. He was so close that I had no time to run, only to brace myself as he lurched toward me. I raised my arms to shield myself, expecting to feel the sting of the blade slashing through my thick sleeves. As the knife came hurtling toward me, I shut my eyes instinctively.

Instead, I heard a groan.

When I opened my eyes, I saw that Freddie's knife was shiny with red. And that Bram was holding a hand to his chest. The scene in front of me almost didn't make sense, but the blood seeping through Bram's fingers painted the picture for me. He stumbled backward, looking just as shocked as I felt. He turned to Freddie, as though to ask him why he'd done that, but when he opened his mouth to speak, only blood came sputtering out.

As Bram slumped to the ground, Freddie turned to

face me. "This is how it's going to go," he said, out of breath and sweating. "I'm going to tell the police that you were scared, kept talking about some guy from your break-in last year who followed you all the way to the city. You were afraid he was going to kill you. I'm going to say that it turned out to be Bram. I tried to fight him—I tried to save you, I really did—but I was too late. He got to you. He killed you."

Hearing Freddie narrate my death made me choke back a sob.

"And when he came after me, well"—Freddie used the back of his hand to wipe the moisture from his forehead, never letting go of the knife—"We both know how easy it is to lie about 'self-defense.'"

I shook my head, my ears ringing, my eyes stinging with tears. "I never lied about that."

"Yes, you did." The force of his words seemed to propel Freddie forward. "You want to know why all of this happened? Why I picked you? I did it because you lied, Rachel. You killed Matthew Marshall."

It was like he'd just pushed me off a cliff. Matthew's name sounded so foreign coming out of Freddie's mouth. It didn't belong to him. I wanted to reach out, stick my hand inside Freddie's mouth, and pull his tongue out. I would hold tight with my fingernails. I would pull until it tore off, until his face didn't look a face anymore.

I could've done that. And in another life I might have. But as I watched Freddie, fixing his grip on the knife, I recognized something in him. The monster inside.

Freddie and I were two sides of the same coin. Fear had created me, lured out the monster who reacted recklessly, who'd killed Matthew. For Freddie it was anger that made him this way. I could see it so clearly now. Freddie was a puppet to his anger. But I wasn't going to let my fear control me anymore. I wouldn't be reckless.

I would fight—I would do everything to stop him. But I knew now who I was. I might have done a monstrous thing once, but that did not make me a monster. I was a survivor. And that was much stronger.

Freddie closed the gap between us until there was nothing but me and him. He raised the knife, but as he brought it down, the blade was wrenched out of his hand.

Bram, risen from what I had thought was death, had the knife. He plunged the blade into Freddie's back.

The two of them fell to the ground.

53

I WOKE UP screaming. No nightmare this time, just blackness. I swallowed in air, reaching for the switch on my bedside lamp, but I was all nerves and my arm bolted out like a live wire, hitting the lamp. It teetered, but my mom's hand caught it before it could fall to the floor.

"Shh, here," she whispered and turned the lamp on. The light immediately bathed everything in a warm glow. Mom sat on the edge of my bed and smoothed back my hair.

I almost broke down and cried just seeing her. She told me she'd spend the whole night in my room, even after I pointed out that the only chair, perpetually piled with my worn clothes, was creaky old wood. I was so glad she hadn't listened to me.

"I'm sorry about the lamp. I'm such a mess. You shouldn't have to stay up with me like I'm a child."

"Rachel, the lamp is fine. It's okay to be a little on edge right now. You just went through something . . . unbelievable."

She sighed, a crease forming between her eyebrows. I knew my mom's tells as well as she knew mine. The way she looked down at her hands because she didn't want me to see her tears. The way her lips settled into a tight, straight line, mustering up resolve, strength. I recognized her tells because they were the same as mine.

"I'm sorry, Mom."

She looked at me, exasperated. "You didn't even break the damn lamp."

"Not for that."

Mom sighed. "Jamonada. You don't have anything to be sorry about. *I'm* sorry that these bad things keep happening to you. I was really hoping the city would be a fresh start."

I didn't deserve her pity. I'd brought this on myself. I'd practically knocked on trouble's door and begged to be let in. And now my mom was blaming herself.

"So what happened?" she asked. She'd waited until now to broach the subject. She'd given me room to breathe when she'd gotten a call from the police, come to get me, sat with me in the back of the cab as the night blinked into day.

The police had given her the facts—the pieces

they'd found scattered in the little corner of Central Park where my nightmare had come to life. They'd found Freddie dead, with a rubber mask on his face, which they used to connect him to Lux's accident. They were also going to reopen their investigation into Saundra's death. They'd found both Bram and Thayer alive, Thayer barely breathing. Felicity hadn't turned up, though, and I didn't mention that she'd been there.

And then there was me, curiously without any major bodily harm. They seemed suspicious, which meant they obviously weren't horror fans. There was always someone left standing at the end. A Final Girl.

I told my mom a version of what I'd told the police. Freddie attacked me. He attacked Bram. And Bram did what he did because Freddie was about to kill me.

I hated upsetting my mom, but she deserved to know what happened. It was the truth, which was something I had fought hard to tell.

"I can't believe it," Mom said finally. "Freddie Martinez. He was such a good kid in all of my classes. I never would've guessed that he could be so violent."

Neither could I. But "violent" wasn't the word I'd use. Freddie was evil. It was difficult enough facing your monsters when you knew what they were, but that was nothing compared to inviting them in and not having a single clue. Freddie had pulled the wool over my eyes since the first moment I'd looked at him. I felt like such an idiot, thinking about how his smiles had made me swoon, when really they were meant to blind me.

Freddie's death had only left me with more questions. That time he told me his deepest, darkest secrets, was he saying that all in a grand plot to deceive me? Every time we kissed, did he hate it? Did he want me to fall for him just so he could stab me in the back on the way down?

The only answer that felt honest was *yes*. To all of it.

Mom put her arms around me and let me cry on her shoulder.

"I'm sorry," I told her again.

"None of that," my mom said. "You're safe now. You don't have to be scared anymore. But I'll stay in your room for as long as you need."

"Go to bed, Mom."

"You sure?"

Mom pinched my cheek as she searched my face, seeming to go over every freckle. Normally, if anyone looked this closely at me, I'd freak. I was sure they could see me for what I really was, the horrible person I'd become the night of the attack. But I knew better now. I wasn't a monster.

I was the one who'd defeated the monster.

"I'm beat," I said, meaning it. "I should get back to sleep."

Mom hesitated, like she was afraid to leave me alone. But eventually she pulled the blanket all the way up to my chin, tucking me in.

"You've got a guardian angel," she said. "I'm so grateful Bram was there."

The last I'd heard, Bram was in surgery, but it seemed like he was going to pull through.

He had to. Because we needed to talk.

54

THE LAST TIME I'd seen Bram, my hands were covered in his blood. I'd used his phone to call for help in the park and stayed with him until it arrived. I'd tried to staunch the bleeding with my hands, and then I took my coat off and applied as much pressure as I could to the wound in his chest. By the time paramedics arrived, my arms were sore from pressing so hard. It'd been terrifying, being alone with him as he lay unconscious, bleeding into the snow.

I didn't know what state he'd be in now. Whatever it was, I'd thought it'd be more difficult to see him. Like maybe there'd be guards posted at his door, or restricted visiting hours and rules, or maybe he'd be flooded with too many visitors and I wouldn't get a chance to talk to him. But all I had to do was say his name and a lady behind a desk told me his room number.

Mom let me stay home from school. Well, she *made*

me take the day off. But I couldn't sit still at home. And when I told her I wanted to see Bram, she understood.

I found his room and knocked, and after a moment I heard his voice. That distinctive low rumble. "Come in."

I opened the door slowly and peeked inside. It was a private room, and Bram was alone. He was sitting, propped up with two pillows, in his hospital bed. There was a bandage wrapped over his shoulder like a toga, and on the rolling table beside him was a pink plastic jug of water. I stepped inside and watched as he reached for the jug. He winced as he gripped the cup. I walked straight to him and took the cup from him. The sound of the liquid glugging from the spout was the only thing to break the silence. I handed him the cup and he nodded his thanks before sipping from it. Bram didn't seem surprised to see me, but then, he never had. "You're alone," I said.

"My parents were here all night," Bram said. "I sent them home. My mother said she'll be back with my favorite pajamas."

"You have favorite pajamas?"

"They have a sushi print."

It was a tiny detail, but this was Bram. He did not divulge details, tiny or otherwise. I took it as a sign. Maybe it meant that he'd be more open with me. That there wouldn't be any more secrets. I hoped, at least.

"How do you feel?"

"Like I've been stabbed in the lung."

The weight of that statement was enough to plop me down into the chair beside his bed. It was the harsh reality of what had happened, of how lucky he was to be alive. And how grateful I was that he'd been there.

"Thank you," I said. The words were really not enough, but they were all I had.

Bram shrugged, or attempted to, then winced again. "Thank you, too."

I shook my head, confused. He was the one in the hospital bed. He was the one who'd almost died. "For what?"

"You saved my life," Bram said. "You stopped the bleeding."

I wasn't sure what to say, but there seemed to be an unspoken understanding between us. He knew what it was like now to end a life, to do the worst thing you could possibly do to another human being. We shared that. But Bram wasn't a bad person. He'd done what he had to do.

I was finally learning to look at myself with the same kindness I was extending toward Bram. We were both fighters. We'd saved each other.

"Bram, there's something I have to know. Were you really not in on it with Freddie?"

"Freddie picked you as his target and we let him," Bram said slowly. "But I didn't think it would go this far—none of us did. When he told us the plan for his Fear Test, we let him do it because we thought there was no way he would be able to pull it off. We didn't think he'd have you hooked for months."

It stung, hearing this. And the look on my face must've been easy to read because Bram added, "No offense." He gave me a small smile, as if realizing how ridiculous it sounded.

Offended? Because I'd managed to get strung along by a maniac? *Nah.* "Thayer, too?"

"Thayer really thought you'd beat Freddie at his own game. He didn't think it'd go as far as it went either. We both wanted out."

I realized now that when Bram had told me to leave the club it was because he was trying to warn me. "I wish you would've told me."

"I couldn't. It was one of our Fear Test tasks. Lie and wear the mask whenever Freddie asked."

I was consumed by a morbid desire to hear about Freddie's plans to deceive me. I leaned into the curiosity. "Tell me his plan."

Bram took a deep breath even though it looked uncomfortable. "Freddie wanted to slowly weave in the mask any chance he got. He wanted you to hear about it. I guess he was hoping it'd trigger you or something, that you'd be freaked out because of your break-in."

He'd been right. "So at my Fear Test, when Lux claimed she saw someone in a mask?"

"That was Freddie."

Of course it was. My gut had told me as much. Bram himself had told me it was him, too.

"I knew he'd worn that stupid mask, but chasing after Lux went too far. I was pissed at him for what happened to her. He told me that Lux tripped. He swore he didn't touch her."

"And the night of Felicity's Fear Test? I was right, wasn't I? It was you who Sim kicked in the ribs."

Here, Bram looked even more contrite. "Yes."

I nodded, feeling vindicated, and somewhat relieved that all the pieces that had seemed so scattered before were now clicking into place. But with the clarity came biting anger. I had to remind myself that Bram had fought for me. That if I could trust anyone, it was the guy who had a hole in his lung for my sake.

"So it was Freddie who spray-painted Saundra's plaque?"

"He would rather get us all in trouble than risk the game ending prematurely. There was only his Fear Test left and he was going to make sure it happened one way or another. He didn't tell any of us he was going to vandalize her plaque. We were as shocked to see our names up there as you were."

"Why did you go through with the game?" I asked. "After Lux got hurt, didn't you know something might happen to Saundra?"

"By then I'd started to believe that what happened to Lux must've been an accident. I didn't think Freddie was actually capable of really hurting anyone. But I was wrong."

I felt a twisted sense of relief in knowing I wasn't the only one who'd been fooled by Freddie. But the feeling was fleeting. "How could you go through with all of this?"

"The rules—"

"Screw the rules," I snapped. I could chalk up Freddie's reasoning to keep this messed-up game going to him being out of his mind, but Bram? He was trying to defend himself, even now. And I didn't get it.

"The club was important to me," Bram said, finally. "My life—my parents, Lux, my friends at school—I always had to live up to their expectations. The club let me breathe."

I couldn't relate to Bram's woes of having everything but still feeling trapped. Though the way he'd acted at his after-party was starting to make sense. He'd looked like an actor in a play, and now I finally understood why.

But I could immediately relate to the safe-haven part, and how important it was to have something you could always turn to. How absolutely life-sustaining it was. Selfishly, I'd figured I needed the Mary Shelley Club more than anybody. The comfort of a group of people who were like me, who understood me, who accepted me. I guess Bram needed that, too.

"I loved the club," Bram continued. "I wanted it to keep going, just like it always had. That's what I was fighting for. Even as Freddie started to poison it—I fought for it even more."

I could get that. But in the end . . . "It was just a game, Bram. It was a stupid game."

"It was more than that. I know you found the folder on my computer, the one titled *Chaps*."

I'd forgotten about that. "Yeah?"

"*Chaps* as in chapters." Bram looked me in the eye, the familiar unwavering stare that reminded me that he was still the same Bram I'd known. "There are chapters of the club all over the country. We didn't invent the game."

"What?"

"The game is much bigger than just our club," Bram continued. "It always has been. Matthew Marshall was a member of a Mary Shelley Club on Long Island."

What happened with Matthew had been a separate thing, something from my past life, before I'd come to the city, before I'd met anyone in the Mary Shelley Club. "That isn't true."

But Bram nodded. "It is. The break-in at your house was a Fear Test. Matthew's Fear Test."

I let the news wash over me. I'd always wondered what Matthew was doing at my house that night. Why a typical, popular high school boy and his friend would break into a house wearing masks. It was wild. But not any wilder than anything I'd participated in these last few months.

"So Freddie chose me because, what, he wanted to avenge Matthew?"

"That was only part of it," Bram said. "When you broke that Fear Test—when Matthew died—the game got thrown off course. Freddie couldn't have that."

"So he had to punish me."

"He thought that was the only way to reinstate order and to make sure nothing like this happened again. Freddie cared about the club more than anything else."

I listened to Bram as though through a fog. He was supposed to be the incoherent one, on pain meds, but it almost felt like it should've been me in that hospital bed for how mentally and emotionally banged up I felt.

I couldn't speak. I could barely even think. All I could do was look down at my hand, resting uselessly on my thigh, when Bram's hand covered it. When I looked up Bram was leaning forward, closer than I expected him to be.

"Sit back, you'll hurt yourself." I didn't mean it to come out like an order, but even so, Bram ignored me. His serious look was gone, replaced by something softer. "I'm sorry," he said.

It wasn't an apology from Freddie, but this was the closest I was going to get. And I needed it.

"Freddie was loyal to a club that's bigger than all of us," Bram said.

I stayed with Bram a little while longer, until he fell asleep, and then until his mother returned with his favorite sushi pajamas. I did it for him, but I also didn't want to be alone. Eventually, though, my mom texted, wondering where I was, and I decided I'd given her enough scares to last a lifetime.

Outside, the Upper East Side of Manhattan got on with the day as usual. There were patients and their families leaving the hospital, nurses in scrubs coming back from their breaks, ambulances clogging the busy street. I passed them all like it was a normal day. But it wasn't, and it wouldn't be again.

I walked, thinking about this game I'd played, and all of those who'd died. I thought of Saundra, of Freddie, and even of Matthew.

Since the incident on Long Island last year, I had done everything in my power not to think about it. I didn't ever want to revisit the ugliest moment of my life. Now I did just that, but from the perspective of the Mary Shelley Club.

Two high school boys in repurposed Frankenstein masks. One left, one stayed. I'd always figured Matthew wanted to hurt me, but if he was playing the game then all he'd wanted was to hear me scream. For a primal, guttural roar to be unleashed. I must not have ever screamed that night, not once.

I'd thought it was just the two of us alone on that kitchen floor. But now it occurred to me that there must have been other people from Matthew's Mary Shelley Club somewhere around my house that night. They must've been watching the whole Fear Test go horribly wrong. Maybe they hid in the bushes outside. Maybe they saw everything through the windows. All of them quietly watching. All of them wearing masks.

I couldn't ignore the creeping sensation of dread in my veins. Because if what Bram had said was true, then there was reason to believe that this nightmare wasn't over.

As I walked away from the hospital and toward the subway station on the corner, I could have sworn there was somebody watching me.

I looked over my shoulder.

ACKNOWLEDGMENTS

THANK YOU:

To my agents, Jenny Bent, who believed in this story when I pitched it to her, and who worked tirelessly to find its perfect home; Gemma Cooper, who took it over the pond with love and care; and Debbie Deuble Hill, who loved this story before she'd read a word of it and got it into the right TV hands before anyone else had read it either.

To my incredible editor, Tiff Liao, whose suggestions and ideas (over plates of vegan cashew cheese) made this novel so much stronger. If not for Tiff, there would be no Bram after-party, and that would've been a real shame. And Sarah Levison for loving scary movies and finding that this story was a worthy homage to the genre.

To my family: my mother, Sonia, and my mother-in-law, Irina, for the invaluable gift of babysitting and giving me time to write. To Alex, for your time, your encouragement, and your impeccable brainstorming skills. You helped me figure out who the killer was! You rightly concluded that Bram should have had a shirtless scene! And I'm pretty sure you thought up the names for Freddie and Rachel. For all that, and more. It is so neat having a partner who thinks your work is amazing and valuable. I thank you. To my sister, Yasmin, who might be my biggest fan. My scary movie partner, since we were way too small to be watching scary movies. I really hope you like this book! And to beautiful, funny, smart, tender Tove! Hi, Tove.